CHARLOTTE WALSH LIKES TO WIN

A NOVEL

JO PIAZZA

Simon & Schuster
New York London Toronto Sydney New Delhi

Simon & Schuster
1230 Avenue of the Americas
New York, NY 10020

First Simon & Schuster hardcover edition July 2018

SIMON & SCHUSTER and colophon are registered trademarks of Simon & Schuster, Inc.

For information about special discounts for bulk purchases, please contact Simon & Schuster Special Sales at 1-866-506-1949 or business@simonandschuster.com.

The Simon & Schuster Speakers Bureau can bring authors to your live event. For more information or to book an event, contact the Simon & Schuster Speakers Bureau at 1-866-248-3049 or visit our website at www.simonspeakers.com.

Interior design by Carly Loman

Manufactured in the United States of America

10   9   8   7   6   5   4   3   2   1

Library of Congress Cataloging-in-Publication Data
Names: Piazza, Jo, author.
Title: Charlotte Walsh likes to win : a novel / Jo Piazza.
Description: First Simon & Schuster hardcover edition. | New York : Simon & Schuster, July 2018.
Identifiers: LCCN 2017057730 | ISBN 9781501179419 (hardback) | ISBN 9781501179433 (trade paper) | ISBN 9781501179426 (e-book)
Subjects: LCSH: Women politicians—Fiction. | Working mothers—Fiction. | Marriage—Fiction. | Women—United States—Fiction. | Political fiction. | BISAC: FICTION / Contemporary Women. | FICTION / Family Life. | FICTION / Political.
Classification: LCC PS3616.I214 C47 2018 | DDC 813/.6—dc23 LC record available at https://lccn.loc.gov/2017057730

ISBN 978-1-5011-7941-9
ISBN 978-1-5011-7942-6 (ebook)

For Charlie—May you grow up to be the kind of man who wants women to win

In politics, if you want anything said, ask a man. If you want anything done, ask a woman.

—MARGARET THATCHER

If I didn't define myself for myself, I would be crunched into other people's fantasies for me and eaten alive.

—AUDRE LORDE

CHAPTER 1
July 15, 2017
479 days to Election Day

Tell people one true thing before you tell them a lie. Then it will be easier for them to believe the lie.

It wasn't the best advice Marty Walsh ever gave to his daughter Charlotte, but it had stuck with her for almost forty years. Marty had been a garbage collector by trade, though he insisted "sanitation specialist" had a smarter ring to it. He wasn't a successful man by most people's standards and he died drunk in his bed before his fiftieth birthday. Now his daughter was running for the United States Senate and Marty's words held a new utility for her.

Charlotte hadn't expected her campaign to begin with an interrogation—an aggressive one at that—but the questions just kept coming.

"Have you ever used any drugs besides pot?"

"No."

"Paid any undocumented workers under the table?"

"Nope."

"Ever killed anyone?"

"Not yet."

"Ever get an abortion?"

"No."

"Infidelity in your marriage? Affairs? Secret ex-husband?"

"I love my husband. We don't have anything to hide." *One of those things is true.* Charlotte punctuated her sentence with a chuckle, hoping the laughter would sooth her nerves and add confidence to her answer.

Josh Pratt, who if all went well today would sign on to be her campaign manager, twisted his mouth in a way that told Charlotte he wasn't sure he believed her. He had a tiny blob of something yellow, maybe mustard, on the side of his thin lips. As he asked his questions, Charlotte had a hard time focusing on anything except for the golden dribble.

I'm running for national political office, she wanted to answer back. *Ask me my thoughts on immigration, on the flat tax, on school vouchers, abortion rights. How much do I think we can raise the minimum wage? Can I bring more jobs to Pennsylvania? Will I create more affordable housing? Will I fight for college tuition assistance? What do I think about trade with the Chinese? Why does my marriage matter?*

"You're thinking, 'Why does it matter?' Why does your husband matter?" Josh read her mind. "Your husband matters. Your marriage matters. As a woman, you bear the burden of having to appear to be charismatic, smart, well-groomed, nice, but not too nice. If you're married, you need to look happily married. If you have kids, you should be the mother of the year."

"Goddammit. It's 2017. There are plenty of women in Congress. A woman ran for president. It shouldn't matter that I don't have a penis." Charlotte rolled her eyes. "It's unbelievable that we have to deal with that kind of shit anymore."

"Well, I'm sorry, but it matters a lot." Josh shot her a stoic stare. "You do still have to deal with this shit. No one likes to say that out loud, but it's true. You're running in a state that's never elected a woman to the Senate or as governor. That should tell you something."

"Tug Slaughter is a serial philanderer," Charlotte fired back at Josh. Pennsylvania's longtime incumbent senator Ted "Tug" Slaughter had been married three times—his current wife was thirty-five years younger than he. The man was a walking cliché. For more than forty years, Slaughter had reigned as the senior senator from the state. Most men in Congress would be easy to miss in a crowd. Not Slaughter. Pushing eighty, the man still oozed raw ego. He was known to strip his shirt off and perform sit-ups onstage at events. Just last month he'd climbed the trestle of the Black Bridge in Marshfield Station with a pack of teenagers and leapt into the icy Delaware River below. Last winter he announced that he donated a kidney to a complete stranger he'd met at an Eagles game.

"It's true, Tug does more cocktail waitresses than he does lawmaking, but he's not the one who needs to create a legitimate candidacy. You do." Josh had an answer for everything.

"That's bullshit."

Charlotte drummed her nails on her desktop, an expensive slab of glass through which she could see her boot tapping the wooden floor. She'd flown Josh here to Palo Alto from Philadelphia on her dime to convince him to run her campaign. He'd insisted on first class because he knew she could afford it, and Charlotte took this as a sign that he didn't think he needed to impress her. All the right people told Charlotte that hiring Josh, a political wunderkind with four consecutive congressional wins under his belt, could give her a solid shot at winning. She needed him more than he needed her money, though she knew that if he said yes to working with her, she would be paying him in the high six figures for a little more than a year.

Josh paused and smiled. "You curse like a dockworker. You don't look like someone with such a foul mouth, with your expensive linen suit, sitting in this glass-walled aquarium in the heart of Silicon Valley."

She was suddenly conscious of what she looked like to him. At forty-seven, Charlotte was often complimented on the fact that she had aged well, and she'd heard it enough that she allowed it to be something she took pride in. She had what her mother once described as a plain face and a sturdy build, meaning she had broad shoulders and a flat chest that persisted into adulthood. She knew her hair was her best feature, more chestnut than brown, with strawberry highlights and just a few strands of silver she easily extracted at the roots.

After half a lifetime of feeling insecure about her looks, in her thirties she'd learned to accentuate her best features and had come to see herself as pretty but not beautiful. She knew the distinction had made it easier for her to succeed in a male-dominated industry.

Meanwhile, Charlotte thought Josh looked ten years younger than his actual age, which Google informed her was thirty-five and, with his baby face, husky belly, and enthusiastic acne sprinkled across his cheeks, nothing like the kind of man who played the kind of three-dimensional chess required to get a person elected to national office. He wore dark jeans, a blue blazer, pristine Stan Smith Adidas with black laces, and a rumpled Phillies T-shirt. It took swagger to waltz into a business meeting in sneakers with mustard on his face and Charlotte knew it gave him the upper hand.

"Well, I curse more like a teamster," Charlotte corrected Josh. "I spent too many nights at my dad's union meetings." Marty Walsh might have been a drunk, but he'd been a happy drunk, and because happy drunks are endearing to children, like Santa Claus and puppets, from an early age Charlotte had wanted to be around him all the time. On evenings when her mother couldn't get out of bed, he brought her to his union meetings and sat her on the floor while deeply angry white men—the room was always all men—cursed and complained about how the world owed them better. Years later, at Marty's funeral, the same men had the same conversations. Back then those men were still progressive Democrats. Mistrust for authority and misplaced expectations had been the central tropes of Charlotte's upbringing. When she closed her eyes, Charlotte could smell the Swisher Sweets and cheap beer and hear her father say: "These men work hard, Charlie. They deserve a good turn. Anyone who works an honest day deserves a good turn." He'd had plenty of flaws, but above all Marty had been a hard worker, and it was that quality Charlotte chose to remember above the others.

"That will play well in rural PA—the cursing, the garbageman dad," Josh said now. "Easy on the union talk though. Only 10.7 percent of Americans identify with a union these days. Play up the white-trash angle. When you run for office, your life history gets reduced to character points: 'Daughter of trashman turns Silicon Valley executive and comes home to help voters get jobs like hers.' That's your brand now. It's a better brand than 'California millionaire who grows heirloom tomatoes, contributes to the Silver Circle of public radio, does yoga, and tries to save the spotted owl.'"

"It's actually the Chinook salmon we're more concerned about these days," Charlotte whipped back.

There were other stories Charlotte could have told Josh. Sometimes Charlotte's mother, Annemarie, had picked up cleaning shifts at a retirement home in Scranton, scraping vomit off the bathroom walls while wearing thick yellow latex gloves. Unable to afford childcare, she'd brought Charlotte with her, placing the little girl on a stool with a book in the corner of the bathroom. But Annemarie had lost that job when they'd found out she was stealing pills from the patients. Meanwhile, Marty had been among the first laid off when Elk Hollow merged municipal services with Abington. He'd picked up some hours at the gas station before it went self-service. In his later years he'd worked as a janitor in the food services department of the University of Scranton. Some months they'd gotten food stamps that her dad was too proud to ever use at the Rainbow market, even when the electricity got shut off for five days. These were memories Charlotte had packed away into dusty boxes in her brain, and when she'd unpacked them, she'd been startled to realize she'd become the kind of woman who bought fifteen dollars worth of organic kale and thirty dollars of non-GMO chia seeds at the Menlo Park True Food Co-op. The trajectory from there to here was vertigo-inducing.

Charlotte's eyes wandered to the couch on the other side of the room, where Leila Kelly, her executive assistant, raised her bushy eyebrows in tandem as if to ask, *Do we really need this guy?*

Josh glanced at his notes and continued. "You and Max Tanner have been married for twelve years, with three daughters under the age of six. You're the COO of Humanity and he's the head of engineering and product for the same company. How will that work exactly when you run? What will your husband be doing when you move your family to Pennsylvania?"

"Max is taking a sabbatical from the company and taking care of our girls."

"Don't say the word *sabbatical*. You sound elitist, like the kind of person who says 'holiday' instead of 'vacation.'"

Sitting in her corner office as the chief operating officer of the technology company that was single-handedly changing how the world did business, Charlotte felt assured in her use of any damn word she pleased. "We call it a sabbatical here at Humanity. We both chose to take one when I decided to run—when *we* decided I should run. We made a joint decision that Max would help raise our daughters so I could focus on the campaign."

Charlotte cringed, remembering the intense marital negotiations it had taken to convince Max that her running for office and him becoming the primary caregiver for their small children would be good for them as a family. Even though she understood what he was giving up for her, she also felt vindicated that she deserved this and more from him after what he'd put her through.

"We can talk about how to spin your husband's so-called sabbatical later," Josh countered, wagging his head and making exaggerated air quotes with his hands around the word *sabbatical*. "Maybe Max works on a top secret project from home. Something with virtual reality. People love the idea of virtual reality. They have no idea what the hell it is, but they think it will change their shitty lives. Always say 'Silicon Valley,' never 'San Francisco,' by the way. San Francisco conjures up images of tie-dyed, pot-smoking, free-loving hippies and transgendered people who want to use your bathroom. 'Silicon Valley big shot' is more aspirational than 'reality television star' these days, and you and Max hopefully come with less baggage."

Josh dredged up his next unpleasant topic. "Speaking of baggage, Max has a reputation for being a flirt. There are a few women who claim he made inappropriate remarks to them in the office."

Adrenaline tiptoed up her spine, but outwardly Charlotte maintained total calm, a skill honed in years of boardrooms filled with other puffed-up men with expensive haircuts.

She took a sip of her lukewarm coffee, allowing her front teeth to clink against her mug. Her husband *had been* a flirt. It was a reflex for him, the way he made both men and women like him. He made inappropriate, vaguely vulgar jokes at the wrong times. He was a toucher. There was a time, not too long ago, when he would stroll into a team meeting and give both men and women uninvited shoulder massages during pep talks. He used to joke, "An unwanted shoulder massage is an oxymoron." She'd made him stop telling that joke.

"All men flirt." Charlotte held her breath and glanced again at Leila. When she made an excuse for her husband, she faltered and raised her voice an octave without intending to. "Do you have any evidence he did anything wrong? No Humanity employees will ever speak badly about Max or me. Everyone signed ironclad confidentiality agreements."

"How do you know they're ironclad enough?"

"I wrote them. I'm the COO." She crossed and uncrossed her legs.

Josh's chapped lips stretched into a smirk. "People talked to *me*, and if they talked to me they'll talk to your opponent and to the press. But you make another excellent point. You have a bigger job than Max. He's the VP of product and engineering. You're one step away from the CEO. You run this company." He waved his hand in an arc sweeping the room, indicating what lay beyond it—the 500,000-square-foot office complex designed by Zaha Hadid, her final project before she passed away. Outside Charlotte's window she could see the ten-acre rooftop park with its man-made waterfalls and brutalist concrete climbing wall.

Josh continued. "I'll bet that was tough on Max, having his wife as a boss, the big dog at one of the most powerful companies in the world."

"My husband is a very evolved man, not a dinosaur."

Josh rolled his eyes. "That would be a cute sound bite if we were living in Sweden. Don't say that out loud on the campaign trail."

He left Max behind for the moment. "Your girls. The twins, they're five now and you conceived them through IVF?" Josh clearly enjoyed toying with people, had the look of a child dangling a pork chop in front of a starving dog as he asked his questions.

Charlotte allowed her eyes to narrow and her annoyance to rise to the surface. "Yes."

"Designer babies."

Don't talk about my kids like that. I will strangle you with my bare hands. "Oh, Christ! Like hundreds of thousands of women, I had trouble getting pregnant and used modern medicine to help start our family." Getting pregnant had been the hardest thing she'd ever done. It had convinced her over and over that she was a failure and had nearly broken her. She despised talking about it.

"Because you were old when you got pregnant? Forty-one?"

"Yes, among other things." Charlotte glared at him. "I'd like to think you know better than to refer to a woman as old."

Unfazed, Josh continued. "What other things?"

"My uterus sits at an inopportune angle for sperm to properly reach my eggs without assistance. I have sonograms of it, actually. Do you think we should release them on Instagram in advance of announcing the campaign? Maybe they could be our Christmas cards."

Josh ignored her sarcasm. "IVF is an expensive procedure."

"The company paid for it." It was one of the things Charlotte was proudest of—not the fact that the company had paid for her own procedures, but that they paid for all fertility procedures for all Humanity employees. In an effort to keep more women at Humanity, she had instituted a policy of paid family planning for all employees. The plan included compensation for IVF, egg freezing, egg donation, and adoption. At the time, she'd had no idea she would need to take advantage of the benefit herself. With Humanity's female retention at an all-time low, she'd seen a problem and fixed it. Solving problems and knowing how to fix things was the defining characteristic of Charlotte's adulthood and had earned her a nickname in certain tech circles—the Fixer.

It didn't matter that she wasn't the most creative thinker or most analytical person in a room: When she was presented with a problem, Charlotte Walsh could always fix it.

She'd done it quietly, but when the press had asked her about it in 2014—because funding family planning was still considered a rogue move in the twenty-first century—she'd explained, as if she were responding to a very small and not terribly bright child, that it was the right goddamned thing to do to keep talented women in the workforce. That quote had caught the eye of some powerful women's groups: EMILY's List, She Should Run, and the Pink Pussy Brigade, which had begun selling Pepto-pink T-shirts emblazoned with the words THE RIGHT THING TO DO on the front and CHARLOTTE WALSH FOR PRESIDENT on the back. After that, a publisher had asked her to write a book, a request which was flattering and daunting. She wrote every night after the girls went to sleep. Her editor offered her a ghost writer, but that felt too easy, and dishonest. She finished the thing in four months, beating their original deadline by sixty days because she secretly feared someone would realize they never should have asked her to write a book in the first place. *Let's Fix It* stayed on the bestseller list for thirty-two weeks. When she'd become an unwitting hero for women in the workplace, the kind of people who talk about such things—political pundits, cable news journalists, political strategists, and under-stimulated men who live in their parents' basements and spend twenty hours a day on Twitter—had started debating the merits of her running for office. Once someone suggests you'll be good at doing something, it's not long before your ego kicks in. From then on, Charlotte hadn't been able to stop thinking about running.

"I'm not ashamed of getting IVF, or of how it was paid for, Josh." Punctuating a sentence with someone's name always made Charlotte feel like an unseasoned primary school teacher. "The policies I created for family planning at Humanity paved the way for a better future for women in corporate America."

Josh rolled his eyes. "Save that for a tweet," he said. "You should talk about it, but not too much. You can be a strong female candidate, but not a feminist candidate. There's a difference. The subtle path is the surer one. It's all in the nuance. And the hair."

A gurgle of nausea swept through Charlotte's belly as Josh reached out and twisted a lock of her hair around one of his stubby fingers.

"Thank God you didn't chop off your hair when you had kids. At least seventy-three percent of male voters prefer women with long hair. Too many liberal lady politicians get that mom helmet. They look like a crop of nuns, or dykes, and men don't like it even if they won't admit it in an exit poll."

This was part of his shtick, semantics as offensive as those of a cable talk show back when talk show hosts were still celebrated for being rude. Charlotte couldn't believe she needed to hire someone she already couldn't stand, but she didn't have to like him; she liked what he could do for her.

Josh pivoted again. "Well, it's nice that Humanity paid for your fancy treatments, but you could have afforded it with your fancy salary, no? Since you earned . . . let's see. . . ." He paused while he looked down at his notes. "A salary of 1.7 million dollars last year. That doesn't even include your stock options, which are more than fifty million. You know you could probably buy this race if you sold half those options?"

Josh carried on with something of a sneer even though, if he agreed to work with her, she would be paying him a salary that was pretty damn fancy. "Are you worried you're too rich and fancy for the hard-working people of Pennsylvania?"

"Being rich worked for the guy sitting in the Oval Office, didn't it?" she growled. "I was compensated for successfully running one of the fastest-growing companies in the world."

Josh held his palm open in front of her face and snorted. "Don't be angry. No one likes an angry woman."

She wanted to bite his chubby hand. Instead, Charlotte batted his paw hard enough to hurt him.

"Goddammit, I *am* angry. That's why I'm running."

"Focus on the reasons why you're angry so that people know you aren't running just because you have the money to do it. But remember to speak softly and sweetly when you talk about those reasons."

Perhaps sensing her disdain, Josh paused. The next time he looked at her his combative edge softened in a way that made him look almost friendly, like he was about to consider her as a human instead of a project.

"Look, I don't like being the dick all the time, but you need someone like me to do this now. It isn't going to be easy. You're going to lose your privacy. The press will dredge up things you said and did twenty, even thirty years ago. You might not even remember them. Forget about personal liberty. You may need to do things you're uncomfortable with, say things you don't agree with, maybe even lie. Probably lie. Let's be honest: You're gonna lie a lot. Normal rules don't apply any more. You're running against a guy who spews fantasy like it's gospel."

Lying. If he only knew. Charlotte sucked a deep breath into her rib cage and wiped her hands on her black linen pants. Her palms were sticky with sweat. She didn't fully comprehend yet what the campaign would ask of her, but she knew she was willing to do it. She was prepared to go all in, whatever it took. Just the potential of it exhilarated, terrified, and energized her in a way she hadn't felt in years.

"We're the good guys, Josh." Charlotte realized how naïve she sounded only after the words left her mouth.

"Everyone thinks they're the good guys. But we can't all be good, can we?"

"I get it. I realize it's not going to be easy." She focused on Josh's pumpkin-shaped head and called to mind the best advice Rosalind Waters, her old boss and mentor, had given her regarding difficult men. That had been more than twenty years ago and Charlotte had only just started working for the Maryland governor when a right-wing conservative radio host baited Rosalind by telling her that deep down some women really just wanted to be sexually harassed. "How do you handle it?" Charlotte asked afterward, disgusted, curious, and enraged on Rosalind's behalf. "How do you listen to pigheaded crap like that and keep a straight face?"

Rosalind answered with her signature spiky wit. "I picture them with a ridiculous mustache. Any time a man talks down to you, or at you, or overexplains something to you, picture what they would look like with an excellent mustache. It could be a classic Tom Selleck, a Fu Manchu, a petite Hitler." Rosalind, known to her friends as Roz, explained this with a sly smile. "If he already has a mustache, just give him a more creative one in your mind. It takes the sting out of whatever they're saying and lets you concentrate on how to respond. Better than picturing them naked. No one wants to see those men naked, even their wives—*especially* their wives." Charlotte also recalled Roz's more recent advice, the advice she'd offered when she'd encouraged Charlotte to enter this race: "Only let the world see half of your ambition. Half of the world can't handle seeing it all."

Now Charlotte directed her gaze to Josh's upper lip and gave him a Salvador Dalí, long and narrow, with the ends pointing toward the ceiling and just covering the smudge of mustard.

"This campaign isn't about the fact that I'm a woman. It's not about how I got pregnant and it's not about my husband. It's about the voters of Pennsylvania. It's about disrupting a broken system."

Josh delivered a pointed look and raised an eyebrow. "You're good."

"You have shit on your face." Leila finally spoke, as she stood and walked halfway around the table to Josh and used her thumb to remove the yellow stain from his lip. Charlotte loved that about Leila, her willingness to inject herself into any conversation, to save Charlotte when she would never ask to be saved, to lick her finger and swipe it across a stranger's mouth for her.

"None of this is going to hurt us," Leila declared. "Charlie got IVF because she has a medical condition. Max was a shoulder rubber? A flirt? News flash . . . everyone likes to flirt with Max. *You* might find yourself flirting with Max. He's going to be an asset on the campaign trail. He looks like Jon Hamm. He's got the sexy day-old beard down pat. He wears flannel like a guy who works with his hands, has dimples for days, and can change a diaper in public in thirty seconds flat. Yes, women like him. But, more important, women voters will like him, a lot. You have nothing to worry about there."

Leila strode confidently back to her seat in the corner of the room and returned to her note-taking.

"What are you?" Josh asked then, looking at Leila and tilting his head to the side, inspecting her face.

"What am I?" the young woman shot back with a smirk that indicated she knew exactly what he was asking.

Leila was asked this question on a weekly basis by colleagues, business associates, strangers on the street. The features inherited from her Sudanese mother and Irish father, a mismatched pair who parted ways shortly after their only daughter entered the world, caused confusion for anyone who wanted to place her in a particular box. Her parents' intense but brief union had produced a child with cinnamon-colored skin, light brown freckles, bright green eyes as vigilant as an alley cat's, and thick dark hair that she wore in a meaty braid on top of her head, coiled like a cobra. Charlotte had heard all of Leila's responses to the "what are you?" question, ranging from the polite "I'm just an all-American mutt" to the cynical "I was created in a lab to breed the women of the future" to the defiant "What are *you?*"

It had been nine years since Charlotte hired Leila at Humanity just after Leila had finished her classes at San Jose State on a full scholarship. They had the scholarship-kid thing in common. Leila waltzed into that first interview wearing scuffed teal pumps from Goodwill and delivered an hour-long PowerPoint presentation about how she would make Charlotte's life easier. She was likable because she didn't need to be liked, she only wanted to be seen as capable. Charlotte appreciated her ambition and confidence and hired her as a personal assistant later that afternoon.

Leila leaned back onto the couch now. She tugged at her ruby-colored pencil skirt, the one with fat brass buttons up the front. She'd tucked a man's oxford into the high waist and topped it with a black bolero jacket. Leila called seventies-era Anjelica Huston her personal style muse. She regularly chided Charlotte for her simpler, more conservative taste in clothing. She'd insist: "Charlie, we live in a world where male billionaires dress like they're homeless. It's our duty to bring the style to this valley."

Leila gave Josh her honest answer. "I'm half Sudanese, half Irish, born and raised in Oakland. My mom came here when she was sixteen, applied for political asylum because being Christian in Khartoum could get you killed. My dad played the fiddle and had kind eyes. And even though she was a sweet Jesus-fearing girl, he introduced her to the glory of the Irish car bomb one night in a bar called McGlinchey's and they made me. Happy?"

Josh bit his bottom lip. Leila clearly unnerved him. "You might want to reconsider the nose ring on the campaign trail. If you're coming, that is?"

It was never in question that Leila would accompany Charlotte to Pennsylvania, even though Charlotte had warned her it would mean putting her personal life on hold for more than a year.

Leila fingered the black hoop through her septum and shrugged. "I'll think about it."

Josh turned his attention back to Charlotte. "Speaking of families . . . your brother? Some guys in Elk Hollow told me he's . . . Hold on, let me get the wording right." Josh threw a glance at his notes. "'A drunk just like his dad and a pill-popping freak.' How accurate is that?"

Charlotte had no idea how accurate it was. Paul, older than her by two years, had a long history of abusing any substance he could get his hands on. His vices were tempered only by his long-suffering wife, Kara, and his inability to afford to maintain a serious addiction. But Charlotte hadn't spoken to him in about five years. During their last conversation he'd asked her to loan him $100,000 to start a hydro-ponic marijuana business in his basement. When Charlotte refused, Paul stopped returning her texts.

"I'm not sure."

"You need to figure it out. Spend time with him. Talk to the wife. Get a better sense of what we're dealing with. You should have a strong family connection in the state since you've been gone for so long. You're planning to move back to Elk Hollow? Yes?"

Elk Hollow, in the far northeastern corner of Pennsylvania, was just forty-five minutes from Scranton and three hours from Philadel-phia when there was no traffic on the turnpike. "Yes. We're moving into the house where I grew up."

Charlotte glanced at her phone as it buzzed in her lap. This was the third time Max had called. "I need to call my husband."

Josh raised an eyebrow and shook his head. "Your husband can wait. This is my time right now."

People didn't tell Charlotte Walsh what to do, or at least they hadn't in a long time.

"Fine. I'll send a text." She looked at the phone again. Max had beaten her to the punch.

Charlie-bird?? How's the boy wonder campaign manager?
Pick up phone!

Josh craned his neck to see her screen. "Boy Wonder—I like that." He nodded his approval, showing no qualms about his invasion of her privacy. "Nicer than what people usually call me. But Charlie, I'm going to need your full attention right now." He smiled when he used her nickname, plucked the phone gently from her hand, placed it in his own back pocket, and picked up where he'd left off. To her surprise, Charlotte let him do it.

"Elk Hollow . . ." Josh let the name of the town dribble off his tongue. "It's good. You're smart. Any path to regaining power in Congress has to go through the small towns. Moving back to your hometown is what I would have advised you to do if you'd hired me three months ago, but you called me late. You're behind already. How much money have you raised?"

Charlotte was ready to loan the campaign the initial chunk of funding, $500,000 out of her personal bank account to get up and running. Because a cadre of very rich people saw her as part of what they liked to refer to as the Resistance with a capital *R*, she'd been promised a handful of six-figure and even a couple of seven-figure checks.

"A couple million."

Josh whistled through pursed lips. "You'll need at least ten times that." He leaned back in his chair and spread his legs wide. His next few sentences sounded to Charlotte more like an internal dialogue.

"I feel good about this. According to early focus-group data, voters like you. They appreciate the no-bullshit, take-charge attitude. They think you're nice-looking. That matters more than you think, and even though they have no idea what you actually do at Humanity, they think it's the kind of job an important person would have. Voters remember someone they think is important." He paused and looked directly into her eyes. "But one last question. Be honest. Why you? Why now?"

"Does this mean you're going to work for me?" She'd expected to feel relief, but instead felt a charge like a static shock—the feeling she'd just gotten away with something, the feeling that she might just be able to pull this off.

Josh held her phone in his hand now like he was considering whether to give it back to her. "I'll call you tomorrow to give you my answer," he said as he placed the device facedown on the table. "If we do this, I'll always call. You will always pick up. I never text. Texting is for teenage girls and teachers trying to have sex with their students. If we work together, I'm the first person you talk to in the morning and the last person whose voice you hear before you go to bed. If you need to take a particularly difficult shit, I should probably know about it."

Tomorrow was soon. Tomorrow was good. She flipped the phone

over. There were five more messages from her husband, but she didn't bother to open them.

"But answer my question," Josh repeated himself. "Why you? Why now?"

Can't it be as simple as "I think I can do a better job than the guy who has the job"? She imagined all the answers she could possibly give about why she wanted to run for office. There was the earnest one: the fact that politicians were failing Americans. Corporations were failing Americans. She hated the hate she saw every time she read the news. She felt terror and anger when she scrolled through Twitter. Americans were at each other's throats and it was disgusting. She was scared to death of raising her daughters in this country. She wanted to help the kinds of people she'd grown up with have a better life. After the last election, she'd had a real road-to-Damascus moment where she'd stayed up nights wondering if she was doing enough of the right thing, if her corporate job was all bullshit.

All of that was true.

Then there was the honest answer: Her decision to run for office had been born of a combination of idealism, guilt, and ego. The more she had thought about it, mostly late at night when she couldn't sleep and the voices in her head reminded her she was crazy for even thinking she had what it took to run for political office, the more clearly she'd begun to recognize her motivations. In the two decades she'd worked at Humanity, their innovations in productivity had put hundreds of thousands of Americans out of a job, and entering government could give her the tools to help fix what she'd broken.

And there was another answer, the one it had taken her years to be comfortable articulating. But it was the one she knew Josh would appreciate. This was the first time she allowed herself to say the words out loud, and she grinned with a small shrug of her shoulders when she said them. "I like to win."

Partial transcript of keynote interview between Charlotte Walsh and news anchor Erika Cabot at the Women Are the Future conference in New York City on August 1, 2017. Segments of this talk were broadcast on MSNBC.

Erika Cabot: In the past five years you doubled the number of women in management positions at Humanity. Some of the men both in and outside of the company have claimed that you actually favor female employees over men, that your goal is to marginalize men. What's your response to that?

Charlotte Walsh: It's ridiculous. For the record, I love men. The majority of the men I know are really good men and I adore them. I'm happy to see any employee stand up for themselves in the face of what they perceive as discrimination, even though I've said over and over again that I don't promote anyone based on their sex or the color of their skin. I hire and promote people based on merit and merit alone. If I've done anything, it's make it easier for highly qualified and talented women to have children and then to stay in the workforce after they've had their kids. That's what contributed to doubling the number of women in management at Humanity. Those women are there because they deserve to be.

Erika Cabot: In your book *Let's Fix It*, you devoted an entire chapter to how the government could follow Humanity's lead by implementing similar policies and incentives to help keep women in the workforce. You were attacked by

Tom Broadbent and Jim Sanders, two congressmen from Wyoming and Florida, respectively, for those statements as being a bleeding-heart West Coast liberal and a hysterical woman. What was your reaction to that?

Charlotte Walsh: At a certain point you have to stop caring whether people like you. Their comments just made me think, and not for the first time, what hateful, smug men run our country.

Erika Cabot: That brings me to the elephant in the room. Will you be the one to change it? Are you planning to run for national office?

Charlotte Walsh: This is where I tell you I'm flattered and have no plans to seek political office, right?

Erika Cabot: That's usually how this works.

Charlotte Walsh: I'm not good at keeping things a secret, so I don't see any point in giving you the runaround. Yes. I'm seriously considering a Senate run in Pennsylvania.

Erika Cabot: That's the most honest answer I think I've gotten from a future politician. You've already got the support of plenty of women's groups. You've got quite the tribe behind you. Do you think the future is female? The future of politics?

Charlotte Walsh: I'm hoping the future of politics is competent and hopeful and ready to fix the problems facing Americans. I'm proud to be a woman and I'm proud to be a candidate.

CHAPTER 2
August 21, 2017
442 days to Election Day

Charlotte woke with a twitch, her body sweaty and stiff, with a sharp pain in her neck. It took her a moment to register her surroundings—the front seat of their minivan. Outside the window a vast parking lot. The pain was from the seat belt digging into her left shoulder. More agonizing, though, were the remnants of the all-too-vivid dream she'd been having. It lingered in her mind, as suffocating as the air in the car.

In the dream she and Max were rock climbing in a beautiful park, somewhere out West, with rust-colored rocks and vast plains. Max climbed above her, his wide hands exploring the crags ahead for the next place to clip in, the sinewy muscles in his back flexing and strained. Suddenly, she lost her grip, the rock crumbling into dust in one hand, her feet dangling beneath her into a vast nothing, a gaping blackness. Her safety rope frayed. She opened her mouth to scream for Max to turn around and help, but no sound came. He swiveled his head to look down at her. "I need you!" she screamed over and over. In the dream his eyes went blank, as if he didn't recognize her. She summoned her remaining strength to reach out to him. If he just reached down he could grab her wrist, but instead he turned his body away from her and continued his climb.

She began to fall.

The nightmare often came when she least expected it, always when she let her guard down, when she finally felt happy and in control of her world again. It had begun almost two years ago. The first one came a week after she found out about Max's affair.

Going back to that moment was like picking a scab—painful and sickly soothing at the same time. She'd been in their bedroom in California, half-heartedly watching some police procedural on network television while soothing four-month-old Annie to sleep by rubbing small circles on her belly. Max giggled down the hall with the twins in the bathtub. The baby smiled big and wide and Charlotte grabbed Max's iPad to try to capture it on video to show him when he came to bed. That was when she saw the unfinished email open on his screen. In her memory of that moment, she heard Max's voice read it out loud, as if it were a monologue coming from the television and not her life.

> We can never do this again. I'm sorry if I led you on. Sleeping together was a mistake.
> This has to be over.

Her hand trembled and she dropped the device on the bed. It bounced and made a loud thud as it hit their thick oak floor. The baby jerked at the sound and began to wail. Max called out from the bathroom.

"You okay?"

When she didn't answer he ran into their room in just his boxer shorts, his chest and arms dripping. In real life, as in the dream, it felt as though the world had dropped out from beneath her. She searched for something solid to grasp onto, something to anchor her in reality, and her eyes locked on the baby's face, crumpled and red and needing her.

Confronting Max had to wait while they finished putting their girls to bed. It was amazing how she could tuck her rage away when she needed to in order to go through the motions of pajamas, bedtime stories, dream feeding, and cuddles. When the night-light caught Max smiling as he kissed both of Annie's cheeks in her crib Charlotte considered pretending nothing had happened at all, letting their idyllic lives continue as if she'd never seen that email.

But she wasn't that woman.

After the kids were snoring sweetly in their rooms she stood over him once he lay down in their bed, straightening her shoulders and occupying her entire height.

"Tell me about the woman you've been fucking." Charlotte kept her voice even. She knew how much it unnerved him when she used that kind of language.

His tearful confession came with the few details Charlotte could handle listening to—the woman worked at Humanity, it had begun at a developer conference in Boulder, and had happened only a couple of times after. It was over. He promised it was over.

"She was an employee. Someone who worked for us? Do you know how that looks? What that could mean for the company if she decides to report you? How could you be so fucking stupid?"

"I'm sorry."

Max assured her that Margaret (her name echoed over and over in Charlotte's brain as she imagined Max whispering it, moaning it, screaming it in passion) had no interest in making any trouble for them.

Charlotte placed her hands over her ears. "I don't want to hear any more." She moved one hand in front of her in a gesture of surrender.

"Charlie, please, just listen to me. You've been different. We've been different."

She recalled the past few years of their marriage. More fights, less sex. Her body from her feet to her bleeding nipples felt ravaged by wild animals, children who insisted on sleeping between them in bed. More work, so much work.

Months later they met with a therapist named Carol who tried to give them rules and strategies and ways to cope.

After a year of therapy, it was clear Max would do anything to win her back, even move back home to a place that he hated, even give up a job he loved and take care of their three small children. He would do it because he owed her. They both knew that.

So she told him she wanted to run for office in Pennsylvania. The timing was perfect. When the last election had turned into an unprecedented disaster, with both sides in an almost comical death spiral, the party bigwigs had been dazed, weary, shell-shocked, and searching for out-of-the-box candidates to create a populist surge. They needed to win back five Senate seats in the midterms to regain control. The national party asked Rosalind to ask Charlotte if she would ever consider running in Pennsylvania, her home state.

When Roz came to see her, it had been nearly a year since the affair, but Charlotte was still shattered. Men cheated on their wives every day. Charlotte knew there was no specificity to her situation, and yet what was happening to her felt completely unique and unfair. She'd worked so hard to craft a life that looked perfect on paper, the opposite of the one she'd anticipated she'd have growing up. Max's affair put her hard work to shame and made her feel like a failure.

"You need to do this," Roz said over two bottles of her favorite cabernet. At first Charlotte had wanted to keep the affair a secret, but there were no secrets from Roz. Her mentor said all the right words, the ones Leila couldn't say because young women in their twenties knew nothing about real heartbreak, real marriage. Roz's husband, Richard, the chair of linguistics at Georgetown, had a liking for coeds who majored in Sanskrit and had pert breasts. Charlotte remembered too well how she'd judged her boss for putting up with her husband's infidelities when she was a twenty-six-year-old staffer, how she had thought Roz was a damn fool for staying with him.

"Your entrance will put a national spotlight on everything that is wrong and corrupt in a state that's never elected a woman to the Senate," Roz insisted. "Why not go home again? Besides, Max owes you this and so much more."

The challenge made it even more appealing, and having a new purpose chipped away at the sadness that had settled into her bones since learning about Margaret. Momentum was what she craved. You couldn't get stuck if you were always moving.

Charlotte began to plan her campaign and set up the meeting with Josh Pratt. She felt guilty about lying to Josh about the state of her marriage: The last thing she wanted was for this race to devolve into a tabloid game of cat-and-mouse, but it was Roz who instructed her to keep the affair to herself. "He only takes clean candidates," she had explained. "And you need him. Apologize later if it all goes to shit. It's a gamble, but it'll be worth it when you win."

Besides, she and Max had been good recently, as good as the parents of three young kids could be. It had taken time to get here, but that was the story of a marriage. There were highs and lows, and those lows could last for months, sometimes even a year; sometimes you didn't love the person or even like the person, but they'd made it through.

And she'd made sure, during her one and only meeting with Margaret, a memory she buried deeper than all the others, one she never let herself revisit, even in her dreams, that the other woman would never breathe a word about what had happened.

Charlotte looked for the keys now to roll down the window of her new family minivan to release the hot stale air. She swiveled her neck to figure out where they were. The last time she was awake they'd been in Wyoming. Now she caught a glimpse of a grove of Ponderosa Pines just obscuring the perfect Roman nose of a granite George Washington. She was in the parking lot of Mount Rushmore.

This minivan was Josh's idea, as was the great American road trip to travel from California to Pennsylvania. Good optics. "Approximately sixty-seven percent of Americans and fifty-three percent of Pennsylvanians still road-trip once a year," he informed her. She wondered where he got his statistics. "It's a show of your down-home authenticity. Drive your minivan and sleep in dumpy motels, ride a tractor, talk to diner waitresses and take pictures and videos of it for your social," he instructed.

Josh came on board to work for Charlotte three days after their meeting with two conditions—that she take his call every morning at 6:30 a.m. and that he'd get a $300,000 bonus if they won. Win bonuses were standard, but this amount would be a record for a Senate race. She agreed to both. In their first few weeks together he'd already made her give the family's nanny a leave of absence. "It doesn't look good to pay someone to take care of your kids, especially a Mexican, even if she's legal. You need to be people who can take care of their own. Money hasn't changed you," he explained. He'd also counseled her to purchase two nondescript American-made minivans to replace their Prius and Tesla because she needed to "seem middle-class where it matters."

Yet the road trip was not the romantic adventure she'd hoped it would be. Day five felt like month five, and Charlotte had already checked twice to see whether they could get on a plane in Sioux Falls and pay someone to drive their car; their dog, a half-blind rescue bulldog named Bob; the twins' bearded dragon, George Washington; and their obese coon cat, Jack the Fat, the rest of the way across the country. Kid squeals, screams, and bloodcurdling cries had ricocheted through the van since they crossed the Bay Bridge. Ella, in particular, knew how to make a noise that sounded as though someone was trying to murder her. One child always needed something. Ella had an insatiable appetite, Rose had a bladder the size of a thimble, and Annie could often only fall sleep if someone was holding onto her left foot.

Bob released a low, sad yowl that announced he was sick of sharing such small quarters with the cat and the lizard and that he probably had to pee if he hadn't already gone in his crate. Charlotte opened the door instead of the window and swung her legs around to put her feet on the pavement. She placed the heels of her hands into her eye sockets as if she could push the dream out of her skull and gulped swallows of hot, dry South Dakota air.

When she lifted her head she could see her family in the dusty rear-view mirror. Max held the hands of the twins, who gripped rainbow lollipops as large as their heads in their opposite fingers. Annie, their youngest, sat proudly atop her father's shoulders in nothing but a diaper and a too-large safari hat.

"Why'd you let me sleep?" Charlotte called out, standing with her hands on her hips and head cocked to her side in mock frustration as the twins, Ella and Rose, let go of their father's hands and galloped toward her.

"Watch out for cars," Charlotte shouted, running to cross the distance between them to block their small bodies from unexpected vehicles.

Max grinned. "I figured you needed rest more than a visit to the most self-congratulatory public works project in the history of our great nation. We spent most of the time in the gift shop anyway."

Charlotte closed her eyes and took a breath to remind herself to sound pleasant when she spoke next. Having the nightmare often left a residue of resentment as if the affair had happened only yesterday.

Her jaw clicked when she yawned. "I did, baby. Thank you."

"Did you see the picture I texted you?"

"Not yet." Charlotte pulled her phone from the van's center console and opened the text from Max. He'd somehow managed to position their three children in perfect line with presidents Washington, Jefferson, Lincoln, and Roosevelt.

"How'd you get them to pose?"

"So much sugar." Max lifted the dog out of his crate and placed him by the back tire, where he let loose a much-needed pee on the baking rubber. "Maybe too much. I can Photoshop you into it." He smirked. "Put it on your Instagram. Boy Wonder would love that, right?"

They were back on the road for less than five minutes before everything devolved into chaos. Rose started, first a whimper that graduated to a yowl. "Annie bit me," the five-year-old twin wailed, raising a bloody pinky finger toward the front seat. Charlotte stole a look behind her to find her two-year-old smiling with a smear of blood on the side of her mouth like an adorable elfin cannibal.

Without missing a beat, Rose's twin, Ella, reached over the car's headrest and punished Annie with a yank of her black curls so hard that fine dark strands came out in her hand. Now two children wailed like flaming banshees. Charlotte climbed into the back of the car and pulled her smallest child out of the car seat and onto her lap on the floor, simultaneously inspecting Rose's finger to ensure she had nothing more than a simple flesh wound. The floor of their minivan was caked in a thin layer of graham cracker crumbs. The windows were smeared with peanut butter, snot, and now blood. Charlotte's ass ended up in something wet.

She leaned in to kiss Annie's head, delighting in the sweetly sour infant scent that still clung to her youngest, and rubbed her cheek along the girl's downy neck even as she reprimanded her. She could feel the child's fragile ribs flutter against her breast. Two-year-old Annie, their perfect accident, was a clone of Max, with her dark curls, sulky mouth, and mischievous blue eyes. Her daughter and her husband both used their entire faces to laugh, throwing their heads back with glee.

After working so hard to have the twins through IVF, Charlotte hadn't been able to imagine getting pregnant again on her own, which was why she and Max hadn't bothered with birth control. "You want an IUD?" the doctor asked when the twins were two months old. Charlotte laughed. "I'm practically geriatric. I'd rather not bother with the hormones." Then came Annie. The surprise of her and the way she burst into the world as a preemie with a vengeance made Charlotte's love for their younger daughter all the fiercer. It wasn't fair to have favorites. *Favorite* was the wrong word anyway. The twins had each other, and Max doted on them because they'd been the first. Annie felt completely hers.

Annie smiled at her, tears still glistening in her eyes. She leaned in as if to give her a kiss and bit Charlotte on the soft part of her ear.

"Owwwwwww."

Max turned toward her shriek and carefully eased the car onto the creaky gravel shoulder, got out, slid open the rear door, reached into the backseat, and pulled Annie from Charlotte. Without a word he marched her into the woods lining the road, every muscle in his body devoted to soothing and admonishing the girl so Charlotte could turn her attention to the twins. Annie bucked her head like a wild thing, her fists tight in his hair.

Thank you, she whispered even though he couldn't hear her. It was these small moments that reminded her how much she needed him. In the weeks and months following Max's affair, Leila had asked Charlotte over and over again: *Why stay? Leave him. Do it on your own. You have plenty of money. Hire people to help. Kick him out for good.*

But it wasn't that simple. She loved Max. Though in the wake of the affair she had to constantly and consciously remind herself of the reasons she loved and was attracted to her husband. She made an exercise of finding new things she enjoyed on his face and body, small imperfections that delighted her because they were incongruous with how handsome he appeared to the rest of the world. One week it had been his nose. It was slightly squashed and crooked, like he'd gotten into a bar fight or been sacked in a violent rugby match. It had the effect of making his other features seem rougher. In truth, he'd fallen flat on his face while roller-skating when he was ten. She came to enjoy the fact that the base of his shoulder blades were still sprinkled with acne. Began to love his giant caveman feet, shaped more like flippers that fanned out wide around the toes. The nails on both of his big toes were mangled beyond repair from rock-climbing accidents. They were the ugliest feet Charlotte had ever seen and she adored them.

Then there was their shared history—the deaths of Charlotte's parents, Max's skin cancer scare, IVF, and then a premature baby. But one of the reasons that was harder to articulate to someone like Leila, someone who'd never been married or had children, was that Charlotte didn't want to do it on her own. And while some days she would have brought the plumber into her bed if it meant he would share the burden of parenting their small monsters, she also didn't want to do this with someone new, to start from day one. She wanted the life she had *already* worked so hard to build.

★

Fifty miles farther on they found a motel with a pool on the border of the Badlands. A sign out front featured a neon image of a prairie dog with his eye burned out. For sixty dollars they got a room with two beds, one for all three girls and a second for Charlotte and Max. The girls were fast asleep now, arms and legs tangled together, the violence in the car forgotten. Charlotte envied her children's ability to dismiss pain and indignities so quickly. She wanted to kiss each of their six tiny feet. She loved having her whole family asleep in one room, loved having the three girls so close she could touch all of them from her bed.

Charlotte could just make out her husband's silhouette in the dim light of the hotel bathroom, tall and lean in his boxer shorts, his toothbrush dangling out the side of his mouth, one hand tapping absentmindedly at his phone.

Who's he writing to? Who's he texting? The hairs on the back of her neck and arms pricked. Every time Max picked up his phone she wondered whether he was texting another woman. An affair does that to you. It doesn't just crumple your soul in the moment you learn about it. You question the little things, maybe for the rest of your life. Even if you heal from it, it's like a bone that's set following a bad break: It will always be a little stiff and a little uncomfortable.

When Max caught her looking at him his mouth moved into an easy smile.

"Checking the weather for tomorrow."

She placed her index finger to her lips to warn him to keep his voice down and walked into the bathroom, softly shutting the door behind her. Charlotte grabbed her husband around his waist and, not for the first time, marveled at the fact that as he approached fifty he managed to stay in such good shape. Rather than enjoy it, she allowed it to be a reminder of her own loose stomach and the fifteen pounds of baby pooch she'd never lose.

He dropped his hand holding his phone down to his side. Charlotte placed her forehead against his chest. "What are you reading me tonight?"

In their twelve years of marriage, they'd cobbled together a few traditions that had stuck and Max reading to her was one. He'd been doing it since their first date, a date that wasn't supposed to be a date. It wasn't supposed to be a date because Max had a girlfriend at the time, some pretty public relations assistant at Apple. The girl couldn't, or wouldn't, go with him on a camping trip to Yosemite, so he'd invited Charlotte instead. Good old Charlotte, reliable Charlotte, just his friend. Roz had pushed her to go on that particular trip. "Jesus, can you please have some fun already? You can't bury your face in a computer screen for the rest of your life. And wear a little mascara."

At a small lake in a grove of redwoods, miraculously empty in the otherwise crowded park, Max stripped off his clothes and ran screaming into the frigid water, his boldness echoing off the sheer granite cliffs. *Take a chance.* For once in her life she did. Charlotte ran in after him.

As they hiked to their campsite he warned her not to touch any plants she didn't recognize along the trail, but she hadn't paid attention. She'd let her hands wander over the leaves and regretted it later that night when she touched her face, spreading poison oak all over her cheeks and eyes. Max covered her in calamine lotion, wrapped her in his sleeping bag, and read to her from a tattered copy of *On the Road*.

"You're such a cliché." She laughed quietly.

"Me?" he replied in mock offense. "You don't like Kerouac?"

"Am I allowed to say out loud that the Beats were immature misogynists?"

"I'll never read it to you again," he whispered, and shut the book. "I like making you happy. I like taking care of you."

She used water from the canteen to wipe the crusty pink lotion from her lips and made the first move, kissing him tentatively at first. Then she grasped a handful of his thick, curly hair and hungrily brought his mouth onto hers. Everything she'd ever done before that trip had been safe. Max made every day seem like it could be a brand-new adventure. When they got back, he dated the PR girl for six more months before he and Charlotte became exclusive, but they never told that part of the story. The narrative of any marriage is mostly revisionist history. Charlotte often wondered what would have happened if she hadn't made the first move. Would they be here now?

Charlotte watched the smile fall from Max's lips in the harsh fluorescent light of the motel bathroom. "Don't you have work to do?" he said.

She made an effort not to look back at her computer, where Leila's hundred-page policy briefing on why gun control was still a wedge issue for Pennsylvanians was waiting for her. "Not right now." Charlotte ran her finger beneath the waistband of his boxers, tracing his stomach and the curve of his hip, avoiding the ticklish spot close to his belly button, the spot that could make him squeal like a girl. She kissed the peach fuzz on his chest, the taste of his skin lingering on her lips as she tried to remember the last time they'd had sex. There were plenty of conversations about potentially having sex, even texts and emails about having sex. But when had they actually done it? There was the Fourth of July, when Max was drunk and couldn't get it up. There was her birthday, when she'd fallen asleep with him inside of her. Having sex after kids was like jury duty. You tried to put it off, get out of it, even demonized it; then you realized it wasn't half bad once it was all over.

Max cracked the bathroom door and they looked at the girls.

"Do you like them today?" he asked in a low whisper.

"No."

"Do you love them?"

"More than ever." They said this most nights.

"We could get our own room," he said into her neck.

"That would make us terrible parents."

"I won't tell if you won't." She loved him like this.

Of course they didn't get their own room. She brushed her teeth and peed, and ten minutes later Max was snoring next to her as she immersed herself in gun control in the Keystone State. She stared at his profile in the glow of her laptop. His resemblance to Annie was even more pronounced when he slept, his jaw slack, his bow-shaped lips slightly pursed.

She turned her attention back to her computer and spent the next four hours emailing potential donors, pressing her hip against the soft flesh of Max's thigh because it felt nice just to touch him while she worked. When she finally put the computer away, she rolled toward him and buried her face in between his shoulder blades. They'd spent twelve years of nights in beds like this together—sleeping, talking, fucking, laughing, crying, bullshitting, screaming—yet sometimes he still felt like a complete stranger. In moments like this she felt his betrayal the most. Then she remembered the ways she had also betrayed him.

Faced with falling asleep, the outlines of her earlier dream came back, that feeling of the world falling out from under her. She pulled herself closer to Max as if to steady herself, to hold onto something solid. But still, she couldn't stop her own voice from echoing in her head, two thoughts on a vicious loop.

I need to tell him what I did.

You can't. It will ruin everything.

Hattie Wyatt Caraway (February 1, 1878–December 21, 1950), the first woman elected to the United States Senate, only went to Washington because her husband, Arkansas senator Thaddeus Caraway, died of a blood clot in his coronary artery.

Everyone expected she would step aside once Thaddeus's original term was up. It was, after all, the polite thing for a woman to do—to let the men do the running for office. Hattie, who never remarried, wasn't a particularly political woman prior to taking her husband's Senate seat, didn't even show a real interest in the issue of women's suffrage, said that adding voting to her duties was the same as adding more cooking and sewing. In other words, just another pain, but when it came time to abandon her place in the Senate, Hattie surprised everyone when she decided to run for reelection. "The time has passed when a woman should be placed in a position and kept there only while someone else is being groomed for the job," Hattie declared. She wrote in her journal that she planned to test "my own theory of a woman running for office."

One of Hattie's theories involved employing an army of male campaign workers to rally new women voters and soothe their crying infants with lollipops so the women could listen to Hattie's speeches without being distracted by their wailing children.

After winning the general election of 1932, Hattie became a champion of President Franklin D. Roosevelt's New Deal policies, veterans' benefits, and farmers' relief. Her relative silence in the chamber was often derided by male journalists who gave her the nicknames "Silent Hattie" and "The Quiet Grandmother." Her response to this was accompanied by a calculated smile. She simply didn't want to take a minute of public pontificating away from her male counterparts, she explained, since "the poor dears love it so."

This is a place you get stuck. It was what Charlotte thought of Elk Hollow when she left home at seventeen. If someone had told her then that she'd be moving back into the house she grew up in thirty years later, she would have told them to go straight to hell.

The town felt familiar and unfamiliar at the same time, both her past and her present. Driving along the Hollow's main drag triggered a montage of memories, some of them as clear as if they'd happened yesterday, others fuzzy and distorted by time and self-preservation. In her grandfather's day, Elk Hollow had been a bustling suburb of Scranton, with homes painted in vibrant Rockwellian strokes of color. But, like those of plenty of other planned suburbs near cities built on coal and manufacturing, the main street of the Hollow was now dingy, lackluster, and gray, filled with shuttered shops covered over in rusted barbed wire, OUT OF BUSINESS signs, and phallic graffiti. Social media reminded Charlotte that the people she'd gone to high school with, the ones who'd stayed in town, were out of work or struggling to cobble together enough gigs to make ends meet as factories all over the Poconos closed and relocated. Those jobs were never coming back, no matter how much Tug Slaughter promised to write legislation that would revitalize the iron and steel mills. According to the policy papers Leila had prepared for her, felony filings had increased by 70 percent in the county in the past five years.

Domestic violence statistics had doubled, and drug addiction was at an all-time high. Citizens of the county were twice as likely to kill themselves as the rest of nation. The average family earnings were $20,000 less than the rest of the state, and 30 percent of the homes were vacant. Barstools in Elk Hollow's two bars were filled by noon with drunk, lonely men, bellies full of $1.50 Coors Light draft beer and pickled red beet eggs, mourning the loss of their place in the world. The minivan drove by O'Puddy's, the town's old-man bar that would probably die with the old men. It was legendary for two-dollar mystery shots and fire meat: bologna pickled in vodka and Tabasco sauce and sold for a quarter. Jars of the stuff fermented on top of the cash register and remained a curiosity. When she was a kid her dad's idea of babysitting had been giving her a Coke topped with a cherry and a roll of quarters to play pinball in the back of the bar while he caroused in the front with his friends and favorite bartender, Linda. Sometimes he picked her up in the garbage truck and let her hang off the back as they drove down the hill they were now driving up to the house where she grew up.

As they unpacked the van in the driveway of her childhood house, Charlotte gazed down the street of single-family homes, more than a few with rusted cars rotting in the yard—the kinds of houses most of her friends and colleagues had only ever seen on TV shows about poor people. Chain-link fences protected parched lawns guarded by mangy dogs tied to stakes in the dirt.

It had felt less dismal when she was growing up, when each of these houses had contained a child within spitting distance of her age and their parents had left their doors unlocked until well after dinnertime. Packs of kids roamed between the yards and kitchens—nothing like the meticulously planned playdates Charlotte attended in California where mommies chatted politely and unironically about the challenges of raising privileged children.

The house she grew up in was smaller than she remembered it. The paint was now dulled by sun and snow and peeling off in large swaths near the roof.

Max dragged the dog over to the cluster of trees around the side of the house to pee. The twins stood tentatively by the car, holding onto each other at the waist, confused about whether this was their destination or just another stop along the way.

"Who's that lady?" Rose asked, pointing behind Charlotte.

Charlotte whipped her head around to see her sister-in-law hollering at her through the window of her truck as she pulled into the driveway behind them.

Kara slammed the rusty door and crossed the distance between them to wrap Charlotte in a suffocating hug. She was a stout woman who wore her curves with comfortable pride in a pair of skinny jeans and a tight black T-shirt that read I JUST WANT TO DRINK PINOT AND PET MY DACHSHUND. If she made her eyes go soft, Charlotte could still see her as the wild sixteen-year-old who'd sported a bright-red fauxhawk, carried Dr Pepper bottles filled with rum to class, sold weed to the rich kids at Scranton Prep, and gotten a tattoo of Jon Bon Jovi on her left bicep.

"I like your shirt." Charlotte squinted at the cursive letters as she stepped out of the embrace to take in all of Kara.

"I made it." When Kara's face lit up, her deep dimples bounced high on her cheeks. "I'm sellin' them on Etsy for nineteen bucks. I make my wine money with the shirts, but I don't tell Paul how much, 'cause then he'd never get a damn job."

"I shop on Etsy all the time." Charlotte smiled. She'd once bought a reclaimed-barn-wood bird feeder as a housewarming gift on the site, but she was far from a regular. She could hear Josh's voice in her head: *Tell people exactly what they want to hear. Make them feel good about themselves before you try to make them feel good about you.*

"I can't believe I'm finally seein' youse." Kara grinned and began helping Charlotte unload suitcases.

Charlotte saw her girls cock their heads at the addition of an *s* on the word *you*, a tic of the northeastern Pennsylvania accent that meant "all of you." It had been years since she'd heard the NEPA accent. Charlotte and Max had both worked hard to eradicate the distinctive vernacular in college, avoiding the use of *youse* and pronouncing the majority of their consonants.

Kara kneeled in the gravel. "Heya. I'm your aunt Kara. You can call me Kiki like the other kids does," she said to Ella and Rose, who were old enough to know their mom had a brother who lived far away that they had never met. The girls smiled politely and extended their hands the way they'd been taught to greet strangers. Kara would have none of their niceties. She leaned in and grabbed the two of them into a hug, smushing their faces into her breasts. "It's so goddamn good to get my hands on you girls."

"Thanks for letting us move back into the house," Charlotte said, once Kara released the children.

Kara waved her hand in the air. "Rental market ain't great lately."

"You know we'll pay you for it," Charlotte insisted.

"I told you not to worry about it."

Charlotte and Paul's grandfather had bought the two-story pre-fab with a $15,000 settlement he'd gotten in 1955 from losing two fingers in a mining explosion. Back then it was a mighty good deal. Everything about Elk Hollow seemed promising during the optimistic days of Pennsylvania's industrial boom. The house was deeded to Marty and Annemarie after Charlotte's grandfather passed. When Annemarie died seven years ago, she'd left the house to Charlotte along with two unpaid mortgages. Once Charlotte had paid the debt she'd offered it to her brother and sister-in-law free and clear. Paul didn't see it as a gift but rather as the tip of the iceberg of what his rich sister owed him. He called it Frack House, convinced someone would pay him to mine natural gas beneath the foundation despite surveyors telling him there was no shale to frack within ten miles of the place. Charlotte's sister-in-law had quietly fixed up the old Walsh place, filling it with furniture from Goodwill, and tried to manage it as a rental.

Sunlight flashed on Charlotte's mom's charm bracelet encircling Kara's wrist. Charlotte had given it to Kara after Annemarie passed, knowing it would have made her mom happy. Her mother had referred to Kara as "the one good thing my son ever gave me." The bracelet was covered in tiny charms of places Annemarie would never visit: the Eiffel Tower, the Leaning Tower of Pisa, the Statue of Liberty. "It's my bucket list," Annemarie said with a wry smile on one of her good days. "Easier than writin' it down." Charlotte fingered the slight gold chain at her own neck that held her mother's simple gold-plated wedding band. The doctor had handed it to her in a plastic bag when she'd flown home to claim her mother's body in the morgue after Annemarie suffered a fatal nervous episode. In layman's parlance she'd committed suicide with a mixture of four different pills—oxycodone, Klonopin, Xanax, and Demerol—all prescribed legally by her doctors for the pain, anxiety, and depression that had gone largely undiscussed from the time Charlotte was a child. Kara had called Charlotte a week before her mother killed herself. "Annemarie's not pickin' up my calls. I went up to see her and it looks like she ain't eating." Charlotte assured her sister-in-law there was nothing to worry about and said she'd check back in the following week after she finished closing a deal with the largest petrochemical company in São Paulo. "She'll still be crazy next week." Except she wasn't crazy next week. She was dead.

When Annemarie died, Charlotte sold a chunk of her Humanity stock options to contribute $1 million to build a mental health facility in northeastern Pennsylvania and lobbied the federal government to provide a matching grant. Creating a project, making a plan, and executing it prevented Charlotte from dwelling on the fact that she could have seen her mother alive one last time.

Still, Annemarie was a subject she rarely talked about, even with Max. Their youngest daughter was named partially in honor of Charlotte's mother. Annie was a name close enough to her mom's to assuage Charlotte's guilt at not doing more to save Annemarie, but not so close she would ever resent her little girl. Charlotte hadn't been back here to Elk Hollow since her mother's funeral. Walking away from the grave that day, Paul had asked Charlotte if he could have the remainder of their mother's oxycodone. "Now that Mom's in the corpse house, you know . . . she'd want me to have them. For my kidney stones," he explained half-heartedly about the medical condition he didn't have.

"I'm not a fucking moron," she said. "If you want to get high on Mom's pain pills, then ask me if you can get high on Mom's pain pills." She'd told him to take what he wanted and later regretted not flushing them down the toilet.

She'd never mentioned it to Kara, but thought about it now as she cleared her throat and asked after her brother.

"How is Paul?"

"Same. Thinks the man has it in for him." Kara rolled her eyes.

Before Charlotte could ask anything else Max rounded the corner of the house, a bag of dog poop in one hand and Annie in the other.

"Goddamn, Charlie, that child is gorgeous," Kara whistled.

Not a day went by when someone didn't remark on what a strikingly beautiful child Annie was. Strangers grinned politely at the older girls, who took after Charlotte, with their chestnut hair and sweet smiles, but Annie took people's breath away. Charlotte often wondered how beauty would shape her youngest. It thrilled and worried her in equal measure that her daughter would be the type of woman for whom good looks would be a defining characteristic for better or for worse.

"She takes after Max." Charlotte reached her hands out to her husband to take the toddler.

Kara sauntered over to Max with a sassy sway in her hips and smacked him square in the ass. "Bet you never thought you'd be back here, Maxie."

He slung an arm around her broad shoulders. "I sure as hell didn't." Max loved Kara, but he didn't have an ounce of nostalgia for Elk

Hollow. Charlotte knew nostalgia, in general, pissed him off. He hated any book or movie where the hero returned to small-town America to shed the sins of big-city living.

Together they made their way up the concrete stairs attached to a screened-in porch and through the front door, which had been painted a defeated shade of green as long as Charlotte could remember. The movers had beat them there. Boxes filled with clothes and toys and computers filled the small living room. Charlotte touched the light-gray walls of the downstairs hallway. Kara had ripped out the floral wallpaper and gotten rid of the brown mold that grew in the corners of the ceiling. There used to be family photos on the wall above the sofa—pictures of Charlotte missing a tooth, Paul at age eleven with a trout as big as his leg, the two of them in the tree house in the back-yard, the one Paul built for her out of two-by-fours and tires when she was six and he was eight. It became their sanctuary, a place to hide when Annemarie was in one of her moods and Charlotte became a target. Back then, Charlotte and Paul had still been allies, confused kids trying to survive a dysfunctional childhood. Those survival skills had served Charlotte well as she built a life outside the Hollow. *Why did I make it out and he didn't?* It was a thought that had plagued Charlotte since she graduated college—a version of survivor's guilt that made her feel angry and lucky and sad all at the same time—when she let it. That was the thing about coming home—it was like you never left.

Anyone looking at that wall of photos would have imagined Char-lotte's mother meticulously printing the pictures and selecting the frames from the local Woolworth, hanging them with care. In truth, it was Charlotte who'd done those things after seeing similar walls of photos in her friends' homes. Creating an organized wall of photo-graphs required a focused energy Annemarie Walsh never could have mustered.

Charlotte planned to move herself and Max into her old room and put the girls in the one where Paul used to sleep. The third bedroom would be an office. Charlotte couldn't bear anyone sleeping in the room where her mother had died. As she walked in, she noticed Kara had kept the heavy curtains in that room, the ones Annemarie always tied shut to keep it as dark as possible. Charlotte fingered the thick fabric now and held her breath.

"Could we take these down?" she asked herself as much as Kara. The curtains evoked a sudden despair and sadness she hadn't anticipated. For a brief moment Charlotte saw herself back in that room forty years ago, a nervous little girl thinking she was being helpful to her mother by opening a window.

"It's such a nice day, Mommy. I want you to see the sunshine. It'll make you feel better."

"Where's your goddamn father?" her mother grumbled, rubbing at her red eyes, her hair unwashed and clinging to her clammy forehead. "I told him to keep you the hell out of here."

"I should've gotten rid of them." Kara stood behind her and placed her chin in the crook of Charlotte's shoulder. "I'll get 'em down. Let's go see the rest of the house. I put some of my grandbabies' toys in the rooms for the little ones. There's quality hair products in the bathroom—Paul Mitchell. I wanted to make it real nice for youse."

"You did a great job. You shouldn't have to do anything else. I'll order blinds." Charlotte swallowed the lump in her throat.

"Hey, girl. You cheer up now. Take a few hours to get settled and then come on over to our place for dinner. See your brother. The two of you need to make peace," Kara said, spinning Charlotte around to face her. "It's time."

Talk to Paul was one of the forty-seven things on Charlotte's to-do list for the month, but it was the last thing she felt like crossing off. With six months to go until she officially announced her campaign, making up with her brother hovered well below finding a campaign headquarters, organizing town halls, hiring thirty staff members, and kissing the asses of the local pols who could lend her their constituent mailing lists and vouch for a stranger from California.

"How would Paul feel about me coming?"

"It's my damn house, too."

"Kara?"

"You know how your brother is. Right now he's got a bee in his bonnet about you runnin' for Senate. He thinks youse guys need to hire him to work on your campaign. Thinks you'll pay him big money to work for you."

"We don't have big money. The campaign doesn't. I just started fundraising."

"How much money you gonna raise?"

Charlotte didn't want to say the actual ridiculous number out loud.

"More than a million." It was what she needed to raise by the end of September. "We have a big staff, door-to-door canvassers, mailings, television ads, yard signs, a lot of expenses I never even thought about. It adds up."

Kara whistled. "Whooooeeee. Must be tough. Askin' folks for money."

"It's the worst part of the job. But look, I'm sure there's something Paul could do." Charlotte chose her words carefully. The last thing she needed was Paul running around town and maybe even talking to the press, crowing about how his rich sister wouldn't hire him.

"He'll be disappointed you can't pay him a gazillion dollars. It's all he's been talkin' about." Kara's laugh echoed through the empty room. "Come over tonight. Tell him you love him, you missed him, and you ain't payin' him shit."

"I don't know, Kara. Everyone's so tired from the drive. Maybe another time."

"You'll be just as tired if you try to unpack and make your own dinner. I ain't takin' no for an answer." Kara turned and began to make her way back downstairs. "Hey, Max," she yelled. "Youse comin' for dinner tonight."

Charlotte heard Max clear his throat. "I was going to go for a run." Before they'd left California Max had announced his plan to train for an Ironman taking place next December, which seemed to Charlotte the least reasonable thing to do when your wife is running for Senate and you're the primary caretaker for three small children, but she bit her tongue and let him have his thing.

Kara held Charlotte's hand and pulled her back down the stairs. She stepped right into Max's face. "Running's for horses. I'll see you at the house at six. Bring some buns. I got meat."

Charlotte looked at Max and shrugged her shoulders at his wary smile.

"This should be interesting."

★

"Thank God my relatives all moved to North Carolina," Max said as they crossed Kara's lawn to her front door, balancing a tray of brownies and plastic-wrapped supermarket roses.

"You paid for your mom and uncles to move to the beach," Charlotte reminded him. Family was as sore a subject for Max as it was for Charlotte, and early on they'd bonded over their shared dysfunctional upbringings. His dad had taken off a week after his son's third birthday, absconding with the family's entire meager savings and leaving his mom so broke she moved in with her older brother and then eventually with a string of deadbeat boyfriends and then again with her older brother. When he was twelve, Max learned his father had died in a car accident in a suburb outside of Tampa. Not realizing how young he was, the Pasco County morgue sent him a box with the contents of the car: a plastic digital Timex, a pack of playing cards with women in bikinis on the back of them, and a Walther P99 semiautomatic handgun, which his mom pawned for two hundred dollars. Much in the same way Charlotte didn't like to talk about Annemarie, Max didn't talk about his father. The one and only time he'd mentioned it was in the hospital the day after the twins were born. Charlotte had fallen asleep after forty-seven hours of grueling labor, and when she woke, both tiny babies were asleep on his bare chest, their bodies hardly bigger than his palms. She looked over at him and saw tears in his eyes.

"How could he have just left?" he asked. They both understood he meant the father he'd never known.

Charlotte was sure that at least some of Max's drive and success was meant as an "F you, I didn't even need you" to his absentee dad.

Max shrugged. "That was money well spent. Keeps them happy and out of my hair. Besides, I like the Outer Banks, and none of them has asked me for money since. You should have done the same with Paul."

"He would have kept asking for more."

Charlotte rang the doorbell.

"It's open," Kara hollered.

The inside of the house was neat and homey, decorated with comfortable things and messy in a good way, lived in, enjoyed. Photos of children covered every available surface. The wine-colored carpet could hide any imaginable stain. Cat scratches crisscrossed an overstuffed plaid couch.

They found Kara in the kitchen. She'd changed into a pink cowlneck sweater woven through with a sparkly thread. Two chubby dachshunds panted happily at her feet. Through the screen door Charlotte could see Kara's grandkids bouncing on the trampoline in the backyard—two boys and two girls with Charlotte's chestnut hair.

"I got the grandkids more often than I don't got 'em," Kara said, shooing the twins outside to meet their cousins. Max followed them, helping each girl onto the trampoline.

"I like havin' them, though. Keeps me young."

Charlotte kept herself from saying *We are young. We aren't even fifty.* Instead she asked "How old are they now?" It struck Charlotte that Kara had been caring for children, her own and her children's children, without a break for thirty years. Charlotte had been fifteen when Paul got Kara pregnant for the first time. Kara's devout Catholic mother had called the baby a blessing from heaven and insisted Paul move in with them so she and her husband could help take care of the baby. Kara and Paul had stayed in that house for the next thirty years and had two more kids. Charlotte always wondered how different Kara's future would have been if her mother hadn't been so insistent about her sixteen-year-old daughter keeping her baby. Kara and Paul's premature responsibilities had made Charlotte uncomfortable as she watched the frightened teenagers turn into uncertain adults overnight. Kara grew up. Paul acted out.

"Mattie's twelve, Bella's ten, Mikey's seven, Little Marty's five, Hailey and Jada are four." Kara ticked each child off on a different finger. "Six! Can you believe it? The littlest four are here now. Are you gonna send the girls to Elk Hollow Elementary? It'd be nice for 'em to be with their cousins."

Josh had already made the declaration that the Walsh kids would attend the local public school, the same one Charlotte had gone to forty years earlier. Max groused about how it couldn't compare to their school back in Atherton, but Charlotte maintained mixed feelings about the $50,000-a-year private school the twins had been in since they were two. The Wonder School was one of those alternative-learning institutions reserved for the offspring of Valley titans, where children who still pooped in their pants studied things like Greek mythology, Indo-African pottery, and how to forage for mushrooms in the wild. Two months earlier she'd sat through a thirty-minute G-rated interpretation of *Antigone* for the school play. Several times every month Charlotte wondered if the Wonder School would make her children unable to function as normal people when and if they were released into the harsh reality of the world beyond Silicon Valley.

"They'll start next week," Charlotte said. "Ella will be fine. She finds friends everywhere. I'm worried about Rose, though."

Kara pointed out the window at the smallest of the boys, his face covered in mud or chocolate. "Little Marty will be in their class. He'll watch out for the girls. I love 'em all but he's my favorite. He's a foul-mouthed little delinquent and he's the best of 'em."

Kara heaved a cardboard box onto the kitchen counter in between a ragged Elmo doll missing his left arm and a five-gallon water jug filled with grimy pennies and nickels. The surface was piled high with grocery store circulars, Bass Pro Shop catalogs, and unpaid bills. "I got a present for you." She plucked T-shirts from the box. "You can pick which one you want. She handed Charlotte a black scoop-neck tee that read NETFLIX, NACHOS, NAPS. Charlotte shook her head. "I don't think that's exactly the image the campaign wants me to portray."

Kara thought for a moment and grabbed another shirt. RED, WHITE AND BOOZE. . . . "Not this one. Okay. I got it." The last shirt said simply WAKE UP, KICK ASS, REPEAT. Charlotte tried to picture herself wearing it. Maybe on a run.

"I love it. Thank you."

Kara busied herself making coffee while Charlotte hopped onto a barstool facing the linoleum counters, Annie in her lap.

"Now, remind me why you're runnin' for office again?" Kara asked as she poured the old grounds down the drain. "Politics is nasty. I watched all seven seasons of *The West Wing*. I know what it's like."

Charlotte laughed a real laugh. God, she'd missed this woman. "I promise you real-life politics isn't all fast-paced dialogue from adorable liberal optimists with perfect hair."

"What do I know? Politicians ain't never gonna do nothin' for someone like me, so I don't get involved."

"Who'd you vote for in the last election, then?"

"You ain't allowed to ask me that, are you?" Kara's eyes narrowed.

Charlotte felt her face flush. "Oh, you don't need to tell me."

"I'm just fuckin' with ya. I voted for Tom Hanks. Wrote him in and everything. But for real. Far as I can see you have a right perfect little life in California with a big fancy job and a big fancy house and sunshine and palm trees and beaches and movie stars."

"That's Los Angeles, not San Francisco."

"Still prettier than here. Why would you want to give it up to audition for a job that don't sound all that great?"

"Nice weather makes people boring anyway." Charlotte tried to make a joke. "I want the girls to be proud of me. I don't want my tombstone to read 'She made a lot of money for a big corporation and then she died.'"

"First woman president's still up for grabs." Kara chuckled. "I'm lucky. I don't have to do much to make the kids think I'm the queen." She curtsied with a Rubenesque grace.

"Where's Paul?" Charlotte accepted a cup of coffee as Kara plunked down a cylinder of powdered creamer and a box of Sweet'N Low.

"Takin' a nap. He was up half the night watchin' Netflix and playing PS2. I'm gonna wake him up in a few."

Charlotte's stomach did a flip and she released the air from her lungs in a sharp burst. "He didn't know we were coming?"

Kara rolled her eyes. "I've been tellin' him for weeks we got to have you over. He don't care, Charlie. He ain't mad at you. It's just that the two of youse went too long without talkin'. He's gonna be happy to see ya."

"Is he working these days?"

"What do you think?"

Through her research on voters in Pennsylvania's northeastern corridor, Charlotte had learned Kara wasn't alone in using Etsy as a side hustle to support her family. In the past ten years, working-class women in America had been screwed over in equal measure to working-class men, probably more so. Humanity's automation software alone had been responsible for the eradication of hundreds of thousands of cashier, bank teller, and customer service jobs typically held by women. Those women didn't get headlines. Instead, they took part-time gigs or became entrepreneurs on Etsy selling T-shirts, jewelry, and crocheted reindeer. They slogged through seasonal work in distribution centers for online retailers like Amazon or Stitch Fix that had moved into the formerly abandoned warehouses in the Lehigh Valley, patrolling miles of cement corridors on foot for twenty cents an hour above the minimum wage with no benefits. They enrolled in job retraining courses funded by the previous administration seven times more often than men. When Charlotte visited the state meeting voters last spring as she was trying to decide whether to run, she was faced with plenty of working-class men who demanded their old jobs magically reappear. There were hundreds of men who told her they were holding out for a coal comeback. The women never complained. They'd found ways to make it work. Charlotte was sick to death of being told to feel sorry for the working-class white man. *Being a mediocre white guy doesn't mean you deserve to be crowned a king, get a job, or get laid. The cavalry is not coming for you.* Of course, she could never utter these thoughts out loud to anyone.

Charlotte felt the fine hairs on the back of her neck tingle and knew without turning that her brother was standing behind her.

"Youse talkin' about me?"

Max walked back in the screen door and crossed the kitchen to give his brother-in-law a pat on the back. "Hey, man."

"Hey, asshole," Paul said with genuine affection.

Charlotte blinked as she took in the middle-aged man in front of her. What had happened to him? Paul was a tiny person, a head shorter than Kara, but now he seemed even smaller. He'd aged quickly since she'd seen him last, and even though he was practically the same age as Max, he looked ten years older. His nose was long and red at the tip. He had a small black mustache, a goatee, and a day's worth of stubble that covered a weak chin. He wore an Eagles jersey two sizes too big for him and black jean shorts with high-top sneakers like an overgrown teenager. When he sat, his shorts crept up his legs, exposing pale white thighs crisscrossed with blue veins.

"Charlie Mary Grace." He turned to her and nodded, using the names no one had used since her father died. Mary Grace had been

Marty Walsh's mother's name. Charlotte wasn't supposed to be named Charlotte at all. In fact, Annemarie told the nurse her daughter's name was Scarlett, for Scarlett O'Hara from *Gone with the Wind*, Annemarie's favorite movie. But the nurse had heard Charlotte and wrote that on the birth certificate. Annemarie was too exhausted and afraid to correct her, and Marty was already at the bar.

"Git me a beer," Paul barked at Kara as he led them outside and settled down at the white plastic patio table.

"Git it yourself," she barked right back, sitting down next to him and placing her bare feet up on the table, the soles black around the heels. "How many beers you gonna have today?"

"A couple. Two, three."

"Git me a wine while you're at it. There's a box in the fridge. Charlie, you want wine? It's nice stuff. They put nice stuff in a box these days. Better than the jug." Kara winked at her. Charlotte managed a sad smile in return and sat next to her. Annemarie used to polish off half a jug of Carlo Rossi before Paul and Charlotte got home from school. Uncertain which version of her mother would be there to greet her, Charlotte had never invited friends over. One day Annemarie would be pleasant and smiling and watching *Donahue* like a completely normal person, and the next she'd be sprawled on the kitchen linoleum in just a ragged T-shirt and her underwear at three in the afternoon.

"I'm good with the coffee." A few yards away she could see the twins attempting forward flips on the trampoline, and her heart fluttered every time they jumped into the air. Annie stretched her arms toward the older girls from Charlotte's lap. "Me play too, Mommy."

"You're too little. Maybe I'll take you on later when the big kids get down."

Paul returned with three beers and a juice glass filled with wine. Kara stood to get an actual wineglass and scowled at her husband. "Nice of you to get your doopa out of bed in time for dinner."

Charlotte muffled a laugh at local slang word for backside. It had been years since she'd heard anyone use the word *doopa*.

"I'm allowed to be tired. I watched a seven-part series last night on geniuses on the Discovery Channel," Paul said, his eyes just glassy enough that Charlotte felt confident in her assumption that he'd taken something before gracing them with his presence. "You know Mom and Dad never got me tested to find out if I was a genius or not. I bet they tested you." Paul shot an accusing glare in Charlotte's direction.

"I have no idea."

"They did, because they put you in all smart classes. Anyways, then I found all these tests online that tell you whether or not you're a genius and you know what? I scored off the charts. I'm like one of those, what you call it, a prodigal."

"A prodigy?" Max gently corrected him, and opened one of the beers from the middle of the table with an expensive polished antelope horn he kept on his key chain expressly for that purpose. He took a long sip that must have drained half the can.

"Yeah, one of those. And all these years no one has had any idea."

"Oh, I always knew you was somethin'," Kara muttered under her breath, used to this kind of talk.

"It got me thinkin' that I need to do something with all of this genius I got in my brain and how I should be running your campaign for youse." Her brother placed his right index finger inside his nose and felt around for something inside the nostril while he talked.

It was a wonder to Charlotte that Paul's ego and self-importance had never resulted in the ability to succeed at anything other than becoming a professional waster of time. She cast a glance at her husband. They'd placed bets on how long it would take for Paul to insist she give him some cash. "You win," Max mouthed ever so slightly, his mouth half hidden by the beer. Charlotte wagered that Paul would hit her up before anyone had had a single bite to eat.

She was prepared. "You know, we've got a campaign manager already. I wish I'd known you'd be interested in something like that," she said in a voice she hoped sounded genuine.

"Too bad. Because I woulda been real good at it."

Of course you think that. Of course you think that's not the kind of job that requires years of experience or high-level thinking or the ability to speak in complete sentences without sticking your finger up your nose.

He finally found what he was looking for and wiped his finger on the bottom of the patio table before setting to work on something on the inside of his left ear. Charlotte looked away, knowing she'd crinkle her nose in obvious disgust if she continued looking at him.

"But I could be some kinda advisor. I could give you advice on things. You remember that poem Dad used to tell us all the time—the one about the bird and the worm." He extracted his finger from his ear, its tip tinged with something orangey-brown, cracked open a second beer on the side of the table, and flicked the cap into the grass. She did remember. It was a Shel Silverstein poem from *Where the Sidewalk Ends*. She still read that one to her girls.

> *If you're a bird, be an early bird and catch the worm for your breakfast plate. If you're a bird, be an early early bird—But if you're a worm, sleep late.*

"You're the bird, Charlie, and I'm the worm and you need a worm. I sleep late and I think about things in my sleep, Charlie." Paul tapped his temple with his index finger.

She felt seized by a desire to tell him exactly what he could do with his advice, grab her children, and get the hell out of there. Instead, she made her voice low and soft and sweet to disarm her brother. "Great. We'll let you know when we need it." Kara raised a skeptical eyebrow.

Paul cut to the chase. "And is it a thing youse pay someone for?"

"Most of our staff are volunteers."

"Why the hell would anyone work for free? Don't they know you're rich?"

"They want to work in public service, I guess." Charlotte made an effort to keep her voice even.

Paul stood, walked around the table to her, put her in a headlock, and rubbed his fist into her hair. "Remember when I gave you noogies? Oh, you hate that, don't you? We've had our differences, but I always support you. You could use a man like me." *To do what? Sell my staffers bad weed and prescription pills? You're disgusting. I don't know how we came out of the same woman.* She felt intense shame over how ashamed she was of her brother.

She cast a glance at Max. *Save me.* But he was tapping away at his phone, ignoring the fact that she was drowning. She looked at Kara. "So, what are we having for dinner?"

"I'm just gonna throw some burgers on tha grill and I got a tray of pizza I can nuke," Kara said as she rose and began to walk toward the kitchen. "Plenty a fixins, too."

"I'll help." Charlotte stood and followed her, hoisting Annie onto her shoulders, feeling the little girl's body vibrate as she giggled.

Her brother called after her. "I'll bet we can work somethin' out, Charlie. I scratch your back and you scratch mine." It was a favorite saying of Paul's, one he'd picked up from *The Sopranos.* "I can make being back here real easy for you." He paused. "Or I could make it real hard."

Is he threatening me?

"I'll see about it." What was it worth to keep him quiet and moderately well-behaved? Would she pay five grand? Ten grand of her own money to shut her own brother up?

"Ignore him. You know how he gets," Kara said once Paul was out of earshot. She pulled an industrial-size vat of macaroni salad, large enough to feed a family of eight, out of the refrigerator. "I got this on sale down the Acme."

Charlotte used her fingernail to pick at a smudge of food stuck to the counter. "He makes me nervous. There's going to be a lot of press coming around. Was he threatening me?"

"He's harmless. That's how he talks. He thinks he's a gangster and not just some dingus who got fired from the junkyard last month 'cause he couldn't even guard da junk."

"Ted Slaughter's gunning for me. He'll be looking for ammo. If Paul does one stupid thing . . ."

"I can keep him in line. I'll kick him right in the doopa if he does one wrong thing."

Kara reached over to smooth Charlotte's hair out of her face.

Her touch released something in Charlotte. She leaned into the rough, warm hand and felt tears prick the corners of her eyes. Charlotte wasn't a crier, but less than five hours back home had her nerves wound tight as guitar strings. One pluck sent vibrations of fear through her entire body.

"He could ruin this for me. Paul could." His words rattled around in Charlotte's brain with a pestering persistence: *I could make it real hard.*

Paul was a liability, that much was clear. And he wasn't the only one.

EMILY'S LIST ENDORSES CHARLOTTE WALSH
FOR SENATE IN PENNSYLVANIA

January 3, 2018

WASHINGTON, DC – Today, EMILY's List, the nation's largest resource for women in politics, endorsed Humanity chief operating officer Charlotte Walsh for Senate in Pennsylvania.

Stephanie Schriock, president of EMILY's List, released the following statement:

"As an executive and champion of women's issues, Charlotte Walsh has dedicated her career to improving people's lives. Now she wants to continue that work in the Senate. At a time when the anti-woman, anti-choice Senate Republicans continue to erode women's rights in the home and in the workplace, Charlotte's perspective running a multibillion-dollar company that instituted more policies to keep more women in the workforce than any other company in the country is needed in Washington now more than ever. EMILY's List is proud to stand by her side. This is a must-win race, and Charlotte is the only candidate who has what it takes to flip this seat.

"Walsh joined the cloud-computing productivity giant in 1999 and quickly rose through the ranks to become, within five years, the first female COO in Silicon Valley. Many in the Valley credit Charlotte's ability to manage difficult personalities and bring organization to a company that was once on the brink of chaos with turning Humanity into a multibillion-dollar global powerhouse that Mark Zuckerberg once described as 'the most important tech company you've never heard of.'

"There are plenty of female executives in the past year whose shallow claims of support for women have not been backed up by their action or deeds. Charlotte didn't just pay lip service to the concept of advancing women in the workplace. She put her money and her time where her mouth was and made real change happen for women in Silicon Valley. Her improvements at Humanity have served as a rocket booster for the careers of the women there.

'I loved every minute of building Humanity into what it is today,' Charlotte said in a statement to EMILY's List. 'I plan to bring the skills I learned in the private sector to the public sector in order to help improve the lives of Americans in the same way we have improved the lives of hundreds of thousands of Humanity employees and clients around the globe.'

"Charlotte is simply brilliant. That's all there is to it. She has the rare combination of common sense, the compassion of a saint, and drive," Humanity founder Kumail Chatterjee said. "In a world that is violently shifting beneath our feet, she is the bedrock."

Since the 2016 election, more than 20,000 women and counting have reached out to us about running for office. To harness this energy, EMILY's List has launched Run to Win, an unprecedented effort to get more women to run at the local, state, and national levels.

Learn more at www.EmilysList.org.

CHAPTER 4
March 2, 2018

249 days to Election Day

Walsh (D)	Slaughter (R)	Spread
34	47	Slaughter +13

New mothers and candidates for elected office quickly realize how much caffeine and adrenaline will allow you to accomplish. In the six months since Charlotte returned to Elk Hollow she hadn't slept more than four hours a night. Now she was on her fifth cup of coffee of the day. Coffee might have been counterproductive to soothing her nerves, but without it she'd have been facedown on the floor. She longed for the coffee even before she closed her eyes at night, anticipating new exhaustion even as she dispelled the old.

The learning curve on the campaign wasn't just steep, it was treacherous. Her first few months had felt like skiing down a sheet of ice.

"The speech needs to be at least ten minutes shorter," she instructed Alex, a speechwriter, and Leila, who was better at writing for her than any of the new kids on her staff. "No one needs to listen to me blather on. We don't need to talk at them for an hour."

"Good point." Josh crept noiselessly behind them. "Trim it to eleven minutes for good measure. Voters want you to answer three questions: 'Can you get me more money?' 'Will you keep my family safe?' And—my personal favorite—'How are you like me?' You never need to answer anything else."

Everything Charlotte had heard about Josh was true. He'd thrown himself into her campaign deeply and completely, applying a laser-like focus to winning at all costs. He didn't even mind wading through hundreds of résumés with the subject line "I'm the Next Olivia Pope." He went thirteen rounds with a yard sign manufacturer who managed to mangle the slogan CHARLOTTE WALSH CAN FIX PA thirteen different ways. They'd already crisscrossed the state together twenty times hosting intimate barbecues and spaghetti dinners with small groups of voters and local stakeholders in the hopes that free food would make people remember Charlotte Walsh nearly a year from now.

But even after six months together Charlotte was still learning her campaign manager's idiosyncrasies, and one of them was that Josh rarely wore shoes or socks indoors.

"I spent some time in Tibet" was his brief explanation when she questioned his bare feet.

A consequence of this was that it allowed him to slither silently around the office like a wild cat stalking its prey, making it easy for him to sneak up on Charlotte. When she turned, he was just two inches behind her. "What's up with your eyes?" He asked this in a way that was neither insulting nor curious, but merely indicated he'd identified a problem. As he examined her crow's feet he bent at the waist so his sweater crept up his spine and exposed the crack of his backside to the rest of the room. He smelled like Cool Ranch Doritos.

"Hmmmm?" Charlotte barely looked up from her computer screen.

"Your eyes. They're droopy. You look tired. We should have gotten you Botox last week."

"Has anyone ever told you that you possess all the warmth and delicacy of a Russian gymnastics coach?" Leila stood, elongated her spine, and stretched her arms high above her head to make the most of her five feet two inches, her tightly braided topknot giving the impression that she was taller. She raised her brows into symmetrical parabolas.

"Da." Josh smirked. "Prekratite suki. Vy imeyete v vidu zhenshchinu."

"What the hell does that mean and why do you speak Russian?" Leila recoiled at his guttural pronunciation.

"It means 'Stop bitching, you mean woman,' which I don't mean, of course, because I would never say that to a woman, but it's one of five phrases I learned when I ran a campaign in the Ukraine."

"Oh, I think you mean it." Leila narrowed her eyes. "Well, here in the States, a man should never tell a woman to get Botox."

"Blame Hollywood. No one on television looks like they're between the ages of twenty-five and fifty-five. You go straight from Miley Cyrus to Helen Mirren. In the world of the high-definition screens you hold in your hand, everyone gets Botox. If Nixon could have gotten injections that made him stop sweating during that televised debate with Kennedy, he would have begged for the needle faster than you can say 'Deep Throat.' "

Josh faced Charlotte and placed his index fingers at her temples as if he were about to give her a massage. Instead he pulled the skin back toward her ears. Charlotte swatted him away.

"I don't do Botox." She didn't meet Leila's eyes.

He shrugged and moved on. "Suit yourself."

Josh padded away, his feline feet hardly making a sound on the linoleum floor of the Walsh for Senate headquarters in Scranton, Pennsylvania. They had found the place in January. The owner of the building was desperate for cash after the previous tenant, an EZ-Rent-a-Car, packed up and left Scranton with a week's notice. It was just a single story with one large room, strip lighting, well-worn green carpet, concrete walls, and a grid of tinted windows at eye level; the building had seen better days, but the addition of tables, computers, phones, and WALSH CAN FIX IT placards and lawn signs covering every available surface provided a patina of authenticity.

They'd tacked an enormous map of the state of Pennsylvania cordoned off into sixty-seven counties and further segmented by voting district on the wall. Charlotte quickly learned there wasn't one type of Pennsylvanian. There were plenty of coastal elites due to the Ivy

League college and abundance of law schools. There were old men who used to work in coal mines and younger men who used to work in steel mills, truck drivers, hippies, rednecks, cis-feminists, queers, white trash, Quakers, the Amish, the working poor, union thugs, self-proclaimed hillbillies on the border with West Virginia, illegal immigrants, and upwardly mobile second-generation Latinos. Parts of Pennsylvania had become a breeding ground for leftist anarchists and neofascists. The state was a microcosm of America, which made it less surprising it hadn't yet elected a woman senator or governor.

Charlotte tasked a former chief people officer from Humanity, Arlene Atlas, to help Josh hire a staff of thirty, including five county directors, two fundraisers, two data scientists, a digital strategist, and a media buyer. There were three press officers, all former reporters for Pennsylvania newspapers—one from each end of the state and one from the middle.

"It's not normal that he walks around barefoot," Leila remarked as Josh padded away.

"He says it keeps him Zen." Charlotte squinted at his feet. "If this is what he's like Zen, can you imagine what he'd be like if we made him wear shoes all day?"

"At least he has decent-looking toes." Leila rolled her eyes with intention and freed a lock of her shiny dark hair from its bun to twirl it around her index finger. "You know I saw him reading *Eat, Pray, Love* the other day."

Before Charlotte could respond, her phone chirped. A text from Max.

Dinner at 6??

It was nearly five thirty. The drive home would take at least forty-five minutes and she had more work to do. As her fingers hovered over the screen, the phone chirped again with a text and photo.

Ravenous munchkins

In the picture Max had texted to her Annie was naked and covered in glitter. Rejecting clothes and then smearing things on her body was a new stage of the child's terrible twos, one Max had no idea how to deal with, and so he ignored it. Just about every time Charlotte looked at her kids, in person and in photos, she felt a rush of accomplishment and awe—*I created that*—quickly followed by anxiety: *How am I messing them up? I'm definitely messing them up, right?*

Charlotte examined her staff, all of them diligently pecking at three screens at once. Spending her days surrounded by brilliant kids right out of college, all of them convinced their next tweet would change the world, wasn't so different from running a company in Silicon Valley. The office buzzed with polite enthusiasm as staffers made fundraising calls, cold calls, press calls, all extolling the virtues of Charlotte Walsh. She'd made it clear she was entering the race six months ago. There'd been no need for a primary, since no other Democratic candidate had emerged this year to take on Ted Slaughter. Before Charlotte had come along, the DNC hadn't seen the point in seeding a candidate who didn't have a chance. On good days, she believed their support for her candidacy meant they thought she had a chance.

Next Monday's speech would be her first big televised speech as an official candidate, a fact that exhilarated and terrified her. Her staff would be here for at least another few hours tonight, and then again tomorrow and again on Sunday. The guilt of leaving them hardened into a knot in her stomach. But the guilt of abandoning Max and the girls felt heavier.

"I've missed dinner with the kids every night this week," she said out loud to no one in particular, even though Leila was the only one within earshot. Back in California, both Charlotte and Max had worked eighty-hour weeks, but they'd always made it home in time for dinner, and they wouldn't touch their computers or phones again until after the girls went to bed.

"You'll never make it home in time." Leila informed her of what she already knew.

"Are we done for the day?"

"No. You need to meet a prospective Instagram producer."

"Why do I need to meet her?"

"She'll be working more closely with you than anyone else on the social team."

Leila gave her a rundown. "She last worked at one of those celebrity lifestyle sites that promotes five-hundred-dollar socks and lotion made of dolphin placenta. Josh calls her a genius at aspirational marketing. I don't think you'll like her, but you'll tolerate her. She has a lot of energy. I'll go get her."

"Good energy?"

Leila rolled her eyes. "Just a lot of it."

Charlotte tried not to appear taken aback as the extremely pretty redheaded elf of a girl rushed at her with a hug and then held her at arm's length like an old great-aunt and smiled, her blazing hair partially obscuring a tiny face the color of Ivory soap.

"Lovely to meet you. Just lovely." She spoke with the contrived and practiced accent common to overeducated young women with trust funds—partially New York, a little Cape Cod, and slightly British. She wore just the right amount of lipstick.

"Hey."

"Charlotte, meet Lulu." Josh made a more formal introduction.

"Lulu is such an unusual name," Charlotte remarked. "Where does it come from?"

The girl had clearly been asked this question many times. "It was my great-grandmother's name. Lulabelle, actually. She was from Poland but was adopted by a German family during World War Two. After she died, my dad tracked down her adoption records and discovered that a family had taken her in when her birth parents were taken away to Bergen-Belsen. And that's how we became Jewish."

It was clear to Charlotte that Lulu used this story to convey that she was interesting in addition to being beautiful.

Josh interrupted her and offered rare praise. "Lulu's a wizard when it comes to accessible aspiration."

"Excuse me?" Charlotte wasn't sure how those words were meant to create a phrase. "I've got an Instagram already."

Lulu patted her hand. One of her navy-blue nails, and only one of them, was crisscrossed with white stripes. "Don't worry, honey." The girl took on an affected nurturing tone. "You want your life to seem just thirty percent more amazing and wonderful and beautiful than that of the person who is consuming the content—the Instagram user, the Snapchatter, whatever. That means things like family photos on the beach in Saint Lucia are alienating, but well-dressed children in color-coordinated outfits playing on the local playground are good. Those are aspirational because no one color-coordinates their children's outfits, or even finds a clean T-shirt on most days. Another good example: I don't want to see a picture of you hugging Jay-Z and Beyoncé. I saw a pic of you three at the Hurricane Alfred fundraiser last year. So cute. Love Bey. But it could be alienating. I *do* want to see beautiful lemon squares baked in the shape of Pennsylvania for the school bake sale."

"I hate to break it to you." Charlotte put her own hand on top of Lulu's like they were playing that children's game where everyone races to pile their hands the highest. "I don't have a whole lot of time to be focusing on baking lemon squares or making my Instagram accessibly aspirational."

Lulu didn't blink. "You don't have to do anything. You smile and comb your own hair and I do it all for you. I Photoshop most of it, smooth over the rough edges. Public figures have no choice but to reveal so much of their lives online these days. But it pays off. It really pays off. It's one of the reasons Gwyneth has been so successful."

"It's a little different." Charlotte tried to stifle a laugh. "Gwyneth Paltrow isn't a politician."

Lulu wasn't put off. "Oh, but she could be if she wanted to. Trust."

"Does Ted Slaughter have an Instagram?"

Leila chimed in. "His granddaughter runs it. It's mostly pics of his daughters and their children. They don't put pictures of him on there." From three marriages, Ted Slaughter had eight daughters, aged nine to fifty, all of them achingly beautiful except for the fourth, who Charlotte thought made up for being homely by being the thinnest. They'd produced a pack of sixteen well-groomed grandchildren and six great-grandchildren, each of whom attended every one of Slaughter's campaign events, often lined up by height and occasionally singing like Von Trapps.

"Of course they don't." Lulu shuddered. "He doesn't photograph well! He looks like the Crypt Keeper on a good day. Besides, it's different for male public figures. Their personal lives aren't as interesting to the public. No one cares about how they look when they wake up in the morning. Let me tell you a little about my vision. We'll schedule a day, maybe two, of photo shoots, make it look like a year's worth of photos. Next, I'll do your husband's social media. I assume that's fair game. We need to use him to appeal to women voters. Not that he doesn't. He's very handsome. But I want him softer. More pics with the kids. I want him covered in children, like a delicious lactose-free chocolate sundae smothered in toddlers instead of fudge."

Leila cut in. "You'd need to be on the campaign trail with us. This isn't a desk job. It sounds fancy, but it's shit. We don't stay in nice hotels. Strange hours, a lot of work."

"I don't mind," Lulu said with conviction. "I'm good at roughing it. I did a semester at sea."

Josh seemed amused by her answer. "That must have been really rough," he said with the appropriate amount of sarcasm. "Your work is good though. We'll talk about it and get back to you by Monday." One of their aides appeared then to whisk Lulu out of the office and point her in the direction of the bus station for her return to New York.

"If she survives that Greyhound ride she can have the job." Josh snickered. "Last time I took it some guy peed on me."

With Lulu out of the way, Charlotte sank into her chair and yawned.

"Why don't you have Max and the kids meet you at a restaurant in between here and home?" Leila said, two steps ahead of Charlotte.

"Good idea. You're brilliant."

"I'm practical."

Charlotte tapped at her phone.

Meet me at the Fridays on Route 6??

Three blinking dots showed Max responding. *Why am I holding my breath?*

I started a meatloaf.

Once in a while, Max got a wild hair to do some cooking, and he relished making an elaborate performance of it. Charlotte rubbed her temples and pictured her husband chopping onions while wearing his swimming goggles so his eyes wouldn't tear up, an act that always made the girls laugh from their bellies no matter how ornery they were by dinnertime.

A restaurant will be nice. And easy. No cleanup

fine

She hated these single-word texts, how aggressive they could feel.

Maybe put some clothes on the baby?

Anything else boss?

He'd begun referring to her as "boss" only recently, in the past couple of months, after she was no longer technically his boss. She hated it. They'd both forced themselves to pretend the move to Elk Hollow would be an exciting adventure, and in the beginning there was an enlivening sense of something old becoming new again, like the exhilaration of finding your favorite sweater in the back of your closet after not seeing it for five years. Max had almost seemed to enjoy their new life through December in Elk Hollow, when snow pummeled the valley and he could go backcountry skiing a few times a week. But a brief warm spell followed by a bitter cold front turned the snow to slick black ice, making it difficult to even go running on the trails behind their house. He was relegated to training for his race on a treadmill in the basement and finding ways to occupy the three girls in the house on weekends. At least one of the three always had a cough and a snotty nose.

"Sometimes I feel trapped," he complained. "Like I'm a prisoner locked up with these children."

It wouldn't do much good to tell him he was experiencing the crisis nearly every professional woman who left work to take care of her children felt at some point.

Max had been momentarily enthused at the prospect of helping Charlotte manage her digital staff. "I can build you a tool that will identify and retarget voters with unique, highly personalized content," he told her one night before bed. She was excited at his excitement, but Josh quickly shot down the idea. "No spouses work on my campaigns. It's a recipe for disaster. Every day would be like an episode of *Mad About You*."

Charlotte knew Max felt humiliated when she told him they didn't need his help.

It was a lie that eating at Fridays would be easier, and Max would be in a terrible mood now when she arrived at the restaurant. Nothing about eating with a toddler and two five-year-olds in public was easy, but it was better than missing dinner with her family again.

Charlotte glanced sideways at Leila. "Come to dinner with us?"

"You want a buffer," she said. It wasn't a question.

"You have to be starving." *Of course I want a buffer. Max and I get along when you're around.* "And I don't want you to spend another night sleeping at the office. It's not healthy." *Grateful* wasn't a strong enough word to describe how she felt every day that Leila had uprooted her own life in California and moved into an Embassy Suites just a couple of blocks from here to continue as her right-hand woman.

"Okay. Let's take separate cars though. I'll be right behind you. I want to read the speech out loud with Alex again."

"Print out a few copies of the speech and bring it with you. I'll go over it more tonight. It has to be perfect." *Better than perfect. It has to be the best fucking speech I've ever given in my entire life.*

"Did Josh tell you Slaughter is giving his own rally this weekend, on Sunday?"

Now that Charlotte had watched more than fifty hours of her opponent's speeches, his low, booming voice haunted her dreams. She handwrote pages of notes about him on yellow legal pads, clocking his strengths and weaknesses. He appeared strong, imposing, and looked the part of an old-school politician straight from central casting, with his broad shoulders and well-sculpted hair. It became quickly evident to Charlotte that he was more a chameleon than a strict party booster. As a man who adored the superlative, Slaughter shifted his shape to suit whatever crowd cheered him on. To former factory workers he was a laborer who'd gotten his first job at age fifteen, helping lay concrete for the foundations of some of Pittsburgh's most prominent skyscrapers. He consistently promised to bring the steel and iron jobs back to the state, and when it didn't happen, he blamed the lazy bastards in DC. To the businessmen, he advocated lower taxes, smaller government, the eradication of the minimum wage. He was a god in rural counties that benefited from his lenient policies on fracking. And despite his conservative policies on abortion rights and the fact he led the charge to defund Planned Parenthood, to the young women he was a kindly, if slightly senile and racist, grandpa. No one local wanted to waste the money to run against the man with the rare gift of electrifying his party's base and fringe Democrats who voted on guns and abortion. Slaughter's peculiar likability was only one of the reasons he handily destroyed anyone who dared run against him until few even bothered to try. There were even whispers that the Slaughter campaign paid out six-figure checks to keep opponents out of the race. Anyone interested in national office in Pennsylvania just ran for the House.

"I have three trackers attending Slaughter's rally." There was Josh again. He'd probably been listening behind them the whole time. Charlotte had only recently learned of the existence of the campaign trackers—a small army of eager junior staffers who followed the opposition on the campaign trail to document their every move. They employed ten of them in total. A single video of a candidate going off script or saying the wrong thing could go viral and do as much service or damage as a multimillion-dollar ad campaign.

"One will film it in case he says something ridiculous, which he will. It also gives us the chance to chat with the press he has covering him. You'll get more ink than he will this week. He hasn't had a formidable opponent in years and certainly not one as camera-friendly as you. We paint him as the status quo, a DC insider, untrustworthy, an old man without the stamina to bring about real change. What has he really done for the voters of Pennsylvania? Absolutely nothing. You're an agent of change. You're young and vibrant and you get shit done. We keep reinforcing that narrative over and over and over until you won't be able to stand hearing it one more time. We've got this covered."

Charlotte took comfort in his words. She knew Josh used "We've got this covered" as a recurring refrain to reassure the parts of her that believed what they were doing might be impossible.

"Now, I've also fixed your Google problem."

"Which one?" Charlotte sighed. Facebook and Google search were the bane of a modern candidate's existence.

"We've bought Google sidebar ads against search terms containing your name to show only positive articles about your accomplishments at Humanity. We bought ads against Slaughter's name that lead to a landing page that lists all of the campaign promises he's broken in the past ten years. Now it's just a race to see who can throw the most money at it."

"And how much money are we throwing at it?"

"Two hundred fifty thousand for this month."

"Jesus Christ, Josh."

"It's working. And it reminds me, we need a million more by the end of this month."

★

By six thirty Charlotte was behind the wheel. Relief at being alone, at not having to be anybody's boss or mother for a blessed ten minutes, took over her entire body. It felt like she'd been wearing too-tight shoes for a week and had never even thought, *I could just take these off.*

She texted Max.

On my way

We ordered already

I'm coming as fast as I can

Don't text and drive. Isn't that part of your campaign platform?

Charlotte's phone buzzed a minute later with a final text from Max.

You know you're the most beautiful girl in the world

Charlotte felt her face grow red at the compliment before her mind went to a dangerous place. *Was this text meant for me? Who else would it be for? Stop it. Do not allow yourself to go there.*

She'd grown up going to TGI Fridays on special occasions—birthdays, graduations, that time her brother's Little League team won the state championship—but she hadn't set foot inside a chain restaurant once she'd moved to the West Coast. They mostly frequented restaurants where the phrase "farm to fork" had long ago become passé in favor of "heirloom nose to tail" and other obsequious descriptors that allowed food to cost five times what it should. In the six months they'd been living in Pennsylvania, Charlotte had reacquired a taste for the loaded potato skins, blooming onions, and endless breadsticks of Fridays, Outback Steakhouse, and the Olive Garden.

Charlotte bypassed the cheery hostess inside the door and turned right at a canoe holding two taxidermied raccoons paddling upstream. She kept a brisk pace with her shoulders back and heard her mother's voice in her head: *Girl, who you tryin' to impress?*

Max and the girls were already seated in a roomy corner booth, grabbing at a plate of quesadillas so large it could feed an entire football team. As she watched them she thought you'd never know she'd uprooted their entire lives and moved them across the country. They'd tried several ways to explain the move and Mommy's new job to the twins, but by far the most effective explanation was Leila's:

"If Voldemort became president, wouldn't you want your mommy to travel to Hogwarts to fight with Harry to defeat him?" This led to enthusiastic approval from her children for both her candidacy and the state of Pennsylvania.

All three girls held separate iPads while Max tapped on his phone. They'd once had rules about screen time, particularly at the dinner table, rules Max now ignored as their primary caregiver. Charlotte could say something about it, but that would give him an opening to complain about how late she was and the rest of the night would turn to shit. She took her own phone out of her pocket to see if he was texting her.

No new messages.

"Hey, Nuggets!" Charlotte leaned in to kiss Max on the lips but missed and got the nub of his chin instead. She smiled through a jab of anxiety and tried to sound unrushed and cheery.

Annie pointed a chubby finger at her. "Mommy's late!"

"You can't tell time." She kissed Annie's tangled curls and lifted her out of her high chair and onto her lap. Max might have gotten the toddler dressed, but she'd clearly chosen the tiara, purple-sequined tutu, and pint-size Philadelphia Eagles jersey. Upon closer inspection, Charlotte noticed that both the twins and Max were also wearing sequined tutus around their waists. Her heart went to butter.

"What'd you order me?"

"Nothing," Max grunted, his mouth filled with tortilla and cheese. "I didn't know what you wanted."

She blinked a couple of times before responding. "Where's our waiter?"

Her husband slid a menu from beneath his bread plate. "I kept this for you. He'll be back in a minute." Max's jaw twitched like he wanted to tell her something else, but he pushed a piece of quesadilla toward her instead. She doused the grease-covered triangle in Tabasco and opened the menu.

"Charlie Walsh? Is that you?" Charlotte looked up to the grinning face of her high school boyfriend standing a few feet from her husband. Her brain struggled to make the connection as she checked the name tag drooping from the pocket of his green Fridays-issued polo shirt tucked into black pleated pants a size too big for him. How had Max neglected to tell her that the boy who'd taken her virginity was their waiter at Fridays?

Charlotte ran her tongue over her teeth to catch any stray pieces of food. "Jack? What are you doing here? You're working here? That's great." She said it with too much enthusiasm. Sunken hollows had taken up residency beneath Jack's solemn brown eyes, and he looked like he'd recently lost ten pounds he hadn't needed to lose.

She really ought to get up and give him a hug, but there was a child on her lap. A handshake felt too formal for someone who had seen her naked.

She'd fallen hard for Jack Seligson when they were lab partners in sophomore AP chemistry. They were a perfectly imperfect match of weirdos. He had a stutter. She was painfully shy. It took a semester for them to speak about anything beyond thermodynamics. Once he finally asked her out on a date—well, if driving around town and singing along to Queen songs, then watching *Back to the Future* in his parents' finished basement counted as a date—they became inseparable.

His dad was a dentist, which made his family relatively well off. They had two cars and owned skis. Their relative wealth often made Charlotte feel like the protagonist in a John Hughes movie even though their town didn't have railroad tracks. One night she overheard Jack's sister talking about her to their mom when they thought the two of them had already left the house. "That Walsh girl is so sweet even though her family's such trash," his sister said. The memory of that comment still stung to this day.

Jack and Charlotte spent most evenings studying and eating frozen Tombstone pizza in his parents' kitchen. She'd leave at night and he would sneak into her bedroom window three times a week for fumbling and groping, and eventually unprotected sex in the filigreed princess canopy bed her dad had rescued from the curb. They talked about forever in the abstract way you imagine forever at sixteen.

For college, Jack had gone to Kutztown and Charlotte to the University of Pennsylvania, a school she'd chosen from the stack of glossy catalogs from her guidance counselor, who told her it was the best college in the state and that no one from their town had ever gotten in. That made Charlotte desperately want to be the first. Late one night after a six-pack and before the eleven o'clock news, Marty had told her he'd find a way to pay for the Ivy League college if she could get herself accepted and even though it was the well-meaning fib of a well-meaning drunk, she'd believed him. She'd worked her ass off, joined all the extracurriculars, including volleyball, where she got her nose smashed in the day before prom. She made valedictorian and got into Penn with a small amount of financial aid. Even though she'd made it happen through sheer force of will, Charlotte was surprised when they accepted her. Marty apologized over and over that despite his bluster, he couldn't cover the rest of the tuition. Charlotte took out more than $100,000 in student loans in her own name and worked the night shift at Arby's to cover the room and board.

At Penn her hall mates were the privileged offspring of the men and women who ran Wall Street, giant media conglomerates, and small countries. They were kids who took both their opportunity and their hope for granted. Charlotte's advantage was that having grown up without those things gave her a resourcefulness and adapt-ability those kids didn't have. She was never going to lose her mind when the dorm ran out of hot water, when the commissary didn't stock tampons, or when a professor told her that her ideas were pedestrian.

Captivated by the conspicuous arms race for status at Penn, for the first time Charlotte knew she needed to do something both interesting and important with a capital *I*. The first semester of freshman year, high on possibility, she vowed she'd never live in Elk Hollow again, that she would join the elite ranks of her classmates' parents, the am-biguous moneyed class that ran the world: the winners.

One of her roommates, Blair, pruned bonsai trees and bragged that Simon Le Bon's cousin had been her babysitter. She gifted Charlotte a six-month-old Calvin Klein clutch because the tan shoulder bag Char-lotte used was "sad." Her other roommate, Anne Stratton, could have bought and sold all of them, but you'd never have known it looking at her in her flannel pajama bottoms, moth-eaten sweaters, and beat-up Doc Martens. She never talked about how her grandfather was the eleventh-richest man in the world and her father the ambassador to Japan. Her family minted their own money, which in turn minted its own money. She offered Charlotte her first lesson about wealth: When you had a lot of it you didn't show it off.

"My mom's name is Anne—well, Annemarie," Charlotte said dumbly when they met, struck by the girl's easy beauty.

"Do you like her? Your mom?" Anne asked as she spread a ragged wool blanket over the top bunk beneath a concert poster for Mano Negra in Mexico City. Charlotte thought hard about her answer, knowing it could set the tone for their entire relationship.

"She can be a real bitch sometimes and she's addicted to pills."

Anne smiled and lit a Parliament, not bothering to open a window.

"We're going to get along just fine."

It was Anne who took her to get an IUD and her first bikini wax, who convinced her it was ridiculous to keep dating a high school boyfriend a hundred miles away. Anne drove her to Elk Hollow for Marty Walsh's funeral during their junior year and sang along to "Danny Boy" with drunk, sweaty union men. It was Anne who got Charlotte the job with Rosalind Waters a few years after college because Aunt Roz and Anne's dad used to be poker buddies. Then, just six months after Charlotte moved to Maryland, Anne died in a collision with a tractor trailer on the icy Merritt Parkway. It was a heartbreak that Charlotte folded away, aware that if she let it, it would have upended her. Instead, she threw herself into work—Anne's voice always echoing in her head: *You got this, bitch!* Still, it was like losing a limb—you always felt the absence—and for years she ached for a friendship so familiar and perfect. To a fault, she held all new acquaintances to the standard of Anne, one they would never be able to live up to. When Marty and Anne were gone Charlotte felt like an orphan, like there was no one left in the world who would willingly take care of her.

Now Charlotte looked up at Jack's easy grin and felt an echo of delayed guilt that she'd never properly broken up with him, had just stopped returning his phone calls.

Last Charlotte saw on Facebook, Jack was married to a girl who was a year behind them in high school and had three kids, teenage boys. He was a teacher at the local high school, lived in the house he grew up in, inherited from his parents, and he played on a softball team called the Elk Hollow Buglers, comprised mostly of middle-aged teachers.

Early last year, when she'd felt defeated about herself and her marriage, she'd sent him a two-word message on Facebook: *Hey you.* He hadn't responded. If he'd received that message or if he still held a grudge for how badly she'd treated him twenty years ago, he didn't show it now as he stared at her holding a hot-sauce-drenched quesadilla. Now his grin was wide and honest.

Why was he working at Fridays?

Max cleared his throat. "You look real busy tonight. Charlie wants to order something quick. The girls are getting sleepy." Of course Max blew Jack off. Her husband always had a real chip on his shoulder about him. Max was two years older than both of them, but she'd hardly known him back in high school. Max, then known as Maxwell, had been tall, quiet, and shy, preferring the company of computers over people and doodling dragons all over his textbook covers. He had a slight lisp and a gray tooth. He'd gotten a full scholarship to Penn State, where he'd become a whiz in computer science and engineering, and then escaped the East Coast for the Bay Area. That began Max's transformation from dweeb to big swinging dick. Of course, a man's teenage insecurity could linger forever like a bad smell. *Did I consider that when I made him come back to the place where he'd once felt small and insignificant? Am I still punishing him?*

Jack addressed the elephant in the room with a hollow chuckle. "I'll bet you're wondering what I'm doing here. I'm still teaching. So is Emily. But last year Em got sick. Cancer. School's insurance doesn't cover a lot of the treatments, so I picked up shifts here and odd jobs there." When he cracked a lopsided smile, Charlotte remembered what it felt like to bite his lower lip and caught herself feeling a stitch of jealousy toward Emily, whose husband was so willing to do whatever it took to keep her healthy, whose eyes still smiled when he talked about her.

"You can only donate blood so many times." Max's lame excuse for a joke fell flat.

"And it's less stressful than dealing meth," Jack volleyed back, making Charlotte laugh.

Her stomach lurched at the idea that two people who'd dedicated their lives to teaching children didn't get adequate medical care to treat cancer. She couldn't think of what to say and immediately felt guilty about their own health care—Cadillac insurance accompanied by a concierge doctor on retainer for $80,000 a year who had the ability to get any member of her family an appointment with any specialist in the country at a moment's notice.

She hoped her smile didn't show her pity. "And it's so hard to get good meth across state lines." She hated herself the most when she tried to make jokes. "Do you want to sit down? Has the health care in the district always been this bad?" She rooted around in her purse for a pen with which to take notes.

Charlotte logged Max's scowl and chose to ignore it. She stared at Jack's hands, which were larger than average and made her think of his penis, which was long but narrow, and then she saw her child push her lemonade in the waiter's direction and she felt hot and ashamed.

"Would you like to share my lemonade?" Rose offered. The twins were learning about sharing in their Elk Hollow public school, which Charlotte preferred to ecstatic dance and Greek tragedies. The offer was almost always followed by "Hereyougo. Takeit."

"Charlie, you should order your food." Max took his own sip of Rose's drink and began spinning his phone like a top on the table, letting it clang against their water glasses.

She looked at the menu again and remembered Jack was working. "I should have a salad. How about the Cobb. Can I get it as soon as possible? So I can eat with my kids." Her stomach grumbled. "Stop. Scratch that. I'll have the steak fajitas. I'd love to talk to you more later about health care in the state."

He nodded. "It's a long story, the health-care problem for teachers here. But, yeah, it's a mess. They scaled the benefits back in the past year. Your food can all come out at once. I'm glad you came in tonight, Charlie. I read on Facebook that you're running for Senate and I think that's great."

If he'd read that on Facebook, then he must have gotten her message and ignored it. She felt a blush creep up her neck at the knowledge of this and his praise, in addition to the feeling of pride that she could be the one who could fix his problems.

"We need people like you—people who left and were successful. You've got my vote." He'd smiled more at her in the past five minutes than she'd seen Max smile all week.

"Thank you," she said to Jack. "And I want to hear more about you and your situation." Charlotte groaned inside. Situation *is a terrible word, the kind of word used to describe someone's second marriage to a woman young enough to be his daughter.* "Maybe Leila, my chief of staff, could call you and we could set up a meeting to talk about what it's like for teachers here and how I might be able to help."

"I'd like that. Let me go back to the kitchen to get those fajitas." He produced a couple of stubby red and blue crayons from his back pocket and placed them in front of the girls. "You know the tablecloth is paper. You can draw your mom a pretty picture."

Thank God Leila arrived just then. When Max shifted his attention to her his sneer morphed into a smile. Max was never a jerk when Leila was around. He was always trying to impress her, to endear himself to her in a way Charlotte found touching instead of irritating, because she loved the girl so much. Max changed the subject completely. "Ella, Rose, Annie, and I were having a serious discussion before the two of you got here. Leila, would you rather be a giant rabbit or a tiny elephant?"

"Tiny elephant, no question."

"Give it a real think before you answer. Imagine the inferiority complex a tiny elephant might develop," Max said.

"But it would be so cute," Leila said.

"Would it?" Ella asked with surprising intensity. "Would it really?"

Leila plucked Annie from Charlotte's lap and lifted her shirt over her head to blow wet raspberries on her stomach as she squeezed in next to Max.

He slung his arm over Leila's shoulder. "Lee, did you pick this place knowing that Charlotte's ex-boyfriend was a waiter here?"

No question, no matter how random, ever rattled Leila. "I picked it for the extra-large margaritas and tasteful taxidermy. Which ex-boyfriend?"

"High school. I don't think I ever mentioned him," Charlotte said, turning to make sure that Jack was out of earshot before she filled Leila in on their encounter.

"But can you believe it?" she asked the two of them once she'd gone through Jack's story.

"That your high school boyfriend is starting to lose his hair?" Max snorted. "I can believe that."

Max's hand moved instinctively to the back of his own head, where his usually thick hair was just starting to thin, where there were maybe even the beginnings of a bald spot.

"No. Can you believe that he's working here?"

"Like he said, it's better than dealing drugs. The world's going to hell. Isn't that why you're running for office? To change the world and improve the lives of the middle class." Max assumed the teasing and slightly patronizing tone their Silicon Valley friends and associates used when discussing the general population of America. Max, much more than she, preferred the tech-world bubble, the idyllic utopia detached from the rest of the country where dreams still came true and where if something bad happened, if your search engine failed or your start-up fell to pieces, CEOs and entrepreneurs still walked away with millions of dollars and the ability to launch their new dream the next day. He'd forgotten about what real desperation could look like, and that disappointed Charlotte, how thoroughly Max had lost touch with his roots.

Charlotte turned her attention to the girls. "Tell me about your day."

Annie twisted her head around to look at her mother. "I pooped in the toilet." Charlotte looked at Max.

"She didn't," he mouthed. The baby laughed so hard her face turned purple.

Charlotte flagged Jack down with an overly enthusiastic wave of both her hands when Max left the table to go to the bathroom after dessert. "Let me get your number?"

"I'll send you a Facebook message with it." He grinned at her. Was it an acknowledgment of her stupid note to him?

"He's cute," Leila remarked once he was out of earshot. "Like a mixture of Coach Taylor with post-*Matrix* Keanu Reeves."

Charlotte rolled her eyes as if to say that she didn't notice those kinds of things, even though she had immediately noticed the exact same thing. Leila looked past her shoulder to the door of the men's bathroom to see if Max was about to return to the table.

"Meeting Jack gave me an idea for your speech next week."

"Oh yeah?" Charlotte said, picking up her napkin and twisting it into a rope. Just the mention of the speech quickened her pulse.

Leila gave her a reassuring wink. "Stay calm, girl. It's a good one. But it's definitely going to piss Max off."

CHAPTER 5
March 4, 2018
247 days to Election Day

"Remind me why I had to meet you in this dingy motel after I drove two hours to get here from Manhattan at the crack of dawn on a Sunday morning?" the handsome young man asked Charlotte, a sly smile on his lips.

"I didn't want Max to see you."

"And what would he say if he knew we were meeting like this?" Langston Kade, who had the plastic perfection of a Ken doll dreamed into life, raised an eyebrow and placed his thin fingers on her shoulders to sit her on the edge of the bed while he studied her face, his navy blue eyes wide and alert. The room smelled like unwashed laundry and sex. There were fingernail clippings left in the sink. These were the kinds of places Charlotte's family had stayed in during their summer road trips to the Baseball Hall of Fame in Cooperstown or Atlantic City, where her dad tried to sneak them into a heavyweight fight.

Charlotte looked at Kade and rubbed her hands along the light-brown comforter that was about as soft as a grocery store paper bag.

"Max would laugh at me. He'd tell me not to do this."

She'd been seeing Langston behind her husband's back since just before her fortieth birthday, usually on business trips to New York.

"You want the usual?"

"Maybe a little more." Charlotte cringed. "Make sure the swelling isn't too bad."

"More? Are you sure?"

"I need it."

Langston opened his alligator-skin briefcase and extracted two bottles from a cooler, one containing Botox, the other Juvéderm filler.

Vanity, Charlotte believed, was something to be ashamed of, a holdover from her Protestant upbringing. And yet she cared more about looking old than she'd ever admit. It had only gotten worse after Annie was born and her chin seemed to melt into her neck. It was worse still that she knew she'd be photographed on a daily basis from unforgiving angles with iPhone cameras containing HD lenses. She had figured she could wait until next month to meet with the doctor when she would be in New York for the Humanity board meeting, but Josh's scrutiny made her second-guess herself and she'd paid Kade triple what he usually charged to drive here on short notice.

"How'd you get here?" Kade filled his needle with the clear liquid and eyed her jogging clothes. "You're sweaty," he said with a look of obvious distaste.

"I jogged. Told Max I was going for a run."

"You can't run back. You'll sweat everything out."

"I'll walk. It's fine," she replied evenly.

"You look tired."

"I know. That's why I need you."

"Everything okay?"

These were the most words they'd ever spoken to each other. Charlotte caught her reflection in the cracked dresser mirror. Her face was pale, her eyes rimmed red. Leila had come home with them from the restaurant and they had stayed up most of the night before sitting at her kitchen table writing and rewriting her speech. Charlotte forced a smile for Kade. "Run-of-the-mill mom exhaustion, wife exhaustion, running-for-political-office exhaustion."

"Mmmm-hmm." Kade was already bored by her.

Ten little pricks in strategic places on her forehead, at the corners of her eyes, and around her lips and it was over.

Kade handed her an ice pack. "Keep this on for about five minutes. You'll look as fresh as a baby's ass by tonight."

★

The parking lot of the motel was empty except for Kade's cherry-red convertible BMW, an eighteen-wheeler, and a family of scrawny stray cats. Charlotte stood there for a breath and allowed the crisp morning air to soothe her raw skin.

Five minutes into her walk home, she stood in front of what was once Regent's drugstore. The pharmacy had closed five years ago when a Walgreens opened a mile away, but the building still stood, the façade cracking, the G in the sign missing, probably stolen by a teenager named Gavin or Gabe for his dorm-room wall. She ran her hand along the peeling paint of the doorframe, and when she closed her eyes she could picture Max, eighteen years younger than he was today, leaning inside this doorway, cocky and oblivious to anyone who might want to pass by him. It was the first time she'd seen him since high school.

It was 1999. She was twenty-nine and working in public service as an aide to Maryland governor Rosalind Waters. She'd been a systems wonk at Wharton and had drunk the Roz Waters Kool-Aid when she heard her speak about how to run a state government like a business. Charlotte was home for a rare weekend in Elk Hollow that coincided with the annual Fourth of July parade. She was also tipsy. Not drunk, though. Charlotte didn't like getting drunk and usually set her limit at two drinks, enough that she could get a buzz without being sloppy. The fact that she was drinking at all—during the day, no less—was her brother's fault. She and Paul had quickly fallen into their long-ago-assigned roles of screwup older brother and eager-to-please little sister. It was almost fun, until it wasn't. Until beer and warm gin weren't enough for Paul and he got pissed at her because she wouldn't lend him a thousand bucks to bet on Holyfield in Atlantic City the following weekend. She tried to explain to him that she made less than thirty grand as a governor's aide and had more than $100,000 in student loans.

"Then you shouldn't have gone to those stupid fancy schools," he spat at her and stalked away. Charlotte didn't bother to chase him. She needed Advil and maybe a packet of Little Debbie donuts to soak up the booze. But Max blocked her way into the drugstore as he fiddled with a PalmPilot and lazily nipped at a cloud of gauzy cotton candy. She hadn't seen him in more than ten years. He stood straighter now and had fixed his gray tooth. His face had grown into his nose and he radiated confidence like a Hollywood movie star.

"You got cute." Charlotte was both surprised and delighted by her uncharacteristic boldness. Though coming from her lips the words still had the tone of a fact rather than a flirtation.

An amused expression touched his eyes before he laughed. He had a good laugh. "Hey, Charlie."

"Hey, Max."

He produced a water bottle from his back pocket and handed it to her. She chugged it quickly and gratefully, drops spilling onto her chin. He reached over to wipe them as the two of them settled onto the curb to watch the last remnants of the parade pass: a Buick carrying the mayor, his wife, and their sad-eyed poodle; a squad of high school girls in glittery shorts tossing batons into the air.

Charlotte quickly filled Max in on her job with the governor of Maryland, emphasizing that she'd grown to become Roz's right-hand woman. She hoped she was impressing him.

He let her finish before he began his own boasts about his big job out in Silicon Valley at the start-up he insisted would change the world—Humanity.

"But what do you *do*?" she pressed, commandeering the rest of his cotton candy and letting the sugar dissolve on her tongue. What did any of those tech companies really do?

He grinned and closed his eyes like he was about to tell her something special. "Everything. We make companies more productive. Our software, operating systems, and applications streamline everything from human resources to payroll to benefits, customer management, and internal and external communications. We use artificial intelligence to predict what a consumer wants before they know what they want."

Humanity, whose mission was based on its founders' impudently naïve adoration of John Maynard Keynes, had begun nobly, in the abstract way most Silicon Valley start-ups do, with the goal of maximizing the efficiency of productivity software to usher in an age of automation such that workers could eventually have a three-day work week. Less time working would give Americans more time to spend with their families and enjoying their interests and hobbies outside of work. The founders, Kevin Rogers and Kumail Chatterjee, dreamed of a world where everyone learned Italian atop a surfboard on Thursdays.

Max nattered on to Charlotte in slick tech jargon—first-mover advantage, scalable best practices, core competencies, the vast expansion of human potential. The irony to Charlotte was that a company called Humanity was doing its best to make humans obsolete. She wasn't wrong. Once Humanity grew legs in the next decade, mostly due to Charlotte's organizational skills, once it streamlined the productivity software necessary to fulfill its destiny, it never delivered a three-day work week: It merely ushered in a Cambrian explosion of automation that eliminated millions of jobs around the globe. At the end of the day, altruism was trumped by the Silicon Valley dictum to move fast and break things. What they broke was the American worker.

But Max and the founders wouldn't have known that yet. Back then, they were still just going to save the world by expanding the weekend and it was cute.

"You're really full of yourself," she said.

"Is it turning you on?" He looked amused.

"Not yet." The truth was, she hadn't been so attracted to anyone since Jack in high school. Pickings were slim in Annapolis, and working eighty-hour weeks for Roz didn't leave much time for socializing with the city's few single men, most of whom popped their collars and wore boat shoes despite never getting on a boat—not that any of them had asked her out. Even knowing what he had been like in high school, this new version of Max Tanner felt completely out of her league.

His hubris and metamorphosis since leaving Elk Hollow intimidated her and made her wonder if she was really all that different from the girl she'd been when she left this town. Had she changed enough to intrigue him?

After the parade wound down, they decided to stroll through town, the edge of a hand occasionally brushing the other's thigh or a hip, but never explicitly touching. The conversation returned to the superficial—was Y2K as big a deal as everyone said it would be, whatever happened to people they'd both hated in high school. But before they parted ways he turned to look directly into her eyes, daring her to look anywhere but at him.

"We could use people like you at Humanity," he said to her. In that moment, she knew she'd succeeded in impressing him and she liked the way it made her feel. And then he said ten words that would turn out to make all the difference. "Politics is dull. Come to California. It'll change your life." He grinned and Charlotte was a goner.

After witnessing her parents' unhappy marriage, Charlotte was in no hurry to chase a man, even one as captivating as Max had turned out to be, but she *was* looking for a new challenge. Roz was going to run for Congress once her term as governor was up and Charlotte had grown wary of the inertia of lethargy that dominated DC. Silicon Valley felt like a place where shit was getting done, where she could make a real difference. The possibility of something happening with Max intrigued her more than she wanted to admit.

Nine months later, she left the East Coast with a single suitcase of

Ann Taylor suits she'd never wear again, a few books, and her clunky old answering machine that no longer worked but held something precious: her best friend Anne's last voice mail she'd left for her, the day before the car accident.

"I fucking miss you. You'd better be out raising hell and making the world a better place if you're too busy to answer my call. Love you, Moo."

Before she'd taken off for California, Max had vouched for her, promising Kevin and Kumail in grandiose verbiage that Charlotte Walsh would be the best thing that had happened to the tech world since Google began indexing the World Wide Web. Silicon Valley welcomed newcomers without a pedigree. When Charlotte joined the operations and project management staff at Humanity, her East Coast–establishment work ethic helped her to thrive. She reveled in overseeing the arrogant children as they disrupted industries around the world. She told herself over and over that she hadn't made the move for Max. In those days she found it easier to lie to herself than to lie to other people.

Moving to California gave her a front-row seat to watch Max court a never-ending parade of ever prettier women while he treated her like an adorable younger sister. "I'm making up for lost time," he would joke. "I didn't lose my virginity until after college." When she thought back on those years, Charlotte felt like she was watching a buddy comedy, the kind that made you cringe for the female protagonist with the unfortunate haircut and thrift store skirts. When Max would get too drunk in the city to go back to his tiny apartment in Palo Alto he'd sleep on Charlotte's futon at her small apartment in the Mission or sometimes snore alongside her in her bed, never laying a finger on her. They'd commute to the Valley together, eating breakfast burritos and mocking their founders' interest in things like Transcendental Meditation and forest yoga. He'd shave his Etch A Sketch stubble while she drove.

Max understood her ambition from the beginning and he nurtured it, encouraged her to speak up in meetings, challenged her to think in new ways. It felt like some of his charisma, the charms that endeared him to everyone he met, wore off on her.

The question loomed for her, of course: Can best friends become lovers?

It was easier to stay infatuated with him than to balance a real relationship with her job. She had a brief crush on the woman who ran the de Young Museum in Golden Gate Park that went nowhere because Charlotte was too self-conscious to properly flirt with a woman. There was one guy. He was older, a San Francisco hippie, the kind who made money in an ambiguous way and always had enough of it, even though he preached it was the root of all evil. She'd sleep with him on his houseboat in Sausalito, an experiment in forgetting about Max. It was nice to fall asleep on the bay, a reminder that the world beneath you would continue to shift, sometimes violently, sometimes with soft and gentle waves, even if you did nothing at all. She had only a small handful of friends from college in the Bay Area, and they met up once a month or so for overpriced beers or quick manicures. But they all moved to Marin once they had babies, which might as well have been New Jersey if you lived in the city and worked in the Valley. Then came that trip to Yosemite, the poison oak, the thoughtful sex at night, the hard and quick sex in the morning, followed by more waiting, more patience.

Max got weird. Busy.

"I'm thinking about moving to DC. Roz called last week and she wants me back on her team and I'm considering it," she told him one night at the bar after work, six months after they'd first slept together.

"But I love you," he replied.

"Okay," she responded as calmly as she could with her heart thrumming against her rib cage, her breath quickening.

"Marry me?" Even though she'd never been a romantic, it wasn't how she imagined a marriage proposal.

Charlotte forced the next words out of her mouth. "Too late."

She flew to DC for a week under the guise of attending job interviews, but spent most of her time wandering the city. The orderly anonymity of the grid was her favorite thing about the nation's capital. She ducked in and out of museums and had coffee with Roz. When she returned to San Francisco she agreed to meet Max for a beer at one of those tourist traps in Fisherman's Wharf she knew he despised.

"We should probably date first," she proposed to him after they'd each ordered a bowl of clam chowder in a sourdough-bread bowl. She liked regaining the upper hand.

"Fine."

They spent four months making out like teenagers all over the city and in dark closets in the office before he proposed again for real during a trip to the Grand Canyon.

Once Max chose her she finally felt validated, chosen, and comfortable in her own skin. It felt like she'd won something, and the fact she'd never expected victory made it all the sweeter.

CHAPTER 6
March 5, 2018
246 days to Election Day

Charlotte woke to the unmistakable sounds of her children vomiting.

"Twins are sick." Max stood next to the bed, clutching a bundle of stained sheets to his bare chest. His hair stuck out in a clumsy way. It was getting long and Charlotte made a mental note to make him an appointment for a haircut.

It was still dark outside. She fumbled for her phone to look at the time. Four thirty a.m. She'd finally fallen asleep near two. How many times had she revised her speech? How many masochistic notes had she left for herself in the margins, long-buried insecurities brought to life on the page? *Do you really think you can pull this off? Try harder.* At one point she'd gotten out of bed, gone to the kitchen, and recorded herself saying it out loud and then played it back, hating every second of listening to her voice as she lay on the cold kitchen floor.

Her laptop screen glowed blue next to her pillow.

"Sick?" She rose and rubbed her eyes. It had always been she who heard the kids in the middle of the night. Since the twins were born, her hearing had heightened such that she could perceive a pacifier drop from their mouths from clear across the house. Max was the one who slept like the dead, but last night she'd heard nothing.

Her husband's eyes had a zombielike quality to them now. "They're back in bed. Both of them puked. I stripped the sheets and put on new ones. I'm throwing these in the wash."

Her brain finally snapped to full attention. "Annie? Is she okay?"

"Didn't wake up through the whole thing. Go back to sleep. You need a few good hours before the big speech." Sometimes, when she least expected it, her husband gave her exactly what she needed.

"So do you."

He set a glass of water from the bathroom tap on her bedside table. "I'm fine. I'm just the help. I can survive without sleep." And just as quickly he turned sarcastic and mean.

"Thank you for letting me sleep," she whispered without acknowledging his tone. She woke two hours later to both girls sleeping in between her and Max, Ella curled into her body like a snail, her light snores vibrating against Charlotte's fleshy belly.

I'm running for national political office today. The words flitted across Charlotte's consciousness like a headline or a Facebook update. *I'm officially running for Senate today. I'm a harried, middle-aged mother running for Senate. How did this happen?*

Ella rolled over and let out an adorable burp that still stank of vomit. Charlotte wrapped her arms around her warm daughter and squeezed her as tightly as she could without waking her before wiggling out of the bed to answer Josh's early-morning briefing call.

★

A naked Annie crawled on all fours into the kitchen and bit Charlotte on the ankle as she scraped cold butter onto raisin toast for the twins.

"Mama, I brought you shoe!"

"Thank you, baby," Charlotte hoisted her onto the ledge of her hip. "I need my shoe. Thanks for bringing it to me." As she retrieved the black snakeskin flat from her daughter's hand she noticed bulldog teeth marks. "That little fucker."

"Fucker!" the baby parroted. *Shit.* They'd been so good about not cursing in front of Annie, who absorbed all of the words, particularly the wrong ones, like a sponge.

Charlotte texted Leila as she dangled the remains of the shoe between two fingers like a soiled diaper.

The dog ate my shoes

Better than your speech . . . you have more than one pair of shoes. We have a bigger problem

Don't tell me that

Your makeup girl canceled. She's sick

Why is everyone sick? Twins sick too. Up all night throwing up

Gross. The worst. Can you do your own hair and makeup?

Charlotte had never been particularly talented at painting on a face or making her hair look presentable. Left to her own devices she would have gotten dressed in the dark and avoided mirrors for the entirety of a day. When she got her first job with Roz she made an effort with some lipstick and smudgy eye shadow and at some point in her thirties she'd embraced professional blowouts to tame her hopeless frizz into something manageable. To this day, when she attempted to put on her own eyeliner she resembled a drag queen impersonating Marilyn Manson. Because she assumed makeup didn't suit her, she went without when she could. She texted Leila back.

It won't be great

I'll find someone else

"Joe Biden never had to go through this," Charlotte said out loud.

"Fucker!" the baby shouted.

"Good morning to you, too!" Max emerged and smiled at his daughter's potty mouth as he kissed her square on the lips.

"I'm a terrible mother."

"I said 'douchebag' last week. Child services should come and take them away."

Laughter loosened the tension knotting her neck and shoulders. She placed Annie back on the floor.

"Drop and give me ten, monster," Max hollered at the little girl, falling next to her and performing his own skilled push-ups. The baby bent her elbows, pushed her butt high into the air, and bobbed her head up and down.

"You know what the secret to ten good push-ups is?" Max bounced to his feet.

Charlotte shook her head, raised an eyebrow.

"Doing eleven push-ups! Want me to take that toast up to the girls?"

Where did he get his energy? She flashed him a grateful smile. "Yes, please. Oh. The woman who was doing my hair and makeup this morning got sick, too. She can't come."

Max glanced over his shoulder from the stairs. "You look gorgeous without makeup. Why don't you call Kara? Isn't that what she does now?"

Charlotte clapped her hands in delight at his compliment and simple solution to her problem. Surprise flickered across his face when she leaned in to kiss him in gratitude.

Her sister-in-law responded to her text within minutes. She instructed Charlotte to wash her hair and keep it wet. She'd be there in twenty minutes. Did they need bagels? She could bring bagels. Did the girls like theirs with scrapple? (A delicacy mainly found in Pennsylvania and New Jersey made from the discarded parts of the pig even the hot dog manufacturers wouldn't touch.) Her grandkids were crazy for it.

"Problem solved." Max grinned.

"Why are you so chipper this morning?"

"I'm excited for your speech."

She didn't bother to muffle a skeptical laugh.

"Uh-huh?"

"Well, also I got an email from Travis last night. He wants me on the board of ePay." Travis Coot lived down the street from them in Atherton. He was one of five actual billionaires in their social circle. Three years ago he'd founded that app that eliminated the need for cash by allowing you to text money to your friends. His recent technological leap allowed users to "pay with their face," leveraging cornea-recognition software to activate the transfer of money. Max enjoyed, envied, and loathed Travis. Max and Charlotte had grown close with Travis and his wife Lucinda, a Googler, by virtue of them having kids around the same age, two boys named Bear and Magellan. Then, last summer, Lucinda had cheated on Travis with a Google intern, a French-Canadian boy genius half her age, and they hadn't seen much of either of them since. Charlotte heard Lucinda had gone to live with their two boys in a spacious apartment in the city overlooking the Bay, leaving Travis alone in the giant house in the valley.

This wasn't a conversation Charlotte felt like having right now. "You can't work for Travis. I need you here. And you still technically work for Humanity. And we don't live in California."

"I'm not working for him. It's a board position."

"But you'll need to be there for board meetings in California, what, once a month, twice a month? Who will take care of the girls?"

Max turned away from her and busied himself with sifting coffee into his fancy glass Chemex. Charlotte despised the Chemex and how long its intricate preparation took to get her her caffeine fix compared to the ten-dollar Mr. Coffee machine. Max's voice lost its shine. "I don't know. We could figure something out."

The news was irritating to Charlotte for reasons she didn't have time to articulate. She glared at the thin liquid as it dribbled slowly, too slowly, through the filter. "Can we talk about it later? I need to get in the shower."

"Whatever you say, boss."

Stop calling me boss. Charlotte brought Annie with her into the shower to save time and spent most of it bellowing "Let It Go" at the top of her lungs while the toddler tried to slip out of her hands and rub shampoo in her mouth.

Ella burst into the bathroom and peeled back the shower curtain, spraying water all over the floor. "Rosie puked again."

"Oh God. Did Daddy clean it up?"

"Bob cleaned it up." She said this sensibly, as if a dog lapping up a child's vomit was the most natural thing in the world. Instead of disgust, Charlotte felt appreciation.

Five minutes later, Kara was there setting up a miniature beauty parlor in her living room. "Sit your bony doopa in the chair and have at least a nibble of some bagel, otherwise you're gonna pass out on da stage," her sister-in-law instructed. She pushed the pads of her fingertips onto the skin above the bridge of Charlotte's nose. "Your forehead is puffy."

The swelling was supposed to have gone down by now. For a moment Charlotte considered telling Kara about Langston Kade and their secret meeting over the weekend. She craved someone besides Leila and Roz to really talk to, to share her insecurities with, to confess her secrets to. On days when she was particularly hard on herself, Charlotte found it pathetic that her closest friends were her husband, her old boss, and her aide. She often wished she were better at prioritizing genuinely intimate new friendships as an adult, at connecting with other women in a meaningful way. It felt complicated after losing Anne, and once she rose to the top of Humanity it was hard to tell whether fellow women in tech wanted to be friends or simply wanted something from her.

"I didn't get much sleep."

Kara raised an eyebrow. "Let's start with the hair. You have such pretty hair. Always loved this color. You can't get this in a box." She began brushing from the top of Charlotte's scalp and pinning it back in four-inch sections with tiny claw clips. "I heard old man Slaughter on the radio talking about you this morning."

"What'd he say?"

"He said he wanted to welcome you to PA and wished you well in your new state of residence."

"Of course he did."

"Then he called you a sweet little girl."

"That's condescending."

"That's Tug Slaughter. His compliments come with a side of arsenic. He also said he wasn't sure if your values were in line with those of voters here since your company paid for employees to have abortions."

Humiliation reddened her cheeks. Charlotte felt like she'd been slapped across the face. She also wondered, not for the first time, what kind of grown man insisted on being called Tug.

"So, did you? Pay for abortions?"

"No. Jesus Christ. That's a lie. A blatant lie. No one would ever do that."

"He said something like it was part of your family-planning benefits. Said it was 'cause you didn't want women employees to be burdened with children. Said you told them to kill their babies so they could be bosses." Kara repeated the terrible accusation in a monotone voice as if she were reading something off a teleprompter. The news, particularly political news, had grown so salacious and violent in the past two years that no one even bothered to muster any emotion when repeating something rotten.

Charlotte closed her eyes and spoke the truth. "We offered family-planning benefits to women to help them have children. We paid for things like fertility treatments and adoption. How can he lie like that?" Her question was a reflex from another time, a time when politicians and people in power at least feigned honesty.

"Everyone heard it. It's on Facebook now. My friends posted about it."

"Shit. Now I'll have to defend myself during my speech. That's exactly what he wanted to do. Put me on the defensive." Charlotte picked at a loose cuticle on her thumb until it bled. She raised it to her lips to remove the blood.

"Stop that." Kara pulled Charlotte's hand out of her mouth. "You want to look like a meth head with bleedin' fingers? It'll be okay. I wrote all my friends back on Facebook and told them to vote for you and told them we need someone like you who is gonna get us jobs back and help people like us get to be people like you."

Charlotte shifted uncomfortably in the chair. "I'm not all that different from you."

Kara looked at her like she'd just stepped off a rocket ship. "That's like saying Haiti ain't all that different from Tahiti, honey."

A naked and still-wet Annie flung herself at her aunt like a slippery baby seal.

"Oooof. My God, Charlie, this child gets prettier every day!" Kara picked Annie up and balanced her on one hip while she finished blowing out Charlotte's hair with the other hand.

"I know it," Charlotte said, seized with a fierce love and pride.

"Now, before I start your makeup go splash cold water on your face. Gets rid of da Botox bloat."

Charlotte opened her mouth, but Kara cut her off before she could say anything.

"Girl, don't even try to hide that shit from me."

The doorbell rang as Charlotte returned to the chair. "Come in!" Kara hollered.

Since she'd begun working for her in her twenties, Charlotte had always been able to tell when Rosalind Waters entered a room. She wondered if Leila felt the same thing about her, if her skin tingled and her nerves shivered in anticipation. Roz, once her boss and now a genuine friend, was a force of nature, a natural-born politician. When she swept through the door the air changed, like a celebrity had arrived. Roz knew it, too, and acted the part, as if her presence were a marvelous gift to any room. Usually it was.

Before giving anyone a hug, Roz strode purposefully into the kitchen and grabbed an everything bagel dripping in grease and scrapple.

"I'm on that dinosaur diet, the paleo, all week, but one day a week I eat what I want, usually Sunday. You know, because it's the Lord's Day. Let's pretend today is the Lord's Day." Roz winked at no one in particular. "Good morning, ladies. What a beautiful day for a political spectacle." Leila slipped in quietly behind Roz, one phone at her ear, a second device in her hand. She paused in her conversation for a second to survey Charlotte from her bare feet to her tired eyes.

"You need to do a five-minute livestream on Facebook of you getting yourself together and getting the kids ready and leaving for the announcement," Leila said. "We agreed to stream parts of the whole day. Facebook will promote it. Mark said he would post to his ninety million followers. It doesn't have to be real. We can fake it. I'll wait until you put on eyeliner. Lulu's on her way."

Kara put the hair dryer down and stretched out her hand to Roz. "Nice to see ya."

Roz grabbed both of Kara's hands in hers. "You must be Kara." Roz's indoor voice was always slightly louder than other people's in case you weren't already paying enough attention to her.

After eight years as governor of Maryland; twelve in Congress, four of those as the majority leader; followed by another four years as the ambassador to the United Nations, Rosalind Waters was finally semiretired. But though she called it retirement, she'd recently spearheaded a nonprofit to revisit the passage of the Equal Rights Amendment to the constitution and she'd become a major player behind the scenes of the national party as they tried to figure out what the hell had gone wrong in the last election.

"Do you miss it?" Kara asked Roz with a mixture of genuine curiosity and innocence. "Workin' in politics every day?"

Roz's chuckle originated deep in her gut. "Not for a second. People seem to enjoy me much better when I'm not running for office." It was true. Politician Rosalind had had every single aspect of her personal and professional life scrutinized by pundits and the press, every haircut, every hemline, every tweet. Private citizen Roz Waters became instantly beloved, a feminist icon, revered as a reluctant heroine, and referred to as Auntie Roz when she posed for selfies with strangers on the street. "I'm huge with millennials. They've got a thing for mature women. I have a theory it's because *The Golden Girls* and *Designing Women* were in syndication when their brains were forming. Plus, now I can sleep in and drink red wine with lunch every day."

Leila put her hand over the phone. "Julia Sugarbaker is still my screen saver."

"And apparently you can wear leather?" Charlotte surveyed Roz's sleek fitted leather blazer and black designer jeans. She'd never seen the older woman in anything other than single-breasted wool in the winter and a linen blend in the summer, and never without power shoulders. She'd definitely never seen her in jeans.

"I call it grandma biker chic. Don't look so surprised. I'm sixty-seven. I'm allowed to let my hair down a little." Roz shook her conservative bob and Charlotte noticed for the first time she'd stopped updating it with her typical honey-blond highlights and had allowed the natural silver to fill in. Roz was a tall woman, nearly six feet in flats, which she never wore. She'd lost weight since Charlotte had seen her back in the fall. Her cheekbones were sharper, her face newly angular.

She rubbed Charlotte's shoulders and dug her thumb into the meaty part of the blade. "How's my girl? Are you ready? Slaughter's on the warpath. It's all over Twitter. That means you've struck a nerve. Good job." She brought a chair next to Charlotte.

Charlotte nodded, her nerves resurfacing. She could still see Leila pacing on her phone in the hallway, speaking in hushed tones—her birdlike frame made more mature by a conservative shift dress with a disorienting pattern.

Leila glanced over at Charlotte and mouthed: "Did you tell him?" Charlotte shook her head.

She'd told herself there hadn't been time to talk to Max about Leila's brilliant plan for who would introduce Charlotte at her speech this morning. They'd originally thought Roz would be the right person to lend some gravitas to the campaign, but Josh had nixed that idea more than a month ago. "We're targeting Slaughter as the DC lifetime politician and he's already painting you as an angry power-hungry woman. You can't have an angry lady lifetime politician on-stage with you."

It was Leila who came up with the alternative after dinner at Fridays: Jack. And, to Charlotte's surprise, Josh had been equally enthused. "Jack the Gym Teacher!" he exclaimed. "It's even better than Joe the Plumber. I like it."

Max wasn't going to like it, and the truth was, Charlotte hadn't found the time to have an argument about it, because it was the last thing she felt like doing.

"I got you a present." Roz handed Charlotte a glossy bag with black cursive writing that signaled it contained something expensive and disposable. "You shouldn't have." Charlotte peeked inside and let out a snort. "Panty hose? You really shouldn't have."

"European princesses and women politicians. You've got to wear them." Roz managed a straight face. "Being a woman in the public eye is an endless series of indignities, and panty hose is just the beginning."

"Gross." Charlotte hadn't worn hose since her First Communion. She pulled it from its cardboard packaging. The beige nylon dripped through her fingers like dead skin.

Roz was insistent. "Just put on the panty hose. I promise someone will notice if you go up there with bare legs. I hate them too. They're a yeast infection waiting to happen. Get some scissors and cut out the crotch so your lady parts can breathe. I tried thigh-highs, but they squeeze your thighs like an overstuffed sausage casing."

Max plodded down the stairs, his wet hair slicked back after a shower. With his face cleanly shaven he looked younger. Roz poked him in the ribs like he was a child. "Can you believe all this is happening?" she asked him. "I brought a pair of Don Arturos we can smoke later."

He shook his head and glanced at Charlotte. "I always said I married up." His smile, so easy an hour earlier, was forced and never reached his eyes. He turned back toward the stairs. "I need to pick out my tie."

Roz gave Charlotte a look, grabbed her by the elbow, and ushered her into the hallway. With a maternal calm, she placed her arms around Charlotte's neck and pressed her forehead to hers. Roz had three sons, all investment bankers, all of them bachelors over forty who dated women fresh out of college. She said often, in earshot of her male children, that Charlotte was the daughter she would have given at least two of those sons to have. Roz needing a daughter and Charlotte needing a mother was partially what had allowed the two of them to grow close and stay close long after Charlotte quit working for her.

"How are things with you and Max?"

It was Roz who'd once told her it was okay to think about divorce. "Every married woman with children fantasizes about divorce or her husband dying in some benign and painless way and leaving her a widow. If she doesn't think about those things, then she's too happy, which means she probably married her gay best friend," Roz had told her one night over too much wine.

Charlotte breathed in Roz's scent, Chanel No. 5 and a spicy cardamom soap Richard used to buy her by the dozen on his research trips to Jordan. "Max and I are status quo," Charlotte said. "No better. No worse."

Roz placed both Charlotte's hands in hers. "If I learned anything about men, it's that they need to feel needed. They need to feel important. Be good to your marriage right now. You need him. You know the saying—behind every powerful man there's a great woman. Well, behind every powerful woman there's a man, any man, a mediocre man, a perfectly acceptable man. But it's easier when there's a man. Now get dressed and let's get this show on the road. I'll get some clothes on your beautiful naked child."

★

Elk Hollow High School, Charlotte's alma mater for ninth through twelfth grade, was one of those grand old structures built during the time when high schools and mental institutions were designed with a sense of panache and civic pride. Two stories, with a majestic clock tower containing a now-broken clock, the public institution had held up well over the years. Because most graduates of EHHS went to trade schools or community college, Charlotte was a local celebrity to them, and it had taken little convincing for them to allow her campaign use of the auditorium on a Monday afternoon.

"Who are you wearing?" A beautiful sylph wearing a tight black skirt and red sweater was the first reporter to approach Charlotte as she walked toward the school.

"Excuse me?"

"Who are you wearing? What designer?"

Josh moved between them. "Charlotte, this is the lovely Carly Meeks from *Teen Vogue*. How was your trip to the Milan shows, Carly? I loved your Instagrams." While he was odd and uncomfortable to be around in private, in front of the press Josh became a charismatic show-man, likable, self-deprecating, even engaging. Before Charlotte could ask what interest *Teen Vogue* had in a Pennsylvania Senate race, Josh answered the question for her. "The suit is J.Crew. The shirt is from Theory, and I'm not sure about those shoes." How did he know that?

"The flats are Tory Burch," Charlotte replied with a careful smile, trying to remember what they had cost.

"Can I Snap them real quick?"

Josh shook his head like a wet dog. "We'll be answering more questions after the speech. Thanks so much for coming, Carly. Will you be livestreaming the speech?"

But Carly would not be silenced so easily. "And what's that nail color?"

Thank God I got a manicure.

The name of the color was Russian Red, but she'd be damned if she'd say that now. "It's Ruby Slippers. So nice to meet you, Carly."

"You too, Charlotte." It felt strange for the girl to call her by her first name. "One last question. Do you think the bipartisan Pregnant Workers Fairness Act currently being reviewed in the House goes far enough to enact protections for women in the workplace?" A look appeared on the young woman's face that dared anyone to underestimate her.

Charlotte was more prepared for this question than she was to talk about her clothes or nail color. "No. I do not. It needs to go further to protect both nursing mothers and women in their third trimester, particularly those working for hourly wages, and I hope the bill is revised before it goes for a vote. I can send you the policies we put into place at Humanity that I hope to introduce into a more progressive bill when I am elected. Thank you for the thoughtful question."

Carly's intense brown eyes considered Charlotte from her feet to the crown of her head in a way that made her feel naked and exposed. "Of course. We're making an effort to cover every woman candidate running this election season from the very beginning. You're my woman."

The young reporter's false familiarity inclined Charlotte to give the girl a hug, but she shook her hand firmly instead. "Then I'll be seeing much more of you."

Charlotte waited until Carly was out of earshot. "Teenagers can't vote, Josh."

"Don't be a snob. *Teen Vogue*'s search results come up before *The Hill*. No one knows where stories come from these days. Their website has millions of social followers who aren't children."

"Are they pedophiles?" Leila managed with a straight face.

Josh just rolled his eyes. "Pedophiles can vote."

"Hey, Charlie!" Jack Seligson strode toward her with two teenage boys who shared his kind eyes and hunched shoulders.

"Thanks for doing this, Jack." Charlotte felt a warm blush creep from her sternum to the nape of her neck as she leaned in for a stiff-armed hug.

"No problem. I hope I do okay. These are my boys Aaron and Caleb. Boys, meet my friend Charlie Walsh. She's gonna be the next senator for Pennsylvania."

The gangly teenage boys reached their too-large hands toward her. "Pleased to meet you, ma'am."

Their "ma'am" made her channel Roz's authority and presence. "You're even more handsome than your dad." She turned back to Jack. "Leila will mic you up and get you ready to go onstage."

★

Jack Seligson wasn't a natural public speaker. But that was the point. He smiled sheepishly as he adjusted the microphone. Those who knew him grinned and nudged the person sitting next to them. The press was clearly thrown. Who was this handsome stranger? A local in JCPenney chinos?

"Most of you here know me. I teach here and I'm the baseball coach. Charlotte said she thought it would be nice to have someone who knew her way back when come introduce her. And so that's why I'm here. I have to tell you that you're less scary than some of my tenth graders. And you look way more interested in what I have to say." The crowd laughed at that.

Charlotte had delivered her valedictorian speech right here in this same auditorium thirty years ago. It was another speech she'd worried over for weeks, writing and rewriting and finally settling on the perfect closer, a Muhammad Ali quote beloved by her father:

He who is not courageous enough to take risks will accomplish nothing in life.

Jack knew enough to wait for the crowd to settle down before he continued. "I saw Charlie—Charlotte—for the first time in years last week. She brought her family, Max and their adorable girls, in for dinner at Fridays."

From the side of the stage, Charlotte gazed over the crowd to see her husband's face contorted into an uncomfortable shape. *I should have told you. I'm sorry.*

"Charlotte and her family were eating at TGI Fridays, where I was their server. I work a few shifts there during the week. My wife, Emily—she's right over there." He blew a kiss down to a pretty brunette in a wheelchair. "Emily's getting some serious cancer treatments this month and our insurance doesn't cover all of it, so I'm trying to make ends meet. Just like a lot of you. And that's why I'm happy to introduce Charlotte Walsh. I know her. You all know her. She cares about us. She cares about helping get us back to a good place. I trust her to do that. But I'll let her say a little more for herself."

Stepping onto this stage is the beginning of something. Notice this moment. Film crews from CNN, MSNBC, Facebook, YouTube, Cheddar, and a handful of local Pennsylvania stations gathered in front of the stage. Someone launched a drone that hovered overhead with the lazy disinterest of a cloud. Charlotte turned to look at her campaign manager. Josh grinned like a jackal. "Well, he was goddamn perfect. Remember, don't mention Slaughter. You don't have to. Don't give him the satisfaction. And don't forget to thank Jesus. Just once. Only one Jesus." With that he nudged her toward the stage.

Banners announcing WALSH CAN FIX IT bounced in the air. Others declared THE RIGHT CHOICE and MORE JOBS FOR PA—bold simplifications of vague concepts. They were pure poll-tested shorthand. Cheers and claps blended into a single cacophonous beat like rolling thunder that vibrated through her entire body as she walked to the podium. She took in the bright faces of her staff and their friends in the front two rows—young, shiny, eager—waving their signs and phones in the air. "It'll look great on television" was how Josh explained why he'd strategically placed only young and good-looking people in the front row. A few rows back her high school classmates, older, less shiny, rounder around the middle, people who'd lived lives, greeted her as though she were a hometown hero. Mr. Thayer, her AP government teacher, was there, an old man now, coughing into a handkerchief, flabby and sullen. Kara had gotten Paul there in his best jeans and a button-down shirt. Behind them was an entire row of pink, the Pussy Brigade, wearing their flamingo-colored T-shirts declaring IT'S THE RIGHT THING. The remaining rows were filled mainly with senior citizens, bussed in from two local retirement homes, fed donuts and coffee en route, and gifted WALSH FOR SENATE baseball caps to hide their gray heads in aerial shots of the crowd. The irony, Josh had explained, was that the elderly were the lifeblood of any political event. "It will always be the like the movie *Cocoon*. You will usually be the youngest person in the room. Just smile and tell Wilford Brimley you like his hat."

She extended her hand to Jack for a formal handshake and turned, as she'd been instructed, to pose for the cameras for a beat. "Never stop smiling," Josh had warned. "Smile until you feel like your lips will fall off. A woman who doesn't smile is an angry woman. You cannot be an angry woman, even for a second." It was hard work to keep the corners of her mouth turned upward, to keep her eyes wide and maintain an expression of both excitement and happiness and gratitude and poise. *Thank God for the Botox.* Still, she worried her face would go completely slack if she stopped concentrating for even a second.

She stepped up to the mic.

"I'm Charlotte Walsh and I'm running for Senate."

Her body recoiled slightly at the sound and pitch of her own voice filtered through the sound system. It was the first time she'd said those words out loud and they felt foreign, like a language she was just starting to learn.

"I left this town almost thirty years ago, when I was still trying to figure out who I was. I didn't realize until much later that this was the place that truly defined me."

She paused, as instructed by the campaign's $500-an-hour speech consultant, for cheers and applause.

Fifteen minutes passed like fifteen seconds. She thanked Jack; talked about the failure of a state where two teachers couldn't afford fundamental health-care benefits; talked about jobs, real jobs that paid a living wage; talked about growing up right on the mountain with a dad who drove a garbage truck and a mom who scrubbed other people's floors.

She knew Josh would kill her for what she was about to do. *But goddamn if I don't say it.*

"Ted Slaughter is a liar. He lied to you this morning. I never paid for my staffers to have abortions. I never told anyone they had to have an abortion. When I was the chief operating officer of Humanity, I implemented a plan to help both women and men have happy and healthy families, and I made sure the company gave them the benefits to do that. Look, I'm not here to play games or politics. If someone tells a lie about me, I'll tell you the truth. When did it become acceptable for politicians to lie like this? Why are there no longer consequences for distorting reality in such a disgusting way? You deserve the truth. I'll give it to you."

The Pussy Brigade rose to their feet and threw their WALSH FOR SENATE hats into the air like modern Mary Tyler Moores. Charlotte froze the smile on her face to allow the audience to tweet and Facebook exactly what she'd said. Her words made their way to the various cable news networks and within seconds scrolled across the bottom of millions of screens in millions of households on an otherwise uneventful Monday morning.

"The fight to bring honesty back into American politics begins today."

That wasn't what she'd intended to say. She'd been swept up

by the eagerness of the crowd. But she'd hesitated long enough for a dark thought to flit through her mind. *Who am I to champion honesty?*

For weeks, Roz and Josh had reminded Charlotte that the end of any speech is the most important part, the part that sticks with people, the part that inspires enthusiasm and loyalty from complete strangers. Charlotte had practiced a half-dozen different closers. In the moment, she'd discarded them all and ad-libbed something new.

"Our country is badly broken. In the past two years, American politicians have revealed both the very best and the very worst of human behavior. I think you can safely say none of you is better off. Something is very wrong. I left Elk Hollow so I could come back ready to make a real difference. That was also the right thing to do. I'm here for you. I'm here to serve you. I have confidence in our future. Together we can fix this."

She closed with a different Ali quote, another Marty favorite.

"God bless Ted Slaughter, but like the great Muhammad Ali once said, 'If you even dream of beating me, you'd better wake up and apologize.'"

The crowd stamped their feet and cheered. Even the senior citizens tapped toes and canes. Her heart stammered with pride and exhilaration. The energy of it all touched a primal nerve inside Charlotte, something almost sexual. She lifted her hands over her head in a V. *You can win this thing.* The thought came with a rush of confidence and excitement.

According to their script, Max was supposed to bring the girls up to the stage. He'd kiss her. Sweet and chaste. Josh had pulled an old video up on YouTube of Al Gore French-kissing Tipper at the 2000 Democratic National Convention. "Don't do that," he'd warned. Next, they'd pose as a family and smile.

Suddenly Josh was the one standing behind her instead of Max. He thrust Annie into her arms. ("She's the most photogenic one," he'd insisted earlier.) Roz led the twins up the stairs, their illness a distant memory. Rosie wiggled self-consciously and made disco hands in time to the marching band parading behind them. Ella skipped next to the drummer and gave a strangely provocative shoulder shimmy she must have seen in the Justin Timberlake halftime show. The crowd kept clapping. Charlotte kept smiling.

But where the hell was her husband?

CHAPTER 7

"You went off script."

The adrenaline coursing through her body and the memory of the cheering crowd, the way their applause had echoed off the walls, the way they'd looked at her like she really was a person who could make their lives better, made it easier for Charlotte to defend herself against Josh's irritation. Her team was gathered in the boys' locker room, the only private place for a quick postmortem of the speech. They had thirty minutes before the next gym class came barging in. She breathed and laughed through the smell of boy funk that bleach could never erase.

Roz interrupted them, her voice big and brawny and full of pride. "Our girl did good. Slaughter wouldn't have anticipated an attack like that from a female opponent. Not out of the gate. It was perfect."

Charlotte expected Josh to disagree, imagined him roaring at Roz to get the hell out of the locker room. Instead he leaned his forehead against the pale-green metal locker for a minute before turning to face them. "You did do good."

His compliment came with a begrudging lesson in political maneuvering. "Making an enemy of Slaughter is a good thing. Having an enemy gives your supporters a reason to be energized. A bitter race brings in more voters. Gets more attention. Raises more money. Most politicians want to be loved by everyone, but smart politicians know that it's just as important to be hated. Just tell me before you go off script next time. And be careful. Edgy won't play well for you anywhere but ten blocks in Center City, Philadelphia."

Charlotte sipped a cup of warm water with lemon, her voice hoarse.

"Thank you," she mouthed. "Any sign of Max?" It had yet to fully set in that her husband had abandoned her during one of the most important moments of her career. She knew she'd eventually feel sadness, anger, even rage, but for now she was able to tuck those emotions away.

"I can't find him." Leila's cringe crinkled the lines in between her eyebrows, expressing frustration on Charlotte's behalf.

"Where are the big girls?"

"Kara took the twins home." Leila played with Annie's hair as the girl sat on the floor in between her legs. "You look great right now. Happy."

Lulu chimed in, "Totally great. Hold on a sec. I'm going to Snap you."

"Now? We're in a locker room. There are toilets behind me."

"So real! So au naturel. Smile."

The muscles supporting Charlotte's cheeks ached from all the smiling.

"Instant gratification!" Lulu dropped down next to her on a bench, handed her an iPad, and scrolled through her Twitter mentions, each of them heavy with undeserved significance. "Here's one hashtag: '#SLAUGHTERLIES.' Ooooh, I love this tweet: 'Charlotte Walsh is my Beyoncé!' That one came from Jasmine, that actress on that zombie show. You know which one. Also, you're a meme." There was a GIF of Charlotte riding a tiger beneath the words *Charlotte Walsh Is My Spirit Animal*. It felt impossible to remember a time when this wasn't how she consumed her information.

"And you've been trolled." Charlotte gagged at the next tweet—a picture of her head Photoshopped onto the body of a pig. **@PatriotMan:** Look at that bitch squeal.

She kept going.

@AmericaTheBrave1776: Charlotte Walsh is a threat to America.

@ProudBoy20: Our women need to stay home and make more babies. Charlotte Walsh is a shitlib bitch marginalizing men. Must b stoped.

@ImperialDaddyHorseface: Walsh hates the hardworking men of PA

@DeplorableMac: Soon the truth will come out about who Charlotte Walsh really is.

"Who do they think I really am?" she asked out loud. *And what do they know?*

"Don't be triggered into showing emotion. First rule of dealing with trolls," Josh said, his lips set in a grim line.

"You can't live in FOMT." Lulu patted her on the shoulder.

"In what?"

"Fear of Mean Tweets."

"That's not a thing people say."

"It is now," the girl said with authority.

Charlotte continued to scroll.

"Are those my feet?" She looked down at her shoes and back to the picture on the screen. There was no mistaking her slightly pigeon-toed feet, bony ankles sheathed in Roz's panty hose. *Why would someone tweet a photograph of my shoes?*

@Politibabe: What's up with these nun shoes on C. Walsh. Gross!

@MomsForPAPols: She couldn't even get dressed up for her first big day at work. Can't take her seriously.

@America4FREE: Hey @CharlotteWalsh real women know how to run in heels.

@Jenny5: My new superhero @CharlotteWalsh don't take no shit from anyone in those badass shoes.

@FashionGurl: Luv the flat action on @CharlotteWalsh. Screw heels.

@PinkPussyBrigade: Sensible shoes for the win @CharlotteWalsh

"My shoes? Nothing about policy? No substance?" She looked up at Josh.

"Excuse me, Charlotte?" The reporter from *Teen Vogue* pushed open the heavy oak doors from the gymnasium with both of her hands.

Josh tried to stop her. "Sorry, Carly, we're done with questions for the day. Shoot me an email and we'll get you what you need."

"Just one more. My editor texted and I need to ask about the candidate's shoes?"

"No, you don't," Josh said.

Charlotte stood and sucked in a deep breath, then another, smiled, and willed herself to be pleasant. "It's cool. Hi, Carly. What do you need to know?"

"This is a real statement?"

"What's a real statement?"

"Your decision to wear flats?"

"It's a statement?" *I haven't worn a pair of high heels since before you sent your first tweet. I'm five eleven in flats and heels turn me into a monster. I have freakishly large size-twelve feet. I have three children under six, and the idea of teetering on something the size of a pencil makes me want to stab myself in the eye with a stiletto. I've had bunions since I gave birth to twins. Wearing flats is a professional calculation. Because I'm usually the boss of all the men in a room and it's easier if I don't make myself more intimidating.*

Charlotte snuck a glance at the girl's feet and saw they were covered in dove-gray suede ankle booties with a three-inch heel and tassels on the side.

"Everyone on social wants to know why you didn't wear high heels. Is it a feminist statement?" Carly repeated.

It wasn't easy for Charlotte to hold back a snort. More report-ers appeared behind Carly, forming a scrum around the two women, holding phones and cameras high, urinals and shower stalls promi-nently in the background of this intense conversation about footwear. *Breathe. Speak in sound bites.* Charlotte felt something click in her brain. "I wore the first shoes I pulled out of the closet this morning. What does Ted Slaughter have on his feet right now? Do you know? Let's find out. Because I'm pretty sure he didn't wake up this morning and decide he should be wearing heels. But if he did, I would certainly applaud that decision. Thank you, everyone. I'm looking forward to seeing much more of all of you."

Smile. Smile again. Wave. Exit gracefully. Josh grabbed Annie from Leila and handed her to Charlotte. The child blew kisses to the reporters.

"Awwwwwwwww." The crowd made the right sounds at the baby and moved easily out of her way. One of Charlotte's hands clutched the back of Annie's soft head, the other her sweaty back, allowing the child to become a shield in her arms.

★

It was Paul who found Max slumped in a bathroom stall outside of the auditorium. He texted Charlotte: "I just saved your husband's life," and congratulated himself for being a good Samaritan with a fifth of whiskey.

"I'm sick. I've got what the girls had," her husband whispered hours later as he lay in their bed.

Charlotte's guilt over jumping to the worst possible conclusion about Max's whereabouts that morning made her overcompensate in her efforts as nursemaid, stroking his feverish forehead and prepar-ing his favorite comfort food—grilled cheese with cut-up hot dogs in it. She was often at her best in their marriage when she knew he needed her.

"I watched your speech on YouTube. You can win this thing, Charlie-bird," Max said, his eyes half-closed.

It surprised her how good praise from him could make her feel. Before deciding to run, she'd read the studies about how narcissism runs rampant in politics: Those seeking office have a lust for power, prestige, status, and authority, the desire to be an object of admiration. Political office provides evidence to confirm a sense of superiority to others. Now, more than ever in her life, she wanted to feel admired, particularly by this man.

"The crowd loved you. You're a natural."

Her arms found their way around her own shoulders. She hugged herself and closed her eyes.

"You really believe that?"

"I do, baby. I really do."

"Could I have done anything better?" When he didn't answer, Charlotte realized he'd fallen asleep.

Downstairs, Kara put on *Moana* for the girls. *God bless you, Kara.*

"Where's Paul?"

"In the garage, I think."

"Doing what?"

"Dunno. Said something about lookin' for an air conditioner."

The garage—or carport, as Marty Walsh always called it—was a separate structure from the house, built by Marty himself to protect the family's one car, a thirdhand Buick, from harsh Elk Hollow winters, with enough room for a punching bag, with which he'd taught her to throw a left hook. "You never know when you'll need it, Charlie," he'd warned her. "Remember what Tyson said before that fight back in eighty-four: 'They all have a plan until I punch them out once and then the plan is out the window.' You never know when the plan will go out the window."

The carport was just up the hill behind the house. She knew Kara had moved some furniture and family keepsakes—old trophies, pictures, art projects, and yearbooks—in there when she cleaned the place out for renters. It wouldn't have surprised Charlotte if Paul kept his stash of weed or pills or whatever he was on these days out there, far away from his own house but still easily accessible.

If Charlotte went upstairs now, she could avoid having to deal with Paul when he came back in, half-lit and overly confident that she should give him some money for rescuing her husband. She kissed Kara good night and told her to let herself out.

With her family occupied for at least the next fifteen minutes, Charlotte felt justified in running a hot bath. She dropped a few dabs of lavender oil into the water before reading the rest of the speech coverage on her phone from the tub.

In the hour she'd been away from a screen, Slaughter's campaign had issued a statement standing behind their earlier "facts" about Charlotte providing abortions for her employees. "That's what we were told," Slaughter's campaign manager, Annabel Gest, said with a straight face. Gest, a sixtysomething woman with bright green contact lenses and an astronaut's helmet of white-blond hair, next branded Charlotte a California hippie billionaire out to hoodwink the voters of Pennsylvania to advance a nefarious West Coast agenda. She let the word *agenda* hang in the air like a puff of smoke. The way she'd said it, you could be compelled to believe West Coast was shorthand for "hell."

In some places, Charlotte's speech was praised by pundits, both professional and amateur, as solid and brave, but any serious analysis was eclipsed by Charlotte's footwear.

#Heelgate: The Senate Candidate Who Refused to Put on High Heels

BY CARLY MEEKS

You've probably heard of Charlotte Walsh. She's the badass Silicon Valley exec who shook up the tech patriarchy by giving her female employees actual benefits and real time off to start their families. But did you know she's running for Senate?

Here's what you need to know: Charlotte Walsh officially kicked off her campaign this morning against incumbent senator Ted Slaughter (if you're not familiar with him, he's the thrice-married old guy who has dominated Pennsylvania politics since before you were born. Check out this video of him mansplaining how your vagina works). Walsh has a warm presence and a sharp wit off camera. You'd like her if you met her at Starbucks, and she'd probably let you cut in front of her in line if you were in a rush. She has sweet freckles, good bone structure, very Julianne Moore, Tom Ford muse.

She announced her campaign wearing a chic pair of Tory Burch flats Monday morning. But it turns out not everyone was in love with Walsh's choice of footwear. Slaughter's campaign manager, Annabel Gest, derided Walsh for wearing "her bedroom slippers" to speak to Pennsylvania voters. It was a real sign of disrespect. "Dress like a grown-up if you want to be taken seriously."

Conservative pundit Kris Krispman took to cable news to ask whether Walsh was a closet lesbian. "Not that I care if she is. But you'd just think a woman like that would want to wear a nice pair of high heels on one of the biggest days of her career. I feel bad for her husband."

Walsh addressed her sartorial decision to *Teen Vogue* just moments after her speech (watch the video below and vote to tell us what you think). "I wore the first shoes I pulled out of the closet this morning. What does Ted Slaughter have on his feet right now? Do you know? Let's find out. Because I'm pretty sure he didn't wake up this morning and decide he should be wearing heels. But if he did, I would certainly applaud that decision."

The shoes have since sold out on the Tory Burch website. Young women across the country are now Instagramming their own photos of sensible shoes in Walsh's defense using the hashtags #HeelGate and #RealWomenWearFlats.

Charlotte had prepared to be excoriated for her policies, her positions, and even some of her personal choices, but she hadn't expected this. She sank under the water, holding the air in her lungs until she could no longer stand it, the physical pain a relief from her rushing thoughts.

Her phone dinged insistently from the ledge on the back of the toilet. She stepped out of the bath, put on Max's robe, and wiped her hands in its folds so she could answer it.

Josh's voice was labored with excitement. He sounded practically giddy. "*Vanity Fair* called. They want to do a shoot with you and the family. They assigned Julia Schulz-Davies. She's perfect for it."

When Charlotte didn't respond right away, he brought his voice up an octave.

"This is a big fucking deal, Charlotte. To get a glossy profile with a Pulitzer Prize winner for a goddamned Senate race. It means the campaign has taken on national importance and we haven't even gotten started yet."

"It's really great," Charlotte agreed and tried to focus, already wondering how hard-hitting a profile Julia Schulz-Davies planned to do, how much she'd dig into the past. "When?"

"Next month. It'll run in June."

"And they want Max and the girls, too?"

"They want the whole family. That okay? You need to ask Max?"

Of course she'd have to ask him, but he wouldn't say no. She shoved a lock of wet hair out of her eyes. "He'll be fine. This is amazing, but what do we do until then? When will we get poll numbers?"

"Soon. FiveThirtyEight might have something by the end of the week. I think we'll be pleasantly surprised. In the meantime, I need you to get out there and kiss some rich ass. We're out of cash."

CHAPTER 8
April 6, 2018
214 days to Election Day

Walsh (D)	Slaughter (R)	Spread
40	44	Slaughter +4

The trick was figuring out what to say to someone who'd just paid $50,000 to have dinner with you.

"You're right. There's such a bias against successful people in this country right now." Charlotte agreed with the biggest real estate developer in eastern Pennsylvania over a white-tablecloth fundraising dinner of five courses donated by a James Beard–winning chef. It was hard not to feel like a high-end escort as she pandered to each of the twenty-five potential donors. Josh called it speed dating for money. Charlotte had run a company that made more money than anyone in the room, and yet she had no choice but to prostrate herself to each of them. They were all white. All men. Because their sizable checks bought them face time and access, Charlotte smiled when one man suggested he'd make an excellent ambassador to Switzerland, when another gave her a detailed description regarding how he could personally make the peace with North Korea, and even when one insisted the problem with America was all the "fucking Asians." Charlotte gave them Leila's email, showed some teeth, and asked them to stay in touch. For $50,000 a night, she never said no. She never laughed in their faces. She never showed her disgust.

The one time she came close was when a particularly intoxicated octogenarian attorney—the head of the Bar Association, she'd later learn—palmed her ass while they stood in line to get a drink at the bar. His fingers tickled the insides of her thighs while his wet whisper landed in her ear in a voice that was gruff and stale. "Let me help you get to the real money." She shifted her elbow so that it jabbed him directly below the ribs, eliciting a grunt that could have been a cough to anyone listening. "I don't want your fucking money," she said in a barely audible whisper.

Against all of her better instincts that told her to scratch at his eyes and announce his impropriety to the room, she backed slowly away from the bald, yellow-skinned man with sloping shoulders and rheumy eyes, worried one cross word spoken any louder would ripple through the testosterone-filled room like a pebble disturbing an otherwise placid pond.

"You should have had that motherfucker thrown out of here for touching you like that," Leila said with anger and outrage in her eyes as they washed their hands in the bathroom. "We don't have to tolerate this anymore. Hashtag Me Too." Charlotte's reaction to the impropriety was more muted. Yes, she was disgusted, but she was from a generation of women who normalized bad behavior from men in power. Less than twenty years her junior, Leila would lead the battle against those kinds of men.

Charlotte looked in vain for paper towels and then shook her hands futilely beneath the dryer. "I handled it my way. When it happens to you, then you handle it yours." She was exhausted.

Charlotte had been in the southern part of the state for one of the longest days of her life. She'd spent the morning in Section Eight housing on the edge of West Philly planning to speak about sentencing reform and then changed her tune when the women there wanted to talk about STEM education for young girls in PA public schools. "Black women voters are going to be key in this race," Josh counseled her afterward. "One woman told me that if a girl like Leila worked for a woman like you then you had to be doing something good."

Their next stop was the Muslim Women's Association at Penn, where a young woman described having her head scarf ripped from her head on the subway while a group of otherwise innocuous students spat on her and called her a sand nigger.

In a meeting with the campus newspaper, the head of the editorial board, a short blonde with jaunty freckles wearing a BLACK LIVES MATTER pin the size of her head, grilled her. "As a cis hetero white lady who makes more than a million dollars a year, what do you know about the plight of the Latino immigrant?" Charlotte told her it was such an astute question and delivered the right kind of answer even as she inwardly rolled her eyes at a girl whose heart was in the right place but who had probably never ventured past the wrong side of Forty-Third Street. *I'll bet you're from Connecticut. Your mom teaches Pilates and drives a Range Rover, your dad works at a hedge fund, and you once kissed a sorority sister after drinking too much grappa at the Sigma Chi formal. I see you.*

She heard Leila murmur low enough that the young woman couldn't hear. "Congrats on being so woke."

Charlotte's next stop was the local fire department, where she met the crew for lunch—bologna on white bread—and posed for a picture driving their fire truck. She stopped by a farmers' market where she listened to complaints about everything from terrible cell phone reception in the state to the slow legalization of recreational marijuana. In the afternoon she shot a Facebook video at the Philadelphia Zoo with a three-legged baby giraffe that had recently been described in the *Philadelphia Inquirer* as a "paragon of the balance we should all strive for in challenging times." Charlotte next made a grand show of eating cheesesteaks from both Pat's and Geno's, competing franchises in South Philadelphia with rabid fan bases. They were nearly identical, both covered in imitation cheese, fried onions, and peppers, and dripping grease onto her lap. She'd declared a tie between the two sandwiches. "Cheesesteak diplomacy," Josh called it.

It was easier now to understand why and how Slaughter tailored his talking points to match the crowd. She often found herself doing something similar, and the awareness of it ate at her. There was such a fine line between pandering and tailoring her message. With people under thirty she talked about legalizing marijuana and eliminating student debt. With people over fifty she proposed expanding Medicare. With the lower and middle classes she promised jobs and job training. For the rich she promised tax breaks that would make the government less likely to expand Medicare and pay for job training. Charlotte needed the money from the wealthy voters, but she needed the minority voters in the urban areas like Philadelphia and Pittsburgh to turn out on Election Day to secure a win.

They exited the fundraiser through the kitchen.

"We should always go through the kitchen, shake hands with the staff," Josh insisted. "No matter how nice a place you're in, always leave through the kitchen." He talked to himself as much as to her, checking off the basics. "When you start ignoring the kitchens, you've lost touch."

They took twenty minutes to wind through the large industrial kitchen. Most of the staff were pleased to steal a moment away from a blistering stove or sink piled high with wineglasses and coffee mugs. They were mostly Latino, some of them Chinese. More men than women.

They cheered when she walked in.

"They know me," she whispered to Josh. "They know me better than the people out there."

"Half of them are smiling because they don't want to be deported. The other half are smiling because these people still believe a politician can help change their lives. They still believe in the American dream. No one dreams it harder than these guys. They aren't jaded. It's a shame only half of them can legally vote. Keep smiling. Keep shaking hands." The men's hands were strong, rough, and wrinkled from soaking in water all day long, their grins wide and honest. She thanked each of them enthusiastically and earnestly.

They didn't begin the three-hour drive home to Elk Hollow until shortly after midnight. It was important to Charlotte to sleep in her own bed and be there when her girls woke up as often as possible. It wasn't always possible. The state was wide, five hours from Philly to Pittsburgh.

Humanity's founders had eagerly offered her use of the company's private jet, but when she'd mentioned it to Josh he'd given her a look as though she'd suggested they use the skin of puppies to fashion their yard signs.

Leila produced a bottle of Purell and an apple from her own purse. The skin on Charlotte's palms had chapped and scabbed from hundreds of handshakes and reapplications of the hand sanitizer. Politicians on the campaign trail contracted nine times more colds than the average person. Long after the campaign ended, the smell of disinfectant would make Charlotte nauseous. The other night, on a similar drive, Leila had handed her a bottle of Ambien.

"I don't need these." Charlotte pushed them away.

"You need sleep."

"I hate pills."

"I hate you when you don't sleep."

Leila's Mary Poppins purse also contained Band-Aids, Advil, nasal spray, a solar phone charger, a small flashlight, and gum.

"I want to be next to you in an earthquake," Josh remarked the first time he saw its contents.

Leila wagged her head. "No, you don't. Right now, I'm support staff. In an earthquake it's every man for himself."

On her way home Charlotte texted Max, but he didn't answer.

She fell asleep somewhere near Allentown, the illuminated road signs blurring and burning into her dreams.

★

A crew had come by to clean the first floor of Charlotte's house the day before, but it didn't make much of a difference. By Saturday morning, the day of her *Vanity Fair* interview, the place had once again been hit by the tornado of three small girls—the carpet coated in a shroud of puzzle pieces, tiny white teacups, pink clip-in hair extensions, and Annie's purple feather boa that shed a piece of itself everywhere it went. Charlotte straightened the cushions on the couch and swiped crumbs off the coffee table with the pinky edge of her palm.

Julia Schulz-Davies was due in an hour. Julia Schulz-Davies, who'd won a Pulitzer Prize last year for her investigation of labor abuses in smartphone factories, who'd once confronted the president on inaccurate unemployment statistics during an official White House dinner, who'd written a bestselling memoir about her two years covering the war in Afghanistan, during which time she'd almost been blown up by an IED on three occasions and had fallen in love with a marine and adopted an Afghan baby boy. Julia Schulz-Davies would be there any minute and Max was still out for his morning run, a run that had already taken over two hours.

Charlotte yawned and swallowed a long gulp of her coffee as Kara attempted to erase the violet circles beneath her eyes with a tool that resembled a sea sponge and smelled like a wet sock. Her presence made Charlotte feel anchored in the world. She needed Kara's calming energy as much as she needed her concealer.

"How'd you get here?" Charlotte peered out the front window, hoping to see her husband huffing his way up the driveway.

"Paul dropped me and ran down the Acme to get an egg burrito. He'll be back in a few."

"When?"

"Wipe that look off your face, girl." Kara placed her hands on her hips. "Don't worry about him, Charlie. He's gonna be good today." Charlotte's decision to include Paul in the interview hadn't been made lightly, and if it had been up to her she'd have kept him out of it. But the reporter wanted to talk to her whole family for this story. A few days earlier she'd hired Paul as something called a "special advisor for local affairs," giving him $2,000 a month out of her own pocket in the hopes that the money would keep him from behaving like an asshole.

"You know he's only drinkin' Thursday through Sunday now, and he laid off the sauce today so he could do this interview with you. He's real excited. He got a tie."

"I'm not worried," Charlotte lied.

She heard the creak of the front door. Max continued to jog slowly as he made his way through the house. Seeing him in his absurdly tight high-performance running pants that left nothing to the imagination made Charlotte's blood boil. It must be nice to have enough free time for a two-hour jog.

"Where were you?" Charlotte asked her husband.

"Running," Max replied like she was stupid for asking. "Fastest time yet. I texted you my MapMyRun. I'm taking the quickest shower that's ever been taken and I'll be down here in ten minutes. I have plenty of time. You worry too much."

True to his word, in less than five minutes Max was hovering over the stove frying bacon and onions.

"You can't walk into a house that smells like bacon and be disappointed," he remarked to no one in particular. "Unless you're a vegetarian. Shit. Do you think the reporter might be a vegetarian?"

The sound of the doorbell brought Annie hurtling toward the door, stark naked, to greet their guests. When she realized it was a stranger she came to a halt, collected herself, and extended a formal handshake to the woman.

"I am peas to eat you," Annie said to Julia Schulz-Davies. The twins erupted in giggles behind her.

The reporter was the tiniest woman Charlotte had ever seen. She had to be four foot eleven, but Charlotte imagined she told people, with certainty, that she was five foot one. Her movements were quick and rigid like those of a captive mongoose. She wore a severe black bob, black pants, a crisp white silk shirt, and chunky tortoiseshell glasses that magnified her little eyes and made her resemble one of those Japanese cartoon characters.

"I am peas to eat you, too," she said kneeling to Annie's level. Behind her a giant of a man in his fifties with a shock of gray hair and generous eyebrows to match struggled with an enormous camera bag, tripod, and light in the doorway. Ella held George Washington up toward the reporter.

"Would you like to kiss him? His beard is softer than you think."

The little girl pushed the lizard in the direction of the woman's mouth. The reporter reached out her hand for a polite pat but made no attempt to put her lips on the bearded dragon.

When Julia stood back up, her forehead just reached Charlotte's shoulders. "Ms. Walsh. Wonderful to meet you. I'm Julia Schulz-Davies. We spoke briefly on the phone. This is Jackson Strait. He'll be shooting the pictures and some video for the digital version of the piece. It smells absolutely delicious in here." The reporter flashed a charming smile.

"Max is making a late breakfast for everyone. He figured you'd be hungry after the trip down from New York."

"That will be a wonderful shot. Max in the kitchen. Jackson, why don't you get it now? Do some stills and get some b-roll." She pivoted back to Charlotte so quickly it looked like a ballet pirouette. "Your daughters are beautiful. You don't mind if we snap them?"

"We don't mind at all," Josh's voice boomed from the living room. "Julia, so good to see you again."

Charlotte thought she saw a cloud pass over the reporter's face when she laid eyes on Josh, though it was quickly replaced with a professional smile.

"Josh. Lovely as always. Thank you for giving us such great access to the candidate. This will be a really special piece. You're an inspiration to a lot of women, Ms. Walsh."

"Please. Call me Charlotte. Sit down. This is Leila Kelly, my chief of staff. She came with me from Humanity. And my sister-in-law, Kara. We hired her to do my hair and makeup for most of my events. My brother should be here shortly. After this we can go down to campaign headquarters if you like and you can meet the rest of the team—fundraising, community outreach, et cetera."

Julia waved her hand in the air, tracing a figure eight with her index finger.

"No need. This profile is about you as much as it is about the campaign. You're the first woman who truly has a shot at a Pennsylvania

Senate seat. And of course your work at Humanity is incredibly interesting to our readers, too."

"Thank you," Charlotte said, gesturing at Julia to take a seat on the couch. "I think so, too. We do have a real shot at this."

Julia leaned back into the cushions and positioned a digital recorder on the table as she extracted a small blue notebook from her purse. "I like to take notes while I record. I don't trust technology." The reporter tapped on the recorder's tiny microphone with skepticism before she continued. "I'm going to ask you the question everyone is asking you first, and I'll probably ask it again in an hour or so and one more time before I leave. Why are you doing this? You're one of the most powerful women in business today, certainly in Silicon Valley. You have three young children. Why enter this rat race?"

"Most people don't ask men why they want to run for office or mention their children," Charlotte countered.

A sly smile spread slowly over the reporter's lips. This was the parry she'd come for.

"No. No, they wouldn't, would they? Let's stick to the first part of the question then. Why give up your big and important job in the most disruptive field in the country to essentially become middle management in a staggering bureaucracy that takes years to accomplish anything worthwhile?"

Charlotte liked her. "You have a bleak view of our federal government."

"I prefer to think of it as realistic."

Now she could give the answer she wanted to give. "I'm running because I can do a better job than the guy who has the job right now. I have three daughters. I want them to see more women who lead."

"But you already lead. You may not be the CEO or president of Humanity, but you're certainly one of the big bosses there. In fact, more people know your name than know those of the founders of that company. Your book was a bestseller. Every time a CEO position comes up out in Silicon Valley your name is on the very short list."

Charlotte smiled and nodded in a way she hoped came across as humble. "I'm proud of those achievements. But I can do more. Let's go back to what you said about Washington being a staggering bureaucracy where it's difficult to accomplish anything. I'm an outsider to Washington and I think that's a good thing. Americans don't seem to give a shit about left and right anymore. They care about whether or not they're one of the haves or the have-nots. I've been both. At Humanity we employ more than a hundred thousand full-time employees around the globe. We've figured out how to improve each and every single one of their lives in addition to improving the lives of our clients and our consumers. I'm used to getting things done, to fixing things. I can bring that to Washington." She was getting more and more adept at saying a lot without actually saying anything at all.

"Why Pennsylvania?"

"I'm from here."

"You haven't lived here in nearly thirty years."

"It's my home. I grew up here and went to college here. It's a state that needs my help right now more than California does."

"So why not open a Humanity office here instead? Something with a lot of jobs?"

"We've already looked at moving an engineering hub to Pittsburgh near the Carnegie Mellon campus and a marketing office to Philadelphia instead of opening a new one in New York. Those things have been in the works for a couple of years now."

"Who wants bacon?" Max waltzed into the room with a platter of sizzling meat.

Julia raised her hand like a schoolchild.

Balancing a plate of bacon and eggs on her knees, Julia turned her attention to Max. "Besides being a whiz in the kitchen, what else are you working on these days?" Josh had coached Max to tell reporters he was still consulting for Humanity while taking on full-time parenting duties. It suited both Max's ego and a traditional media narrative of masculinity. In other words, he still had a job.

"I'm here to support Charlotte. That's my number one priority right now." He shot Julia a grin.

"You seem too good to be true."

Charlotte had to remind herself that she wanted this woman to be charmed by her husband. "He is," she said.

"Do you two fight?" Julia was smooth, knew when to flatter her subjects, when to befriend them, and when to blindside them with a question they weren't prepared to answer.

Julia spoke in Max's direction, but Charlotte answered first with an uneasy laugh. The question overwhelmed her more than she'd expected, and she began to wonder how much Julia knew about her marriage. "Every couple fights. We have three kids under six. That struggle is real. We both had high-stress jobs. We just uprooted our lives and moved across the country. There's stress. But we don't have big blowups." The truth was that in the past week they'd fought about whether the girls should be allowed to be here for this interview, whether Max had time to fly back to California to run a half marathon to qualify for his stupid Ironman, and twice more over why they couldn't hire a regular cleaning lady and nanny. The house had also been thick with new tensions Charlotte couldn't figure out the source of, nor did she have the energy to sit her husband down and discuss everything that was bothering him.

Josh intervened. "Charlotte's an open book. It's part of what makes her so appealing. She doesn't have that politician's filter." He cast a loaded glance down at her kids, who were building a fort in the corner out of discarded pizza boxes Max saved specifically for that purpose ("So sustainable!" Julia commented). Josh's gaze at the children signaled that it was unsavory to ask more probing marital questions in reach of their delicate ears. Charlotte's children once again became armor, protecting her from further inquiries about the state of her marriage.

Paul knocked and let himself in the front door. He was dressed in one of Max's heavy Fair Isle sweaters that Charlotte had shrunk in the wash. She could see a red tie knotted in the collar of a blue oxford underneath. His hair was combed behind his ears.

"The NRA is a terrorist organization," Charlotte insisted.

"It's a terrorist organization that can get you votes and get you elected so you can take them down."

"And what are your politics, Paul?" Julia asked, once Charlotte's brother settled himself in the armchair.

"I'm a patriot." It sounded like something he'd heard someone say on television or in a bar.

"And what does that mean in today's world?"

Her brother squirmed in his seat like a child. He seemed completely focused one moment and twitchy and self-conscious the next. "Hell if I know." That made Julia laugh out loud.

"Did you vote for Ted Slaughter?"

"Weren't any better options."

"Would you vote for him again if your sister weren't running?"

"That's a stupid question to ask, since she is."

"Touché." Julia smiled. "How about this: What was your sister like as a little girl?"

Paul shot Charlotte a look asking permission to speak. She nodded and flashed an encouraging smile.

"Brainy. You know, she was on the gifted track and all." He didn't use the words he used to use to describe her when she was a girl— *bossy*, *know-it-all*, eventually *bitch*. "Always readin'. The best shot in Lackawanna County."

"Pardon?"

"Girl hit her first buck at age twelve. Eighteen-point whitetail in one shot."

Charlotte had expected this, but it still made her uncomfortable. It was a setup. They'd practiced it. Josh had been adamant that she needed to find a way to appeal to voters who typically voted for Ted Slaughter, rural voters, blue-collar voters, farmers, hunters.

"I'm going to need you to shoot a gun," he explained to her.

"Doing this doesn't make sense. I support stricter gun control," Charlotte countered.

"So do most reasonable people," Josh said. "But you can't make it happen if you don't get elected. Get the votes, then change the law."

"It's a trick. We're tricking people."

"These voters won't remember it as a trick if their kid doesn't get shot up at school."

"Maybe some of your fellow liberals will scoff at the thought of their candidate as a twelve-year-old girl wielding a Winchester, but it doesn't matter. They'll vote for you anyway. Guns and abortion are still the major wedge issues in Pennsylvania. These rural voters will drool. Pretty lady has a gun just like me." He affected a dopey and slow and completely inaccurate interpretation of the northeastern Pennsylvania accent.

"You know they're not stupid, Josh," Charlotte shot back, more offended than she'd expected to be at his caricature. When she'd been a little girl her favorite thing to do had been to go hunting with her dad. She hadn't talked about it in thirty years and soon the memory had faded as though it was something that had happened to someone else a long time ago. She used to love being in the woods with Marty, squishing through marshes of cattails and crunching through shrubs and groves of sturdy-trunked trees to reach the duck blind before five in the morning. Charlotte went there sometimes by herself. It was her favorite place to read and where she'd devoured all of the Laura Ingalls Wilder and Nancy Drew books. She reveled in the patience it took to be a serious hunter and still believed in the sport as long as people played by the rules and ate what they killed. When she was little, the Walsh household had had a winter's worth of venison steaks in their freezer. There was a difference between owning a gun to hunt your food and owning a semiautomatic weapon that could kill a hundred people in the blink of an eye, and Charlotte had never understood why the two ideas couldn't be separated by politicians to create reasonable gun control legislation.

Josh actually waggled his finger in her face during their discussion. "I'm not saying rural voters are any more stupid than liberals when it comes to voting on superficial characteristics. The left puts their own labels on you without thinking—woman, Ivy League, feminist, pro-choice. They think they know, without asking, that in your heart you believe in single-payer health care and free tuition at public colleges. Everyone is a simpleton when it comes to identity politics."

Julia turned to Charlotte. "The best shot in Lackawanna County, huh?" the reporter repeated with an eager smile. "Now that's something I'd like to see."

They'd practiced this part, too.

"Charlie can show youse." Paul gestured toward the backyard, perfectly playing the part of the hokey older brother. He was earning his two grand. "We've always got cans set up out back for target practice. Come out. You ever shot a gun before, Julia?"

"A time or two."

Charlotte cleared her throat and pretended to protest.

Max hated this hunter narrative, and it had been the subject of another fight this week. "How do we explain this to the girls? They're not old enough to discuss the cycle of life and death or that Mommy once killed Bambi."

"We explain it to them the same way my dad explained it to me." In northeastern Pennsylvania, hunting was a part of life. Kids wore blaze-orange jackets and camouflage pants as soon as they could walk.

Max snorted. "I'm sure that was eloquent."

"It was. The same way your family explained it to you."

"They didn't. I just saw a bloody deer corpse on the top of my uncle's car one day and was told to skin the bastard. There's a reason I left this damn town, Charlie. I hate this shit."

Charlotte grabbed a green canvas hunting coat that looked old, stained, and beaten, but had been purchased by Josh at Walmart only twenty-four hours earlier. The small deception brought Charlotte a twinge of shame. Her dad's old Winchester was real enough, a rough-around-the-edges, no-frills, functional gun. Charlotte had been practicing with it for days and had been surprised to feel her muscle memory kick in alongside the sense of calm and immediate purpose she felt with the heavy wood in her hands, the acrid smell of ammonia and smoke clogging her nostrils.

"Get this on video," Julia ordered her cameraman.

Max told Leila to keep the girls inside the house, but Ella raced into the backyard.

"Mommy's got a gun!" Ella jumped up and down. "Mommy's gonna shoot it!"

They led the reporter carefully away from a few bits of dog shit Max had forgotten to pick up. Charlotte squinted at the three cans of Keystone Light lined up on a two-by-four supported by cinder blocks. She widened her stance. She'd gone ten for twenty earlier in the week, but now she just needed to hit one. Preferably the first one and they could go inside and start talking about the minimum wage, eliminating student debt, and paid parental leave.

The gun cocked hard against Charlotte's cheek. It would leave a mark. Her fault for not getting it settled before she took the shot. She was off, but not by much. She closed her eyes, visualized the target, the way her dad had taught her. He'd had no idea at the time that he was teaching her a way to meditate, to still herself in the most difficult of circumstances. It was a tool she'd used over and over as an adult. *I forgot this was where it came from.*

She always felt it in her bones when she nailed a shot. The second bullet sliced through the can, sending a spray of foam into the air.

"Your turn." Paul turned to the reporter. If Julia Schulz-Davies knew this was a setup, she didn't seem to care. The story was a good one. The pictures and videos would get a lot of traffic.

Julia raised her hand in protest. "Maybe next time."

"Come on. Just one shot." Charlotte's brother was persistent. Julia took the gun reluctantly. When she rolled up her sleeves, Charlotte was both taken aback and delighted by an intricate black-and-white tattoo of a bald eagle spread across Julia's forearm. She expertly nailed three cans in four shots.

As they walked back into the house Julia linked her arm through Charlotte's. "It's always nice to surprise people, isn't it?"

CHAPTER 9
June 1, 2018
158 days to Election Day

Max and Charlotte were attempting to have sex when the profile of her went online. They had removed the right items of clothing and stroked the parts that required stroking when both of their phones buzzed with a Google alert and continued with texts from Leila, Josh, and Roz. With the momentum toward intercourse interrupted it was easier to stare at their screens.

IS THIS HAVING IT ALL? The headline hovered over the lead photograph, a shot of Max manning the stove with Charlotte standing behind him. She leaned against the ugly mushroom-colored fridge, a stern smile on her lips, the girls playing at her feet. The saturation on the photo was boosted to brighten the red of Charlotte's lipstick and the lime of the linoleum kitchen counters.

"They took two thousand pictures when they were here and that's what they chose?" Max's left eye twitched as he read parts of the story out loud in a tone that did nothing to hide his irritation.

"'While she brings home the bacon, he cooks it. Literally . . . He gazes at his wife adoringly as she talks about accomplishing something no woman has ever accomplished in the state of Pennsylvania. . . . Max Tanner is the unique man who doesn't seem to mind that his wife's ambitions outpace his own.' What the fuck?"

"What's wrong with it?" Charlotte knew the answer. She shouldn't have asked him the question in the first place. What did all those marriage advice books she thumbed through periodically and furtively in the self-help aisle warn about asking your spouse a question you didn't want to hear the answer to?

"She makes me sound like a gigantic pussy." Max snorted. "Your ambitions outpace mine? What the hell does she know about how ambitious I am? This isn't what I expected her to write."

Charlotte suspected part of the problem was that it hit too close to home. In the past five years, Max had coasted as the head of engineering for Humanity, allowing his younger and more intense staff to do the work and take the credit. He was ready to cash out, tired of striving, ready for the next generation to disrupt things.

"Welcome to politics."

"I'm not a politician. I hate politics. I didn't ask to be here." He let out a sigh of exasperation and tossed his phone onto the nightstand. "It's not like I had a choice." He stood, walked to the dresser and opened a drawer, looked inside, then banged it closed. "I have no goddamn underwear." It was an accusation, his lack of clean underwear her fault—a consequence of her ambition.

Why don't you do some goddamn laundry then? She bit the inside of her cheek and pushed past him to close their bedroom door as he rifled through the hamper to find the pair of boxer shorts he'd thrown off the bed with alacrity moments earlier.

"You had a choice. You've always had a choice." Charlotte sat down quietly, the lie vibrating in the air between them.

"Well, it didn't feel like it." He picked up his laptop and continued to read while she got up to pee and finish reading the story on her own, in peace, on the toilet.

When she returned, he was jabbing his finger accusingly at the computer screen. "These comments! Take a look at this one: 'Hey Max Tanner, it must be hard for your children to grow up in a house without a masculine influence. Oh, never mind. There's your wife.' "

Before she could stop him, Max typed a response. "Would I be more masculine if I punched you in the face?"

"Jesus Christ, Max. Is that your real name on that?" she yelled. "You just threatened violence against an Internet troll. You're giving them what they want. They exist to get a rise out of you. Delete it."

He knew he'd crossed a line and for a brief moment looked properly chastened. "How do I delete it? I don't see a way to delete it."

She grabbed the computer and stared at it for a full minute before finding a complicated drop-down button that allowed users to erase their comments.

Why is he so pissed? The story made Max seem like a goddamned saint. Not that she wasn't grateful for the things he was doing. She was. But come on. What the piece didn't capture was the fact that she still did the majority of the housework and a good deal of the parenting every single minute she wasn't at work. Max was forgiven for dropping the girls late at school or forgetting to pack juice or emergency underwear because he was the adorable stay-at-home dad. Other mommies swooped in to help him, so sorry for the hapless man whose wife made him shoulder the burden of parenting three young girls. *You have it so easy. You're a goddamned hero just for being a man who takes care of your own children.*

"Bitch all you want, but keep it in this house," she said. Her voice went cold.

"I want to go back to California for a few days. I need a goddamned break from all this." This was his constant threat: *I'll leave. I'll go home.*

"That's cute, Max. Wouldn't it be nice if we could all just take a break? I'd love a break from this campaign, too. And from being a mom every once in a while. And from our marriage." She knew she shouldn't say what she was about to say, but when she said it the words came out slowly, infused with contempt. "Oh, right. You already took a break from our marriage. I almost forgot."

She wasn't sure he heard her as he stormed down the stairs.

★

"The bacon! The gun! The naked child running around the house!" Josh raved over breakfast the next morning. "You seem so real!"

Is that a compliment? I seem real.

Josh slapped his hand on the table, rattling their cups of coffee. "I love it. This is perfect. You can't buy this kind of publicity. You can't blow someone for this kind of publicity." For a second she thought Josh would lean over and kiss her on the mouth, he was so jacked up. "What did Max think? I can't get enough of that picture of him with the bacon."

Charlotte forced a smile. "He didn't love it."

"No?"

Leila interrupted as she motioned for the diner waitress to bring more coffee. "I'll bet he didn't. Sure, it's a feminist woman's wet dream—sexy dad who stays home with the kids and cooks and cleans while Mom goes out and conquers the world—but that part about ambition and how Max doesn't have much, I bet he fucking hated that. How would you like it?"

Josh bit hard into his sausage and wielded its speckled stump at Leila like a scepter. "I'd love it. Want to marry me and be the bread-winner? I'd give this rat race up in a heartbeat."

"You're not my type," Leila scoffed.

"Even better. Then we can still have sex with other people. It would be the perfect relationship for me."

Charlotte slapped her palm against the table. "Enough. Where do we go from here? This is a good story. How do we use it to our advantage? And will the voters of Pennsylvania even care?" The high from the article felt a little like the one time Charlotte had taken a friend's prescription diet pills in college. She'd felt wired and strong and brilliant and liked it so much she never let herself do it again.

"Ninety percent of registered voters won't read it, but enough of them will see the headline in their Facebook feed and think, 'Wow that's interesting, maybe she's interesting,' and then on Election Day they'll at least know your name and that's half the battle," Josh said. "Folks filter for political agreement. Everyone who reads it was already going to vote for you anyway by virtue of the fact that they read a liberal commie rag like *Vanity Fair*."

"Reassuring," Charlotte said.

"But none of it matters. Because Mary Ann from the *Today* show called. She wants you on next week for the eight a.m. hour. You're gonna get Hoda-ed. She's gonna love you. They asked for Max, too. I said he wasn't available."

"Max wants to head to California next week anyway."

"He can't. Bad optics for him to go and leave you here alone. You have five events in the next three weeks he's expected to attend. Maybe he can go next month."

"He'll be pissed if I tell him he can't go."

All of Josh's previous excitement and cheer evaporated in a single sentence. "Keep him here, Charlotte. You get one chance at this. Don't let your husband ruin it for you."

Why Does a State Like Pennsylvania Still Have a Glass Ceiling?

BY TOM SULLIVAN

There are few places or industries in America that can still be referred to without irony as a "man's world."

Strangely, Pennsylvania politics is still one of them.

Consider the statistics: Pennsylvania has never elected a woman governor or US senator. The state's 18-member congressional delegation has no women. Our 253-member legislature had one of the lowest percentages of women in the nation and the lowest among northeastern states.

"Harrisburg definitely tends to be a good-old-boy network," Allison Latch, former female state senator, revealed about why she chose not to run for a second term. "The best way I can put it is that the men in this state are very good at making a woman feel small even when she has a big job. I can accomplish way more in Pennsylvania now that I work in the private sector. There were times I felt like my male counterparts fought me on issues just because I was a woman."

Ms. Latch added: "Campaigning in this state is brutal. It's not easy to be an intelligent woman and not go insane over some of the things voters and even politicians will call a woman running for office in this state."

Now tech executive Charlotte Walsh has moved home to northeastern Pennsylvania to try to break at least one of the glass ceilings here by becoming the state's first female senator. Incumbent Ted Slaughter has tried to use the fact that Walsh is the mother of three young girls against her in new iterations of his stump speech.

"Will she be running home from Washington every time someone gets a cold? And what does it say that she thinks nothing of abandoning her young children, children who depend on her, for long stretches of time?"

Slaughter's tactics of painting Walsh as a potentially ineffective legislator due to what he portends is her handicap as a mother and as a bad parent for abandoning her kids has done him no favors with suburban women voters, and Walsh has narrowed the spread between herself and the incumbent by just two points.

Story cont. on page B8

CHAPTER 10
June 8, 2018
151 days to Election Day

Walsh (D)	Slaughter (R)	Spread
41	43	Slaughter +2

Every day of the campaign brought a new indignity.

Picketers with signs declaring CHARLOTTE WALSH KILLS BABIES besieged her as she walked out of the *Today* show. Shocked and curious, she approached one of the Latino men holding the cardboard placards. "Why are you doing this? Your sign doesn't even make sense." He fixed her with a dull stare.

Josh dragged her away. "They don't speak English. Slaughter paid them to be here. They probably don't even know what their signs say."

Next came the photographs in the *Daily Dispatch*. The headline read: "Senate Candidate as a Young Hottie."

"No one has ever referred to me as a hottie," Charlotte snorted to Leila. There were other adjectives that, as far as she knew, had never been used to describe her—*beautiful*, *adorable*, and *sexy* all came to mind.

"Enjoy the vaguely complimentary misogyny," Leila replied drolly.

There was a photo of Charlotte as a teenager in a relatively chaste two-piece bathing suit water-skiing on Lake Winola. In another she held a red Solo cup and leaned provocatively against a telephone pole smoking a cigarette, wearing a too-large army jacket, a black beret, and maroon drugstore lip liner on her way to a Smiths concert in

Philly during her junior year of high school. The pièce de résistance was her in a gray negligee with the word ID written across the filmy white fabric in puffy paint. During her senior year of high school Charlotte and two other girls from the honor society had decided to be Freudian slips for Halloween. In the photo she curled her shoulders in and stood a step behind Jessica Kelly and Jenny DiGiorgio, who hadn't wanted to include her at all except they didn't think they'd win the costume contest with just an ego and superego.

Paul. The pictures must have come from Paul. He'd probably taken them when he was mucking around in the garage after her announcement speech. *How much did they pay him?*

He denied it when she finally got him on the phone, but Kara didn't rule it out. "I'll get to the bottom of it, honey. If he's got money, I'll figure it out sooner rather than later. He'll do somethin' stupid with it."

I've been running a multibillion-dollar company for fifteen years and yet my fuckup older brother can still humiliate me. Losing her mind at Paul would be as fruitless as smacking Bob the dog for eating her shoes or Jack the Fat for peeing in them. All of them were too stupid to know they'd done something wrong. The difference was the animals showed remorse.

Josh was less concerned than she expected him to be. "You had a nice rack as a teenager." He clicked through the photo gallery, lingering on the bikini picture.

"Find more pictures of you as a hot kid. We can make a joke out of it. Turn this into a humanizing moment for you. Get me more Halloween, college, you as a kid with a gun. We'll make an album on your website. It'll drive traffic through the roof."

While she was in New York she met with a young actress, that one from that show with the teenage zombies. Roz had recommended her as a surrogate to attract young voters. She was from Conshohocken and still registered to vote in Pennsylvania. Jasmine Yates had been acting since she was five years old and had gone to rehab twice as a teenager. Then she'd gotten into Yale, reinvented herself as America's brainy sweetheart, and had been nominated for an Emmy and a Golden Globe last year.

Charlotte arrived late in the afternoon to a television studio in Queens that used to be a sugar factory and waited an hour in the actress's dressing room, cursing the waste of time. The walls were painted a soft yellow. One contained a corkboard vision board of pictures cut out of magazines and printed from Instagram that actually said "Jasmine's Vision Board" across the top edge. Charlotte used the time alone to review a briefing memo Leila had crafted for her on the last four seasons of Jasmine's show.

"Pretend you're a huge fan," Josh had instructed.

"Because I'm the demographic for teenage zombie romance?" Charlotte replied with a sarcastic smirk.

"Their audience is mostly thirty-five- to fifty-year-old mothers who no longer have sex with their husbands and fantasize about being held hostage by a nineteen-year-old zombie," Josh said flatly. "I don't know what's in your Netflix queue."

When she finally appeared, Jasmine's face was washed of the heavy makeup used to render her a member of the living dead. Her hair was chopped into a pixie cut that wasn't exactly becoming but could be called cute, and her wispy white dress was practically see-through in places that didn't matter. Charlotte could see through the veneer of wholesomeness that Jasmine was going to great pains to project. The girl placed her hands on Charlotte's shoulders and gazed into her eyes. "I feel like I know you."

Charlotte remembered this young woman had once overdosed on heroin. There had been pictures of it where her head was cocked at an unnatural angle in the passenger seat of an expensive car, her tongue flopping out of her mouth. That had been five years ago, and look at her now.

"I love your show." Charlotte gave her an easy smile. The girl looked down to insinuate that her "work," the things she did on television, was insignificant compared to what she was engaging in right now, her political activism.

"How can I help your campaign?" Jasmine asked. "Can I come on the trail with you? I have 4.1 million Instagram followers." It was the battle brag of the newly minted social justice warrior.

Charlotte knew Jasmine's robust Instagram following proved the actress's worth more than any awards. Lulu would love her. Charlotte imagined a future where the two young women would eventually become best friends, briefly lovers in an experimental way, and later bridesmaids in each other's first weddings to handsome young men, both of them named Tom.

"I can introduce you to my Instagram manager, Lulu. We'll get you to Pennsylvania in the next few weeks."

Within the space of a breath the girl's demeanor shifted. "I know how I look gets people's attention. I don't mind using it to get the right things done. I'm passionate about connecting with young voters. The first time I voted was like an out-of-body experience for me. I mean, it was, like, almost orgasmic. So many feels. Do you know what I mean?"

Charlotte made a herculean effort to smother a laugh.

"I know exactly what you mean."

"I'm writing a song about it."

Jasmine leaned in toward her like she was prepared to tell her a frightening secret.

"Let's take a selfie before you leave." The actress pulled Charlotte in close to her before Charlotte could protest.

Charlotte felt the need to cock her chin so it looked smaller and more angular.

No matter how many times she looked at herself in the mirror or in photographs, her appearance as a woman in her late forties could still surprise her, as it did now when she saw her tired eyes and sunken cheeks on the screen next to this glowing, shiny young woman.

Jasmine crossed her eyes and stuck out her tongue. "Smile."

★

Her staff sat in a Burger King halfway between New York and Scranton following Charlotte's weeklong media blitz.

"We should Instagram this." Charlotte looked to Lulu, who pecked furiously away at her phone's screen. "The glamour of the campaign trail."

Lulu hardly even looked up from sipping her ice water through a straw. "You just promised to put healthy food in school lunches."

"But I also promised hourly workers, like the ones who work here, I would fight to increase the minimum wage for them."

"The lighting in here is really yucky." Lulu's eyes darted around the restaurant as she wiggled her nose.

Lulu was still sullen from a slap on the wrist from Josh after she'd played Billy Joel's "Allentown" in a Snapchat earlier in the week.

"It's about Allentown," she had argued.

"Yes," Josh replied. "About how they were closing all the factories down. It's a song about despair and misery and how Pennsylvania is a terrible place to live. Listen to the damn lyrics next time."

"Seventy-seven percent of Pennsylvania voters eat in a fast-food restaurant at least once a week," Josh volunteered now. "But forty-three percent of those are ashamed of it. Maybe hold off. On another note, we need to dangle something or someone shiny in front of voters this month to get more cash."

"Do you want me to see if Oprah is available?" Leila asked with a half smile.

"She's not," Josh said with a straight face. "I checked. I have a call into Nick Foles."

"I met with that Jasmine girl. She's going to be a surrogate and do voter registration events. I raised half a million this week, Josh. We're doing okay." Charlotte had no idea if that was okay.

"We're still short." Josh took a large bite out of his Whopper. Orange sauce slopped out of the bottom and dripped onto his wrinkled khakis. "We need something new to get people's attention, and we need it fast."

"I can make up the difference," Charlotte whispered, almost to herself.

"How?" Josh asked. "Yourself. Your money?"

"If I have to."

"Hopefully it won't come to that. How do you feel about Jimmy Buffett? Can you be a Parrot Head?"

She buried her head in her hands. "I'm exhausted trying to be everything to everyone." *I'm a pathetic people-pleaser.*

"Then you shouldn't have run for office," Josh answered wryly. "It's the reason you're leading with both black women in urban areas and white men in rural areas. It's the reason persuadable independents are coming over to our side for the first time in twenty years."

She'd heard this before. Some days Josh actually ended their day by saying, "Did you talk to some brown folks today? Some old white guys? Anyone under twenty-five? Okay, then, you done good today." Charlotte could see the chewed-up lettuce and meat in Josh's mouth as he spoke.

"I feel like a liar."

"I warned you about that from the beginning. But you aren't lying. You're just telling people what they want to hear. There's a difference."

She felt like one of those Russian dolls stacked inside one another, constantly unpacking a new version of herself painted over to look like someone else.

I am a liar. I am a rich woman pretending to be a middle-class woman. I am terrified of losing my husband and my family, but I pretend everything is perfect. I don't trust the government but I'm asking people to trust me to be in the government. I don't always trust myself.

"And we need you in more parades." Josh kept going. "PA loves a parade and Slaughter doesn't do them anymore since the Pussy Brigade pelted his float with tampons soaked in cherry Kool-Aid."

Charlotte excused herself to go to the bathroom and was irritated to find it locked.

"You need a key." The obese teenage boy who had served them their burgers now stood too close behind her, holding a silver key attached to a spatula. His breath smelled of warm French fry grease and rum and Coke.

"Thank you."

He bowed his head slightly and she recoiled when he leaned in as if to sniff her.

The floor of the bathroom was strewn with damp, crumpled paper towels. Someone before her had attempted to bathe in the sink. One of the paper towels in the corner was covered in blood.

She lowered the toilet seat, sat on the lid, and dangled her head between her legs.

A tentative hand rapped on the door and jiggled the handle.

"Just a minute," Charlotte said.

"It's me. Can I come in?" Leila shook the handle again.

Charlotte reached over and flicked the lock to the right.

Leila's red sandals stuck to the paper towels on the floor. She bent her knee and picked one off without even a grimace and handed Charlotte a black coffee.

"I'm so tired."

"Drink this."

"I don't think coffee works anymore."

"Want me to get you some speed?"

"I'd like it too much. I don't think I can do this anymore, Lee." In that moment, Charlotte was too exhausted to leave a fast-food restaurant bathroom, much less campaign for five more months.

Leila grabbed Charlotte by the elbow and pulled her to her feet.

"You've got this, mama. You're almost home."

★

Charlotte arrived at their house to find a sullen-faced teenage girl picking at fresh acne scars on her cheek and playing Candy Crush on her phone as she channel-surfed on their couch.

"Hey there." Charlotte slipped off her shoes next to the twins' glittery high-tops, dropped her bag on the floor, and surveyed the mess in the living room—an empty pizza box on the coffee table, damp children's bathing suits hanging on the backs of chairs, an unfinished board game and colorful paper money in the middle of the floor. "Who are you?"

"Bailey," the girl replied with a roll of her eyes, as if the answer were tattooed on her forehead. "The babysitter." She was the fifth Bailey Charlotte had encountered in Elk Hollow. *What happened fifteen years ago that inspired all these couples to name their babies either Bailey or Riley, names better suited for cocker spaniels than little girls?*

Bailey stared at the television screen for a moment and then looked back at Charlotte. "That's you."

It took Charlotte a beat to recognize the unflattering photograph of herself used in the advertisement. Watching herself on television, a distorted version of herself, made her feel trapped, cornered. The quality of the photo was so degraded she appeared cadaverous and frightening. The words CHARLOTTE WALSH THINKS SHE'S SMARTER THAN YOU were writ large and angry and red on the screen. A voice read them in a low, ominous tone, giving them the cadence of a eulogy. Then came a montage of more photographs: Charlotte getting her diploma on Franklin Field (caption: IVY LEAGUE GRADUATE), Charlotte attending a gala for the New York City Opera (caption: ELITIST), Charlotte standing at an altar officiating a wedding ceremony for two male employees (caption: GAY PRIEST), footage of an interview with Charlotte for a TED Talk where she laughed and said, "I'm a total nerd at heart," and audio of her saying the words "That's just stupid" (where did they get that?). The spot ended with bright-red letters declaring CHARLOTTE WALSH THINKS YOU'RE STUPID. It was paid for by Patriots to Reelect Ted Slaughter.

It was still early in the year for an onslaught of attack ads, and Josh speculated it was because Slaughter thought he could humiliate her into quitting the race. The quality, or lack thereof, of local political ads astounded her, particularly when she considered that the cost of producing them ran into the hundreds of thousands of dollars. A drunk monkey with an iPhone and the first version of Adobe Photoshop could have made better stuff.

"It must be totally weird to see yourself on TV." Bailey's eyes moved from Charlotte's wrinkled pants to her face. "You're less scary in person." The teenager had the yearning look of a girl who believed, more than anything else, that she should already be starring in her own reality television show.

"Thanks. It *is* totally weird. Are my kids asleep?" She didn't bother to ask where Max was. Her ignorance regarding her own husband's whereabouts was none of this teenager's business.

"Yeah. They've been out for an hour. I also saw you on Facebook this week."

Overcome with the need for some sugar, Charlotte opened the fridge to find a jar of applesauce, a package of string cheese, six cartons of Girl Scout cookies, and some sparkling water. The trash bin overflowed with pizza boxes and Chinese takeout containers.

"You did?" Charlotte ripped into the box of Thin Mints and wondered what the going rate was for babysitters here. In Atherton it was twenty-five dollars an hour. They had to pay for an Uber each way and order the sitter an expensive dinner. How long had this girl been at her house? She fumbled in her purse, hoping to find a few twenties. Bailey puffed out her bottom lip to blow flat bangs out of her eyes and flipped her hair behind her ear as she thumbed the screen of her zebra-print iPhone. "I'm gonna text my boyfriend to come pick me up. Cool?"

"Cool."

★

The floorboards of the bedroom creaked. Charlotte flicked on the light. Their bed was unmade. Dirty clothes coated the floor, chair, and desk. Charlotte picked up the socks and underwear she encountered on her way to a much-needed shower. Her hair stank of fast food. Bob woke to the sound of running water and emerged from under their bed. She squeezed the scruff of his neck and tapped his butt to send him out of the small bathroom.

She heard Max come into their bedroom, remove his shoes, and drop his shirt in a pile on the floor like he was spending the night in a hotel.

Her husband walked into the bathroom and wordlessly lifted the toilet seat to pee.

"Hey." She tried to keep her voice friendly.

"Hey." He stopped and didn't flush. The ancient plumbing made the shower lose hot water when you flushed. She wanted to believe he was protecting her from being frozen rather than being lazy.

"There was a strange girl on the couch when I got home." They were out of shaving cream so she used conditioner to shave her legs, not bothering to go above the knee.

"I texted you I got a sitter."

"No, you didn't."

"Must have forgotten to hit send. Sorry. I thought I'd be home earlier. Were the girls good for Bailey?"

"Sounds like it." *Why don't you ask me about my week? About New York. About anything. Yes, Hoda smells good—like mint and apple shampoo. I missed you. Talk to me, please!*

"Is the water warm?"

"It's fine. Hey, why do you think all the teenagers in this town are named Bailey?" Charlotte asked him.

"I dunno." A surge of disappointment settled over her. When things were good between them Max would have liked this game. He would have manufactured an elaborate theory of the town's many Baileys involving algorithms, weather patterns, global birth rates, and some pop-culture phenomenon. "I'm gonna run down to the basement to check on the hot-water heater. It was acting up again this morning. Oh . . . and we're out of toilet paper."

Then why don't you replace it? It's under the sink, in the same place I always put it after I buy it.

Charlotte wiped the soap from her eyes so she could lean out of the shower for a kiss, but Max was gone by the time she got her face around the plastic. She stood under the water longer than necessary, attempting to wash her frustration with her husband down the drain.

Her phone buzzed on the bedroom dresser. She ignored it as she turned off the tap and towel-dried her hair. The next time it buzzed she picked it up.

This wasn't her phone. It was Max's.

She saw a text from someone named Abby. Charlotte typed in his code and scrolled up to see the entire exchange.

♥ ♥ ♥ I miss your face. When can I c u? 😶

Before u know it. Booking a trip to Cali soon. Excited to see you too. Lots to talk about.

Not soon enough. Did you tell C. about me?

Not yet. No time. She's ALWAYS busy.

Too busy for you?

Especially me.

That's too bad.

Tell me about it. You're sweet.

We'll have some fun when you're here.

A familiar humiliation overtook Charlotte. *Goddammit. Not again. Not now.* Buried memories assaulted her. *Stop it, Charlotte. Don't go there. Focus on what's happening right now.* She closed her eyes and exhaled through her nose as she read the messages a second time.

She flipped through her mental Rolodex to pinpoint an Abby in Max's life. Andrea was a former assistant. Abigail? No, Abigail was his seventy-two-year-old masseuse who didn't own a cell phone. Abby, Abby, who the hell was Abby? Then she had it. Of course. Abby was a wunderkind engineer Max hired two years ago from Apple to work on Humanity's Artificial Intelligence team. Charlotte only met her in person once, but didn't find her particularly memorable, couldn't even recall her face. Why was Abby sending her husband kissy-faces and hearts and why was Max telling her she was sweet? Why were they planning to meet and what was the urgency? *Don't be simple, Charlotte. You know the answers to these questions. You knew this would happen again.*

This can't be happening again. Not now.

Charlotte scrolled to the contact information and committed Abby's phone number to memory for no other reason than it gave her something to do. Charlotte was good at memorizing numbers. She'd won a contest in the fourth grade for memorizing pi to twenty-three places. Max poked sweet fun at her for it and asked her to recite the numbers at cocktail parties and weddings.

Still naked and wet, she replaced the phone on the dresser and sat on the edge of the bed, allowing conflicting emotions to swell inside her—rage, sadness, fear, guilt, doubt, and blame, all competing to see which would rise to the surface first. Charlotte stood, picked up the phone again, and threw it against the wall. Rage. It was going to be rage. The shiny black rectangle bounced on the carpeted floor.

Get it together.

She drew it all back inside and pulled on a ratty Penn State sweatshirt Max had left on the chair. His smell disgusted and comforted her in equal measure. She walked downstairs and directly out the front door.

They were far enough away from any city lights that the stars looked like the kind projected on the ceiling of a planetarium. Out of the corner of her eye she saw one light begin to move west, too small to be a plane—a satellite, most likely. Charlotte hadn't known you could even see a satellite with the naked eye until that long-ago camping trip with Max in Yosemite, when he'd pointed them out to her one by one. He'd described in careful detail the names and paths of each of them. There was the International Space Station, China's Tiangong-1 space laboratory, and Russia's Mir.

"I used to track them with my telescope when I was a kid," he'd explained. "There was a kit you could mail away for from NASA, before the Internet, you know, that showed you the orbits."

Charlotte was touched by the idea of a small boy with a gray tooth and a crooked nose entranced by star maps and amazed such a faraway thing was visible with just his eyes.

"I had no idea," Charlotte had whispered to him.

He smiled at her the way men smile at women before they've had sex with them. "I like telling you things you don't know. It makes me feel good."

Does Abby make my husband feel good? When is the last time I made him feel good?

She texted Max.

Left something at the office. Back soon. Don't wait up.

He'd see her text at the same time he saw Abby's. She got in the car and drove with nowhere to go, just down the street and through the neighborhood, trying to stay in motion.

When they were first married, Charlotte had believed she and Max had no secrets. Their lives had been open books to each other, sometimes to a fault. It was one of the things she loved about them, that frank and sometimes painful honesty that can only be born out of a true friendship. Sometime after they'd had kids, though, her husband had become a mystery.

How had he found the time and energy to have an affair the first time around? As far as she was concerned, sex with anyone, Max or someone new, seemed like too much work. It wasn't that she'd never thought about what it would be like to be with another man. But the thoughts alone exhausted her. There was too much else to do. And now he might have found the time and energy to do it a second time.

An animal, probably a cat, dashed in front of Charlotte's car, forcing her to pump the brakes and catch her breath. When something terrible happens to someone else our brains search for a reason, something that makes them different from us, something to reassure us that terrible thing could never happen to us. She'd thought about that when she first learned about Margaret, the excuses people would make for why Charlotte deserved to have her husband cheat on her.

Charlotte was never around.

She worked all the time.

She let herself go.

I heard they stopped having sex when the twins were born.

She was his boss, after all.

How would someone justify it now? If Max really was having another affair. If Abby was an actual threat to her marriage.

She put the campaign first.

Charlotte was too ambitious.

Didn't you see that Vanity Fair *article?*

Charlotte shuddered inwardly. *I am greedy. I wanted too much. Look at everything I was given, everything I took for granted. I meticulously created a life I thought I deserved and it was too much.*

She needed to talk to someone. There was one person who would understand. Roz was the obvious person to call. She'd endured Richard's infidelities when she was running for office the first time. Charlotte could trust her. Roz would never repeat anything Charlotte said to anyone else, would never say something to the wrong person, who could accidentally say something to the right person, who would turn it into the main story on *Politico* the next morning.

"Is it too late?" Charlotte asked. She knew it wasn't. Roz didn't sleep.

The formidable voice took over the car's audio system. "Never. Just catching up on *This Is Us*. I cry like a goddamned alley cat in heat every time I watch this show. You had quite the week. I saw you on *Today*, *Morning Joe*, *Maddow*, *Anderson*, and a bunch of other shows that didn't exist five minutes ago. I like that one with Mia Farrow's kid. Thank God he got her bone structure. He definitely didn't come from Woody Allen. And you shooting that gun? Very Calamity Jane."

For a brief second Charlotte let herself enjoy her former mentor's praise.

"Did you see me bake gluten- and sugar-free brownies with Rachael Ray?"

"I missed that. I'll bet they tasted like crap, though."

Charlotte lowered her voice, willing it not to crack. "Something happened."

"Yeah?"

"With Max."

Roz's voice contained concern, but not surprise. "Tell me."

"Max has been texting with another woman." Out loud the words sounded juvenile and ridiculous. Texting—something kids did.

She heard Roz suck in a breath and pause the television show. "What kinds of texts and how do you know and what do you know about her?"

Charlotte explained how she'd picked up the wrong phone, about Abby, about everything she knew, and in recounting it she realized what she knew for certain was close to nothing.

"And you never suspected anything between him and this Abby before?"

"I hardly know who she is."

"And that was all there was to it? Those were the only texts?"

She felt uncertain. "That was it." Charlotte wavered in her anger and, for a moment, allowed the possibility that she could be jumping to conclusions, that Max's first infidelity still haunted her and colored the way she interpreted everything he did.

The line got quiet save for Roz's heavy breathing.

"What do you want to do about it?"

"Confront him? Scream at him? Punch him in the eye."

"And what would that accomplish?"

Charlotte moved to the side of the road, no longer able to concentrate on driving. She placed her head against the soft leather of the steering wheel. "Probably nothing. Push Max even farther away. Disrupt our lives even more."

"What do you want to focus on right now?"

Her brain shifted toward task management, damage control, the neutrality of fixing a situation. "This campaign."

"Do you?"

"I want to win."

"Then don't say anything to your husband."

Charlotte's head throbbed, but her hands had finally stopped shaking. She couldn't halt the loop inside her head, recounting all of the times Max could have been texting Abby, or any other woman. She wondered whether he'd really been sick the day of her announcement speech, where he'd been before the *Vanity Fair* interview. Was he really training for an Ironman? One small thing could make you question all of the other things, could begin to unravel the fabric of your memory, making everything fallible.

"Charlotte? Are you there?"

"I'm here."

"You need him to win. You know that too, right?"

Charlotte stayed quiet.

"I'm sorry, honey. Now is not the time to let your marriage fall apart. Confronting him right now will only hurt you worse than you hurt right now."

Charlotte knew she was right. She hung up the phone and drove home to Max.

★

The last thing Charlotte wanted to do before collapsing into bed was check her email, but she was a slave to her inbox. She told herself it would be fast. She'd just glance at it and then go to bed.

Then she saw the name on an unread email in her inbox. Charlotte's hand shook as she opened the message. The email contained links to stories reporting on her campaign followed by one line.

You're going to ruin both of our lives.

Talk of the Town

On a rare morning off, Charlotte Walsh, tech executive, mom of three, and Senate candidate in Pennsylvania, is trying to decide between a deep maroon and a navy blue polish at a nail salon in downtown Altoona humorously named Nailed It.

"My daughters always want me to get purple with sparkles. Which I guess is a nice blend of both parties, right? Like wearing a donkey on the front of my shirt and an elephant on the other. It's strange, but I get asked about my nail color at least once a day. Sometimes I think I shouldn't wear nail polish at all, but that might make people ask me about it even more." She decides on the maroon color named "Party on a Platform."

Walsh speaks quickly and whiplashes from one idea to the next without pausing. When she's not speaking she's listening intently without interrupting.

As she settles into a large black leather armchair, she leans forward to make animated small talk with the nail technician, a petite Korean woman named Jen. They speak in hushed tones for a few minutes before Walsh turns to me to summarize.

"She told me she got health insurance for the first time last year, but now she can't afford the premiums. Goddammit, I hear these stories every day. These are the things we need to fix."

Jen asks Walsh if she wants a pedicure. The candidate shakes her head.

"No one ever sees my toes."

On her feet Walsh is wearing black Nike sneakers with a bright pink swoosh. Following her announcement speech in March, an Instagram account was created documenting her daily choice of footwear. It currently had more than one hundred thousand followers.

Thirty minutes later we pile back into the Walsh family's Chevy minivan.

"Excuse the mess," Walsh says as she gets behind the wheel. "And don't sit right behind the driver's seat unless you want to get glitter all over your butt." The Chevy minivan is a cobalt blue with six seats in the back and no television screens.

"I prefer to talk to people while I'm in the car. Don't you think it's a good place to talk?" she says as she turns on her blinker and checks the rearview mirror.

Charlotte Walsh considers herself an expert at the car game where you attempt to find the letters of the alphabet, in order, on road signs or nearby buildings.

"It's how we taught my twins to read," she says.

"She has an eagle eye," her campaign manager Josh Pratt adds from the backseat. "She's always going to find the *X* and the *Z*."

Somewhere in between Altoona and State College, Walsh collects a *T* when she spies a sign for farm-fresh turkey eggs.

"Have you ever had a turkey egg?" she asks her assistant, Leila Kelly, with a gleam in her eye. "Why don't we eat turkey eggs? Are they inedible or is there some kind of inherent prejudice against them?"

She pulls the minivan into the long driveway leading to the farm.

"It's really hard to keep her on schedule," Kelly says. Walsh, Pratt, and Kelly spend about seventy hours a week in this van as the candidate attempts to fulfill a campaign promise to visit all sixty-seven counties in the state twice before Election Day. Walsh grew up in Pennsylvania and went to college there. She takes care to tell you she went to school in Philadelphia without mentioning the name of the Ivy League university she attended. She took a hiatus from her Silicon Valley job when she moved back last September to take on incumbent senator Ted Slaughter in the midterm elections.

Walsh parks at the end of the driveway, knocks on the door of a split-level ranch house with aluminum siding, and introduces herself to the turkey farmer, Glenn Wright, and his wife, Joanne.

Ten minutes later we are eating scrambled turkey eggs with a sprinkling of goat cheese and chives with Glenn and Joanne while discussing the economics of turkeys.

"Who knew that turkeys take two months longer to start laying than a chicken?" Walsh says with genuine interest as she asks Joanne for seconds and begins to discuss the labor shortage facing Pennsylvania farmers in light of the president's new immigration policies.

Before she leaves, Walsh purchases a dozen of the turkey eggs for twenty dollars. "I'll make a frittata for the staff during our Sunday morning huddle." Because Walsh has worked in Silicon Valley for almost twenty years, she uses words like "huddle" to describe a morning meeting.

As she pulls onto Interstate 99 to Williamsport, home of the Little League World Series, Walsh spies in quick succession road signs for Deer X-ing, Year-Round Parking, and a No Passing Zone.

"Bam!" Walsh smacks the steering wheel with unbridled joy. "I win."

CHAPTER 11
June 30, 2018
129 days to Election Day

"I bet you I can put away more pie than Ted Slaughter." Max smirked from the driver's seat on the hour drive south to Wilkes-Barre, drumming his fingers on the steering wheel to a Tom Petty song Charlotte loved but could never remember the name of. She forced a smile as she dabbed more concealer beneath her eyes.

"I'll bet Daddy eats more pie than anyone," Ella chimed in from the backseat. Josh had insisted all three girls and Max join Charlotte while she emceed the annual apple pie–eating contest in Wilkes-Barre and crowned this year's Appleseed Queen. Apple-picking season was still three months away, but with the Fourth of July imminent, apples felt very American and on-brand for the town, like fireworks and Budweiser. Bob drooled in the way, way back of the car. He was by far their best ambassador on the campaign. Americans loved a special-needs bulldog.

Max picked up his phone and flicked the screen.

"Hands on the wheel," Charlotte said.

For the last two weeks, each time he'd glanced at the damn thing she'd wondered if her husband was expecting a new message from Abby, but she had no way of knowing. He'd changed the password on his phone. She knew this because she'd checked it again last week. His locked home screen glowered at her.

Day and night his phone taunted her with every beep, buzz, and click. *Just say it! Tell him you know. You're losing your mind.* Now that they'd settled back into a routine, the thought of mentioning the text messages or explaining why she'd waited to say something caused her brain to crumple in on itself.

She'd similarly tried to push the email out of her mind when she erased it from her inbox. *I have everything under control,* she repeated like a mantra.

"Slaughter won't be there today," Charlotte said. It amazed her that she'd never met Ted Slaughter in person, but there was an unspoken rule in state races that the two candidates crossed paths as infrequently as possible, that they took their shots from afar. Their staffs took great pains to ensure they rarely had to come into direct contact, with the exception of formal debates. They wouldn't have one of those until October. Most voters wouldn't even realize there was a Senate race until September. She glanced at Max with a plastic smile. "My money's on you to win, honey."

"PIE, PIE, PIE," Annie chanted at the top of her lungs from her car seat.

Sticking with the apple theme, Charlotte had selected a red blazer with slim-fitting jeans for the event. She kept buttoning and unbuttoning the jacket.

"Maybe Lulu could turn it into a whole Instagram story." Despite Max's concerns over not seeming masculine enough, or his worries that the press and social media thought he was a "pussy," he didn't seem to mind Lulu's transformation of his Instagram account—or maybe, Charlotte thought, he just didn't mind Lulu.

Maybe he's fucking her, too. She'd created a new and dangerous game: Who else did her husband want to hop into bed with? Every woman on the street was fodder, and it broke her a little more each time she played it.

Maybe you'll choke on the pie.

Max sneezed and Charlotte took a small amount of pleasure in not saying "God bless you."

"Mommy, why are you a very special guest today?" Ella asked

from the backseat. The girls knew their mom got invited to a lot of parties where she was the guest of honor, like a princess, and that sounded like a lot of fun. They knew that she used to go into an office and that now she drove around and talked and got her picture taken a lot. They also knew people liked to take their pictures more often now than they did before. Annie and Ella enjoyed the attention, but it bothered Rose, who had always preferred her twin to take the spotlight from the very beginning of their lives. She'd even hidden behind Ella in all of their sonograms. In photographs now, Ella and Annie beamed, hammed it up, and made silly faces, while Rose turned her profile to the camera or stared dreamily at the sky, looking fragile and vulnerable. Every time she looked at those pictures, Charlotte wondered how she was damaging her daughter.

"Because I'm running for Senate, baby, remember?"

"What's Senate?"

Charlotte had tried this before.

"You know how Mommy and Daddy are the bosses in our house? How we make decisions and rules for all you girls?"

Ella nodded her head hard. "You make more rules than Daddy." This made Max laugh. *I do make more rules than Daddy. Because Daddy wants to be the good guy and I always have to be the bad guy and that sucks.* "So, we make the rules in our house, but someone needs to make the rules outside of our house. In America we have a president and politicians who make those rules. They're called senators. I want to be one of those people who makes the rules."

"Because you love rules," Ella screamed, and giggled and punched Rose in the shoulder because Rose was ignoring her and she hated when her twin ignored her.

"I suppose I do love rules," Charlotte said.

"That was good," Max murmured. "I don't know how I would have explained it." She rolled her eyes. *Why don't you see how annoying it is to have to be the rule maker all the time?*

★

A teenage boy dressed as Johnny Appleseed, complete with a tin cooking pot on his head and tattered houndstooth pants, greeted them with an enthusiastic wave as they parked the car.

"Carry Annie?" Charlotte asked Max.

"On it." He hoisted the girl out of the backseat and onto his shoulders. Johnny handed the twins their own tin-pot hats and tiny American flags and grabbed each of their small hands to lead them to the festivities, which included a pig roast and a dunking booth. Kids of all ages bobbed for apples in a blue plastic pool, their hands tied behind their backs with red bandanas.

Lulu ran to greet them with all the excitement of a child on Christmas morning, her long legs and wiry arms propelling her insect-like torso forward with the force of a pinball launch.

"How funny is this?" the girl trilled the way a certain class of New Yorkers did when they left the city to play at being rural. "I've been shooting quick Insta lives and doing candid Snaps with people. The people here are so real. They're adorable. The turnout is great for a pie-eating contest, but no one has any idea that a Senate race is happening in the fall. This is like something out of a movie, but with less-attractive people." Lulu shifted all of her weight onto her toes. Charlotte would have bet anything Lulu had been an elementary school ballerina who reveled in tottering around *en pointe*. She was dressed in an ankle-length leather skirt that would have made anyone else look like a cartoon witch with an S&M fetish, but on Lulu it worked. A slight sheen of sweat only made her prettier.

"Hi Max!" Lulu gazed down at his artfully weathered denim that had come that way from the factory and then held her phone in front of him. "Smile!"

"I'm going to eat so many pies today," he responded with a lopsided grin. As usual, her husband got stupid around beautiful women. It was never lost on Charlotte that he chose to get smarter when she was around. She cut through the crowd, introducing herself to people who clearly had no idea who she was or why she was there. The blank stares made her feel like she was crashing someone else's prom.

"I'm Charlotte Walsh and I'm running for Senate," she'd politely introduce herself. Every fifth person, a small glimmer of recognition would cross someone's eyes.

"You're the gal who shot the gun."

"I saw you on Facebook."

"That video of you with that baby giraffe made me cry."

"You have that cute husband. Oh, there he is." A group of women close to her age clustered around Max for a photo. A redhead wearing too much lip liner pantomimed grabbing his butt and he playfully swatted her away.

Would my husband fuck her? Charlotte thought.

Four men quit working the grill and came over to ask her what her plan was to get jobs back to Pennsylvania. Would she reopen the factories? Slaughter had promised to bring steel back to Pennsylvania. Could she promise that? A George Packer quote from an old profile of Peter Thiel reverberated in her head. He claimed that in a *"techno-utopia a few thousand Americans might own robot-driven cars and live to a hundred and fifty while millions of others lose their jobs to computers that are far smarter than they are, then perish at sixty."*

She was supposed to say, *I'm working on it.* That was the answer they wanted, even if they knew, deep down, that it was a lie.

"We're going to bring jobs to this state." She looked them directly in the eye and never said the word *factory*. Those factories were never coming back. *The best I can get you is an Amazon distribution warehouse. I wish I could tell you the truth, but you don't want to hear it.*

One of the men had a swastika tattooed on his neck. Charlotte watched Leila notice it and avert her eyes.

A bespectacled woman with hair an unnatural shade of yellow, like lemonade made from powder, grabbed her by the elbow and patted her hand. She smelled like White Diamonds perfume. "I like you. You're very American-looking. Are you a Christian, dear?"

Charlotte smiled and gave a small nod. She removed her blazer, keenly aware that sweat circles had stained her silk tank top. She resisted the urge to pull her hair into a ponytail, knowing it wouldn't look good on camera. The lack of sleep had caught up with her. The smell of hot dogs, Kool-Aid, and grease made her nauseous.

One of the campaign kids trailed behind her doling out WALSH FOR SENATE swag bags filled with glossy flyers and a WALSH CAN FIX IT baseball cap in bright blue.

The scrum of reporters lounging on a rusted merry-go-round stirred at Charlotte's arrival and formed a circle around her.

"Are you competing?"

"What's your record for pie eating? Har, har."

"Did you bring your gun?"

"What do you say to Ted Slaughter's claim that you think you're smarter than the average Pennsylvanian?"

Charlotte spied a petite young woman, hardly older than twenty, lingering on the fringe of the crowd holding her phone in the air to record all of Charlotte's answers. She was purposefully innocuous in black jeans, a simple black tank top, and a ponytail. Her face was mostly plain and devoid of makeup except for a swipe of nude lip gloss. A birthmark in the shape of Florida along the length of her right jawline was the only feature that set her apart. Slaughter's number one tracker had already recorded hours of footage of Charlotte. There were others, of course. Some of them Josh had yet to identify, but this one tailed her more often than the rest.

Charlotte smelled Josh behind her before she saw him, the thick, musky stench of stale cigarettes. The kids on the campaign trail wore their unhealthiness like a badge of honor, smoking at least a pack of cigarettes a day. They followed Josh's lead and subsisted on Red Bull, Big Macs, and Marlboro Reds. Charlotte had quit regularly smoking right after college and hadn't had a single cigarette since the night of her mother's funeral, but the campaign made her want to start again every day. She reached into her pocket and pulled out a shiny white tab of nicotine gum to keep her craving at bay. Josh was trailed by three of his disciples, pudgy young men in jeans, blazers, Vineyard Vines ties, and expensive sneakers. Their fervor to please Charlotte in order to please Josh made them indispensable. The three of them were all mixed up in her head. She could never remember if it was Mark, Jason, and Tyler or Matt, Jonathan, and Tucker. One of them casually stepped in front of Slaughter's tracker, blocking her shot.

Josh held up his hand to the reporters and stubbed out a cigarette with the toe of his throwback Adidas. "Everyone gets one question. Then Charlotte has some duties to attend to here. If I heard right, Max is gonna eat a lot of pie here today, which should be fun for you vultures, at least the ones with cameras. Let's keep this quick."

A television reporter with excellent breasts and an unfortunately upturned nose grabbed Josh by the crook of his elbow. "When are we getting you on air?" she cooed in a voice filled with ambitious lust.

"I'd rather stab myself in the eye, Samantha." Josh stared at her eyes instead of her chest. "I'm not here to get famous. I'm here to get Charlotte Walsh elected." This was what she appreciated about Josh. Most other campaign managers took the work in the hopes of winning a race that would land them a coveted talking-head spot on one of the cable networks. Josh wanted none of the spotlight. He'd rather be in the trenches. "Let's talk about Charlotte's job-retraining proposals, shall we? Coal miners into coders!"

Carly Meeks from *Teen Vogue* pushed her way to the front of the crowd. She wore a pinstripe blazer and a formfitting shirt that read: RESIST THE GASLIGHT.

"*Vanity Fair* reported that you're more ambitious than your husband. Do you think men find ambitious women attractive?" *Would my husband fuck her?* She glanced across the grass at Max typing on his phone. *Who is he writing to?*

"Ambition should be a virtue regardless of gender. Be right back, folks." It was balmy, the air thick and syrupy, and Charlotte felt too warm in long pants.

She put her hand in her pocket and felt around for another tab of gum, knowing it would give her a buzz, but found only empty foil. There was another pack in the car. She could send someone, but she wanted to be alone for a blessed second.

Charlotte heard the sounds of a fight in the parking lot before she saw it.

"Get your hands off me, dammit. Get 'em off me. I'm runnin' for Senate. I'm runnin' for Senate. I'm an important person."

No, no, no.

A security guard, not a real police officer, had her brother Paul facedown on the parking lot pavement. Her brother's jowls drooped loose and flat against the pebbled cement. She could hear his teeth grinding, his jaw creaking. The guard was thick and stout. His shoulders strained against his white polo shirt and he wore pants an inch too short for his legs so they showed an almost feminine inch of ankle. Charlotte recognized Paul's buddies Jimmy and Jeff standing a few feet away. Jimmy had his phone in the air and was making a video of the spectacle. Jeff crouched low with his hands on his knees. "You better cut the shit, fool. This man's running for president."

All three of them were stoned out of their minds. Fortunately, they had yet to attract a crowd. Charlotte whipped her head around to look behind her. All it would take would be one person with a phone to catch her lunatic brother making an ass of himself in this parking lot.

"Excuse me, officer." She made her voice high and sweet. Guys who weren't real cops got off on being addressed as "officer." "I'm Charlotte Walsh. I'm one of the hosts of this event. Can I help you?"

Paul craned his neck at a painful angle, his pupils dilating, the veins in his neck bulging.

"Charlie you tell this man I am runnin' for president." The look on his face was fixed in a way that let her know that in that moment he believed what he was saying. He began singing his version of "The Star-Spangled Banner."

Oh say can you pee. By my dong's early light.

She could hear the *tap, tap, tap* on a microphone for a sound check. She had maybe five minutes.

"Please let him go."

"I can't, ma'am." The guard had a strangely high-pitched voice. "I caught these three with open containers in the parking lot and this one was smoking marijuana." The Keystone Cop believed he was doing the world a favor.

"Has anyone ever told ya you talk like a fag?" Jimmy stepped into the guard's face.

"Shut your mouth, Jimmy," Charlotte growled, moving between them. "I understand that, sir."

Paul's defense didn't allow her to say she was running for Senate. If she mentioned it now, their dialogue would quickly descend into something from a Wes Anderson movie.

"I work for the mayor's office," she lied, and showed the guard an official-looking pass that was little more than a ticket for free soda and chips. "I can take it from here."

The guard rolled his bulging eyes. She could see his brain slowly working it out, his eyeballs darting back and forth like he was trying to do long division in his head. What would these guys think of him if he let a woman tell him what to do? But what if she really did work for the mayor and he lost his weekend gig? He liked the job. It probably got him laid. He stood and released Paul.

"You gonna take him?"

Be polite. Be submissive. "I'm going to make sure they get on out of here so the families inside can enjoy their day. I can't thank you enough from everyone in the mayor's office."

The guard continued to look at her like he knew he was being played, but he made his way back into the event.

Paul had fallen asleep. Charlotte nudged her brother with her toe and looked at Jimmy and Jeff, who grabbed their wide stomachs in laughter. "Get the hell up."

"What a pussy. You told that pussy who was boss, Charlie. Fucking dickbrain," Jeff chortled and spit a wad of chewing tobacco near her feet.

She glared at them. "You need to get out of here before the real police arrest you. Get him in the car and go."

Jeff saluted her. "Yes, ma'am."

"I'm going back inside. Don't speed. Try not to get a DUI on the way home."

A sudden urge to escape overtook her. *What if I got in the car and just drove away?*

Inside at the concession stand a pleasant woman wearing a hat that said I DO IT FOR THE PIE handed her a can of off-brand cola. Charlotte pushed the cold metal into the back of her neck and felt the condensation drip down the back of her blouse.

"You okay, Walsh?" The shooter from MSNBC cast her a concerned glance.

Saving Paul had sapped even more of her strength. *I can't breathe. What the hell is happening to me?* "I'm fine. Hotter than I expected."

"Put the jacket back on," Lulu whispered in her ear. "You need to hide those giant sweat stains."

"It's showtime." Josh grabbed her by the elbow and turned her toward the stage. The front of her throat tightened and she forgot what she needed to say. "Keep it conversational," Josh said. "Don't forget you're standing in front of a table of pie. And pronounce the town like the locals do: *Wix-Berry*."

Her toe caught the first stair and she stumbled walking up to the stage. *I don't want to do this right now.* After the twins had been born, during the time when they screamed for five hours every sin-

gle night no matter how many times Charlotte had paced the backyard bouncing them or pushed them in the carriage down the street,
she'd often dreamed of not being their mother for just one day. It
had made her believe there was something wrong with her. Now she
wished she could give the campaign up for just a day, just one day, to
see if, once it was gone, this still felt like the right thing to do.

Max sat next to the mayor of Wilkes-Barre. He wore a confident
expression, and a white napkin tucked into his collar as a bib. Five
whole pies were stacked like children's blocks in front of him.

"PIE, PIE, PIE! EAT IT! EAT IT!" the crowd chanted.

Charlotte tapped the microphone. "I'm Charlotte Walsh and I'm
running for Senate." Her voice sounded far away, like she was hearing
it from underwater.

"PIE, PIE, PIE!"

"I grew up not too far from here in Elk Hollow, outside Scranton."

"PIE, PIE, PIE!"

"I'm running because I believe the voters of Pennsylvania deserve
something better." The heat in the air pulsed in front of her eyes. A
bead of sweat dripped over her eyelash.

"Annie Oakley!" a male voice bellowed close to the stage. A man
wearing a T-shirt that said FRACK YOU turned his thumb and pointer
finger into two guns and began shooting at her from the crowd.

Beyond the gunslinger she thought she saw Paul. Then her mind
flashed to her brother lying facedown in the parking lot, his eyes rolling back in his head. She heard him cackle words from almost a year
ago. *I can make being back here real easy for you. Or I could make
it real hard.* Then a woman emerged from the back of the crowd, a
slender blonde with pale skin and light-blue eyes. Charlotte squinted.
Margaret? It couldn't be. A current shot up her legs and her heart
pounded in her throat. The faces in the crowd dissolved in front of
her. She reached for something to hold on to, but she was in the middle of the stage and there was nothing but the microphone in her
hand. *Introduce the mayor. That's all you have to do.* She opened her

mouth to say his name, but no sound came out. Her face felt heavy. Charlotte swayed back and forth and focused on Max. He smiled a real smile, like he was actually having fun. The sun shone behind his head. Too bright. *I need you,* she thought. She watched her husband rise and rush toward her as she sank to her knees. Everything went dark.

Senate Candidate Sparks Pregnancy Rumors After Collapsing on Trail

BY DAN SLADE

Pennsylvania Senate candidate Charlotte Walsh collapsed onstage while introducing a pie-eating competition in Wilkes-Barre, PA, on Saturday afternoon. Walsh, a Silicon Valley executive with Humanity and a *New York Times*–bestselling author, announced her candidacy in April and is running against longtime incumbent Ted Slaughter.

The Slaughter campaign took the opportunity to question whether Walsh could be expecting her fourth child.

"This is her first time running for public office. She just might not be up for it. Not everyone is cut out for this sort of thing. I feel sorry for her. She's got a lot on her plate with three kids, and one on the way," Ted Slaughter said. "I remember when my wife fainted during her first trimester."

The Walsh campaign did not immediately respond to a request for comment.

. . . Story developing

CHAPTER 12

Walsh (D)	Slaughter (R)	Spread
42	41	Walsh +1

It was the sheer absurdity that pissed Charlotte off the most.

"Unless there's been an immaculate conception, I'm not having a baby. Call them now. Fix this." She began to itch at her forearms and the inside of her wrists. She felt as though her entire body were covered in fleas.

Josh actually rolled his eyes at her. "Call who? All of the press? All of Twitter? Stop it. Are you sure you're not?"

"I've never been more sure of anything in my life." It wasn't just the statistical unlikelihood of having another child at her age. It was easy to promise you couldn't be pregnant when you hadn't had sex with your husband in more than six months.

Footage of her collapse was all over the Internet, her onstage, knees buckling, body crumpling, video in slow motion, in fast-forward, one set to circus music and another to a pop song she'd never heard.

"I need to show you something." Josh opened his laptop to reveal four quadrants of Excel spreadsheets filled with percentages. "You're ahead in the latest polls. You're doing great with both college-educated women and non-college-educated women. White men are still a problem."

"That should be on a T-shirt or, better yet, a hat," Leila interjected. "'White Men Are Still a Problem.'"

"What?" Josh pretended not to get the joke. "But they're actually not as big a problem as I thought they would be. We've seen a surprising bump in non-college-educated men over sixty. They look at you and think you could be their successful daughter, or their trophy wife. I don't care if they're into your brain or your vagina as long as it's working for them and they remember your name in November. You're gaining steam with the moderate Republicans in the Philly suburbs without losing ground with the blue-collar base in the western part of the state. The problem now is a pregnancy makes you look weak to male voters."

"But I'm not pregnant," Charlotte reminded him, her voice thick with exasperation. She moved on to scratching a spot just above her knee.

"And anyway, pregnancy isn't a disease, Josh," Leila chimed in. "I traveled with Charlotte to Beijing and São Paulo in her third trimester with the twins. She delivered, drug-free I might add, two seven-pound babies during forty-seven hours of labor. Who's weak?"

Charlotte allowed a smile. "I really should have gotten the drugs that time. Why didn't I get the drugs?"

"Because you're fucking strong," Leila said.

Josh shrugged. "Men don't get it. They think pregnant women are fragile flowers, not United States senators. No woman has ever run for Congress while pregnant, and only a handful have actually served while pregnant."

"Who's picked the story up?" Charlotte scrolled through her Google alerts.

"Everyone," Josh replied evenly. "It's juicy. Forty-seven-year-old woman pregnant with fourth child collapses from exhaustion on the campaign trail. I'd read that. You're trending on Twitter and the lead story on both CNN and Fox News."

"But—" Before she could even finish her sentence, Josh cut her off.

"Don't do this."

"Do what?"

"Don't react like you're a normal person being attacked. It's not personal. It's political. It'll get worse than this." Josh stared at her hard. "I need you on your feet, perky, cheery, happy, awake, and telling the voters you are not pregnant. If I talk to the press, it will look like we're hiding something. You can't seem secretive and evasive. Once they think you lie about one thing, they think you lie about everything. Find your most formfitting shirt. Put on a pair of Spanx, suck in your stomach, and we'll livestream in an hour. This message has to come from you."

Charlotte got up slowly from the couch. Her muscles ached. Her skin ached. The doctor had given her an ambiguous diagnosis of exhaustion and dehydration. She knew what it had really been—she'd seen her mother suffer through plenty of them. This had been her first panic attack.

She made her way to a mirror in the hallway and laughed in her own face, the sound wild, feral.

"What's so funny?" Josh asked.

"I look like death." *What's funny is that someone thinking that I'm pregnant is actually the least of my worries.*

"Kara's on her way. She'll spackle your face. We'll put a filter on you. You'll be fine."

"What do you want me to say?"

"Don't sound like you wouldn't be so happy to be pregnant. Then you sound anti-kid and angry."

"I am angry."

"Not today you aren't."

Kara swept into the house like a mother hen, bringing chicken soup, a carton of Tropicana, and Gatorade. I'm so sorry about Paul honey. I shoulda had better mitts on him."

Charlotte dismissed the apology. "Kara . . . you know this isn't normal. He needs to go to rehab, right? This can't keep happening. You have to tell him to go to rehab."

"I can't tell my husband what to do, Charlie. My house ain't like your house, where I snap my fingers and everyone does what I say. Never has been. I can't make him do shit."

"Maybe I can talk to him."

"Maybe." Kara didn't sound convinced. "I did read him the riot act last night, and then I went through his computer tryin' to figure out what da hell is goin' on with him. I found somethin'."

"Oh yeah?"

"He wasn't out to get you with those pictures."

Charlotte must have looked confused.

"With those old pictures. He wasn't out to hurt you. He thought he was doin' good."

"What are you talking about?"

"Take a look."

She pushed a stack of paper toward Charlotte. It was correspondence initiated by an editor at the *Daily Dispatch* to her brother.

From: Jackson.Blake@DailyDispatch.com
To: PGiddy456@aol.com

Mr. Walsh, good speaking with you on the phone. Like I said, we are working on a timeline of your sister's fascinating life and I want to illustrate it with some photos of her through the years. It's a really in-depth piece and we want to show the human side of Charlotte as more than a candidate. Do you think you could get us some of those old pictures? Things from high school, mainly. I want to show voters she has a sense of humor.

From: PGiddy456@aol.com
To: Jackson.Blake@DailyDispatch.com

Hello Mr. Jackson,
    As my sister's very special advisor for local affairs, this is

something I can help with. How many pictures you need? I should check with Charlotte.

From: Jackson.Blake@DailyDispatch.com
To: PGiddy456@aol.com

No need to check with her as I'm sure she's busy and it sounds like you have the authority to authorize what we need. As many pictures as possible. It will make a beautiful story.

From: PGiddy456@aol.com
To: Jackson.Blake@DailyDispatch.com

Mr. Jackson. I am attaching the pictures you asked for. I chose ones no one else has seen yet. Do my sister proud.

"He didn't get paid for it." Charlotte finished reading the email. "He thought he was doing a good thing." She paused a second before adding, "God, some of these journalists are real scum."

"Let's not go nominating him for sainthood, now. Your brother is still a sonofabitch and right now he's passed out in our bathtub with a shiner and covered in puke." Kara looked accusingly at Charlotte's midsection. "You're not, are you? You ain't pregnant?"

"God, no."

"Three's enough kids."

"Oh, I know."

"Is a camera crew coming?"

"We're streaming it on my Facebook page. Just make me look alive."

When Kara was done with her face Charlotte shut the door to her bedroom to steal a blessed second alone. As she pulled a formfitting white shirt over her head she screamed a little into the soft fabric. She rooted around in the back of her closet for a box she knew contained some of the twins' old toys and a Velcro belly corset she'd worn for nearly a year after Annie was born. Charlotte sucked in the puckered roll of flesh beneath her belly button that had recently expanded due to a regular diet of Wawa hoagies and Sizzlis. She fastened the Velcro around her torso like a tourniquet.

Max was still out for his run. Their conversation that morning had been brief.

"Christ, Charlie. What are you doing to yourself? You're not okay. I want you to rest."

She half listened to him as she watched footage of her collapse played in reverse. "I'm fine."

"You're not. You're falling apart."

"Why don't you go for a run?"

And he did.

Part of her thought, *Thanks for the help, buddy*. Most of her just wanted him out of the house.

The livestream was carefully staged and began with Charlotte holding Annie on her hip from an angle that showed off her flat stomach. The message was "I'm not pregnant, but I love babies." Never before had her parenting been so directed, so performative. It made her feel like a stage mom who forced her girls to tap-dance and wear fake eyelashes.

"We have our hands full already." She delivered a throaty chortle. "Another child would be a blessing, but our family is complete." The twins ran behind her, giggling. She laughed again. *I hate myself right now. I don't even recognize myself right now.*

"One last thing." She went off script. "Pregnancy isn't some kind of handicap. I negotiated a fifty-million-dollar deal with the Chinese government when I was pregnant with twins. I worked up until the day I went into labor. I know pregnant women who get more done in a day than a man does in a year." It was a paradox—this need to portray herself as an Amazon warrior during and after her pregnancy. In hindsight, that was when she discovered she *was* stronger than at any other point in her life. But in those moments, when it was all happening, she'd been convinced that every day with those small babies would be her last. Her sanity, her career, and her marriage had all quietly suffered. But that wasn't what she needed to say right now.

"Ted Slaughter's desperate commentary on my reproductive health reminds me of something my sexist grandfather might say. Now, I loved my grandfather, but he sure didn't belong in the US Senate."

CHAPTER 13
July 26, 2018

103 days to Election Day

Walsh (D)	Slaughter (R)	Spread
44	41	Walsh +3

Charlotte was hiding out in the bathroom of the campaign headquarters when she heard Leila scream for the first time in their nine years together.

It had been a mind-numbing morning of fundraising calls to potential big donors. It would have been easier and more efficient to just make a recording of Charlotte begging for cash. If she'd been a Humanity client, their team of engineers would have crafted voice-recognition software that would release perfect courteous requests on her behalf. Making the calls was somehow both boring and exhausting. Now the only quiet space in the entire office was the handicapped restroom, where she was free to devour a limp spinach salad with anemic carrots and shredded American cheese. Charlotte had balanced the salad on her knees and was about to refresh her browser to read a story on *People* magazine's website about Reese Witherspoon really pulling off a denim kimono to clear her brain with a bit of harmless celebrity fashion news when she heard Leila shriek.

"That racist lying bastard!"

What had Ted Slaughter done now?

Leila never lost her cool. The ability to project outward composure was one of their shared virtues. When Charlotte told people Leila was the strongest person she'd ever met, she meant it. Early on in their time working together, Leila had told Charlotte a story about how her mother was held up at gunpoint at the intersection of Fairfax Avenue and Foothill Boulevard when she was seven months pregnant with her daughter. The robber, a fifteen-year-old kid, had pushed the cold barrel of the gun directly into her abdomen and kicked her in the kneecap, all for ten dollars and a bus pass. Leila's mother claimed that her daughter punched back so hard from the womb that she had the strength to get up and chase the assailant down the street, knock him over, and take her money back. When Charlotte cringed at the story, Leila just laughed. "My mom's sisters were beaten within an inch of their lives by soldiers who were supposed to protect them. Her brother was kidnapped and they never saw him again. I had a lot of reminders growing up that I never had the right to feel sorry for myself or whine because I didn't get new Nikes or an American Girl doll."

Charlotte sat on the toilet for a moment more before standing and slipping her phone into her pocket because she hated anyone knowing she'd brought her phone with her into a bathroom. She swiftly made her way to join Leila on the other side of the room, where she stood over one of their interns, a University of Scranton student who tracked Slaughter on weekends. It was so clear to Charlotte from the way he averted his eyes and picked at a pimple on the side of his face that he was afraid of Leila, and that she didn't realize the power she wielded over him.

"What's up?" Charlotte plucked a sweaty can of Diet Coke from Leila's hand and took a gulp of it. In the past three weeks she'd begun supplementing her coffee with several cans of caffeinated soda. It began when Max started sleeping in the basement. "You're up working all night," he complained. "I can't sleep with you typing." His absence from their bed gave her license to stay awake most of the night reading policy papers. She was getting an average of three hours of sleep a night. Most days she didn't even see Max in the morning. He ran while she got the girls dressed and fed before he took over for the rest of the day, shuttling the twins to camp, taking Annie to the playground; then she tried to make it back for bath time and bedtime stories. They were like soldiers on patrol, parceling out duties, going through the motions, doing their jobs.

When Leila looked at her Charlotte saw anger layered over genuine hurt and dismay. "Ted Slaughter has a nickname for me. Tell Charlotte the nickname, Michael."

Poor Michael looked like he thought he was about to be spanked. He returned his hand to his lap, where he began to tap his index and middle fingers on his thigh like he was playing a scale on a piano. When he shook his head his sandy-brown hair flopped into his eyes like the fur of an ungroomed sheepdog. "I really don't want to. Do I have to say it out loud again?"

Leila grunted. "I'll say it out loud. Ted Slaughter, when he's talking to his aides and to the press and sometimes even to voters, calls me Charlotte Walsh's jihadi handmaid. But that's not all. He let it slip in a private event with donors that he thought my mother might be an actual terrorist."

Charlotte looked around for Josh because he would know exactly what to say, would make an off-color joke so heinous he would diffuse Slaughter's disgusting remarks. But Josh was half a state away in a meeting with the governor in Harrisburg trying to secure an official endorsement. Harrisburg had been dragging their feet and Josh scheduled a face-to-face to figure out why. The governor's lack of support made them nervous. He was up for reelection next year and his silence could mean he was worried about hitching his cart to a potential loser.

"Let's take a walk." Charlotte grabbed her chief of staff by the elbow and led her out of the office into Scranton's muggy summer air.

Leila kicked a discarded can of grape soda down the middle of the sidewalk. "Jihadi? He called me a terrorist, Charlie." Her face twitched with righteous fury. "He called my mother a terrorist. What if people come after her? What if this fucks with her visa? He's a racist, lying old sonofabitch. He thinks all brown people are terrorists or gangsters. I'm American. My mother's from Africa—that makes me

African American, and Irish American, and I was baptized Catholic. I'm not a terrorist and I'm also not your minion."

Leila needed to say the words out loud, because refuting Slaughter's lies, even just to Charlotte, made a difference, made them more real and made him accountable in a world that had stopped holding him accountable.

"Your mom is going to be fine. She has a green card. She's been here thirty years and no one has ever questioned her status."

"He's goddamned terrible. My mom might be fine. But what about her mom and her sisters?"

For the past ten years, Leila had spent a good portion of her salary to help her mother move her family from Khartoum to Oakland. Charlotte had encouraged her to use Humanity's legal staff to wade through the bureaucratic nightmare of the asylum process, a quagmire that had only gotten worse in the past eighteen months.

"Men like him make decisions for millions of people. Men who look at me and think, 'Just another little brown bitch, she's the problem, she's a threat to us.' "

Seeing Leila's frustration swell forced Charlotte to be strong and cool. "Let's sit somewhere. I need sugar." Charlotte stayed silent as she led Leila to Mary's Kitchen, their dingy corner diner where the campaign staff usually hung out eating egg burritos and disco fries at two in the morning. The waiter came quickly and Charlotte ordered a Caesar salad and a brownie sundae to split between the two of them while Leila groaned and rested her forehead on the linoleum table.

What surprised Charlotte the most about Leila's reaction to Slaughter's insult was the effect it had on her, how it brought out a protective instinct she'd previously only felt for her daughters. Leila turned her cheek and laid it on Charlotte's hand like a small child, her emerald eyes widening.

"It's just so fucking ignorant. It makes me want to give up. Or throw up. Or both."

Charlotte stroked the back of her head the way she did the twins' when they were sick. "It sucks. I know it sucks. I know how it feels." For the past six months Charlotte had kept a list of the most ruthless and brutal insults leveled against her on television, the Internet, and social media in a text file on her phone. Late at night when she sat alone at the kitchen table, in the bathroom, or, more recently, in bed, she read them out loud to herself. It was an unhealthy form of verbal self-flagellation.

- *Wicked Witch of the West Coast*
- *Harpy Walsh*
- *A stuttering slob*
- *Mommy Morebucks*
- *A hero to all stupid sluts*
- *A walking vagina with fangs*
- *Silicon Valley Satan*
- *Bitch girl*
- *An artisanal pig in lipstick*
- *Nasty new-money cunt*
- *A burr that sticks right in my asshole*

That last one came from Ted Slaughter himself. Then the comments:

"She doesn't know what the fuck she's doing.
"You're not fit to be a mother."
"You should have been aborted."
"I want to slice her tits off and send her to the gas chamber."
"You will burn in hell."
"I knew her in high school. She cheated on all her exams. That's
  how she got into that preppy college."
"Your children should be taken away from you."
"God WILL take your children away from you."

That wasn't the worst of it. Someone had created horrific memes of her daughters being stabbed using photographs they'd taken from Charlotte's Instagram account. There was the Reddit chain devoted to ways men would like to show her how they would be the boss of her that included acts so disgusting that Charlotte gagged the one and only time she read it. There was the elaborate hate mail that included pictures of men masturbating. It usually came in email form, but she'd gotten several letters to the office written in stilted capital letters, the envelopes containing clippings of pubic hair. She'd become a blank screen for the enraged and hopeless to project all of their anger upon.

When she read the insults, witnessed the hatred on the ground, and despaired at the incivility on the Internet, she sometimes wondered to herself, and only ever to herself, whether America got the president it deserved.

Leila sat up and swiped at the mascara pooling beneath her eyes before she slammed her hand down on the table.

"Fuck it!"

The few other diners, an elderly couple sharing a grilled cheese sandwich and a young mother trying to get her toddler to eat with a fork, turned to look in their direction.

"Keep your voice down," Charlotte warned.

"I can't. Did I tell you someone spit on me on the street the other day, a man, probably your age. He recognized me from pictures with you and he spit in my face and told me that we were what is wrong with this country."

"Why didn't you tell me?"

"You have other things to worry about. But there are days when I don't know why I'm doing this, or why you're doing this. I didn't expect it to be like this."

"Me neither."

When the food arrived they ate in silence, trading bites of salad and ice cream.

"I'm used to eating my feelings, but these are some of the more delicious feelings I've taken down." Charlotte attempted a joke. She just wanted Leila to smile once.

Leila pulled at a lock of hair that had escaped from one of the tortoiseshell combs she used to pin it back behind her ears. She straightened the curl and let go so that it bounced toward her cheek. When she finally spoke again, she'd regained a semblance of her typical determined and professional tone. "I know something. About Slaughter. I have something that can hurt him."

Charlotte scraped the remaining whipped cream from the side of the sundae glass. "Something I don't know about?"

"Yeah. I didn't mention it because it's one of those things that I heard and I was like, this isn't right. This isn't us. This isn't what we do. I want us to be the good guys."

"We *are* the good guys."

"It came from a friend from college. He's a producer on the local news in Pittsburgh. He got this tip during Slaughter's last campaign and they never did anything with it, so he told me about it now and I didn't mention it because it didn't seem like something we'd do, but now . . . my feeling is that we should use it."

Leila explained what she knew. Ted Slaughter's wife, Bonnie, had had an abortion about a decade ago, less than a year before she'd married Ted. The kid had been Slaughter's. It was an open secret that the two had had an affair well before his divorce was finalized. The doctor who performed the procedure wouldn't go on record, but this television producer friend of Leila's had secured confirmation on deep background from a nurse who worked in the clinic in the western suburbs of Pittsburgh. The woman claimed that Ted Slaughter paid for the abortion with a personal check.

"Why didn't they run with the story?" Charlotte asked, motioning to the waiter for their bill.

"My friend thinks Slaughter helped the network's executive producer get his daughter into Pittsburgh's most competitive private school."

Charlotte didn't need to think hard about it. "We can't do it."

But Leila had the crazed look of someone who wouldn't be easily dissuaded from seeking revenge. "Charlie, this isn't just because of what he called me. Ted Slaughter is an enemy of women. You know that. He says birth control is a luxury good. He calls C-sections preexisting conditions and says abortion should be illegal even in cases of rape and incest. He voted to defund Planned Parenthood at the national level. Clinics all over the country and the state have been shut down because of legislation he introduced. And he's a goddamned liar. He's a goddamned hypocrite and we can call him out on it."

Charlotte placed her hand on top of Leila's and told her she had every reason to want to do this before she told her why she couldn't. "It's not fair. Dragging his wife into this. What did she do to deserve to be attacked and humiliated?"

"She married an asshole, for a start," Leila persisted.

Charlotte sighed. "That's not her fault."

"This is an attack on him and his disgusting hypocrisy. He gets up there and hisses about family values and how life begins at conception and I'll bet he made her get rid of it because he knew he'd have to pay more in his divorce. He attacks me. He attacks you. He attacks women every single day. He deserves this and so much worse." She gave Charlotte a pointed look. "We both know that sometimes you have to get your hands dirty to protect yourself."

Charlotte turned and looked out the window for a second to ensure her voice stayed steady and assured. "We don't have proof it was his."

"Why do we need proof? Who has proof for anything anymore? They made up a story about you being pregnant! They call me a terrorist."

Charlotte would have called it opportunistic if anyone but Leila had suggested doing this, but that was the last thing she wanted to think about Leila. Instead, she thought about why she didn't want to do it. There was the fact that it was low, lower than anything they'd considered doing so far in this race. But she also understood why Bonnie Slaughter would want to keep her abortion a secret beyond the obvious reason that she was married to a man who made a career out of exploiting the pro-life right. The reason hit close to home. Charlotte hadn't lied to Josh during their first meeting more than a year earlier when she told him she'd never had an abortion. But what she hadn't said was that she'd been pregnant once before the twins. It had been in high school. The baby had been Jack's. She never told her high school boyfriend she was pregnant. Charlotte had watched a teenage pregnancy derail Kara and Paul's lives. She made the difficult decision on her own.

Pennsylvania required parental consent for a girl under eighteen to get an abortion. Charlotte told Marty Walsh about the pregnancy because telling her mentally ill mother wasn't an option.

This was the version of Marty she remembered best. Charlotte confessed to him in their old Buick after Marty picked her up from volleyball practice. A Peter Cetera song about knights and love and honor played on the radio. Empty cans of Keystone Light rolled over her sneakers in the footwell. "Don't be ashamed," her dad whispered in a tone that was sad, but not sorry. "This is the rest of your life we're talking about."

Marty smoked a pack of Camels a day. He reached into the glove compartment for a new pack, drew two from the foil, and handed the second one to Charlotte. "Don't tell your mother." Charlotte wasn't sure whether he meant the cigarette or the procedure. "You're gonna be a woman with a big life," her dad said, pulling the smoke into his lungs and wheezing on the word *life*. Marty booked an appointment at a clinic outside Philly because there wasn't one in Scranton. Then the pregnancy ended on its own a few days later. She estimated she was maybe eight weeks along, and what came out of her looked like nothing more than a large blood clot. It was Marty who held her while she cried. Together they felt sadness and relief and never spoke about it ever again. Sometimes she allowed herself the possibility that Marty Walsh could have been a feminist if he'd been born in a different time and a different place. The memory was somehow both terrible and beautiful for her.

Now she felt like she was letting Leila down. "Bonnie Slaughter is the one who will be attacked. If we do this, then I'm no better than him. We aren't releasing it."

Leila folded her arms across her chest.

"Let me talk to Josh about it."

This campaign had brought out the worst in both of them.

"This isn't who you are. And don't forget, I'm your boss, not Josh."

CHAPTER 14
August 10, 2018

88 days to Election Day

Walsh (D)	Slaughter (R)	Spread
43	41	Walsh +2

"A chatty old woman handed me a hand-crocheted baby blanket in the Rainbow grocery this morning." Max rooted under the couch for the remote control for the television. "It's the ugliest thing I've ever seen, but I didn't have the heart to tell her you're not pregnant, so I took it and gave it to Bob."

"It's remarkable the story has stuck around." Charlotte discovered the remote beneath a cushion and handed it to him. "Josh likes to say the press and public usually have the attention span of an autistic gnat." Most headlines—"headline porn," as Josh referred to it—lasted in people's news feeds for less than an hour before they were replaced by something that seemed more urgent but would be forgotten just as quickly. The pregnancy of a forty-seven-year-old woman stuck in people's minds like the lyrics to a car dealership jingle.

"He doesn't say that out loud, does he? About the autistic gnats."

"Not when they're within earshot."

Max rolled his eyes. "I don't know how you tolerate him."

"We're ahead in the polls," Charlotte said.

"Well, then, that's all that matters."

She noted the escalating derision in her husband's tone.

Max aimed the remote at the television, flipped through the channels, and landed on one of the late-night talk shows. He unfolded his long torso on the nubby beige carpet in their living room, crossing his ankle over his knee to stretch his hamstrings.

"Of course the polls matter." In the past few months, poll numbers had replaced caffeine as Charlotte's drug of choice and she fiended for new ones like a heroin addict in search of a clean hit. There was a time when she'd measured her self-worth by Humanity's stock price—now she measured it in approval ratings and point spreads.

Max rolled lazily onto his side and continued to channel surf. "Here we go again. I can't watch any more of these," he said to himself.

"No. Leave it." Charlotte backed toward the edge of the couch and sat down ungracefully. It was yet another attack ad from the Friends of Ted Slaughter. This ad opened on the skyline of San Francisco on a bright and sunny day. It cut to a drum circle of gutter punks, their matted dreadlocks covered in grime, smoking joints in front of the Golden Gate Bridge. One of them spoke: "We just love Charlotte Walsh. We can't wait to move to Pennsylvania when she wins." Next appeared a six-foot-tall black drag queen who gave a clichéd snap of her fingers and announced with a shimmy of her broad shoulders: "Charlotte Walsh told me I can use your bathroom." Then the camera panned to a group of young Latino workers wearing bright orange hard hats and red flannel shirts: "Charlotte Walsh is gonna get us jobs in Pennsylvania." Next in the queue came two well-dressed women standing in front of Philadelphia's Independence Hall. "Did you know California is the only state in the country that allows you to choose between three genders on your driver's license?" one woman asked the other. The second lady affected a horrified openmouthed gasp. "What does that even mean?" In a confusing but explosive ending, two self-driving cars crashed head-on into each other beneath the ominous voice-over: "Charlotte Walsh will bring the worst of San Francisco to Pennsylvania."

"What self-respecting drag queen would agree to be in that ad?" Max grunted and thumbed the remote to switch off the television.

Charlotte picked up the phone to call Josh without responding to her husband. He answered on the first ring and she didn't bother with a hello. "This latest ad is the most bizarre one yet." She could hear Josh light a cigarette before he answered.

"Oh, I don't know. It does a good job of playing to rural xenophobia. It's been viewed about ten thousand times on YouTube so far. We should have your new ads ready by next week. I'm particularly fond of 'Ted Slaughter Wants to Kill Your Grandma.' "

Charlotte watched Max narrow his eyes, which should have stopped her from laughing out loud, but it didn't. "That's rich."

"I'm only half kidding. Slaughter cut Medicare for two million senior citizens in Pennsylvania when he voted on the latest health care bill. He quite literally is killing grandmothers. Don't worry. It's done in really good taste." Josh paused. "Better taste than 'Charlotte Walsh Wants a Drag Queen to Piss in Your Toilet.' "

She laughed again.

"Max wonders what self-respecting drag queen would agree to be in that video."

"Size-thirteen Jimmy Choos don't pay for themselves."

Before she could finish chuckling, Max stood and walked upstairs.

Her husband returned once she had hung up the phone and opened her computer to continue working. He sat next to her on the couch and opened his own laptop.

He finally spoke. "How's your boyfriend doing?"

"Excuse me?"

"Boy Wonder. Your new bestie. The first person you talk to when you wake up in the morning and the last person you gossip with before you go to bed."

Are you kidding me? What about your new little girlfriend? What about Abby? For the most part she'd pushed Abby and her adorable text messages out of her head. If she didn't pack away the memory it would linger, like the smell of days-old fish. And besides, she'd been able to forget much worse. Now Charlotte bit down hard on her tongue before she responded and allowed the pain to calm her.

"He's my campaign manager, Max."

"It was a joke. Can't I joke, too, or do you only laugh at Josh's jokes?"

"Stop it. You're acting like a child."

"Whatever, boss."

They sat next to each other for the next thirty minutes, pecking away at their keyboards. Charlotte briefly wondered what Max was working on or reading, or who he was talking to and glanced at his screen, but it was tilted in such a way that she couldn't make anything out.

Max spoke next. "I booked my tickets to California to run the Big Sur Half and go to the ePay Q3 board meeting." After more than a decade of marriage it still surprised her how easy it was to move between irritation and the mundane without acknowledgment.

"I'm leaving Monday like we talked about. We have a ton of miles. I can get free seats for the twins."

"You're taking the girls?" She'd known he was taking this trip, had even planned to come out and meet him a week later. It had been discussed and decided and yet she felt a nagging insistence now to say something she knew she would regret.

The words tumbled out of her mouth before she could stop them. "Won't it be hard to meet your girlfriend with your daughters with you?"

A look of genuine confusion flickered across Max's face. "Huh? What girlfriend? Are you talking about Margaret again? Seriously? We've been through this. She works halfway across the world now. I haven't spoken to her in almost two years."

Why not pretend she did mean Margaret, apologize for dredging up the past, and end this conversation? Max would go to sleep in the basement and she'd spend the rest of the night working. But something in her subconscious had committed to the momentum of this argument, to finally asking Max about the mysterious Abby.

"I'm talking about Abby. You're meeting Abby in California, aren't you?"

There it was. There would be no going back after this.

Max scratched his head. "Abby?"

"Yeah. Abby."

Realization crinkled the corners of his eyes.

"I—" Charlotte started and then looked away and out the window at the headlights on the turnpike down below the ridge. The remaining trees between the house and the freeway were all second growth. The original forest had been sheared during the road's construction. These new trees were thin and weak and the car headlights were strong enough to cast shadows on their walls. In the brief silence that followed, she steeled herself for a confession, to learn that her husband had betrayed her again.

"I saw her texts."

"Her texts?"

Charlotte repeated them from memory in a high-pitched childish California-girl twang. "'I miss your face.' . . . 'Did you tell C. about me?' . . . 'We'll have some fun.'"

"You fucking went through my phone? What the hell did I do now to make you not trust me? What the hell do you think you know?"

They were living a rerun, and even though she was beginning to doubt what she had been accusing him of, she already knew her line. "I know everything."

Max stood and placed both his hands on her shoulders. She squared her body to him and tilted her chin up the slight bit necessary to meet his eyes as he defended himself. "Okay. If you know everything, then you know that I helped Abby get a job with Travis at ePay. You know that I think she's a brilliant engineer with a bright future and it makes me feel good to be able to help kids like that, especially young women. You know she wants to thank me by having me over for dinner with her and her girlfriend, her *live-in girlfriend*," he emphasized. "They want me over when I'm back in the Bay Area. You know that she wanted to have you come to dinner, too, but I told her you were probably too busy, because you're always too busy, and I didn't want to bother you."

At first it didn't make any sense, not when she'd constructed a completely different narrative in her mind for months.

Max helped Abby get a job.

Abby has a girlfriend.

I was wrong. I was wrong. I was wrong.

Her husband let go of her with a disgusted sigh and bent down to pick his phone up from the floor. He handed it to her. "Go through it again. New password is your birthday backward. Look at whatever you want. This campaign has made you paranoid that everyone is out to get you now, but I'm not. I'm one of the only people who still has your back."

She wanted him to keep screaming at her then, because she deserved to be screamed at. Instead he sat down and hung his head, touching his chin to his chest, his voice a whisper. "Charlie, Charlie, Charlie." He said her name in a crescendo he meant to soothe himself. "I've done all the things you've asked. Haven't I?" Max turned his palms toward the ceiling in surrender. "I don't know what else I can do." His voice had an unfamiliar pleading tone, a desperation that cut Charlotte.

Charlotte sat next to him but didn't touch him and didn't speak, because speaking would require admitting she was wrong and she wasn't ready to do that even if it sickened her that she'd been so far off base. She felt more tired than she had five minutes before, or maybe ever. Their marriage wasn't improving. Somehow things had gotten so much worse in the past six months. She supposed she shouldn't have been surprised, but she was.

"Take the twins, but leave the baby with me," Charlotte insisted. "I'll meet you later in the week. I'm sorry. I know this is hard. Sometimes it does all feel like a bad dream, like a nightmare even. But it's temporary. The campaign won't last forever." Her words felt flimsy and small.

A muffled cry came from down the hall. Annie had woken up and needed help getting back to sleep, a glass of water, a hug, assurance a dragon wasn't hiding in her closet. Max made his way to the stairs and didn't look back at her as he mumbled. "But it's not a nightmare. Because the good thing about nightmares is that they eventually end. This is our life, Charlotte, and we're miserable. We can't keep going like this." The familiar anxiety crept into her stomach. *What is the alternative?*

Since becoming a mother, Charlotte had never experienced life with just one kid. The bright side of Max's journey to the West Coast with the twins was getting to know Annie as an only child, one who basked in the singular attention of her mom. The relative quiet of their home on the first night Max and the twins were gone was deafening. Being without her husband felt okay, normal even. Still, being without two of her daughters caused her entire body to ache.

Leila organized a steady stream of babysitters for Annie and they brought her along to events when it was appropriate. She particularly enjoyed a visit to an alpaca farm in Lower Milford, where Charlotte met with artisan yarn makers and took in a felting demonstration. The week went by in a blur. Rubber-chicken dinners in Philly, fundraiser at the art museum, pancake breakfast in DelCo, registration event at the YWCA in Reading where too many people thought registering to vote was the same as actually voting, retirement home talent show in West Chester, ribbon cutting at a car dealership, another tractor ride at another small-town carnival.

The places changed and the words stayed mostly the same. It was the constant repetition that wore Charlotte down the fastest. Every day at Humanity had been different, had brought on some new challenge—one day she'd be negotiating a deal with the CEO of

Apple, the next she'd be arguing with the Chinese government about digital protectionism, a week later she'd be brainstorming with the founders about where Humanity fit in the Internet of Things. Each day on the campaign trail was like a scene from *Groundhog Day*—the same stock speeches, the same requests for cash, the same smile for every photo op. Even her best days on the trail felt like running in place.

Charlotte left Annie at home while she went to visit St. Mary's Hospital near Altoona to hold babies addicted to opioids one morning. That's what it actually said on the schedule:

9 *a.m.*—CW *to hold babies addicted to opioids_limited press_ video*

Her original plan had been to give a speech on the multiplier effect the opioid crisis was having on the Pennsylvania economy. She'd stayed up for three nights reading an in-depth analysis prepared for her by the chair of the Harvard economics department on the billions lost in productivity to the overprescription and subsequent abuse of the drugs and prepared what she considered to be her most significant policy speech yet. It was Josh who nixed the idea and told her all those facts and figures were too hard to turn into a sound bite.

"More voters will watch a video of you soothing a drug-addicted baby. Good optics. Great for sharing. Unless, of course, you want to talk about your mom—suicide by opioids?"

Charlotte turned away from him then. "Let's go to the hospital."

Cradling the screaming, twitchy, crimson-cheeked, too-tiny newborns in her arms reminded her of Annie's first weeks in the NICU. This ward for babies born dependent on drugs was new, due to the tripling of cases in the past two years. It looked like something out of a science fiction movie, the whole space taken up with glass incubators with barely any room to walk. A handful of mothers, many of them still strung out and broken, stared through mesh-caged windows with vacant expressions.

Real tears streamed down Charlotte's cheeks while a local television news crew caught it all on tape. The feet of a little boy named Kevin, no bigger than her thumb, shook uncontrollably. She tried her best to hold them tightly in her hand. It always worked to soothe Annie; maybe it would soothe him. *I'm sorry, baby. You deserve better than a photo op.* Leila rubbed her back as she touched up her mascara in the harsh light of the hospital bathroom. "I think you should have given the speech. Who cares if anyone picked it up? It was a good speech. It was a smart speech."

Before the sun set Charlotte drove another couple hundred miles, raised a few hundred thousand at a young professionals' happy hour, and posed for a picture with the largest pig in the state. *I'll do anything to seem likable.*

"It was a great shot. Perfect optics," Josh said.

Charlotte didn't mask her disgust. "Because that's what poor white people really need. A photo of me clutching an overfed swine."

He shrugged. "They'll all share it on Facebook."

★

With the exception of downtown San Francisco, where the fog creeps into your bones and turns everything gray, Charlotte was quickly reminded when she stepped out of the airport that the world appeared brighter in California than it did in Pennsylvania, as if life on the West Coast were crisper, more alive, more like an Instagrammed photo with the perfect filter.

Charlotte felt like she'd been away from her children for months instead of just over a week. The five of them had FaceTimed every night they were gone, the twins always eager to recount every detail of their days. Max sat with them but rarely spoke, and Charlotte didn't know what to expect from him when he picked her and Annie up.

Her phone had died on the plane. It was the longest stretch she'd been away from the Internet in months. She'd forgotten to pack the plug portion of the charger and she itched to get online but stopped herself from asking Max for his phone when he greeted her with a full and surprising kiss on the lips in the parking lot of SFO. It was an extravagant kiss, the kind of kiss that only happens when you leave a person. Before she could put up her guard she parted her mouth slightly, feeling the tip of his tongue as she leaned her body into his. He pressed his forehead briefly into hers and squeezed the soft part of her hip. She didn't squirm. She wanted to remember this simple welcome, this perfect kiss.

"Ewwwww," Ella groaned. "Grossness. Kissyface! Ewwy!"

"Doesn't it feel nice to be home?" Max said, breaking the spell of his greeting. She stopped herself from telling him that California wasn't their home anymore. At least, California didn't feel like her home anymore. His forehead and nose were sunburned and peeling, the skin around his eyes pale, making him look like a raccoon in reverse. He looked well rested, healthy, and happy.

"I just got here. How was the race yesterday?" It had gone well, she knew, because he'd posted pictures to Facebook of his early-morning half marathon over the Big Sur bridge, through the redwood forest, past Nepenthe, one of their favorite restaurants with a view of whitewashed cliffs and the indigo waves of the Pacific. He hadn't texted any of them to her.

"My best time yet. I'm gonna kill this Ironman, Charlie. Just wait. Want In-N-Out? Animal style? Half-cooked fries." Her stomach grumbled at the mention of fast food.

Once they'd settled into the red vinyl booth, the Formica table covered over in greasy buns and too many petite paper containers of ketchup and mustard, the twins burst into fluttery chatter, filling Charlotte and Annie in on every detail since they'd been separated.

Max brought up the campaign before she did.

"Crazy about Bonnie Slaughter, huh?"

Her ears burned and her mind spun like a top. The fries did a double flip in her stomach. "What about her?" She didn't need to grab Max's phone to know what he meant, but she stretched her hand out for it anyway. He handed it over reluctantly.

There it was. The number one story on CNN: "Pro-Life Senator's Wife Had Secret Abortion."

"Shit."

"Charlie?"

Charlotte could see Max's pleasant mood of the past hour evaporate.

"I need to make a call."

Max rolled his eyes toward the ceiling. "Sorry I brought it up."

Her fingers twitched with every second that went by without calling Leila. "It'll be fast. I promise."

"It's never fast. Can we get home first? I want to make it to a barbecue at Travis's place this afternoon. They've got a bouncy castle and a magician. The girls want to go."

"Will Lucinda be there?" Charlotte asked.

"Travis has a new girl." Max waved his hand as casually as if a new girl were a new laptop. "Divorce was final last month. Lucinda's shacked up with some scientist or archaeologist who works at the Academy of Science. The girls want to go to the party. Can you cobble together a war room at our house and I'll take them over there by myself?" His warm greeting now long forgotten, Max looked desperate to get away from her.

Be calm. Let him win. Do what you need to do to get to a computer and a phone and deal with this. She adjusted her tone.

"Let's get home and I'll make my calls from there. I'll meet you later."

★

Their sparse modern house, all blond wood, sharp angles, gleaming steel, and spotless glass, had the feeling of a posh hotel after living in her parents' rundown place for nearly a year. Walking through the open kitchen with its eight-burner Wolf range and farmhouse sink as big as a bathtub, Charlotte felt embarrassed by how much they'd spent on this house and everything in it. Their home, which had once been featured in the "Tech Titan" issue of *Architectural Digest*, was too big, too fancy, too expensive—five million when they bought it and now worth nine, a not-so-subtle reminder of how easy it was for the rich to get richer. Their dining room table cost more than her father used to make in a year. A wall of windows overlooked rolling golden-brown hills. Olive trees dotted the top of the far ridge, and beyond that grapevines, mostly pinot noir and some cabernet. *Why did you leave this? Because it didn't feel real.* Max liked sleek things, new things. Walking through it, she felt like she was trespassing in someone else's home. Right now it was far too neat for her husband and two five-year-olds to have spent the week here. He must have hired someone to come clean this morning.

She was able to dial Leila's number from memory from their house phone while her cell charged.

Charlotte gulped. "Why'd you do it?" In some ways, the weight of Leila's current betrayal felt worse than Max's so many years ago.

Silence crushed her. The custom-designed bamboo blinds in Charlotte's living room quivered in the soft breeze drifting over the hills from the sea just a few miles away. She could see the digital thermometer outside the window, a perfect seventy-two degrees. It was nearly always a perfect seventy-two degrees in this valley.

"Charlie . . ." Leila stuttered. "Yes. I may have told Josh about it last week. I just . . ." she began again and faltered. "I just mentioned it. Floated it in passing." Leila said the same thing three different ways, possibly in the hopes that it would be taken differently each time.

"After I told you not to." Charlotte hated that she'd taken on the same tone she used when she reprimanded her daughters.

"I wanted his opinion."

Charlotte repeated herself. "After I told you not to."

"Josh said there are some things you're better off not knowing. He said it's better if you're able to tell the truth about whether we leaked this."

"So you lied to me."

"I never technically lied to you. I did it to protect you."

It wasn't the first time Charlotte recognized the lack of control she had over how her senior staff managed this campaign. Josh was often her brain, and her staff was her nervous system. Many days she felt like just a mouth.

Part of her expected Leila to beg her for forgiveness. Part of her wanted that. But the voice on the other end of the line only grew more resolute.

"I did what I thought was right. Look at the conversation this started. He's finally getting called out on years of hypocrisy."

Why couldn't Leila see that wasn't the point? That it didn't justify going behind her back, directly disobeying her, doing something she should have immediately recognized was wrong.

Charlotte slumped down as far as their stiff mid-century Scandinavian couch would allow her to slump. She straightened her legs and pushed the ottoman away so that just her heels were touching it.

"It's not personal, Charlie. It's politics."

"Don't quote Josh to me. Don't do that."

The line went silent. Charlotte's phone beeped with another call. Since she was calling from the house phone she had no way of knowing who was on the other line without getting up and walking to the receiver in the kitchen, but she knew without looking that it was Josh.

When Leila spoke her voice took on a frightening blankness. "Do you want me to resign? I'll resign if that's what you want." Charlotte pictured her back in the office, her features settled into a defiant look.

She wanted to tell her no, to tell her that she couldn't imagine doing this or any job without her support, to say that she attributed much of her success as both an executive and as a mom to Leila simplifying what should have been an incredibly complicated life.

"I don't know. I need to think about it."

The phone beeped again. When she didn't pick it up the second time, her cell began ringing from the other room. "I have to go. We aren't done talking about this."

Leila hung up without responding.

Charlotte didn't bother with pleasantries when she picked up her cell. "What the hell, Josh?"

"Don't be mad at Leila."

"Don't tell me what to do." *Mad* wasn't the right word, anyway.

"I can't tell you enough times not to let these things get to you. I need you to let the news cycle have its way with this. It's a Sunday. You're with your family in California. Come back Tuesday and we'll start from there. This is good for you, Charlotte. Takes some of the pressure off. It will definitely get those Bible-thumping protesters out of your hair. No one will ask you if you're pregnant anymore. Slaughter's campaign is spinning."

There wasn't much else to say to Josh right then, so she cut the call short. After she hung up the phone, Charlotte read every story she could find about Bonnie Slaughter. With few exceptions, the photographs that accompanied the story were ancient, probably fifteen years old. Bonnie had been a different woman then. Today's Bonnie favored Eileen Fisher twinsets, pink oxfords, and sensibly low heels. But the old Bonnie, the twentysomething who'd worked as a fundraiser for Slaughter back when he was already a sexagenarian married father of six, favored tight black pencil skirts, low-cut blouses, and stilletos. She was beautiful, the kind of woman who looked like she smelled incredible, like something spicy laced with vanilla and clove cigarette smoke. Charlotte imagined photo editors combing the archives for a picture that looked like she was "the kind of woman who would have an abortion."

Ted Slaughter denied any knowledge of his wife's "procedure." He always used the word *procedure* and reinforced his pro-life platform. "This is so petty. I remain committed to the belief that life begins at conception and must be protected by the good men and women in our government," Slaughter said. "We've discussed the matter with our pastor, and Bonnie has sought to rectify the wrongs she committed through prayer and service to other women."

Slaughter's team pivoted quickly and used the story as an opportunity for fundraising, sending an email to supporters begging for funds to shut down the evil machine at work against him.

"Together we can stand up to the forces of evil that are attacking the good and honest values of Pennsylvania's hardworking citizens," the email read. "Take a stand by donating to our campaign today."

Progressive pundits on MSNBC came right out and speculated the child was Ted Slaughter's. Both the *Times* and the *Post* ran op-eds pointing out the Slaughter family's intense hypocrisy on women's issues. *Bustle* accused Slaughter of slut-shaming his own wife. Conservative talking heads attacked Bonnie and turned Ted into the victim of a wanton woman who'd hidden her dirty past. There was video of the Slaughter family going to church—Bonnie wearing a conservative khaki shirtdress and taupe heels, striding into the building with one of her step-grandchildren strapped to her chest in a sling, holding the hands of two of her own girls, using the children as shields to keep the press at bay, a tactic Charlotte knew all too well. In one photograph Bonnie crossed her Pilates-toned legs and glared at her husband as he stared ahead at the pastor. Charlotte imagined a thought bubble suspended over her head bearing the words *You fucking owe me*.

It was nearly 4 p.m. before Charlotte could tear herself away from the computer and the relentless comments on every story branding Bonnie a liar, a traitor, a whore . . . and sometimes, a hero.

★

The party should have been winding down by the time Charlotte arrived at Travis's house, but one of the ePay executives began mixing mai tais that gave everyone a second wind and Travis paid the bouncy castle rental guy another grand in cash to stick around for a couple of hours to keep the kids out of their hair.

Charlotte exchanged the requisite air kisses with the women and stiff hugs with the men as she searched the palatial grounds of the estate for Max. Everyone at this party had just the right amount of color—not a tan, just a healthy glow. They were properly fit. Being fat in Silicon Valley was considered far worse than being addicted to cocaine or abusing a dog. She weaved through a sea of khaki and earth tones, flowing skirts, ironic straw gardening hats, and large statement jewelry made with unvarnished wood—outfits meant to convey a sense of simplicity, ease, and lack of attention to flashy things, despite costing what most Americans paid in rent.

This group of their friends and acquaintances was populated with imperfect marriages and arrangements that no one would dare criticize as absurd or abnormal for fear of not seeming open-minded. Just past the bar Charlotte spied David and Tess Gallagher, a Facebooker and a Googler, respectively, who had been separated for two years and yet continued to live under the same roof so they could successfully coparent their triplets while Tess had a serious relationship with a cardiac surgeon named Jill.

Roasting artisanal s'mores over the fire pit was multi-time entrepreneur Astrid Andrews, who'd once been Andrew Andrews before transitioning last spring with the full support of his wife, Anne, who worked in the biz dev department of Humanity. Mike and Sara Matthews had an open marriage and couldn't stop talking about it after they'd had two glasses of wine. Sara was a brassy blonde, a head taller than her petite Asian husband, an ear, nose, and throat doctor who exclusively wore scrubs or too-short running shorts to most occasions. They called their arrangement monagamish, which sounded like emotionally immature verbal vomit to Charlotte after *she'd* had two glasses of wine.

Bits and pieces of conversations wafted through the air, talk of graceful exits, cryptocurrencies, and unicorns. They all blazed with the certainty that technology and money would save the world. She caught a snippet of an exchange about whether a billion-dollar investment in technology to extend human life would pay dividends in the next ten years. This crowd talked about how to solve death while her neighbors in Elk Hollow talked about how to pay a single medical bill. Only wildly rich people, the kind of people who knew they could order room service every day for the rest of their lives, believed life was too short.

Two men standing at the bar spoke loudly and joyfully about whether they should buy land in Wyoming or Idaho, something "off the grid," in preparation for the end of the civilized world. A certain breed of Silicon Valley man fancied himself a rugged survivalist.

Charlotte briefly calculated how much money her campaign had raised from the guests at this party, at least three million. They called themselves angel investors in her campaign and she didn't bother to correct them that they wouldn't be seeing a cash money return. They probably knew that, they were smart people, but they enjoyed the opportunity to say "angel investor." It sounded beatific. These were the new rulers of the free world, the ones who made change happen. And right now the people who shaped the universe were drunk on organic mai tais.

Travis snuck up behind her carrying a large pink drink perfectly rimmed with sharp red rock salt. Travis was keenly aware he wasn't a handsome man and overcompensated for the deficiency with his imposing vitality. He'd practically pioneered the lunchtime workout blast where he led a group of employees, mostly male, on twenty-mile bike rides three times a week through the hills of Menlo Park. He dropped a lei of live orchids around her neck. "Charlotte! How's life in Ohio treating you? Is it as dismal as Max lets on?" She noticed pity in his eyes. What had Max said to him? That life with her was dismal? That their marriage was dismal? *Smile Charlotte. Keep smiling.* Her cheeks trembled.

"It's Pennsylvania, actually. The campaign's great. It's been an amazing experience." A petite Asian girl, no older than twenty-five and wearing an ensemble that looked like men's pajamas, slinked behind Travis and placed her arm around his waist.

"What I want to know is, what happens if you win? Do you really have to live in Pennsylvania, or do you go to DC? I can't stand DC myself. I go wheels up for a day or so on my PJ and then I'm out." It had been more than half a year since she'd heard someone refer to a private jet as a PJ and it was an abbreviation she hadn't missed.

The last thing she wanted to do was explain their postelection living arrangements. "The plan is to split time between DC and Pennsylvania when I'm elected. That's usually how the Senate works."

"Whoa boy. Poor Max. I'll have to find reasons to let him come out here for a break. Great to have him on the board now. We're launching a bunch of new AI initiatives, smart programming that anticipates how you want to spend your money; then we help you spend all that money . . . with your face," Travis said with the kind of smirk only rich or handsome men could get away with. When he paused in anticipation of her laughter she provided the obligatory titter necessary to facilitate a swift exit.

"Have you met Coco yet?" He gestured toward the Asian girl with his cocktail, a few drops splashing down the front of his shirt.

"Hey." Coco jutted a pointy chin in Charlotte's general direction and blinked rapidly behind thick, clear-rimmed glasses. "I read a kick-ass post about you on Pussy Power. Keep it up, girlfriend. I'm obsessed with Max's idea for the new app."

Max and Travis were the kind of men who wrote a dozen new app and start-up ideas on napkins during breakfast. "Which new app?"

"The one that will let people seamlessly donate to candidates through ePay," Travis said. "I think I can roll it out in the next month. Might be useful for you."

Charlotte knew nothing about it.

"I think it's really going to change the way people do democracy."

Do I tell him democracy isn't really a thing you do?

She patted his shoulder and pretended she knew all about the fruits of her husband's creativity. "So do I. Do you know where Max is? I haven't seen him yet."

"He's with Abby by the pool." Travis slapped her on the back like she was a fellow bro. "Good to see you, Charlotte. You've got my vote. I gave Max another check for you. A big one." *You can't vote for me from California, asshole, but I will take your money.*

"Vote early and often, Trav." Charlotte took off for the other side of the pool, where Max stood with three twentysomething girls, maybe half a football field of drought-resistant plants and well-manicured stone paths away. Their heads were close together, one woman's hand on his arm. She wore a Mexican sundress covered in embroidered flowers, probably picked up on a whim during a weekend in Sayulita, paired with worn brown leather huarache sandals.

One of the other young women exclaimed enthusiastically about something with her hands, her gestures almost spastic. Charlotte couldn't remember how long it had been since Max had been able to hold her in that kind of thrall with his idle chatter.

Max caught her eye before she could round the pool.

"Oh, Charlie, get over here!" he said. He was drunk, his legs slightly splayed like those of a man relaxed and completely at ease in a thirty-million-dollar home. "I want you to meet Abby."

Before she knew what was happening, the girl in the sundress wrapped her in an overly enthusiastic hug. Thick Buddhist prayer beads on her wrist rubbed against Charlotte's shoulder blades. As Charlotte stepped away, startled by the affection, she could see Abby's eyes were a little soft, her face slack from the mai tais.

"I'm so indebted to Max and you for supporting me. Thank you, thank you, thank you." Charlotte plucked the drink from Max's hand and licked the salt from the rim.

"I'm glad Max could help."

"This is my girlfriend, Tess, and my sister Jeannine. Jeannine's visiting us from Omaha." Abby and Tess were so squeaky-clean and sweet they looked like they should be starring in a tampon commercial. Jeannine was something else entirely—tattooed up and down her thin, taut arms. She had black hair that looked as though it hadn't been washed in several days. Her elbow was linked through Max's in a casual way. Jeannine was the kind of woman Max fantasized about, the kind he watched in Internet porn Charlotte had once found on his computer. In short video clips these pale, angry, snarling women had bushy pubic hair and gave the finger to the camera while using the other hand to pleasure themselves. Long ago Charlotte had let it worry her, had spent too much time wondering what it meant that her husband fetishized women who looked nothing like her.

Shortly after discovering the videos and a website called Inked Vixens bookmarked on Max's laptop, Charlotte had gotten a tiny tattoo. She'd done it in Amsterdam during a conference for developers where she'd delivered a keynote speech on the future of cloud collaboration to a standing ovation. Max took her for dinner and absinthe and a stroll along the canals that culminated in the red-light district where bored women leaned inside windows advertising their bodies for sale, their C-section scars reflecting the fluorescent light.

Charlotte pulled Max into a well-lit tattoo parlor and asked for a small hummingbird on the convex ridge of her right shoulder blade. "Hummingbird" was one of Max's many nicknames for her. "Because your heart beats faster than other people's." It hurt like hell, a youthful indiscretion at age forty. He told her it was the sexiest thing he'd ever seen.

"What do you do in Omaha, Jeannine?"

When Jeannine smiled she showed a gap between her two front teeth, her face softened, and she became pretty. "I work in an animal shelter. I'm a vet. Mostly spaying and neutering. I read your book. Twice, actually. I underlined almost everything you said."

The muscles in Charlotte's shoulder blades and back of her neck twitched then and she had the distinct feeling she was being watched.

"Thank you. That's so kind of you." Her phone buzzed with a text message.

"Charlie's always on call." Max winked. "She's very important, you know."

Abby rolled her eyes to mock Max and not Charlotte. "Everyone knows that, Max. Charlotte's the real deal."

She pulled the phone from her pocket to see the screen. It was Leila: *I will draft a resignation letter tonight.*

The words stung like a slap across the face. Max must have noticed a change in her demeanor, because he reached over to touch her shoulder. Tears welled in her eyes as she met Max's gaze and hoped he would understand she was telling him she needed him to get the girls and come home with her now. Right now. She wanted desperately to call Leila back then, but needed to get control of herself before they spoke again.

She gave a polite nod to Abby, Tess, and Jeannine and turned to look back toward the house. Hot, fat tears rolled down her cheeks. She swiped them angrily and noticed a blond girl standing strangely among the flowers taking a selfie. She wore jeans, a sweater, and black high-heeled boots and looked both familiar and vaguely out of place.

Charlotte walked back toward the house. Ahead of her Travis waved his arms in the air as he attempted to rap to an old-school Snoop Dogg song about smoking dope in your mother's basement.

Nearing the porch, she came face-to-face with the blond girl with the black boots. Even in the dim light it was easy to make out the birthmark in the shape of Florida running down the girl's jawline.

She was one of Ted Slaughter's trackers.

At first Charlotte wondered how she had gotten in, but it was a ridiculous thing to question. It wasn't like Travis had a guard checking off names from a list at the door. This girl had walked into the party just like anyone else. But how long had she been following her, watching her, watching Max, watching her daughters?

Max kept chastising her for her paranoia, but this proved it had been warranted. Here was an actual person stalking her, a person paid to search for ways to harm her.

The tracker hadn't been taking a selfie at all. She'd been taking photographs of Charlotte's husband. The girl with the oddly shaped birthmark held her gaze now and smiled at the tracks of tears that stained Charlotte's cheeks.

In the morning, Charlotte missed Josh's first call and then his second. She let the phone vibrate and stared at a stack of books on her nightstand, all of them fondly selected by Leila almost a year ago and each bearing a yellow Post-it note scrawled in her girlish hand about why Charlotte might enjoy a particular tome.

Kurt Vonnegut, <u>Cat's Cradle</u> – Interesting take on the dehumanizing aspects of technology

Naomi Alderman, <u>The Power</u> – An alternate reality where women rule. Obama loves this one.

Kirsten Gillibrand, <u>Off the Sidelines: Speak Up, Be Fierce, and Change Your World</u> – A taste of what you're getting into

Ron Chernow's <u>Grant</u> – Importance of being farsighted in politics

Nora Ephron, <u>I Feel Bad About My Neck</u> – Because you need a laugh and I know you feel bad about your neck

Charlotte blinked away another set of tears and took the phone into the bathroom to avoid waking Max.

She sank down onto the floor and leaned the base of her skull against the lip of their sleek granite bath. "I told you I was taking today off."

"There are no days off. We have a situation." It was nine in the morning on the East Coast and Josh would have finished at least three coffees by now. Charlotte longed for just one.

"A situation worse than you going behind my back and leaking a story I didn't want leaked?"

"Check your email." Josh released a long sigh that sounded like someone letting the air out of a balloon.

"Hold on." She clicked on his first email and then to a link to a story on PennPolitics.com to find a headline declaring "Senate Candidate's Open Marriage."

The story was accompanied by a series of photographs of Max talking and giggling with Abby, Tess, and Jeannine as Charlotte stood off to the side, a faraway look in her eyes, an accommodating half smile bending her lips. In the final picture she looked into the camera with tears tumbling down her cheeks. A "source" told the reporter that according to friends of the couple from Silicon Valley, Max and Charlotte had had an arrangement for years. "Charlotte and Max both regularly date other people. It's a very California thing."

"Now we know why whatsherface was at the party last night."

As soon as Charlotte had spied the Slaughter staffer at Travis's place she'd called Josh. Travis had politely asked the girl to leave. Until this moment, she couldn't have imagined why Slaughter would waste the resources to have someone follow her to a neighborhood picnic.

"They've been tailing Max since he flew out of Philly. This, though? This is a quick-and-dirty retribution for Bonnie," Josh said. "I'm sorry. I should have seen something like this coming."

It was the first time he'd apologized for anything. Two voices competed in Charlotte's head: *The work you will do in office once you win this race will be more important than the humiliation you feel in this moment.* The other said, *Quit now. This will only get worse.*

She scrolled down. There were more pictures taken from Max's Instagram—her husband grinning at the finish line of the Big Sur race surrounded by a gang of fellow female runners holding their medals aloft. The article read like something out of a cheap tabloid, the kind found at airports and supermarket checkouts: poor grammar, salacious speculation, unnamed sources, and tangential conclusions. "Max Tanner and Charlotte Walsh took a time-out from their marriage while Tanner was running a race in Big Sur this weekend. 'Tanner is well known to have many close running partners out on the West Coast,'" a source said. "'The arrangement that the pair of Humanity executives have is unconventional but it works for them,'" another close friend revealed. "It's the kind of thing you see all the time in San Francisco and Silicon Valley." Listening to Josh read the article out loud felt like watching a car crash in progress.

One day my kids will read this. What have I done to invite these dangers into our lives? Don't fool yourself, bitch. You've done plenty.

"I'll deal with this, Charlie." Josh's voice was kind. "Spend the day with your family. Pretend it's a day off."

"There are no days off, right?"

"Just pretend." Josh hung up the phone.

Her anger wasn't going to dissipate on its own and it needed a target. Unfortunately for Max, he was the closest warm body over the age of six in the house. Charlotte ripped the covers off her husband.

"Why did you have to be so goddamned friendly with those girls at the party? Why'd you have to get all flirty with those women at the race?"

He reached out to yank the comforter back over his chest.

"Good morning to you, too, darling wife. What the hell, Charlie? What's gotten into you?"

Charlotte paced the room, her left hand rubbing forcefully at her eye as if trying to wipe something painful away. She leaned back into their dresser. "PennPolitics is reporting that we have an open marriage. There are pictures of you flirting with those girls."

Just then, Ella shouted from the bottom of the stairs, "Mommy, are you up there?"

Charlotte changed her tone to the tinkling yoga instructor's cadence she used with their children. "What do you need, sweetie?"

"I think the milk tastes weird and I can't reach the cereal." The child's tone wobbled, revealing her to be on the verge of a tantrum.

"Give me one second and I'll come make you something yummy. Don't touch the milk, Elly-belly. I'll be right there."

"Don't take your campaign shit out on me." Max swung his legs over the side of the bed and stood as close to her as possible without touching her. "I don't deserve it, Charlie. I really don't." He opened their closet, a space the size of their bedroom in Elk Hollow, to search for his sneakers.

"I've been thinking we should go see Carol while we're here," Max said as he grabbed a pair of yellow shoes and began lacing them. Carol was their therapist, the woman responsible for reconstructing the shattered pieces of their marriage in the months after Max's affair. They had met with Carol twice a week for four months, and by the end of it Charlotte had been ready to let Max come back to sleep in their bed on a regular basis even though she never completely stopped feeling resentful. Carol kept telling her that the burden wasn't on Charlotte to punish or sanction Max. She only needed to forgive him. She'd carried that notion around with her every day since. Charlotte couldn't stand the kind of people who lived by inspirational quotes. Still, she'd written one line from Desmond Tutu on a piece of paper and repeated it silently to herself most days last year: "Forgiveness is the grace by which you enable the other person to get up, and get up with dignity, to begin anew."

Carol had saved their marriage once. Maybe they needed her again.

Max stared through her. She could hear what he wanted to say. *Quit this campaign. I want my life back.* "I don't know what else to do. We're already out here. Let's just go talk to her."

She had exhausted him. They had exhausted each other.

★

The therapist told them they could come the next morning. She had an early cancellation that would still allow Charlotte to take an afternoon flight back to Pennsylvania. In the meantime, Charlotte played ponies with her daughters and avoided the Internet.

"How's my favorite power couple?" Carol boomed when they walked into her office, her voice rising and falling on each of the consonants. She probably said that to all her patients.

Carol's office wasn't far from Humanity headquarters, which meant the therapist made a tidy fortune off counseling tech industry power couples, people swimming in privilege, whose individual operating systems no longer synced. She worked out of a small converted barn behind her home. "It used to have chickens," she explained the first time they settled onto her overstuffed purple velvet couch. "Took ages to get rid of the smell." In their first appointment she'd told them that she'd seen it all, personal dramas that wouldn't be believable if written into a Hollywood movie—a wife who burned down her marital bed with her husband in it, a husband who faked his own death for the insurance policy when he didn't get the Series A round for his new start-up, the CEO of a large multimedia conglomerate who'd moved to Thailand to get a sex-change operation without consulting his wife. Nothing fazed her. She was uniquely attuned to the fragile egos and sensitivities beneath the wealth and titles of her Silicon Valley clients.

An obese Hawaiian woman living in a world of fit white people, Carol reveled in her differences and announced loudly and often how much she loved Spam; her coon cats; her small Jewish husband, Harry; and love. It was embroidered on a couch cushion in cross-stitch—I LOVE LOVE. She smelled like patchouli and oranges mixed with pork and cats.

"We're seeing you, aren't we?" Max released a sarcastic laugh. "Clearly things are going great."

"Oh, honey. I just thought you missed me." Carol laughed right back, which made Max smile. He liked Carol. "So what's up? Big changes. Big move. Running for Senate! What's that doing to your marriage? You're, like, living that show, the one with Mr. Big, but in reverse."

Max cleared his throat and narrowed his eyes. Charlotte wasn't looking at him, but she could see the two of them in the mirror behind Carol's fireplace. Him leaning back, his arms folded across his mesh marathon T-shirt, her perched on the edge of the couch, lips pursed in a tight oval. Her hair was greasy. She hadn't had time to wash it this morning. This was how they looked when they weren't wearing their masks: a sullen middle-aged couple filled with resentment.

"Well, the press is reporting we have an open marriage and Max is miserable."

"Why not let Max tell me how he feels?" Carol was supposed to remain objective, but in past sessions Charlotte had the sense that the woman was on her side.

Max cleared his throat a second time. "I'm definitely not happy. This campaign has taken over our lives. It's changed Charlotte."

"Changed her how?"

"She's obsessed with winning. At any cost. She's a different person every day. She does things and says things that don't sound like her."

"Charlotte has always been a driven woman, Max."

"This isn't drive. It's obsession." He turned to face Charlotte. "You're obsessed."

He's not wrong.

"Charlotte, why are you running for Senate?" Carol asked.

It was hard to turn the sound bites off, even with Carol. She'd been so well-trained to be guarded in every single one of her interactions. "I wanted a new intellectual challenge. I want to make people's lives better. I think I can fix a lot of what's wrong with DC."

This made Max snort. He stood and paced, his hands stuffed deep in the back pockets of his jeans. He often did this in their sessions with Carol. He would pace and then he would lie flat on his back on the floor and then he would rise and pace some more.

"She's running to get back at me for the affair."

"I'm not." Wasn't it a little bit true? *After the affair, I craved new-ness, novelty, a life that looked completely different from the one I had the day my husband had sex with another woman.*

"Of course you want to punish me. I did an unforgivable thing. I know that. And now you're getting back at me."

"I'm not."

Carol interrupted her. "Let him speak."

"I messed up our great life."

"By cheating on me."

"Charlotte," Carol warned.

Max exhaled. "By cheating on you. Yes. But now you're fucking everything up again."

Carol's fish tank gurgled nearby the couch and Charlotte let the Crayola-colored fish catch her eye, the sight of them dodging and weaving through the spires of the plastic replica of a fairy-tale castle calming her before she spoke again. "I wouldn't equate running for public office with putting your penis in another woman."

Carol raised her eyebrows at Charlotte's boldness.

"It feels like tit for tat. I hate PA. I've always hated it and you know that. I left the first chance I got." Now his tone fell somewhere between irritated and defeated. "I didn't think this would be this much work. To be honest, I didn't really think you had a chance at winning. I thought we'd look back and laugh about that time you tried to run for Senate and then we'd go back to our normal lives."

Why does he think I won't win? "Thanks for your confidence in me."

"None of this is what I signed up for."

Carol tilted forward, her enormous breasts spilling over her desk, the puckered tan flesh jiggling as she spoke. "That's interesting, Max. What did you think you signed up for when you married Charlotte? We've never talked about this before."

"I thought we were on the same page."

"What does that mean?"

"I thought we both wanted to work hard, make money, retire early, travel the world with our girls, maybe start a foundation, put our money where are mouths are, and do some fucking good in the world instead of just talking about it, and then go live in a hut on the beach in Madagascar."

Charlotte snorted. "You sound like an emo teenager."

He glared at her. "Fuck you, Charlie. I want to enjoy life. I don't give a shit what people think about me. Not like you. I don't need to keep striving. I just want to live. You were on board. We talked about this. We never talked about you running for office."

She thought back to a conversation they'd had right before they got married.

"What do you want to be when you grow up?" Max had asked her. They were lying on the bathroom floor of a hotel room in New York after having sex on the bamboo bench in the shower. She'd tweaked a muscle in her hip trying to get her leg in the right position to keep him inside her, but had ignored it until they both came.

"Aren't we already grown-up?" She crossed her eyes, laughed at him, and tugged on his too-long sideburns.

"We won't really be grown-ups until we're forty-five or fifty. We're still practicing." They were thirty-five and thirty-seven. In two weeks they'd be husband and wife.

She turned the tables on him in a voice she hoped was sexy. "What do you want to be?"

"Rich." He didn't hesitate. "And happy."

She gathered her thoughts and closed her eyes for a moment.

"I want to be important. I want my life to matter."

She hadn't thought of that conversation in years. It was the kind of idle chatter that happened after sex and was promptly forgotten as soon as you'd changed into a new pair of underwear.

Carol nodded at her to speak, but the fight had drained out of her. *Maybe we do want different things. Maybe our desires are incompatible. Maybe this, not the affair, is what the beginning of the end looks like.*

"I wanted you to be impressed by me again," she said quietly, the words surprising her. "I wanted to do something to remind you that I was better than her. Not to punish you."

"Better than who?" Max looked surprised.

"Margaret." She hated saying her name out loud.

"That's ridiculous. Margaret was a mistake."

"A mistake that almost cost us our marriage."

Carol stopped her. "We're not talking about the past. Let's talk about what's happening right now. Where do we go from here?"

Max answered quickly. "I just want to keep the girls in California. I don't want to answer one more stupid question or smile at another sad-eyed old woman or shake the hand of another out-of-work sad sack and promise him I can help him get a job. I want my life back."

Charlotte addressed Carol instead of her husband. "He can't leave. I need them."

"She needs us as props."

"No. I need my family."

Carol blinked and nodded. "Max, do you feel like a prop?"

"Absolutely." The word hung in the air.

The campaign uses us all as props. The entire election process was an act of well-choreographed pageantry, operatic in how it moved its humans onto and off a stage. It was true that the girls and Max were a big draw for her when they went to shake hands and take pictures with voters at pancake breakfasts, beauty pageants, and, once, the opening of a new mall.

Charlotte looked out the window and then back at Max. "Stick it out through the election. I don't want to do this without you. I need you." It was the most honest thing she'd said to her husband in months. Charlotte could feel her eyes getting hot and wet.

"What happens if you win?" Carol asked her.

For a year now she'd focused on that one day in November and hadn't allowed herself to think beyond it. "We'd find a place in Philly.

I'd commute to DC during the week and be home some nights and most weekends. The Acela is just two hours. We would put the girls in school in Center City, Friends Select, or public school at Meredith."

Max sighed. "I'm essentially going to be a single father of three living in Philly, a city where I know no one and have no job."

Charlotte kept going. "I promised Max one term. I won't serve more than that. I'm not a career politician." She meant that. She couldn't maintain this frenetic pace indefinitely. "And after that one term we can follow his dream. We can move to Madagascar if he wants and live in a hut on the beach. We can start a foundation. We can sell all of our Humanity stock and never have to work again. I just want this chance to do this. That's all I'm asking for." She didn't realize she'd reached over and grabbed Max's hand. It remained limp within her own.

Carol asked Max. "Can you live with that?"

He didn't answer.

Carol turned to Charlotte. "And what if you lose?"

Charlotte trained her gaze at her hands. "I don't know. We can go back to Humanity. We can move back here. We could start traveling."

"But how would that make you feel?"

"Defeated."

"So you do want to win?"

"Of course I do."

There was a long pause. Then Max surprised both Charlotte and Carol. "I'll stay in Pennsylvania. We can stay."

Had she simply worn him down? Had the guilt of his infidelity overcome him a second time and made him commit to a compromise? *Is there a small chance he still loves me and wants me to be happy?*

"What if the two of you go away for a little while, take some time for just the two of you, no campaign, no kids. Could you do that?"

Charlotte couldn't remember the last time they'd been alone for more than twenty-four hours. It was before the twins, that much she knew. But where would they go? And what would it be like to be alone now when there was so much bad blood between them? *Do I even want to be alone with my husband?*

She spoke slowly. "We could do it. We could go away for a long weekend somewhere." She tried a joke. "Maybe Madagascar?"

Max didn't smile, but Carol did. "That's my prescription for the two of you. It will do you some good to get away. Spend time in nature. Try not to fight. Laugh. Fuck. Remember how to enjoy each other."

Do Men Want Ambitious Women?

BY CLARE BALL

Last year I found myself in a relationship with a very woke man. He cooked more than I did. He loved to clean a toilet. He drove a VW van to a women's march clear across the country and brandished a sign declaring that women's rights are human rights. He even knitted my pussy hat and got the labial lips just goddamned perfect. He wore a sweatshirt that declared NOT THIS PUSSY above a picture of a uterus and fallopian tubes that resembled the alien in *Alien*. In hindsight it was a little much.

And yet, when I got a job where I made double his salary, when I got promoted to editor in chief, he began to resent me. And then he went and fucked his secretary.

That's when I started to wonder—do men really want ambitious women, or do they just like to pretend they do?

This brings me to the case of Pennsylvania Senate candidate Charlotte Walsh, the Silicon Valley executive looking to unseat incumbent, and enemy of vaginas the world over, Ted Slaughter. It's been well-documented, particularly in a profile in *Vanity Fair*, that Walsh and her husband, Max Tanner, both worked for Humanity and that Walsh was his boss in her capacity as chief operating officer. The two left the company when she ran for office and he became a stay-at-home dad.

Since then, there's been chatter out of the Valley and in their Pennsylvania hometown that Walsh and Tanner are having marital problems. One story claimed the pair have an "agreement" and an "open marriage" that would allow Tanner to enjoy the company of other women as long as he supported his wife in public. This is a familiar narrative, no? Haven't we heard this over and over again when we talk about powerful women in business and politics? Agreements, arrangements, convenience. Powerful men never have these things. They just have marriages.

The Walsh campaign vehemently denied the story, and Max Tanner penned an editorial for the *Washington Post* in support of his wife's candidacy. Meanwhile, Walsh's poll numbers have risen with both white and nonwhite women, perhaps owing to their sympathy to Walsh's personal accusations. They have, however, fallen with white men, bringing me back to my original question: Do men want ambitious women in their lives as their partners and their government representatives? Is Charlotte Walsh paying the price for her ambition?

CHAPTER 17
September 13, 2018

54 days to Election Day

Walsh (D)	Slaughter (R)	Spread
41	42	Slaughter +1

Roz offered both her support for Carol's plan and her vacation home in the Adirondacks. "Take a break. You're running yourself ragged. You've got less than two months of the worst part of the campaign, the part where real people start paying real attention. You're in a sprint to Election Day. You have your only debate in less than three weeks. You need a vacation."

Roz's second home was a four-hour drive from Elk Hollow. They'd leave on a Thursday night and return on Monday. Max drove while Charlotte stared at her phone.

"I won't get service in the cabin," she apologized. She'd canceled seventeen events, ten of them fundraisers, to be able to take the weekend away. "I should just finish some things." The idea of being away for two days had initially sent her into a panic. It was Roz who'd talked her down. "You're not that important. The world will not end if you go dark for two days." And yet, the last time she'd taken a day away, Leila had leaked a story she'd never wanted leaked and the fake-news industrial complex announced that she had an open marriage. While not cataclysmic, both events had been undesirable, embarrassing, and personally uncomfortable. The open-marriage headlines had done little to move the needle for voter sentiment, at least according to the most recent polls and a few canvassers. If undecided voters had been horrified by Bonnie Slaughter's abortion, they were equally horrified by Charlotte Walsh's alleged unconventional marriage. They would find something else to be horrified by the next time they logged on to Facebook.

It was her relationship with Leila that had truly suffered. When Charlotte had returned to Scranton she found a neatly typed, official-looking letter of resignation sitting on her desk. She crumpled it up and held the battered paper in her hand as she went in search of her chief of staff. When she found her sitting outside on a park bench staring into a Styrofoam cup of black coffee, she dropped the ball onto her lap.

"I don't accept." Charlotte didn't say anything else. But since then their relationship had narrowed to professional considerations, and Charlotte had never received the apology she believed she deserved. Instead, Leila tiptoed around her and worked harder than before to streamline Charlotte's life without any of the friendship. They were careful with each other now. Gone was their easy intimacy, and that was a special kind of torture. What stung Charlotte was that she knew Leila still believed she'd done the right thing.

"Do what you have to do." Max flipped through radio stations, paused on a rerun of an NPR quiz show, and then turned it off altogether.

Back roads turned to highway then again to back roads where the borders of New York, Pennsylvania, and New Jersey blurred.

"I've never been to Roz's country house," Charlotte said once she knew she'd lost cell service for good. "I've seen pictures, but I never went up with her. I guess it was in Richard's family for a hundred years or something," she babbled. Instinct made her twist her neck to check on the girls every few minutes, and each time she was surprised they weren't there.

"Mmmm-hmm," Max said. He hadn't shaved that morning, or the morning before. She always liked his stubble even when it scratched her face. She wanted to touch him, to make this easier, to put her hand on his leg or even begin to unbuckle his pants the way she had one time they were driving home from Tahoe a long time ago. She also wanted to scream at him, to hit him in the face, to scratch his arms, to make him feel the pain he'd caused her in the past two years. Instead she sat in silence.

Hills rolled higher and higher. Sugar maples and aspen trees created a canopy over the old country roads. At the higher elevation the leaves changed in small pockets of burnt orange, deep russet, and a cheerful yellow. They passed through a small town square with just a general store, a post office, and a gas station before turning onto a gravel road badly in need of resurfacing. The car bounced along for another five miles, passing three or four turnoffs with multiple mailboxes for hidden country homes. Finally, they found a dirt path and a rickety sign painted in green proclaiming their destination, CAMP WATERS.

"It's more of a compound, wouldn't you say?" Max said as the buildings came into view, four of them in total, all old pine, matching green shutters, solar panels on the roofs.

Charlotte lifted plastic grocery bags filled mostly with wine from the backseat. "She said the spare key is inside the smoker in the back. Can you grab it and I'll get these onto the porch?"

Someone had been by to cut the grass recently and carved a neat path toward the door. Ten feet from the cabin the forest took over the landscape, wild and dark. Dried sticks and leaves made a pleasant crunching sound beneath her feet.

The handle of the bag broke as she walked toward the big house.

"Shit." Two bottles of red wine slipped onto the ground, one shattering on the edge of a tree root, the other rolling over her foot. Charlotte got down on all fours, careful to avoid the glass, in an effort to gather what remained of the groceries.

"Let me help." Max kneeled next to her. He looked young in the soft light, sweet. She leaned over to kiss his cheek. He recoiled in surprise at the touch of her lips.

"I'm sorry." Why apologize for kissing her own husband? He leaned over and kissed her on the mouth. It felt obligatory.

"Don't touch the glass," he warned too late. A crimson stream of blood trickled from the inside of her palm. She hardly made a noise, just clasped it with her other hand. "Leave it all. Let's go inside."

"Animals will get it."

"You're bleeding. Go in and run it under some water." He handed her the key. "I'll be right there."

The interior of the cabin was the opposite of Roz's stately Maryland home. It was filled with mismatched furniture that looked like it had all come from a high-end thrift shop. There was a plaid couch and an orange chair and a red bookshelf with grimy paint that shed strips like an orange peel. The floors creaked. A stack of board games sat in the middle of an end table carved to look like a grizzly bear holding a cocktail tray. An ancient moose head, its fur matted and rubbed away near the antlers, hung over a grand stone fireplace still filled with charred wood and burned bits of newspapers. The entire place smelled lived-in, like dirt, smoke, and marshmallows. Charlotte was so taken by it she didn't notice her blood dripping onto the unfinished wooden floor. The cold water in the sink stung. When the bleeding slowed, she opened drawers in search of a first aid kit and instead found only dominoes, a tattered Yellow Pages, a corkscrew, a dog brush, and bug spray.

"Will you check in the bedroom for a first aid kit?" she yelled to Max as he came through the door and dragged their suitcase down the hallway. She heard him rustling through drawers. Then she heard his laugh. Deep and strong. Real.

"Do Rosalind's kids come up here without her?"

Charlotte shook her head, still clutching a paper towel to the palm of her hand. "No one but Roz has been up here this summer. She's been coming on weekends to write her book and, in her words, told her family to screw off for the summer and rent themselves a damn beach house." Earlier that year, after mouthing off against the president on one of the morning news shows, Roz had inked a memoir deal in the low seven figures. "If I don't tell my own goddamn story, someone else will," she told Charlotte. "I might as well be the heroine."

Max yelled out to her from the next room. "Does Rosalind smoke pot?"

"What?"

Max walked into the kitchen holding a chubby joint between his thumb and forefinger. "It smells fresh. It was in the nightstand drawer. On top of the King James Bible."

"God bless her. Maybe she has glaucoma?" Charlotte said, trying to picture Roz sitting on the back porch staring into the dense forest and toking on the small cigarette.

"Or maybe she just likes to get high." Max chuckled again. "Can you imagine Rosalind Waters high? Do you think she gets even more intense and loud? Or maybe she becomes this soft-spoken introvert who doodles in adult coloring books."

Charlotte thought about it. "I'll bet she's a lot of fun."

"Maybe she giggles a lot."

"I don't think Roz knows how to giggle. She might be pretty bossy. You know those people who get high and then try to get you to help them organize their apartments?" She grinned and steadied herself against the kitchen table with her injured hand. "Ow. Shit. I need that Band-Aid." Max left the joint on the counter and disappeared into the bathroom, emerging a minute later with a roll of gauze and medical tape. He gently dressed the wound. For a minute she expected him to kiss it the way he did with the girls, but he just walked back into the bedroom to finish unpacking.

Charlotte got to work putting away the groceries and cleaning off the old Weber grill on the back porch. She'd brought along two nice T-bones to go with the wine.

"Hey!" she called. "Can you help me light this grill? I'll get started on a salad."

"Sure."

"Should we start a fire?"

"Probably." He busied himself collecting wood and adeptly arranging it into a little log cabin within the fireplace. Max was proud of his fire-building capabilities. Charlotte had forgotten how much she liked to watch him do something he enjoyed. She plugged her phone into a speaker on the kitchen counter and scrolled through her downloaded music to find an old Charlie Parker album.

"I haven't heard this in a while."

"Me neither."

She opened the wine. Her glass was empty by the time "April in Paris" warbled to its conclusion. *I will have more than two glasses of wine tonight. I will try to enjoy more than two glasses of wine tonight.*

Max moved to the grill and left the back door open so she could see and talk to him. Except she had nothing to talk about. How was it possible that they had so little to say to each other? Sentences began in her head but stopped before they could come out of her mouth. She walked toward him and moved to wrap her arms around his waist, but stopped that, too. Instead she spun on her heel, went to the sink to wash the spinach and chop the green onions, and poured herself a second glass of wine.

"Roz has Trivial Pursuit," she finally said, and pointed to the stack of games. "It looks old. Probably from the eighties."

"Oh yeah?" Max flipped the meat.

"Maybe we could play after dinner." She noticed his wineglass was empty and filled it.

"Maybe. These will be ready in two minutes. Grab me plates."

Sitting across from him at the table, she could hear him chewing his steak instead of speaking to her.

"This is really good."

"Thanks." Max poured more wine.

It was so polite, which was worse than when they behaved like assholes to each other. Assholes cared about something, the wrong things, maybe, but something. Strangers were polite.

"Did you use a rub?"

"Just salt and pepper."

"It's really good."

"Thank you."

Their conversation skimmed the surface. When had the house been built? Had Roz gotten much writing done this summer? Should we call to check on the girls? Charlotte was sick of small talk, sick of smiling. They both were. Maybe they needed an excuse not to speak or perform. She thought about the days left ahead of them here in the middle of nowhere, and tension caught in her shoulders and the back of her neck.

"We could smoke that joint." Max picked up both of their empty plates and walked them over to the sink.

"Yeah, right."

"I'm serious."

"Why?"

"Why not? It could be fun. Loosen things up a little."

For a brief moment she wondered if she would be drug tested if she won the election. She didn't like smoking around other people, so she rarely indulged. But the couple of times she'd gotten high with Max it had been okay, maybe even fun.

Max fingered the joint. "And we could play Trivial Pursuit."

She tried to muster enthusiasm equal to his. "Okay."

They used to love trivia games. Got off on them even. Through-out their relationship Charlotte had been the reigning Trivial Pursuit champion, but it was always close. She was the clear leader in both sports and history, Max at science and geography. They were both crap when it came to pop culture. Early on in their marriage, they'd spent hours playing, sometimes using the cards just to pass long flights or sleepless nights.

"I want to screw your brain," Max once said to her after she won a game. "You're the smartest woman I know and it gives me a hard-on." She still thought about it because it was one of the dirtiest things anyone had ever said to her and she enjoyed the way it sounded coming out of his mouth.

"I'll set up the board."

Max rooted around in the drawers for a lighter. He located a green Bic and sat next to her on the couch, thigh touching thigh. She had a feeling of déjà vu, or a flashback, or the sense that she was on a couch in her parents' basement about to make out with a boy for the first time.

"I haven't smoked a joint in a long time." Max stared at the little white roll of paper pinched between his index finger and thumb. Neither had Charlotte, even though every VC they knew had invested in some kind of recreational weed hustle.

"I'll light it." Suddenly, she was eager to begin, to find out where this was going to go. She tucked her feet underneath her like a small child and rolled her thumb over the spines of the flint.

"You look like a schoolgirl when you sit like that."

She liked this compliment, but ignored it and lit the end of the paper, letting it burn down before placing the joint between her lips. She'd never mastered how to look sexy smoking anything, not even cigarettes. She pulled the smoke into her lungs, held it there, pursed her lips to release the smoke, and coughed hard. Max handed her a bottle of sparkling water. They were a middle-aged couple with a troubled marriage smoking pot with a bottle of sparkling water. She swallowed to clear her mind of the cliché and lifted the joint back to her lips.

"Easy there, maestro." Max plucked it out of her hands. "Why don't we get started on the game?"

Charlotte was unprepared for all her muscles and thoughts to relax, for her mental to-do list to blissfully disappear. She'd forgotten what it felt like to let go. She wasn't high exactly, just less anxious than usual; the heavy ball of twine that had taken up permanent residence in her stomach unraveled. Maybe this was how most people felt all of the time. Max stood and reached out his hand to help her off the couch. "I'm going to nail these *Charlie's Angels* questions."

"But I kill at Iran-Contra."

"We'll see about that."

He added another log to the fire, rolled up the sleeves of his well-worn flannel shirt, and jiggled the dice in his left hand a moment longer than necessary. Charlotte could see his wedding ring shine orange in the firelight. Tender memories flooded over her as she looked at that ring. They'd picked it out together in a small shop in Uruguay. Copper could look rough and ugly on some men. It fit Max perfectly.

"You should propose to me," he joked when she bought the ring just a week before their wedding.

Max's proposal only a few months before had been like something out of a movie. He'd taken her to the Grand Canyon. "Keep your eyes closed," Max said, even though his hands were fastened over her eyes as he led her from the parking lot into the national park.

"Don't let me fall over the edge." She laughed.

"Why would I do that? I'm not even the beneficiary on your good life insurance yet. Keep walking. You're almost there."

Max led her on an uneven trail through hordes of animated foreign tourists.

"Okay. Open them."

"Holy shit! What? Wow!" She gazed out at the vast expanse of the canyon, for the first time truly awed by something outside herself. She turned, and Max was on one knee with an emerald-cut solitaire. He had safely steered her right to the edge of the world and held her hand to make sure she didn't fall off.

"My proposal *would* be better than yours," Charlotte teased when they bought his ring. Friendly competition was the core of their relationship. It was how they communicated, how they flirted, their version of foreplay.

She surprised both of them when she dropped to one knee on the dirty floor of the shop in Las Piedras. "Maxwell Tanner, do you promise to love, honor, cherish, and obey me for as long as we both shall live?

He sank down next to her. "I thought we were taking 'obey' out of the vows."

"I'd like to keep it in mine."

He took the ring from her hand. "Whatever you want."

His ring was the first thing Annie had reached for when she'd lifted her hand out of the incubator in the NICU. The nurses said preemies couldn't see much in front of them, but they liked things that were shiny. That tiny hand reached up to grip her father's finger and held on for dear life.

Charlotte wondered if Max ever thought about those memories when he looked at the ring, when he nervously twisted it around his finger as he spoke. Or if the ring had just become a part of him he no longer noticed.

Max plucked the joint from the table and lit the end, pulling in a deep breath as he sat down across from her. "I feel good about this."

But how do you feel about us?

The game continued for two hours. She was ahead and, for a moment, considered losing on purpose.

Then Max took the lead.

"Since when did you know so much about *Charlie's Angels*?"

"I had a thing for Kate Jackson when I was a kid."

Charlotte raised an eyebrow. "Not Farrah or Jaclyn Smith? Kate was the boring one."

"She was the smart one."

"Not the sexy one."

"I think smart women are sexy. You know that."

Is he flirting with me? She busied herself with what was left of the joint, but couldn't get the lighter's wheel to spin. Instead of finding this troubling she found it hilarious. Her laughter was contagious.

"You don't laugh enough anymore." Max focused on her like he was recognizing her for the first time in a long time. He took the lighter from her hand. The flint caught easily beneath his thumb.

A self-conscious blush crept up her neck as she leaned into his offered flame, inhaled instead of answered.

"Seriously, Charlie. We don't laugh that much anymore. I want to laugh with you. I want to crack up every day. We used to do that."

Make him laugh. Say something funny. This used to be easy.

Her face grew hot. "This is good pot." She reached for her wineglass but didn't notice it was empty until it reached her lips. Max passed her the bottle and she took a sip from the narrow mouth, not bothering with the glass. "I once had a sex dream about Ronald Reagan."

There was his laugh. And then hers. The sound of both mingling together was a pleasant surprise.

"The Gipper? Old Ronnie or young Ronnie?" For just a second she luxuriated in this version of herself that was still a revelation to her husband.

"Old. Seventy-year-old, second-term Ronald Reagan. It began with a speech."

"*Challenger* disaster or Evil Empire?"

"Neither. 'Mr. Gorbachev, tear down this wall.'"

Max nodded with amusement. "A classic."

"So he gives the speech and then I end up in the back of the motorcade with him. Alone."

"Was it hot?"

"Nancy Reagan was a very lucky woman." She inhaled the last of the joint and dropped it in the dregs of her red-wine glass.

"You dirty bitch."

They were touching. His hand grazed her thigh, hers moved to the back of his neck.

"We should finish the game," she whispered into his ear, biting into the soft flesh of his earlobe.

"I'll spare you my great victory. We can call it a draw."

"Where's the fun in that?"

"I have a better idea." He gripped the seat of her chair and shoved it away from the table, unbuttoned her jeans, and kissed her stomach. His hands clawed at her thighs. She could feel his fingernails through the denim. They were long. She'd have to remind him to cut them. *Can you just enjoy this?* She tilted her hips forward and in a single swift move he yanked the pants to her ankles and leaned forward to run his tongue below her navel.

★

Max climbed ahead of her, his wide hands exploring the crags above for the next place to clip in, the sinewy muscles in his back flexing and strained. She lost her grip, the rock crumbling into dust in one hand, her feet dangling beneath her into a vast nothing, a gaping blackness. Her safety rope frayed. She opened her mouth to scream for Max to turn around and help but no sound came. He swiveled his head and when he looked down at her he lost his grip.

They both fell.

As usual Charlotte woke early, except this time the nightmare startled her awake instead of Josh calling her on her phone. Her mouth felt like it was filled with cotton, dry and salty. Blinding sunlight made its way through the trees and windows and directly into her eyes. They lay on the floor of the cabin's living room. A crocheted afghan was all that separated her body from the rough wood. Max snored next to her on his stomach, his white pockmarked ass bare to the room. She stared at him while he slept. He opened one eye and reached out for her waist.

"Hi."

"Hi."

"Let's open a hotel."

"A what?"

"A bed-and-breakfast." Max had that gleam in his eye. "When all of this is over. Let's open a hotel up here, one of those places where people can detox from technology and old married couples can re-ignite their sex drives. We'll put everyone's phones in lockboxes and force husbands and wives to talk to each other and do drugs. The girls can grow up in the mountains and never wear shoes."

"When this is over?" She said it tentatively.

He breathed into her neck. "Yeah, when the campaign is over."

Max doesn't think I will win. She didn't say anything. Instead she allowed him to slip his hand between her thighs as she closed her eyes.

Yes, yes, yes.

★

Even as everything began to feel right, Charlotte couldn't escape her desire to check in with the campaign and made an excuse of going into town to get more cheese and some bread that was just a charade to get somewhere with cell service. Roz had promised she'd get a signal if she drove to the edge of town and up a small hill behind the post office.

There were more than one hundred emails in her inbox from the past twenty-four hours and she was able to skim most of them in just ten minutes.

Then she saw it. The subject was in all caps:

WE NEED TO TALK.

Charlotte's palms went slick as she clicked the email open. It was short.

I got a call from a reporter today. He knows something. You
can't keep Max in the dark any longer.

Charlotte read the email from Margaret over and over, closing it and opening it a half-dozen times, looking for more words. She breathed harder. *This is over. The campaign is over.*

Stupid, stupid, how could I be so stupid? She turned her phone off, a futile attempt to keep the past from infringing on her future.

She looked down to see her fingers entwined, already in prayer.

Max wasn't religious, and he'd never understood why she was. None of their friends in California admitted to believing in God. Instead, they openly mocked people who did as simple, stupid, and ignorant. No one even mentioned God without first rolling their eyes. On the campaign trail, Josh encouraged her to pepper her speeches with a biblical quote or two, preferably something from Psalms, but to always go easy on the Jesus talk.

She allowed herself to pray now, to pray and to cry: ragged, primal-sounding wails. She squeezed her eyes shut and spoke to God, repeating the same prayer over and over again:

"Don't let my mistakes destroy my family."

CHAPTER 18

Margaret was right. She'd been right all along. Their secret wouldn't stay a secret much longer. And when it was finally revealed, it might ruin both of their lives—just as Margaret's email had warned back in June.

Charlotte scrolled through her phone to a number labeled XYZ that connected through Singapore to Margaret's cell phone. What time was it there? She did the math. The middle of the night.

It rang and rang, in that odd monotone buzz you get when you dial a foreign number from an American cell phone. No one answered.

Charlotte drove into town and bought a bottle of cheap wine with a screw-top cap and a pack of Parliament Lights from the general store before driving back up the hill. She left her shoes behind in the car and lay down in the grass.

It was time to tell Max. It was time to tell Josh. She would eventually need to tell her girls. They were the reason she had set all this in motion in the first place.

Charlotte took a swig from the bottle of cheap sweet red wine that tasted like jam, letting the alcohol numb her hangover. She stared up at the leaves and opened the door to the compartment in her mind she'd forced herself to keep locked shut, allowing herself to remember the one and only time she'd met Margaret in person.

The image of Margaret's face came back to her sharp and clear—sitting across from her at a café Charlotte had chosen for its anonymity, one of those generic restaurants designed to evoke a sidewalk café in Rome or Paris with wicker tables and chairs and waiters in black vests. It was a place none of their Humanity colleagues would be caught dead in.

In the month since she'd discovered the affair Charlotte had become consumed with an overwhelming, irrational need to see Margaret face-to-face. She cold-called her at the office one day—an act that must have terrified the woman. She all but demanded Margaret meet her the following afternoon, knowing the woman would never have the nerve to say no.

Charlotte arrived to their meeting fifteen minutes late, on purpose—she would be damned if she were the one waiting—and spotted Margaret perched childlike on the edge of her seat in jeans and a flowery peasant top. She had narrow shoulders and wide-set eyes; pale skin with delicate cheekbones; blond, almost white hair; and full lips, her beauty the stuff of pre-Raphaelite paintings. Charlotte scrutinized her with two questions in her mind: *What does she have that I don't have? What about me wasn't enough for Max?* Margaret looked fragile, and Charlotte imagined that could also be attractive to men in the way a wounded bird is attractive to a child. Beauty and fragility were two things Charlotte had never possessed, and being faced with them in the woman with whom her husband had betrayed her was almost enough to make Charlotte want to turn and go home.

Then Margaret looked up and gave a tentative wave and Charlotte had no choice but to continue to the table.

Margaret sipped delicately on a glass of water, her hands shaking ever so slightly, creating ripples in the liquid. She was shivering even though the air was warm. Charlotte felt like a giant standing over the tiny woman.

"I'm sorry," Margaret murmured into the glass. "I'm so, so sorry." She didn't meet Charlotte's eyes. "Please don't fire me. I need my job."

Charlotte knew from a Google search and a glimpse of her Humanity human resources file that Margaret was thirty-nine, never married, no children.

"What?" It hadn't been what Charlotte expected to hear, and she felt queasy in the face of this neediness, the fact that she might be put in a position to grant this woman any favors, and, conversely, that Margaret thought she would use her power to exact retribution. "I'm not here to fire you."

When the cheery waiter arrived to read the specials, Charlotte held up her hand to stop him mid-sentence. "Just two glasses of the house red—and please bring the check when you bring it. I'm in a bit of a rush." He hurried back to the kitchen.

She didn't care if Margaret wanted the wine or not. Ordering on someone else's behalf was a way to stay in control. Maybe Max had made mention to Margaret at one point about how controlling his wife could be. Perhaps it had been part of his seduction. *You're nothing like my cold, controlling wife.* Beneath the table Charlotte's hands compulsively clenched and unclenched a paper napkin.

Margaret stared down at the table. "I've always looked up to you."

Charlotte laughed then, and it was a bitter sound. "You admire me, so you fucked my husband?" The word choice made Margaret shudder and Charlotte liked that, liked rattling her. "Is that why you did it? You wanted to be like me?"

"No." Margaret finally met her eye. "I did it because I was foolish and stupid and lonely. But I deserve everything you just said to me."

"Yes, you do."

"Please, stop." Margaret's voice was quiet and desperate. Their waiter arrived with the wine just then and a vintage cigar box containing the check, which he balanced delicately on the edge of the table. Charlotte took a sip. It was tart and sweet and not very good at all, but it burned the back of her throat as it went down in a way she enjoyed. Margaret pushed her wine toward the center of the table.

"Would you rather have white?"

Margaret shook her head.

When Margaret refused that, too, Charlotte, by a strange instinct, looked at the woman's stomach, which wasn't as flat as one would expect given the rest of her frame. Her blood ran cold then as the woman raised her eyes to meet Charlotte's and said what Charlotte somehow already knew.

"I'm pregnant."

"Excuse me?" Charlotte said, even though she didn't need her to repeat it—she'd heard her perfectly. She placed her wine back on the table too hard, rattling the surface and causing the top-heavy glass to topple over, spreading red liquid across the table. The waiter was on them with a handful of napkins before it could reach either of their laps.

Charlotte grabbed the bundle from his hands and practically threw half of it at Margaret. She hissed at the server. "Thank you. We're fine here."

"I'm pregnant," Margaret repeated more quietly. "It's Max's," she added unnecessarily.

Charlotte's feet tingled, then her hands. Her entire body went numb. What had she expected from this meeting? Closure maybe. Not this. Never this. How could Max have been so fucking stupid? First to sleep with an employee and then to do it without protection. It made her question everything about the man she'd married.

"I want to keep my baby."

Charlotte forced words out of her mouth. "What does Max think about that?"

"He doesn't know. I didn't tell him yet." Margaret's eyes were pleading. "It could be my last chance to have a child."

Her desperation, so thick Charlotte felt like she could smell it, reminded Charlotte of herself eight years earlier as the IVF failed and failed again. "Keeping your child is your decision." Charlotte chose her words carefully. *Should I even be speaking to her without a lawyer?*

Instantly, she had pictured this child—he or she would have Margaret's blond hair and Max's mischievous blue eyes, Annie's mischievous blue eyes. Oh God, the child would look like her daughters.

"I have three daughters, you know. *We* have three daughters— our little one is only a few months old. What would we tell them?" She was asking herself this question as much as Margaret. "Do you want my husband to be a coparent, for us to take the kid on weekends?"

Margaret stared at her hands again. "I don't want anything from you."

"But you plan to stay here and raise the child?"

"I don't really have anyplace else to go. I have no family. Both of my parents died years ago. It's just me. I guess I could move away. But it's not like I can go back home. I don't have a home to go back to and I need my job."

Charlotte tried to unravel a tangle of emotions: anger, fear, and even a little bit of sympathy. "Then why tell me?"

"I thought you might know."

"How would I know?"

"I guess . . . I guess I thought you could have looked at my medical records." Margaret directed her words down at the table.

"That's illegal. Humanity isn't Big Brother."

"Who knows what's private anymore?" Tears streamed down Margaret's face.

Charlotte wanted to rip this woman to shreds and hug her at the same time. But mainly she wanted to figure out how to fix this—or better yet, make it so this wasn't happening. And that's when the wheels in Charlotte's head started turning. She could see the beginning of a plan. She could do this, she could make this go away—if not the problem itself, then at least Margaret. Because if Margaret stayed in the Bay Area, her presence would be inescapable and eventually all-consuming. Max still bore the scars of growing up without a dad. He would never abandon a child. Margaret and her baby would be tied to them for the rest of their lives. Charlotte would be constantly reminded of Max's infidelity. It would haunt her girls. Imagining their future was daunting enough. They didn't deserve to be handicapped with their father's mistake for the rest of their lives, and she couldn't allow it to happen. *I'm not strong enough for this. It will break me. It could break all of us. Margaret and her child cannot stay here.* All these thoughts rushed forward in a tumble.

Charlotte placed both of her palms flat on the table. Her wedding ring glinted in the sunshine.

"What if I transferred you to a new office? London, Singapore, Tokyo. You can raise the kid abroad. Max doesn't have to know about the baby."

Am I saving myself by punishing Max? I will banish his child to the other side of the world and never even tell him it existed? Do I have it in me to be so cruel?

She could tell by the other woman's face that her proposal crossed a line, but also that it was a proposition Margaret was willing to consider.

Charlotte had the sense she was building a house of cards, but she pressed on, becoming more convinced that this was the best way forward, the only way forward. "This could be good for everyone. A fresh start. I could get you on a great team—launching the new marketing and analytics cloud programs in Asia. We need good people like you. Your work in South America was very good." She couldn't believe she was flattering this woman. Clearly she was, because Margaret blushed at the compliment.

"I don't know what to say. You would be okay with that?"

"I'm not okay with any of this. But I'll learn to live with it." And in that moment, Charlotte resolved to do so. Yes, it would be hard knowing that Margaret was out there, that Max's child was growing up in a city far away. But she could do hard things. And if the end goal was saving her marriage and protecting her children, it was worth it.

"You're going to stay with him?" Margaret asked quietly.

Did this woman believe that she wouldn't? Did Margaret entertain fantasies about Charlotte and Max breaking up and him coming to live with her and her child, seeing his three girls on weekends?

"I don't want him," Margaret assured her before Charlotte could answer. "That's not what I'm after. I want this baby. I want us to have a good life. I promise you. That's all." Margaret moved her hand protectively to her belly. Charlotte knew well that from the moment your child twitched in the womb you wanted to feel each of their kicks, rolls, and punches, to bear witness to each part of their brand-new lives. Those were the moments you first became a mother.

Charlotte set her lips in a grim line. "I want to believe you. Please don't repeat anything I've said to you."

"I don't talk to Max."

"Right now, I hardly do either."

Charlotte couldn't stay there another moment. She abruptly got up and threw two twenties on the table. "Let me know your answer by Friday," she said, as if they were wrapping up a business deal. Which, in a way, they were.

It was a deal that had served them both. Margaret delivered a healthy little boy. It was Leila who remained in contact with her and made sure she was taken care of, made sure Margaret took a long maternity leave and thrived in her position. Margaret had a good life.

Charlotte had never wondered if she'd made the right choice, or if she'd do it again. In hindsight, it was easy to see Margaret as a problem that could be solved rather than as the woman who'd changed everything about their lives. But then, she hadn't known she'd run for office, had never thought her life would become an open book, each chapter secret fodder to take her down. Guilt still gnawed at her. She'd felt it just the week before when she saw delight widen Max's eyes as he watched Annie attempt to tie her shoe. *There's another child out there,* she thought. *And he's probably learning to do something right now and you're missing it.*

Charlotte could second-guess herself all she wanted, but the fact remained—she had no choice now but to fix this. She could tell her husband what she'd done, or she could tell her campaign manager.

She picked up the phone to call Josh.

It took her less than two minutes to tell him the worst thing she'd ever done.

"You lied to my fucking face," Josh said, his voice equally pissed and impressed. "The first time we met. You lied."

"I know." She hoped she sounded properly chastened.

"You *are* a really good liar."

"I know."

"You're going to have to do more of it," Josh said in a clinical tone. Had she expected his sympathy? His livelihood was on the line as much as hers.

"You need to get through the debate," Josh said. "If we make it through the debate, we might have a chance. It's the first and only time most voters will pay this race any attention. I can handle Margaret. But do not even think about talking to Max about any of this yet."

CHAPTER 19
October 1, 2018
36 days to Election Day

Walsh (D)	Slaughter (R)	Spread
43	40	Walsh +3

Ted Slaughter made a grand entrance onto the debate stage. When Charlotte went to shake his hand, he dropped to the floor to begin the first of thirty-seven push-ups.

"Your turn." He turned to his challenger once he finished his calisthenics.

What the hell am I supposed to do with that?

"You're adorable." Charlotte winked at the camera.

During the debate, Slaughter gripped the microphone like he was trying to strangle it, his brown-speckled fingers vibrating with the effort, one fist stacked on top of the other. When he made a point, whether it was about Charlotte's inexperience in Washington or his own prowess at slashing taxes, he'd throttle the audio device, causing his voice to warble like a professional wrestling announcer.

Senate debates are odd things. Unlike a presidential contest, there are no set rules for how many times congressional candidates have to face one another before Election Day. An incredibly small percentage of voters actually watch the debate itself. A slightly larger group will read recaps about it the next day or watch a segment about it on the local news. In the age of social media, small moments matter—hence the push-ups, hence the wink. Charlotte personally never enjoyed watching debates and rarely even tuned in for the presidential ones.

She found them grandiose and self-righteous. Voters agreed. Recent polls showed the majority of voters believed political candidates cared more about fighting with one another than about actively solving the nation's problems.

Still, the debate was just over a month from Election Day and its proximity was what made it matter the most.

And now she needed to get through it. Josh had spoken to Margaret, told her what to say if confronted by a reporter, told her to go off the grid, to leave her home in Singapore to take an extended vacation paid for by Charlotte. He'd managed all the details to ensure Charlotte would get her chance to take the debate stage.

Meeting someone in real life after they've been your nemesis for more than a year was like meeting a character from a book that you didn't particularly like. Charlotte felt a complete disconnect between Slaughter the mythical adversary and the flesh-and-blood old man five feet from her onstage. Up close he looked positively reptilian, with weathered, almost scaly skin. His lips were thin, his teeth professionally whitened to the point of appearing purple beneath the bright studio lights. His shock of shoe-polish-black hair from a bottle was plastered against his head in a precarious comb-over.

Charlotte had selected her own outfit for the debate, a tasteful silk white button-down shirt, navy blazer, and wide-legged navy pants with a thin gold belt. It made her feel like Katharine Hepburn.

The debate itself lasted just under ninety minutes. Standing beneath the television lights was like standing under the blazing sun on a day with no wind. Charlotte felt sweat trickle down both her thighs. The stage lights reflected on the faces in the front row. Charlotte's eyes landed on Bonnie Slaughter, her hair pulled back in a French braid, her pink suit severe and conservative, an American flag pin on her right breast, a single strand of pearls resting on her collarbone. Charlotte's people were on the opposite side of the room: her Allegheny County director and ground team, Leila, Josh, and Lulu who mouthed, "I love your pants!" with an animated thumbs-up. Max beamed at her from the front row, Annie on his lap, the twins on either side. He'd been happy since their weekend away, supportive even. For the first time in a long time it felt like they were on the same team. *Get through today. Then you can tell him. You need to tell him.*

Kara was supposed to join them but had backed out at the last minute. "Your good-for-nothing brother has gone missing and I might not let him back in this time," she'd explained to Charlotte the night before.

Damn you, Paul. You can't even find a good time to have a crisis. "I'm sure he's fine. If he isn't back tomorrow, we'll call the police." *I don't have time for his shit.*

Slaughter had rejected three different moderators. The first had been a black woman, the second a white woman. The third and final choice was a black man, a former NFL football player turned local news anchor. He had a penis and a Heisman and Slaughter wasn't going to do any better than that. To his credit, Ned Nolton was a decent guy and a solid newsman who didn't play favorites and seemed more excited to be there than anyone in the audience or on the stage.

What ensued wasn't a debate like the kind Charlotte had mastered during high school debate club, the kind with frameworks, contentions, plans, and counterplans. This was an exercise in showmanship; a physical and mental test of wits; a battle of one-liners, attacks, and counterattacks; a trading of blows and barbs. Slaughter's strategy seemed to be to interrupt her as often as possible. Her counterstrategy was to roll her eyes and affect a bored demeanor. Charlotte hated every second of it. Slaughter would spend fifteen minutes lambasting her and then, the second the cameras stopped rolling, he'd pretend she wasn't there.

During commercial breaks, harried women from the network's makeup department sprinted toward them to touch up their hair and makeup. Slaughter would adjust his tie. One time he took off his jacket and signaled an aide to bring him an identical fresh one. During another break, he beckoned his wife onstage for a kiss. For the final pause, he recited a portion of Rudyard Kipling's "Gunga Din" from memory to no one in particular.

Charlotte stood behind her podium and reread her notes. Josh approached her like Mickey coming to tape Rocky's eye in between rounds. He'd whisper advice and uncharacteristic encouragement. "Perfect answer on jobs." "You've got him right where you want him." Charlotte heard Slaughter's spokeswoman, Annabel Gest, cackle and saw her glare at Josh in a familiar way. She nodded at the handsome woman in her sixties. "Did you?" Josh nodded slightly enough for only Charlotte to see. "Iowa caucuses ten years ago. Don't look so surprised. I have a mommy complex and we bonded over our shared disdain for communism."

On some issues Slaughter seemed detached (cybersecurity) or vague on the details (school choice), on others (abortion, guns) he came alive, babbling in morality tales. Charlotte stared at the space between his nose and his upper lip and pictured the old man with a wobbly handlebar mustache.

When it was over, Slaughter shook Charlotte's hand on his terms, clasping it so hard it would leave a red mark across her knuckles the next day. The plastic smile never left his face. "You're a good candidate," he said. Charlotte could see streams of taupe running from his temples to his jawline, where beads of sweat cut through his heavy makeup. He lowered his voice. "But I can tell you're a cold little cunt inside and out and I feel sorry for your husband."

Ted Slaughter was a pro, but with so many debates under his belt he'd gotten cocky, forgotten the basics. Or maybe his staff was to blame. They should have been quicker to make sure Ted's microphone was off.

Ted Slaughter called Charlotte Walsh a cunt in front of the entire world.

Senator Denies Insulting Opponent on Hot Mic

ASSOCIATED PRESS

Senator Ted Slaughter of Pennsylvania insulted his opponent Charlotte Walsh during their first and only debate last night in Pittsburgh. When the two candidates went to shake hands, Slaughter called Walsh what sounded like "a cold little c-nt." The insult was picked up by a wireless lavalier microphone attached to Slaughter's collar.

"That's not what I said," Slaughter immediately told reporters who asked him about the insult when he walked off the stage. "You misheard me. The microphone jumbled my words."

When asked what he did say, Slaughter responded that it was personal and between him and Charlotte Walsh.

Walsh's campaign manager, Josh Pratt, immediately released a statement: "Tug Slaughter showed his true colors after what we thought was a polite and measured debate on the real issues concerning Pennsylvanians. We're disgusted at his level of incivility and his inclination toward misogynistic insults."

The Pennsylvania race has gained national attention and cost at least $150 million, including outside spending from PACs and political nonprofits, an extraordinary sum even in this extraordinary midterm election year.

Viewership for this debate, broadcast on local CBS affiliates and streamed, per Walsh's request, live on Facebook, was higher than the average tune-in for a Senate debate, due to Walsh's profile in Silicon Valley, recent headlines about both candidates, and the vitriolic spirit of this campaign. . . . [developing story]

🐦 Twitter Thread

@OfficialCharlotteWalsh: THREAD

1/x Nothing to see here. Women have been called worse for centuries.

2/x Here's a list of other things I've been called during this campaign. Let's get them out in the open. (click for more)

3/x Every single one of these insults comes from a man, usually a man who doesn't know me, who's never met me, who prefers to stay anonymous.

4/x Most men go their entire lives without ever calling a woman a c*nt

5/x I won't bother to tell Ted Slaughter he needs to work on his anger issues.

6/x I'm sick of having to explain to men the right things and wrong things to say to women.

7/x Slaughter has done his best to make PA an even more hostile place for women.

8/x I don't have the perfect sound bite for this. I wish I did.

9/x There has to be some good that comes out of this. Women have to feel comfortable saying we're sick of your petty insults.

10/x Why should I have to filter my own truths when men in power have no filter whatsoever.

11/x At the end of the day, this is a b*llsh*t distraction and the last thing anyone should worry about.

12/x I hope the most important thing you read today will not be a tweet.

CHAPTER 20
October 11, 2018

26 days to Election Day

Walsh (D)	Slaughter (R)	Spread
41	41	TIE

"How is it possible that Ted Slaughter's poll numbers haven't fallen off a cliff after he called me a cunt?" She could drive herself insane trying to find logic where logic no longer existed. She paced her kitchen, cell phone pressed to her ear.

Josh replied in a measured tone. "These days a male politician needs to get caught with a dead girl or a live boy in order to see his poll numbers dip. You know that by now."

It was a joke and it wasn't a joke. His words landed with a dull thud.

"But he called me a cunt!"

"Charlotte." His voice held a warning. "I let you blow off steam on Twitter last night. That was enough."

"I get it. It's not personal. Tell me again how the news cycle moves too fast for it to matter." In the past week two hurricanes had battered the nation's southern states, displacing thousands and leaving millions without power. A white nationalist had strapped twenty-seven pounds of dynamite to his body and held a primarily African-American school in Chicago hostage for seventy-two hours before a police sniper was able to put a bullet through his temple, rescuing more than three hundred elementary school children. A man in Milwaukee had been accidentally locked overnight in a beer cooler and drunk himself into a coma. The world had more to care about than Charlotte Walsh being called a cunt. It crumbled each day and rebuilt itself at night, just enough to feed the insatiable demand for content.

"Now, I have some more bad news for you. It's time to tell your husband. It's time to tell Max about Margaret's son."

Charlotte stared at her mouth in the reflection of the window as she spoke next. "Who's writing it?" She practiced keeping her eyes impassive.

"Walt Jones at the *Times*. He has proof. A copy of the kid's birth certificate with no father's name on it, a source from Humanity telling him Margaret admitted the affair with Max to them before moving to Singapore, and a second source close to Margaret claiming the father was definitely Max."

"How long do I have?"

"Less than twenty-four hours before the story breaks."

She needed caffeine. She mixed a spoonful of instant Nescafé into a cup of water and put it in the microwave, noticing red splatters from reheated chili or tomato soup coating the appliance's insides like a murder scene.

"I'll call you back," she whispered to Josh.

Two minutes later, she took a SAN FRANCISCO IS FOR LOVERS mug, purchased ironically by Max years ago before they began dating, into the backyard and sank onto a rickety chaise longue. Bob tagged behind her, tripping over his enormous paws. He dutifully sniffed the back fence, looking for a place to squat. She'd forgotten to bring poop bags outside with her and the mess would have to wait. It was the start of a beautiful fall morning, the sky a perfect shade of light blue that could either remind you of small joys or make you resent the rest of the world's happiness. *It shouldn't be so beautiful. The world should look gray and damp.* She lay back and closed her eyes, the old chair creaking under her weight, her butt nearly grazing the ground.

She didn't know how long she lay there before she heard Max tap on the kitchen window and saw him wave at her. He raised his protein shake in the air, silently asking her if she wanted one. She shook her head and began to stand. Her legs crumpled beneath her and she sat back down and closed her eyes again.

A shadow crossed over the sun, Max standing above her. *No. Go away. Not yet. I'm not ready.*

"Charlie?"

She pulled him down on the chaise next to her and kissed him as tears streamed down her cheeks.

"I need to tell you something." She'd practiced this conversation so many times in her head, each of them leading to different outcomes, none of them good.

"Are you okay?"

"Where are the girls?"

"What's going on? You're freaking me out."

"Where are they?"

"They're still in their bedroom."

"Are they awake?"

"Yeah."

"We need to have Leila take them for the morning." She sounded hysterical.

"Charlotte, what's wrong?" He grabbed her by her shoulders and stared into her eyes. There was love there, real love. *Is it enough?*

"I did a terrible thing. I need to talk to you. I need the girls to be out of the house so that we can talk."

"Just tell me. What did you do? Nothing could be that bad."

You have no idea.

"Please. Get them up. Give them breakfast. I'll text Leila to get them and then we can talk."

Thirty minutes passed in a blur.

"I want you each to bring one fairy costume." Charlotte heard Leila's bright voice explaining to her daughters that they were going to Aunt Kara's for a very exclusive tea party, costumes encouraged.

Bless her, Charlotte thought.

While the girls scrambled to find their sparkly dresses and wings, Leila made her another cup of coffee.

"What are you going to tell him?" she asked quietly. Whatever distance had grown between them had disappeared the moment Charlotte called Leila and asked for her help that morning. Something between them had shifted back to the way things were before the campaign drove a wedge between them.

"The truth."

Leila bit down on her lower lip. "I'm sorry you have to do this." She grabbed Charlotte's right hand in both of hers. "I'm here to do whatever you need."

Finally, Max and Charlotte were alone. They sat side by side on the couch. The interlude between their conversations did nothing to calm Max.

"What the hell is going on, Charlie?"

"I'm sorry. I'm so sorry." Her words sounded hollow because they didn't ring true. Charlotte still felt no remorse for what she'd done. When she'd first decided to keep this secret from Max, when she'd moved Margaret out of the country, she'd been certain she was doing the right thing for her family and for Margaret. Everyone had gotten what they needed out of Charlotte's plan, everyone except Max. She was sorry for the pain she was about to inflict. She was sorry she'd been caught and that made her feel even worse.

Variations of different lies looped through her head. Could she get away with telling him this had all been Margaret's idea and she'd just supported it? Did she have to tell the whole truth?

"I should have told you this a long time ago."

He flinched when she reached to touch him. "Told me what?"

"Margaret has a son."

Confusion flickered across his brow. He blinked like a child who doesn't understand what's happening.

Charlotte forged on. "Margaret has a little boy. He's about a year old. He's yours." *That's not the entire truth.* "I knew about it and I didn't tell you and I asked her not to tell you." *It's still not the entire truth.* "I helped her transfer to a new office and I sent her money to make sure they were comfortable." *Wasn't it close enough? Did he need to know it was all her idea?*

His face didn't change, didn't even twitch. The information still didn't make sense to him. She could see him trying to work it out. For a moment she thought he might accept her lies and machinations in stride, that it wouldn't completely alter the course of their lives.

"And now the story might be public as soon as tomorrow."

Max's features twisted and contorted into shapes she'd never seen or even imagined were possible. Rage crossed his eyes. He hated her in that moment. She was sure of it.

"He's my son?"

"Yes."

"He's my son?" His voice rose by several octaves as he stood and paced around the couch. "How could you do this? How could you keep this from me? What kind of a person are you? What kind of a monster are you?" His voice was thick with resentment as he leaned down over the back of the sofa to look directly in her eyes. His were wild like he wanted to hit her in the face.

"You've punished me for so long," he snarled bitterly. "You've played the victim. I've done everything you wanted. Everything. And all this time you've been playing me like a puppet, pulling my strings, pulling all of the strings, manipulating everyone to get what you wanted. You're sick, Charlotte. You're a fucking sociopath."

But you started it. If you hadn't screwed Margaret I never would have had to do this.

"I didn't create this situation. I just tried to fix it."

"Fix it. Fix it? Fuck your fixing. Look at you, the Fixer. I hated that fucking book. Did you know that? I hated everything about it. I hated the title. I hated your smug fucking author's photo. I was ashamed of it. I was embarrassed when it came out. What kind of man is married to a person like that, a person so smug she thinks she can fix the world? That's when I started thinking about fucking other people. I never told you that, did I? That was the moment I realized you thought you were better than everyone else. That's the moment I started to despise you."

These were the words he'd never said before. In the months spent in therapy neither of them had been honest. All those hours on Carol's couch and they'd only said what they believed the other one wanted to hear. The words that had seemed raw and honest in the moment had been half-truths.

"You knew exactly who I was when you married me."

"I married you because I felt sorry for you."

Charlotte felt a stabbing pain beneath her heart. It was the one line that could destroy her. Neither of them spoke right away.

"I didn't mean that."

"You did."

"I didn't."

"It's fine. I knew. I've always known."

"It's not the truth. I want to hurt you right now. I want to physically hurt you. I want to strangle you. I actually want to put my hands on your neck. I need to get out of here."

"What are we going to do?"

"We? We aren't going to do anything. Call your campaign manager. He'll figure out how to spin it. Maybe your poll numbers will go up. Every woman who has ever wanted revenge on their cheating husband will turn into a Charlotte Walsh evangelist."

"What about us?"

"I'm leaving."

"Back to California?"

"I'm going to start by leaving this house."

"Don't go," she said quietly and half-heartedly, knowing nothing she could say would make him stay.

He pivoted swiftly on his heel and stood just an inch away from her, his breath hot and smelling of sleep. He hadn't yet brushed his teeth.

"How could you have been so stupid as to think this wouldn't come out during this campaign? So cocky to think you didn't need to tell me before you put our family in the eye of a hurricane. And then that weekend when we went away you lied again and again. Said we're done with secrets. Done with keeping things from each other. What you meant was I, me, I was done with keeping secrets from you. Your secrets were something else."

Words failed her because he was right about everything. If she'd never entered this campaign, certain unfortunate things about their marriage could have stayed successfully buried.

He went on, his voice even louder. "You don't deserve to know what I'm going to do next. But I will tell you I want to meet my son and I will do that. I don't give a damn how it affects your campaign. This is my life and I didn't choose any of this and I'm going to start making my own choices."

The part of her that wanted to cry and beg him to stay was silenced by her more rational instincts, the instincts for survival, the same ones that had put them into this position in the first place. The next thing out of her mouth was engineered to strike back, to hurt, to manipulate.

"Think before you do anything rash, Max. Think about whether you want to lose your little girls by gaining a son." Merciless. She wanted to take it back, but she could no more take it back than he could take back telling her he married her because he felt sorry for her. Her coolness and malice achieved their intended effect and she saw, for the first time, that her husband was genuinely afraid of her.

"Go. Cool off. Go home to California if you want. I'll figure this out." *No. That's not what I want. I want you to keep screaming at me. Hit me if you need to and then hold me. I want you to forgive me.*

Max didn't say another word. He stomped upstairs. She could hear drawers opening and slamming. He didn't look at her when he came back down the stairs and walked out the door.

Charlotte went into the bathroom to splash water on her face.

She wandered into her girls' room and lay facedown on Ella's bed. Her face was buried in a foul-smelling Snoopy doll when Josh finally walked in.

"Where did Max go? I can't have any wild cards at this point."

"Let him cool off." Charlotte rolled onto her side. Had she fallen asleep before he walked in? She actually had no idea. Exhaustion had become a part of her, like another limb.

Josh pushed the pile of stuffed animals to the floor and sat next to her on the bed. "The only way to spin this is that you didn't know. That Max paid her to stay quiet. No one can ever know you hid this from Max. You can't be branded a liar."

More lies to cover the lies.

"We can't say that."

"Then you can flush this race down the goddamned toilet." Josh looked like he'd slept in his clothes, slightly hungover with pallid skin and bags beneath his watery eyes. "Charlotte?" He sounded like he'd been hit by a bus.

"Yes?"

He fiddled with a stuffed elephant missing one of its tusks. "Are you still in this race? I can end it now. You can end it now. It still won't be pretty, but I promise it will be easier." He rubbed at his eye with his pointer finger, pulling the lid down until Charlotte could see the filmy pink skin. "I'm not going to tell you what to do. I will see this to the end either way. But if you don't want to move forward no one would blame you." They were the most human words that had ever passed his lips.

As everything else crumbled around her she needed this campaign more than ever, needed both its neediness and constant validation, even its punishments. As grueling and terrible as it could be, the campaign was the only thing in the past year besides her children that had given her purpose. Her healing strategy this entire time had been to outrun her sadness, to work harder and faster and better to fill the pit of uneasiness. How could she stop running now?

Charlotte made her voice equally low. "I want to stay in."

Because what would happen if she ended it all now? She'd be the laughingstock techie who thought she could run with the big boys in Washington. Her downfall would be at best a farce and at worst a tragedy. Maybe she'd be forgotten—just another woman approaching fifty with one broken marriage under her belt reading self-help books about reinvention and pivoting and self-care.

"Okay," Josh said, his voice resigned. "So far, your issues, your marital issues, have actually softened you, kept you the underdog. Underdog is the best position a woman candidate can find herself in. The underdog is easier to like, believe it or not. Your marital shit makes you likable. Congratulations. You're the newly crowned warrior princess of the suburban white woman who thinks her husband is an asshole."

His analysis exhausted her. "I'll do whatever you think I need to do." She tried to imagine what that would look like, ran through the various scenarios in her head, before surrendering to the fact that she had no idea what would actually happen.

"We need to get in front of the story. You need to schedule a big interview with another woman. It's the women who will judge you for this. Men don't care. They don't vote with their hearts. Oprah, Diane Sawyer, Erika Cabot. I'll see who we can get. Maybe Oprah isn't the best, never been married. Sawyer's marriage to Nichols might have been too happy. Cabot could be the right fit. She has the dead husband, new fiancé, two handsome sons."

Josh cleared his throat. "You need to tell the staff. We need them behind us and they can't feel blindsided, can't feel like the press knows more than they do, even if that's true. We should get down to the office right away. I can call in as many of the field leads as we can get in an hour. I would say we could Skype with the rest, but it makes me nervous that someone could record it. Of course, there's always the chance of leaks once we start talking at all, but it's a chance we have to take."

Josh was an elegant machine as he sat on her daughter's bed and created a blueprint for the next forty-eight hours. When he was done the two of them awkwardly faced each other, realizing for the first time that they were sprawled on a child's bed.

"Remember I told you I ran a race in the Ukraine a few years back?" Josh formed a steeple with his two index fingers and used them to prop up his ample chin.

Charlotte nodded, forcing herself to be interested because it was clear Josh wanted to tell her this story and it was rare that he shared anything about his past campaigns or personal life. He never mentioned a wife or husband, girlfriend or boyfriend, and she got the sense he was desperately lonely. "Did he win? Your candidate?"

"She," Josh corrected her. "One of the first women to run in that district, actually. And yes, she did. She was wonderful. Brilliant, tough, didn't take shit from any of the men in the national party, all of them bullies, all misogynists, most of them criminals."

"Good for her." Charlotte believed he was telling her this story to draw a parallel between her and this woman half a world away, to help her believe that, in the end, it would all work out for her.

"Yes and no." Josh said with little enthusiasm. "The day after her victory party her opponent, a mean motherfucker from a family of thugs and gypsies, strapped a bar of dynamite to her cat and sent it running into her house, burning it to the ground. She escaped. No one in her family was hurt, thank God . . . well, except that cat."

"That's terrible. Why are you telling me this now?"

He got a faraway look in his eye like he wasn't sure why he had just told her the terrible story. "Politics is nasty everywhere in the world. Not just here." He paused and picked up the smelly Snoopy. "And you could have it worse. They could blow up your cat and set your house on fire." He stood without looking at her again and placed the doll gently beside her before he walked into the hallway and downstairs.

Leila returned from Kara's without the girls and focused her attention on Charlotte, making more coffee and toast while Charlotte showered and attempted to blow out her hair before pulling it, half wet, into a knot on the top of her head.

"How'd it go?" Leila asked quietly.

Charlotte blinked and shook her head slightly. "I can't even talk about it."

Within two hours forty staffers had gathered at the campaign office, some still wiping sleep from their eyes while others looked rumpled, like they hadn't gone to bed at all.

In the previous two hours, Charlotte had seen Josh drink six large cups of coffee.

She stood in front of the assembled group. "What I'm about to tell you is confidential and off the record. We have a zero-tolerance policy for leaks of any kind."

They'd decided on the ride from the house that Josh would be the enforcer, while Charlotte would play to the sympathies of her staff. She told an adapted version of her story, the one Josh had crafted to paint her in the best possible light. Max had had an affair. The woman had been a fellow employee at Humanity. Max had come to Charlotte when the woman told him she was pregnant. Together, Charlotte and Max had decided to support the woman in her decision to have the child. The woman had transferred to a Humanity office in Asia of her own volition. "The woman." She was always referred to as "the woman," never given a name. Calling her "the woman," calling her son "the child," made them seem less consequential, less real.

She continued to explain. Max and Charlotte had agreed to financially support the child because it was the right thing to do. She paused out of habit after saying "the right thing to do" because it had become her calling card and she was used to making it a sound bite, used to applause when she said it. Now it was greeted with stony silence. She finished with an apology for putting her staff in this position. She told them she still believed they could win this race.

Her western counties director, Erik Oliver, was the only one who couldn't contain himself. "I fucking knew it," he murmured, loud enough for Charlotte to hear him.

When she was finished, no one walked out of the room. They went back to work. Charlotte stuck around in case anyone had questions for her, but when they didn't she went outside for a walk and ended up on a park bench two blocks from the office. It was chilly for October and she hadn't worn a jacket or sweater, but the goose bumps were a modest distraction from the anxiety that came in fits and starts, gnawing at the back of her throat, her belly, the tips of her fingers. In the middle of the square stood a statue of an unnamed coal miner, a battered helmet on his head, a pickax slung over his shoulder, too-large boots covered over in bird shit, eyes glinting with hope.

Josh came to her twenty minutes later. "I just got off the phone with Margaret. She's still technically off the grid and she'll stay that way until after Election Day. The press won't get a statement out of her."

Charlotte breathed a small sigh of relief as Josh continued the logistics of crisis containment.

"Erika Cabot can do an interview with you as a news special for NBC tomorrow. We need Max. I promised the two of you together."

"I don't know if I can get him."

"You have to try. Tell him you'll never let him see the girls again." It gave her chills that she and Josh had immediately thought of the same scare tactic to manipulate her husband.

What kind of a monster have I become?

CHAPTER 21

Max could have been on a plane back to San Francisco already, but Charlotte doubted it. For all his flaws, her husband was a good father and he wouldn't have left their girls without saying goodbye.

Charlotte put on a baseball cap she found in the footwell of their van and pushed the brim low over her face as she walked into O'Puddy's. With her khakis and white button-down, she didn't pass for a regular. Linda, the rusty-haired cocktail waitress who'd fixed her Shirley Temples as a little girl, still worked the bar, and whistled as Charlotte squinted through the smoke. A decade ago, Pennsylvania banned smoking in most bars, but places like O'Puddy's took pleasure in discounting the law.

"Looky what the pussycat dragged in. Hey, girl," Linda hollered in a throaty voice. "Get over here."

Linda had been her father's favorite bartender forty years ago. Maybe she'd been more than that. Thin as a rail with penciled-in eyebrows and blue eye shadow caked into the folds of her eyelids, she wore a purple tank top with lace straps, the flesh below her arms dripping like cake batter that had boiled over the pan. The waist of her jeans was high and tight around the flabby bulge of her stomach.

"Sit down, girl. What can get I you?" The smell of stale beer soaked into carpet made Charlotte's stomach turn.

"I'm good." Charlotte looked around the bar. No sign of her husband. In the back of the bar three guys played a game of dominoes in one booth. A man slumped low in his seat at the next table over, his head resting on the table. No one moved to wake him or ask him to leave. A television bolted into the corner showed a golf tournament being played somewhere warm, tropical, and far away from here, maybe Hawaii. A second TV was tuned to a conservative news network, where an orange-faced pundit opened his mouth in an angry sneer that looked theatrical with the volume turned down. Beneath him were the words AMERICA IN CRISIS. *When is America not in crisis these days?* A mailman recently off his shift parked his metal cart next to his barstool. Toby Keith's "How Do You Like Me Now?!" warbled out of a dusty jukebox: *Do you still think I'm crazy standing here today?*

"Come on, honey. Have a drink," Linda pressed her. "It's five o'clock somewhere." It was currently two o'clock in Elk Hollow, Pennsylvania.

Feeling pressure to be polite, Charlotte settled onto one of the few empty stools. "I'll have a whiskey and Coke."

"That's my girl. You want a cherry in it for old time's sake?"

"Yeah, for old time's sake."

"Hey Walsh," the man to her left said. He could have been fifty or eighty. Ruptured veins along his nose splashed pink down his nostrils and across his cheeks. He was probably closer to her dad's age, Marty's age if he'd still been alive, which would have been what? Seventy? Seventy-one? He weighed close to three hundred pounds and sported a close-cropped haircut that let her know he was former military. His right eyelid drooped toward his cheek, making him appear weak or stupid, but Charlotte could tell he was neither of those things.

"You taking a break from the campaign today?"

His drinking buddy spilled his elbows over the bar and turned to get a better look at her. "You're the girl runnin' for governor."

"Shut it, Mick. She's runnin' for Senate." Mick shrugged and took a sip of his drink. His hands had a slight tremor. "What's the differ-ence." It wasn't a question. "She ain't gonna pay my mortgage."

"Can I buy you a drink?"

"No, thank you. I have one." And she wanted to finish it as quickly as possible. She waved for Linda. "Hey, Linda, you seen Max?" Linda tipped her head to one side to try to find the relevant information in her brain.

"Not this week. I saw him last week. He came in here for a beer last week, I think."

"Today, though? Have you seen Max today?"

Linda considered it again. "I don't think so, hon. I been on since eleven. I don't think I woulda missed him."

"I don't think you would have either." Charlotte took too large of a swallow. Her eyes warmed with the drink. Two more gulps like that one and it would be finished.

"Maybe Paul's seen him."

"I'll give him a call." She knew that she wouldn't. The last time she'd talked to Kara that morning, Paul was off on another bender. He'd sent a few texts confirming he was still alive, but he had yet to come home.

Confusion rippled Linda's forehead. "He's right there. Just go ask him." She pointed a turquoise fingernail toward the back of the bar. Charlotte looked back again at the man asleep in the back booth. Why hadn't she recognized him before? The wiry neck, the thinning black hair. It was her brother, all right.

The man with the red nose and short hair was smiling at her like he needed to say something. He wasn't drunk, but his eyes were watery and glassy.

"We're on your side, kid. You'll get us new jobs. We believe in you." He was missing an incisor on the left side. "I voted for Slaughter for the past thirty years but you got me. I trust you. You won't give us the runaround with that job-retraining bullshit. Who the hell do those people think I am? They think I'm gonna learn to install solar panels for a bunch of fuckin' yuppies. I got good skills. I don't need new ones."

She wanted to say something big and profound, but the words wouldn't come. His belief in her filled her entire body with dread. She would never be able to create jobs this man would qualify for. The best she could do would be to bring more distribution centers for e-commerce companies, maybe plant the seeds for a Rust Belt Silicon Valley, but what would that do for him? She kept peddling hope no one could deliver. Her hand tingled as she took another gulp of the whiskey and was surprised to see the bottom of the glass. Linda grabbed the empty, and before Charlotte could protest, she'd refilled it.

"Thanks," she said with real humility, feeling foolish for not having anything better to say. This could have been the first unscripted conversation she'd had with a voter in months. "I'm gonna do my best."

"You'll be great, kid. I didn't have any daughters. I got three good-for-nothing sons. They all left here. But that was for the best. The young people should leave. But if I had a girl I'd like if she woulda been like you. Real smart-like. Doin' something with her life. Your dad woulda been real proud. I bet da old bastard is lookin down or up from wherever he is right now and thinkin' he done one good thing raisin' youse."

The mention of Marty and the whiskey softened her and made her feel a real affection for the man. She cursed the tears welling in the corners of her eyes. This campaign had begun as a way to heal, but instead it had peeled back layers of emotion she'd believed were long buried.

"Thank you. I should go. But thank you. I appreciate it." She grabbed both his hands in hers and leaned over to kiss him on the cheek. It was rough, and the taste of tobacco smoke and Old Spice lingered on her lips when she pulled away. "I really am going to do my best." She noticed a pack of crumpled Newports on the bar next to the man's sweaty beer mug.

"Can I take a couple of those for the road?"

He handed her the entire pack. "You look like you could use more than two."

Charlotte stood to walk back toward her brother. *I'll wake him up. I'll tell him he's got to go to rehab. I'll pay for rehab.* His head lurched to the side and he let out a long, low burp, followed by the kind of smile a baby enjoys after relieving himself.

Or maybe I don't have to be the one to fix him. Maybe it isn't my job to fix him.

She turned to Linda. "Make sure he gets home okay."

It wasn't until she reached the car that she pulled her phone from her pocket and noticed the four missed calls from Roz.

"Where are you?"

"Looking for Max." Charlotte noticed a tinny, faraway quality to her voice. "Where are you?"

"I'm on my way to Elk Hollow."

"Who called you?" She had never imagined when she first met Rosalind Waters more than twenty years earlier that she would feel such relief at knowing her mentor was coming to help her.

"Leila and then Josh. How are you holding up?" Roz's voice contained the right amount of empathy.

"I'm not."

"I didn't think so."

"How much did they tell you?"

"Everything. Thought it would be easier for them to tell me than for you to have to fill me in. They wanted my advice."

"I can't picture Josh wanting anyone's advice."

"He didn't ask for it."

"How close are you?"

"Just past Philly. Plymouth Meeting. I've always thought Plymouth Meeting was a terrible name for a town."

"Blame the Quakers."

"They got a lot of things right and a couple of things wrong. We would probably have been better off if they'd stayed in charge. What are you going to say to Max?" Roz's big voice echoed through the car speakers.

"I don't know. Beg him to do what we need to do to help me stay in this race?" Charlotte said automatically. "Should I stay in this race?"

"I can't answer that."

"What would you do?"

"I'd stay in the race." Roz didn't say anything else for a minute. Charlotte heard her flick the turning blinker and spin the steering wheel. When she spoke next she changed the subject. "Have I told you that I haven't written the opening chapter of my memoir yet?"

"Shouldn't you do that first? Isn't that how a memoir starts? With a beginning?"

"I couldn't figure out how to start so I skipped it and wrote through it. When I got past the beginning I was able to push through the next four hundred pages. I keep coming up with opening lines like 'There are a few things you probably don't know about me.'"

"It's no 'Call me Ishamel,' but it isn't bad."

"I'm also thinking, 'It's the worst of times and also the worst of times. . . .'" Roz's brawny laughter filled the car. "My book's about regret. It took me twenty years of therapy, twenty-seven chapters, two different editors, and a new ghostwriter to realize that. It's about the road not taken, the road I wasn't allowed to take." Charlotte envied Roz's ability to be so introspective.

"But you had an incredible career. You were a governor, a congresswoman. You were the ambassador to the UN."

"I could have been more."

At the turnout for Bear Cove, she saw Max's car parked just beyond the guardrail where the road turned to dirt. Charlotte pulled in next to it and lit one of the Newports.

"I found him."

"Are you ready for this conversation?"

"I don't have a choice." Before they hung up, there was one last question she needed to ask. Roz's regret had to have something to do with Richard, with all his baggage and bullshit holding her back all these years. "Why didn't you ever divorce Richard? All those other women for so long. Once you made it to Congress, why didn't you leave him?"

"The truth?"

"Of course."

Roz breathed in and out several times. "Richard married his gay best friend."

It took a beat for Charlotte to connect those dots and when she did she felt as though a trapdoor had been pulled out from beneath her. Roz was gay. It was such a simple thing to know and such a complicated thing to learn decades after befriending a person and thinking that you knew everything about them.

"Roz . . ." In shock, Charlotte didn't even know where to begin, what to say. A flood of regret washed through her as she wondered what she could have done to help Roz confide in her earlier.

"Charlie, listen to me. Please, listen to me. For the most part we were very happy. We both got what we needed and wanted—children, stability, the respect of our peers. It was a different time."

It hit her just how long Roz had kept this secret. Charlotte wondered whether this meant that Roz had never really trusted her at all. Her heart ached for her friend and mentor who'd felt like she had to live a lie all of these years.

"I didn't know," Charlotte said softly, completely unprepared for this conversation.

"Of course you didn't, honey. No one did. I was a very good politician. You're maybe the third person I've told. I've got entire chapters written about it locked in a drawer and I still haven't decided whether they'll see the light of day."

Charlotte understood too well the toll a secret took on you and couldn't begin to imagine keeping one as big as this.

"There's more to tell. We have some wine to drink when this race is over. But right now let's focus on you, okay?" Roz's voice had turned bright and it was easy for Charlotte to imagine her smiling. "Now go talk to your husband. Your marriage is worth saving. So was mine, for that matter. No one can judge someone else's relationship. It's all too goddamned complicated. Human beings are too goddamned complicated. But for some reason, we need our politicians to be simple and neat, particularly our women. Speak to Max, and then we'll talk."

★

It was a two-mile hike uphill to reach the lake and the cave that constituted Bear Cove, and Max's favorite place was another mile above that, near a smaller pond made from a spring far underground. He still believed he was the only person who knew it was there at all besides Charlotte and now the girls, who delighted in capturing small turtles in the clear mountain water and covering their faces in mud and pretending to be baby bears.

She was out of breath, but the crisp air sobered her up by the time she reached the first lake. She shivered in her too-thin shirt damp with her sweat. The Poconos were known as rolling mountains, more hills than the kinds of rocky peaks they'd become accustomed to on the West Coast, and yet Max's favorite spot involved a climb of nine hundred feet.

His knees came into view first, sticking up in the tall grass of the meadow as she came around the last bend in the steepest part of the incline. Her husband's eyes were closed but she could see the easy rise and fall of his chest. A fifth of Jameson sat half empty beside his left foot. A second lay in reach of his right fingers. The grass and dirt beside him was wet and smelled like something foul. The odor of stale pond water waiting to be replenished by the winter snow caught in the air. She didn't say anything when she sat down. A family of pill bugs struggled beneath her thighs. She shifted her legs and flicked them away with her index finger. She and Max stayed like that for five minutes. The stillness felt raw and painful and necessary.

She finally spoke first. "Did you really marry me because you felt sorry for me?"

He didn't answer right away. Then he ignored her question.

"Did you start smoking again?"

"No."

"Give me one."

Charlotte brought the crumpled pack and the matches from her pocket, removed two cigarettes, lit one with the last match, and used the first to light the second.

"I miss smoking."

"Me too."

"It was great. Why'd we stop?"

"We grew up. It kills you."

Another long beat of silence, maybe five minutes.

He squinted at her as a cloud passed and darkened his face. "I didn't marry you because I felt sorry for you."

"Then why'd you say it?"

"Why do people say anything? I felt like shit. I knew it would piss you off. I know you think it. I know you better than you think I do."

"Then why?"

"Why what?"

"Why'd you marry me?"

"You were the smartest and most capable woman I'd ever met. You were my best friend. I never wanted to marry a woman like my mother, someone who needed a man to get through life. I knew you'd always want to take care of yourself. You made me laugh. You made me happy. I knew I'd never be bored."

"Were you attracted to me?" It sounded so shallow.

"I've always been attracted to you. We had a good sex life. It wasn't why I married you, though."

He wasn't drunk, but he wasn't sober either. His words traveled slowly.

"Will you please sit up and look at me?"

"I can't."

Charlotte folded her arms across her chest, holding herself close. "That's mature."

"No. I can't. I threw out my back on the way up here." Max hadn't thrown out his back in a decade and the last time he'd been hang gliding in Marin. Were their bodies really reaching the point where a strenuous walk could put them out of commission?

"Were you ever going to tell me about my son?"

His son. He has a son. There's a little boy thousands of miles away who is half Max. When she allowed herself to think about it, the weight of what she'd done sunk her heart lower in her chest.

It was her turn to be quiet. The truth was, she'd hoped she'd never to have to tell him. She'd believed she could keep the boy a secret for the rest of their lives and had somehow trusted Margaret to do the same. It had been audacious and cruel. She saw that now.

"I wanted to."

"No, you didn't." There was something comforting in his accusation, in how well it proved he knew her.

"You're right. I didn't. I wanted it all to go away and I wanted to forget about it."

"And you knew it was terrible, that you were doing a terrible thing?"

"I knew it was terrible for you. It was right for the girls and me. Especially for the girls. I couldn't imagine them growing up knowing about this half brother, especially Annie, so close in age. It's the kind of thing that fucks kids up for the rest of their lives, Max."

"They're going to know now."

"I know that and I hate it. I still hate you for what you did. I still hate you for a lot of things."

"Now we're even. I hate you for a lot of things, too."

Charlotte shook her head and stared up at the sky. She felt as though they'd aged twenty years in the past twenty days. "Do you want a divorce?"

He moved his arm away from his eyes for a moment and rolled his head toward her. "I don't know. Do you?"

"I don't know either."

They didn't speak for a while after that. She twisted the cap off his bottle and took a long pull.

"I'm staying in the race."

"I'll bet you are," he said, his voice tinged with bitterness.

"I can't do it without you." What did she expect from him? She knew what she wanted. She wanted him to stand by her side and smile and nod and cover up her lies.

"And what if I disagree? Then what? Then you withhold my daughters from me? Make them hate me?" He had become a broken man, a man stripped of his ego, his strength, his defense mechanisms. She had done this to him.

"I shouldn't have said that."

"You shouldn't have said that."

"I didn't mean it."

"Yes, you did. You have to tell me the truth. From now on. You tell me the fucking truth."

"I meant it."

He winced as he propped himself up on his elbow and reached for the bottle, now closer to her than to him. "I wouldn't put it past you to do it, either. It was a righteous threat. It would work. You can have me eating out of your hands. That's how you fix things, Fixer. You dangle my children in front of me and threaten to take them away."

"It doesn't have to be like that. I still love you." It was the truth. She did still love him, loved him despite all the pain he'd caused her in the past two years, despite the fact that he could still ruin everything she'd worked so hard to achieve. "Do you love me?"

"It doesn't matter. What matters is whether I agree to do this for you."

"Will you?"

"Haven't decided."

Charlotte stood. Her legs were stiff. She bent her knees and let her head fall down toward her feet to stretch the backs of her thighs. When she dangled her arms down toward the ground she brushed a crumpled leaf from Max's chest. "We're supposed to do an interview together tomorrow morning."

"I'll decide by then."

Erika Cabot was a fierce bitch.

The previous summer, after meeting at the Women Are the Future conference, Erika and Charlotte had a night on the town, or what constituted a night on the town for two professional women and mothers nearing fifty who preferred to be in bed by 10 p.m. After they shared the stage for the conference's keynote interview, the two women decided to go for a drink and decamped to a nameless Midtown bar with low lighting, red banquettes, and good-looking male waiters who were probably models or poets, who posed prettily with a drink before setting it on the table. Erika and Charlotte's plan to have a glass of red wine had turned into three strong drinks, a bourbon for Erika and a 7 and 7 for Charlotte and a molten chocolate cake to split between the two of them that didn't fulfill its promise of being particularly molten.

Ten years earlier, days after Erika had been promoted to be the first female anchor of a network nightly news show, her husband had died in a drunk-driving accident in East Hampton. He nodded off at the wheel, his heel hit the gas, and their Range Rover shot across the median. A teenage girl in the opposite lane swerved to get out of his way and landed in a ditch, leaving the driver and passenger with severe concussions. John Cabot hit an oak tree head-on and was killed instantaneously. The parents of the teenagers sued the Cabot family for their pain and suffering and were awarded an undisclosed amount in the seven-figure range.

John Cabot wasn't an alcoholic. He wasn't even a frequent drunk driver. He was merely a fool. He was a fool Erika loved madly and raised two boys with. When her world fell apart, she took a leave of absence from work. In the midst of the greatest tragedy of her life, the press castigated Erika and her dead husband, branding him a menace to society and holding her complicit in his poor decision-making. Every detail of her marriage and professional character was scrutinized. Then, a couple of years later, she was diagnosed with stage four breast cancer and underwent a double mastectomy. Her book, *Rebuilt*, still topped the bestseller list. The network made her the headliner of a morning talk show, which soon became the highest-rated program on morning television. She still reported for the evening broadcast and for their cable affiliate. Last year, she'd gotten engaged to a professional cellist half her age. Erika understood marriage, real marriage, real heartbreak, but more important, she understood how a woman's personal life was often a liability for her professional life.

With the promise of an exclusive interview, Erika had agreed to be in Elk Hollow with a crew the next morning. It wouldn't be fluff. She wouldn't go easy on Charlotte, but she would let her tell her side of the story.

Charlotte texted Max the details and asked him to be at the house by 8 a.m. She didn't let on to Josh and Leila that there was a chance he might not show. If he didn't come, she was determined to do the interview alone.

★

Every available space in Charlotte's kitchen and living room was occupied with a staffer on their laptop. Leila ordered dinner for everyone, pizza with too much cheese that burned the roof of Charlotte's mouth.

"Why did you keep the child a secret?" Roz asked her in yet another mock interview.

"I wanted to protect both this woman and her child. If the roles were reversed I would have wanted the same courtesy."

"Not good enough," Roz snapped.

"Then ask me a different damned question already," Charlotte snapped back.

Patience frayed, tensions ran high. Charlotte was sick of answering the same ten questions over and over.

"I'm tired."

"I'll brew coffee." Josh rummaged in the cabinet to find coffee filters.

Leila put a stop to it all. "She needs sleep. She's good on her feet, but she'll be shit if she's exhausted. Let her rest."

Rosalind followed Charlotte upstairs and sat on the corner of her bed holding the stems of two red-wine glasses in one hand and a pack of Marlboros in the other. She offered a glass and a cigarette to Charlotte and lit one of her own, not bothering to open a window. "Wretched things."

"Roz?" Charlotte had so many questions for her. Was she coming out? Had she not trusted her after all these years to keep her secret?

Roz raised a hand to put a stop to them. "Not now. We need to talk about what you really want to say tomorrow."

★

Erika Cabot's assistant wore a crisp white shirt and black glasses that were strictly decorative. Their crew of eleven arrived at dawn to construct a miniature set in Charlotte's living room that required moving half of their furniture into the backyard. They brought their own hair and makeup people. Kara was still taking care of her girls.

Charlotte felt ridiculous in a demure violet shift dress made of expensive and itchy fabric with an American flag pin over her left breast.

"I know it isn't you and I don't care. I need you looking 110 percent domestic and contrite in this interview if we want this to work," Josh instructed. "Soft makeup, soft hair, pastels and pearls. Channel your inner Bonnie Slaughter."

Charlotte looked to Roz for confirmation. The older woman nodded. It was strange to have all of these people in her bedroom. "He's right. This is about your marriage. You're playing the role of wife. It's a wife costume."

But she had no husband.

"Where's Max?" Josh finally asked. "If he's not coming I need to know."

He might not come. "He'll be here," Charlotte lied.

Roz shot her a pointed look and seconded her. "He'll be here."

She heard the front door open and saw hope flash through her eyes in the mirror. Leila's voice was on the stairs. "I have bagels." She paused in the doorway and sized up Charlotte's outfit.

"You look like Laura Bush."

"You're not helping, Leila." Josh shot her a simpering stare.

Leila shrugged. "It's true. She doesn't look like Charlotte Walsh."

"That's the whole goddamn point. She needs to look like someone else for five goddamned minutes. Otherwise Charlotte Walsh is the victim here."

"Don't you think the press is going to see right through this?" Charlotte said.

"The press sees what we want them to see." Josh snorted. "Where's your husband?"

"He's finishing up a call in the car," Leila said nonchalantly. "In the driveway."

Charlotte tried her best to conceal her surprise. It was 7 a.m. Who was he talking to? It was just about 7 p.m. in Singapore. Could he be talking to Margaret? Had he already spoken to his son? The front door slammed again.

She smoothed the dress down her hips. "We should go down." Charlotte could hear Erika Cabot's no-nonsense New York accent in the living room asking for hair and makeup. "I look like a dead cat. I need some serious help this morning, Jenny. Get me in that chair before you start on Walsh."

Television lights were rigged all over the family room and three chairs were poised near the fireplace, one on one side, a pair on the other. Family photos of Charlotte, Max, and the girls lined the mantel. There was her wedding photo, her veil caught in a gust of wind and flying behind her at a forty-five-degree angle, Max laughing, his mouth open so wide you could see his molars. That photograph hadn't been framed in this house before. Josh must have printed it out overnight and placed it in a frame as if it had been there forever. There was a photo of the five of them down the Jersey Shore earlier this summer lifted straight from the Lulu-curated Instagram. They all wore white shirts, tan pants, and easy smiles that conveyed they knew their matching outfits were a little much.

"Charlotte Walsh. How the hell are you?" On television, Erika Cabot cultivated a sophisticated and refined insouciance. When the cameras were off she cursed like a sailor, a trait Charlotte appreciated very much.

Charlotte didn't have to force her smile. "I've been better."

"I like the pearls. We'll have a matching pair. They're like a fancy dog collar. Ruffffff!" Erika's laugh was low and deep as she fingered the strand of shimmering beads on her own neck and yelped like a dog. "Fucking pearls." She stared directly at her. "Was that Max in the driveway?"

"He gets better reception out there."

"Did he sleep here last night?"

Charlotte looked out the window for a moment, just long enough to let the humiliation pass from her face. "Of course he did."

"You don't have to bullshit me off camera. I'm so fucking sorry you're going through this. I was rooting for you. I'm still rooting for you. And I can't imagine how it feels to deal with this after everything you've worked to build. I hope that motherfucker is remorseful." That motherfucker was Charlotte's husband. Josh had filled Erika in on Max's affair, painting Max as the villain.

"He is. It's been difficult for both of us." Oh, how badly she wanted to sit cross-legged here on the floor with Erika and admit just how terrible it had been, just how much it all still hurt, how terrified she was of the future. But no matter how fun an evening they'd once had, no matter how much she felt like she could trust this woman who'd gone through so many personal struggles worse than Charlotte's, she knew she couldn't trust anyone outside the inner circle with the entire truth. For a brief moment she realized that this was how Rosalind had felt her entire life.

She needed to give Erika something small, some kernel of truth.

"I'm so tired," she admitted.

Sympathy flashed across Erika's pale-blue eyes. "I know, honey. Trust me, I know."

Charlotte changed the subject. "When's your wedding? Soon, right?"

"Next month. It'll be small. I'm too old for the white-wedding bullshit. Doing it at my house in Sagaponack. Just my boys and his family and about fifteen members of the Philharmonic. Reception afterward in the backyard for whoever wants to come. Simple. Happy."

"That's pretty much what we did . . . well, minus the Philharmonic."

"Palm Desert, right?"

"You did your research."

"My staff's good." Erika's eyes were intent on Charlotte, her expression flush with pity. "So, is there anything you don't want to talk about? Anything you don't want to answer?"

This made Charlotte laugh. "All of it. Can we just talk about who I want to win the World Series this year? Has that happened yet?"

Erika chuckled again and Charlotte wished for a second time they were just two girlfriends having a chat over strong drinks.

"I'm honestly not even sure who's in the running, but I imagine I should say I hope the Phillies win."

"That's probably right."

The front door creaked when it opened. There was Max, clean-shaven in a recently pressed blue shirt and navy blazer over khaki pants, an American flag pin on his left breast.

"You must be Erika." Max smiled wide, ready to be charming. "My wife told me about you last time you took her out. I imagine today will be a little more sobering." *He should be the one running for office.*

Erika stretched her hand toward Max, her mouth now set in a grim line. "A pleasure to meet you. Sorry it has to be under these circumstances."

"So am I." Max managed to look contrite.

"I was just asking Charlotte if there's anything you don't want to discuss."

"We know you need to do your job. We just want to tell the truth here." He sounded as though he'd been coached.

"Your girls, do they know?"

Charlotte looked at Max. "They don't. We'll find the right time to tell them together. All of this happened so quickly. They're still very young. As you can imagine, it isn't an easy thing to explain."

"Ms. Walsh, are you ready to get started with hair and makeup?" A small woman wielding a large brush snuck up behind her.

"I am."

It took an hour to give her a helmet of network-friendly hair, airbrushed foundation, and an abundance of eyeliner. Roz, unadorned, completely without makeup and wearing a simple black hoodie, chatted with Erika.

"Give me five minutes to talk to my husband?" Charlotte excused herself to walk outside where Max was talking on his cell phone.

Max hung up the phone as she approached. "You look like Martha Stewart."

"Leila said Laura Bush."

"Her too."

"I didn't know if you'd come."

"I didn't know if I'd come until Roz came to see me at the motel late last night."

Charlotte was genuinely surprised. "She did?"

"Thought you knew."

"I had no idea."

"We had a couple of drinks and smoked a couple of Cubans. She's very persuasive. Would have made a damn good president, or one of those guys who gets you to upgrade your cell phone plan in the AT&T store."

"What did she say?"

"The short version?"

"That's all we have time for."

"She told me to do what long-suffering political wives have been doing since the beginning of time for their politician husbands—dress to impress, smile with teeth, sit by your side, hold your hand, and lie."

"I assume there's more to it than that."

"You asked for the short version."

"Do you know what you're going to say?"

"I'm saying what you want me to say." He looked her in the eyes. "It's my mess. I created it. You made it worse. Much, much worse. But I'll handle this. I owe you that."

But what about us? What about our marriage? Are you leaving? Are you leaving me?

"I appreciate that."

"Hey kids, it's time to get this party started," Josh shouted from the front door. "You look good, Max. Like a young Republican."

"I hate him," Max murmured under his breath.

"He's an acquired taste."

★

"I want to offer the voters of Pennsylvania an apology," Charlotte began once the cameras rolled.

"What are you apologizing for, Charlotte?" Erika Cabot leaned in close to the two of them. The audience couldn't see it, but Charlotte knew there was a camera behind her that would capture Erika's attentive, inquisitive expression. There was a similar camera behind Erika's back, and that was where Charlotte directed her answers.

"I want to apologize for not being completely straightforward about my marriage. A little over two years ago, my husband and I went through a difficult time. I know a lot of people, women and men, will understand that, will understand how trying and complicated a real marriage can be. We went through a hard time and we separated briefly. We chose to keep this quiet for the sake of our little girls."

"How long did the separation last?" Erika cocked her head to the side.

"A couple of months. It wasn't long," Charlotte said.

"And during that time you lived apart?"

"We did."

"And did you see other people?"

"This is difficult to talk about."

A burnished silver box of tissues had been strategically placed on the low table next to Charlotte.

"I understand," Erika said, as she'd said in so many interviews before. Her ability to adequately convey empathy on camera was part of what made her so good at this job. She picked up a glass of water from the table and pressed it into Charlotte's hand.

"During our separation Max did spend time with another woman. She became pregnant. She had a child." Charlotte reached for a tissue. Her tears were real. They'd promised this mascara wouldn't run.

Erika reached over to touch Charlotte's knee.

Max backed her up. "I made a mistake, a terrible one that I will regret for the rest of my life. It was a time when I should have been working on our marriage, and I was selfish and irresponsible."

Erika nodded at Max but kept her eyes focused on Charlotte.

"You've never told anyone about this?"

"One or two close confidants and that was all. I was protecting my family." Charlotte looked Erika directly in the eye, which she knew meant she was looking the viewer directly in the eye.

"And the woman and her child? What happened to them?"

Now Max spoke. "Of course, I offered to support the child. We agreed to support the child together. Charlotte and I. We've been doing so quietly."

"And have you met this child? Either of you?"

Max winced. "At the mother's discretion we have let her make the decision as to whether she would like me to be involved in his life."

"And do you want that?" Erika pressed. "Do you want to be in his life?"

"I want whatever is best for my family and for everyone involved."

Erika produced a copy of *Vanity Fair* from beneath her chair. "This story. This headline: 'Is This Having It All?' Was this story a lie?"

"No." Roz had prepared Charlotte for something like this. It was the most honest thing she'd say in the entire interview. "This is what having it all really looks like. It's not easy. It's messy and flawed and imperfect." Erika didn't try to conceal her smile at the answer.

"Why talk about this now?"

That was her cue to return to Josh's script. "I don't want to keep secrets from the voters. I'm sick of politicians who say one thing and do another in their personal lives. I didn't want someone else to try to tell my story, our story, and get it wrong."

"Then why not talk about it earlier?"

"I honestly didn't believe that it mattered. Now I understand that it does." Despite all of their practice the night before, each question felt like a hot knife slicing through her heart.

"How will this affect your campaign? Do you think voters care?"

They shouldn't care. It has nothing to do with how I will do my job. It's absurd I have to pretend they should even be allowed to care.

"Voters need to feel like they can trust me, and I will do everything I can to ensure they can trust me. There has been a lot of speculation about my marriage in the press. The press can be terribly vicious, especially to women." There was a long pause to let the audience and Erika know she was referencing how Erika's own name had been dragged through the mud. "I'm here to tell you my campaign is strong. My marriage is strong." *Tell people one true thing before you tell them a lie.* "We're going to win this race, and I am going to accomplish real change in Washington."

Max spoke next, his voice low and sad and sincere.

"What I did was unforgivable and it was a mistake, but it was a mistake between two consenting adults that does not reflect on Humanity or on my wife's work there. Every day I am humbled by my wife's work ethic, by her desire to improve the lives of practically everyone she comes in contact with. No one should be blamed for what I did except me."

★

When it was over, Charlotte and Max drove together to pick up the girls. Sweat stained the purple crepe dress she'd never wear again. She should have changed, but both her mind and body were numb.

They drove in silence for five minutes before Charlotte spoke.

"Who were you on the phone with?"

"When?"

"Before the interview."

"The girls."

"What will we tell them?"

"We'll call Carol or a child shrink. Get a professional opinion."

"Good idea."

He cracked a wry smile. "Didn't our fucked-up childhoods make us more interesting?"

"Depends how you define interesting. It will give one of them enough fodder for a bestselling novel and another one an excuse when they end up in jail or on the pole. Have you talked to Margaret?"

"No. When I talk to her I want us to do it together. I hope we can do it together."

Both of them fell silent. Charlotte squinted into the steely October sky. In all the times she'd imagined the moment when all their secrets were revealed to each other, she'd never pictured this kind of stillness.

At last Max spoke. "Charlie."

She turned her head to look at him, detecting resignation in his voice.

"Max."

"I'll stay through the campaign. Then we need some time apart."

★

Erika Cabot's interview aired at 8 p.m. It took less than five minutes for the Internet to respond.

PA Senate Candidate Reveals Husband's Affair in Interview
Charlotte Walsh's Political Love Triangle
Tech Titan's Husband Has Secret Love Child

By 10 p.m., think pieces from pundits, columnists, partisans, hacks, and a handful of actual journalists appeared online. Some focused on whether Charlotte was to blame for her husband getting another woman pregnant.

A handful came to her defense.

Leave Walsh's Personal Life Out of It
Senate Candidate Brutally Honest About the Reality of Having It All
How Dare We Attack a Woman for Keeping Her Family Together
Don't Blame Her for His Bullshit

Charlotte huddled with her staff in the living room. Slaughter released a brief statement at 11 p.m. "Our hearts are with the Walsh family as they go through this difficult time. Charlotte Walsh may want to consider stepping down from this race to begin healing her family."

"Fuck him," Leila said. "He's acting as if someone died."

"That's the point," Josh said. "He's acting as if her campaign has died. But there's good news."

"Yeah?"

"You've raised more grassroots donations in increments below fifty dollars in the past five hours than you have in the past two months."

"Why?"

"People like an underdog. The more you're attacked, the harder your supporters will fight. Maybe they like your honesty. Maybe they don't like to see a woman beat up by the press. Until now, small-dollar donors didn't think you needed them because you're rich as fuck. Everyone needs to feel needed. You're more likable as a loser? I don't know. But we'll take it. And we'll use it to get boots on the ground for the next two weeks and ads on people's televisions and computers."

"It's unbelievable," Leila muttered quietly.

"It's not. It's close, but it looks like you're inching ahead of him again in the polls." Josh explained. "Never underestimate the power of cutting through the noise."

★

A gang of off-duty strippers, no doubt dispatched by Slaughter's goons, intercepted Max during school drop-off the next week. They formed a circle around him as soon as he stepped out of the car, wrapping their arms around him, pushing their breasts into his sides and back. They played ring-around-the-rosy with Charlotte's husband as their prisoner. Cameras whirred and clicked. Max pushed one woman away, hard. He ran back to their car and refused to come out. Within an hour, the video of the altercation appeared to show Max shoving a half-naked woman to the ground.

The next day, one of the other children in the twins' class told Rose that her daddy told her he wanted to punch Ella and Rose's mommy in the face. That night Charlotte didn't hesitate before buying her children and husband plane tickets to get the hell out of the state of Pennsylvania and back to California.

"Are you sure?" Max asked. "Josh said you needed us for Halloween. Family trick-or-treating, some parade?"

"I'll deal with Josh. Go."

It was for the best. Television news vans turned the road in front of their house into a parking lot, their satellite dishes blocking out the sun. Protesters regularly stood opposite them screaming things like "Media scum!" and "Fuck the fake news!" Charlotte couldn't tell if the protesters were for or against her, but she was relieved her children were gone.

No reliable poll numbers were available until the end of the week. In the meantime, they implemented a strategy Josh referred to as "throw shit against the wall and pray."

"You can hide or you can act like nothing's wrong," Josh said. "The show has to go on or it gets canceled. Act like none of it matters. Voters take their cues from you."

She made an appearance at the Warren County ox roast and farm machinery show, an event that boasted the best braised oxtail in the state. Commercial-grade barbecue grills held boiling vats of bubbling bone broth. Charlotte ate ox seven ways. She complimented a series of ox sculptures made from a half ton of butter before she answered questions vetted in advance by Josh.

"Acknowledge the five-hundred-pound elephant in the room and move on," Josh instructed.

Charlotte smiled humbly when Carly Meeks asked her whether she felt like a hero to women who'd endured crises in their own relationships.

"I thought the most exciting question I would answer today would be about barbecue sauce, but I was wrong."

"Can you say that one more time on video?" Carly held up her phone.

"Do you really think the readers of *Teen Vogue* care, Carly?" Charlotte covered her frown with her hand for a brief moment before mustering the enthusiasm for her flat joke one more time.

Carly stood taller. "I work at the *Washington Post* now. Thanks mostly to my coverage of you. Seriously, thank you."

"You're welcome, Carly. Turn on the video."

Charlotte forced her smile to turn serious without ever becoming a frown and delivered another answer. "There are no heroes here. I'm a wife and a mother doing what's best for my family, and very soon I hope to be a senator doing what's best for the people of Pennsylvania."

I'm not conveying intelligence or the ability to promote policies that would quite possibly make a difference in these people's lives. I'm not speaking truth to power. The only thing I now convey is "Like me," "Forgive me," "Pardon me."

Charlotte felt raw and exposed. Press and pundits labeled her a hero, a villain, and a victim, but each day she felt more like a fool.

★

Josh pulled out his computer and showed her their new commercial.

It opened with black-and-white shots of what looked like a post-apocalyptic industrial wasteland that Charlotte soon recognized as old factories on the outskirts of Elk Hollow. It cut to a picture of Paul looking exhausted, beaten down.

"I've applied for twenty-three jobs in the past year and haven't gotten a single callback. I can't catch a break."

Charlotte paused the video. "When did you film this?"

"Last week."

"My brother didn't tell me about the jobs."

"Did you ask him? Keep watching."

The next shot was of Jack and Emily Seligson. "Because of Ted Slaughter, we can't afford lifesaving treatments for my wife's cancer," Jack said.

The statements came faster.

A woman Charlotte met at a campaign event clutching a crying baby: "I can't afford to feed my child."

A man sitting on a barstool: "I've been out of work for five years. My benefits dried up. I lost my house. It's a living nightmare."

Then, bold words in capital letters came onto the screen. TED SLAUGHTER'S PENNSYLVANIA IS A LIVING NIGHTMARE.

The pièce de résistance was a clip of Ted Slaughter falling asleep in the Senate chamber. It cut to video of Charlotte driving her minivan, lingering on the Chevy emblem, a subtle reminder to the audience that Charlotte drove American. It showed her getting out of the car, speaking to voters, taking notes. It finished with her voice: "Ted Slaughter isn't listening to you. I am listening to you. I will fix this."

It was a fast-paced $30,000 blatant manipulation.

"It's like Nazi propaganda," Leila whispered.

"Propaganda is the only thing the Nazis were good at," Josh managed with a straight face.

"It's exploitation," Charlotte said.

"A campaign is exploitation."

"My brother agreed to that? Jack agreed to that?"

"Are you kidding? Your brother loved doing it. He thinks it made him famous, and we paid Jack enough money that he doesn't need to sling fries for a year and I got Emily an appointment at the Mayo Clinic next week. Now, one more thing. Slaughter had a minor heart attack last week. Didn't tell anyone, not even his staff. We have footage of him in the hospital. He looks gnarly . . . knocking on death's door. Don't ask me how we got it. You don't need to know and you shouldn't know. I am leaving it up to you whether we release it or not."

The voice that came out of her mouth wasn't hers. "Do it."

★

Her poll numbers dropped, then recovered, then dropped again. They plowed a million dollars into a digital ad buy for Slaughter attack ads.

In the last week of October, they ran more than one hundred hours of negative advertisements.

Now was the perfect time to hide behind surrogates to deflect attention. Jasmine, the eager zombie actress, canvassed Philly and Pittsburgh and helped register five thousand young voters and got them a feature in Lenny Letter.

They brought in Harrison Oglethorpe, a beloved rock star who sang songs about the working poor that people danced to at their weddings not realizing the lyrics were about poverty. Born and raised in South Philly, Harrison was now in his sixties and still selling out stadiums. He agreed to do an impromptu concert for Charlotte that drew a crowd of twenty thousand with only twenty-four hours' notice and raised more than five million dollars.

Before the event, Harrison joined Charlotte for a drink at 12 Steps Down, a bar on Christian Street chosen for its popularity with both blue-collar workers and millennials who didn't like to spend money. Lulu Instagrammed a photo of the two of them clinking their beer mugs.

"You're not worried about being associated with me?" Charlotte joked to the rock star.

"I have seven kids with five women. I once overdosed on heroin in the Parthenon." He grinned at her with a smile so famous it still papered the bedroom walls or iPhone backgrounds of women aged eighteen to seventy. "Who am I to judge? Who's anyone to judge? It's all bullshit."

★

The next day US Weekly ran the photo underneath the headline "Senate Candidate Dates Rock Star to Get Back at Cheating Husband."

"I can't do anything right," Charlotte said to Josh on their morning call.

He actually laughed before he answered. "The good news is there's not much you can do wrong at this point either."

CHAPTER 23
Election Day

Walsh (D)	Slaughter (R)	Spread
43	43	TIE

Ted Slaughter delivered an hour-long oration at dawn in Prosperity, Pennsylvania. He said his biggest regret in the race was that Charlotte Walsh wasn't a man. If she were, Ted Slaughter insisted, he would have challenged her to a Hamilton and Burr–style duel.

Charlotte caught a clip of it on the local news and thought about watching the whole thing online before deciding she had better things to do than listen to the ramblings of a senile old man with a chip on his shoulder.

A light rain had them worried early in the morning. Josh had warned for months that potential voters are easily dissuaded from going to the polls by inclement weather or a sale at Target. "It's not that people dislike voting as much as they don't feel like prioritizing it over getting a bargain on a twenty-four-pack of La Croix," he explained. Luckily, it cleared up after ten.

"Ready to go when you are," Max yelled up the stairs. Charlotte brushed her hair one last time and swiped on an extra coat of deodorant. In a few minutes they'd head to the elementary school she'd attended four decades earlier, where she would vote for herself for the United States Senate.

Max and the girls had returned on Sunday night even though Charlotte had told him he didn't need to come with her to the polls.

296 ★ JO PIAZZA

He'd insisted, and she was grateful. She'd chosen a hot-pink pantsuit paired with black sneakers for the occasion. *Fuck off. I'm wearing pink. I'm a woman. I am angry and I am a feminist and it's too late to piss anyone off.* At the last minute, she added the T-shirt Kara had given her—WAKE UP, KICK ASS, REPEAT. When she walked downstairs, she saw her three girls dressed in identical pink pantsuits. It was perfect and sweet because it was a surprise she hadn't known she wanted.

"I put on mascara and now I'm going to cry it all off." Charlotte reached for Annie and smiled at Max. Annie wore shiny yellow rain boots Kara bought her at the Goodwill. She'd finished off the outfit with her hot-pink tutu, and no one told her she had to take it off.

"Did you pick these out?" Charlotte asked Max.

"Roz and Leila helped."

A marriage, it had taken Charlotte more than a decade to figure out, wasn't the sum of the moments like this, the ones that took your breath away and made you thank God for the person you married. It was the totality of the moments that weren't wonderful, the crises you weathered together, and the people you became on the other side.

Savor this time as a happy family. It's fragile.

Annie pulled the handle for her in the voting booth. Charlotte had imagined this moment so many times the action felt like a memory.

Josh surprised her when he told her to relax for the rest of the day.

"That's one of the things I love about you, Walsh," he said. "You never stop moving. Take a break. Usually on Election Day, I tell candidates to go for a run, see a movie, have sex, or think about having sex and take a nap instead. Rest and be in Philly by eight p.m. tonight. We have a ground team knocking on doors and buses driving voters to the polls. Not much you can do at this point."

In the past week she'd crisscrossed the state more than twenty times, finding voters where they lived, worked, ate, got their hair done, took their kids to the playground. She'd campaigned around the clock in diners, high school gymnasiums, mills, barbershops, and malls. People knew her now. Some of them even cheered easily and eagerly when she arrived. Much of a Senate race is invisible to working folks trying to get through their week until just days before an election. That's when pounding the pavement and knocking on doors actually makes a difference. And she did it. She did it for fifteen hours a day, because when it was all over she wanted to say she'd tried her hardest and done everything she could to win. She needed to be able to tell herself that. Her motto for those final days was simple: *Be a goddamned human being.* She went off script, talked about how Kara had finally gotten Paul into rehab for pills and booze, she even opened up about her mom. Charlotte talked about her struggles with IVF with a woman who'd gone into debt for five failed fertility treatments. She refused to ride another horse or drive another tractor. "I'm actually terrified of horses," she admitted. "And I take allergy meds, so I don't think I should be operating heavy machinery."

And now it was over.

She was ready for it to be over.

Freedom felt foreign. When they returned from voting, Charlotte removed her shoes and jacket and lay down on the bed to close her eyes for a precious few minutes, intending to ignore Josh's advice and go to headquarters, make some phone calls, maybe even knock on a few doors. Her limbs were loosened from exhaustion. She sunk into the comforter, rolled on her side, and shut her heavy lids as Jack the Fat purred on her head.

She slept for the next five hours and woke with Max's hand on her hip.

"We should get going," he said gently.

"Or we could stay here all night."

"We'd miss the party."

"Or the wake. Are you packed?"

He planned to return to California in the morning.

"Yeah." He closed his eyes and ran his hand through his hair.

They lay in welcome stillness for a few minutes; then he cupped her chin. "Come back to California."

It will change your life.

★

Rosalind took to the stage in the small ballroom in the Logan Hotel to begin a chant at 9 p.m.

"She will win. She will win."

And another.

"Fix it. Fix it. Fix it."

The chants took on a life of their own.

"Kick the bastard out. Kick the bastard out."

"We deserve better."

The evening's festivities were small, just staff and major donors, at Roz's recommendation. "Honey, you don't plan a wedding unless you're sure the bride is going to say yes."

Outside the building, on Benjamin Franklin Parkway, the police were called to disperse a group of young women burning an effigy of Ted Slaughter in protest. When they saw the officers approaching, the women raced the half block to the Swann Fountain in Logan Circle, tossed the doll in the water, and took off north on Nineteenth Street. The cops looked the other way. Twenty blocks north, a gang of more than one hundred wearing white hoods began marching down Broad Street carrying a banner that read CHARLOTTE WALSH BURN IN HELL.

★

"I feel sick." Charlotte sat on a couch in a hotel suite eight floors above the conference room.

"It's nerves," Max said.

"Maybe you're pregnant?" Leila flashed a wry smile. "Let's start a rumor you're pregnant." In two weeks, Leila would move home to Oakland and start her own exploratory committee to run for the California State Assembly. She'd given her second resignation a week before. This time Charlotte had accepted it.

The loss of Leila would eventually hit her harder than anything she'd endured on the campaign trail, but she would accept it to maintain the girl's sanity and their friendship.

Pundits promised midterm voter turnout would reach an all-time high amidst the political turmoil the country had gone through in the past two years. Fear, depression, and anger would drive people to vote in numbers usually seen during a presidential election year, they all said. "This Election Day will be epic. It's no less than a struggle for the soul of America," they crowed. On the Sunday morning before Election Day the *Washington Post* ran a front-page headline declaring "The End of Apathy." The piece led with an anecdote about a fifty-year-old waitress in Tampa who had never voted in a midterm election in her life and could now recite all of the Congressional and down-ballot candidates and initiatives in her state as easily as she recited the daily specials during lunchtime rush.

So far, turnout was average. Congressional politics would never be sexy.

Charlotte and Josh stood alone in the corner of the room as he smoked a defiant Marlboro. How strange it was to think that after tonight they wouldn't have a reason to speak every morning. They might never speak again. Their intimacy, fostered over the course of the year, would disappear and he would begin the cycle all over again with someone new, possibly as soon as tomorrow. Even though it felt a little juvenile, she wondered if he would miss her.

"I knew this would be close. I didn't expect it to be ball-clenching close."

"How much longer until we know?"

"Any minute or a few hours. We're underperforming in some poll sites where we should be doing better, and I think it's due to low turnout."

Scranton and Philadelphia came in for Charlotte. The suburban counties around Philly were still too close to call. So far Charlotte had upset Slaughter in more rural counties than he'd ever been defeated in before. Polls in Pittsburgh had yet to close, and it was still anyone's race in the steel town. The western part of the state had grown progressively more red in the past two elections, but so far the returns didn't favor either candidate.

"Dems flipped at least four seats in the house so far in New York, Virginia, New Jersey, and New Hampshire," Leila said, her eyes glued to the television.

"What about the Pennsylvania house seats?" Charlotte asked.

"Haven't been called yet. It's all tight."

Charlotte nudged Josh. "I never asked you why you were doing this. You asked me that question the first time we met. You asked why I was running. But I never asked you why you said yes to working on my race."

He paused so long she thought he might blow off the question. "I like money." Josh, in his own way, was often more honest than she was, and his words contained no irony. He pulled on the last puff of his cigarette and dropped it into a tumbler of Diet Coke. The flame sizzled out with a shy hiss. "And I still believe in good guys."

Tears pricked the corners of her eyes. It would be strange now to hug him in front of Max. *I need to be alone.* She excused herself to go to the bathroom.

"Mommy, I want to go with you," Annie moaned. The baby was both wired from all of the cookies and brownies from the hotel-provided buffet and exhausted by all of the people and the frenetic energy in the room. Ella was busy calling out every number she saw on television even if she didn't know what it meant while Rose twirled in the corner, content no one was watching her.

Charlotte didn't want to be a mother right now, but she didn't have much of a choice. "Okay, baby, come on. Let's go together."

"You can watch me pee-pee."

"Yes, I can."

Charlotte closed the bathroom door and stared into the mirror while Annie perched happily on the toilet with a picture book about a talking crocodile who befriends an Australian hunter. Annie loved sitting on an adult toilet, which meant she would remain quiet for at least ten minutes.

Charlotte felt the skin beneath her eyes with her fingertips. The arduous schedule, the punishing criticism, the personal costs had all taken their toll. Who was the woman staring back at her? She looked exhausted, ten years older. In the past month she'd lost fifteen pounds she always thought she'd be happy to lose, despite subsisting on rest-stop Sbarro pizza and half-cooked Cinnabons. Now she thought she had looked better with the extra weight. The bags beneath her eyes were permanent, deepened into thick grooves.

Maybe it would be a relief if I didn't win. Maybe I can do more good outside of office than in it. Maybe my family will be better off if we go back to California. Maybe all of this was a gigantic waste of time and money. Now that she had no way to control the outcome of the situation, she was able to put it in perspective. Maybe the world didn't need her to fix everything. She'd been smug about that, often self-righteous and heavy-handed. Plenty of people glimpsed ghosts of lives they could have lived. She had at least attempted this one. That was worth something. Wasn't it? She fingered a piece of paper in her pocket that Kara had slipped into her hand earlier that day. She'd written down a quote she saw on Facebook and liked. "I've found that the changes I feared would ruin me have always become doorways." Charlotte liked it, too.

She slammed her palm on the sink so hard she'd have a bruise and gripped the edges of the sink until her knuckles turned white. She could read all the scraps of paper with all the inspirational quotes about failure as an opportunity, but why should she fool herself now? She still knew she could do a better job than the other guy. She still wanted this. Even knowing everything it had cost her, she still wanted to win.

"What happens next?" she asked her reflection, the words loaded with fatigue and curiosity.

"Next I wipe." Annie snapped her back to reality. Her daughter had actually gone to the bathroom in the toilet. Charlotte dropped to her knees and kissed her on the mouth, unspooling a wad of toilet paper and thrusting it into Annie's hand.

"Yes, you do, honey. Yes, you do! I'm so proud of you."

I'm grateful to be here right now.

There were moments from the past year that made her heart fill with similar joy—the time Rosie, who loved cheese more than most little girls loved ponies, made a castle of mozzarella that would have made Walt Disney proud at the Human Rights Campaign dinner buffet. There were Annie's impromptu dance performances every time a camera began rolling. There were the long days they spent as a family driving across the state in the van, absorbing the countryside, stopping at every historical marker and photo overlook to take yet another picture. There was the time Ella emptied her piggy bank and asked Charlotte to buy formula for an Ecuadorian immigrant with a tiny newborn. The woman had approached Charlotte shyly at a town hall and explained that since her husband had been deported she had to choose between buying formula and paying for bus fare to get to her job. Ella had been eavesdropping. She was always listening. Her child insisted that her entire year's allowance be used to buy food for the baby. Would her girls remember those things or would this entire year be overshadowed by the time they learned they had a half brother on the other side of the world? They'd taken that news in stride so far, not entirely understanding what it meant. Charlotte picked Annie up off the toilet and climbed into the empty tub, sitting the little girl on her legs.

Max walked in without knocking. He grabbed their child and gently shooed her out the door to join her sisters before he climbed into the tub opposite Charlotte. Her husband reached over to grasp her foot, kneading his thumb into the fleshy part of her heel. She moaned with pleasure. She was sick of speaking, wanted only to feel his hands touch her feet and let the rest of the world disappear for five sweet minutes. She had softened to him again after years of becoming hard.

"I'm proud of you. I never want you to think I'm not proud of you."

She looked at him. Max's hair had more salt creeping away from his temples than it had six months earlier, and the lines in his forehead, the ones that used to appear only when he thought hard about a problem, no longer disappeared when he relaxed his mouth. She could see the man who convinced her to take a risk and change her life, her greatest cheerleader, the exhausted father, the burned-out executive, the good husband, the unfaithful husband, the guy who made a mistake and tried to make all the amends he knew how to make, the love of her life.

He met her eyes. "Josh has results."

"Why didn't you tell me when you first came in?"

"It feels nice to have a few more minutes before we know."

"What are they?"

"He won't say anything until you come back out."

Charlotte closed her eyes. There are moments in life that are meant to define you. This felt like one of them.

She looked at her husband and tried hard to imagine their lives after this night. There were too many possibilities.

"Are you ready?" he whispered.

"I'm ready." It was the truth. In some ways, for the first time in her life, she found the uncertainty of her future exciting. She stood, exhaled with her whole body, and reached down to help Max stand.

Charlotte clutched her husband's hand and his touch made her feel strong. Max squeezed her fingers tight until she felt her knuckles crack as she pulled him along behind her to learn whether she'd won.

AUTHOR'S NOTE

I bet you have a lot of questions after getting to the final page of this book. Namely, does Charlotte win? Does she lose? Does she stay with Max? Does she opt to do it all on her own?

The truth is, I've written six different endings to this book and I've spent many sleepless nights over the past year thinking about what happens to Charlotte. I loved considering and writing out all the possibilities; each meditation on a new path for Charlotte was a privilege. Eventually I began to wonder if that was what I could offer to readers at the end of this book—the chance to ponder the possibilities, to discuss them with friends, other readers, and with me.

In these politically charged times, everything is taken as a statement. A definitive ending to this book would have been seen as one statement if she won and another if she lost. That wasn't the story I wanted to tell. Instead I wanted to talk about what it means to be an ambitious woman and what it often costs us. I wanted to explore how the media treats women and how women treat one another. I wanted to show how difficult it still is for a woman to run for office even though we all know we need more of us in government.

The world is continuing to shift violently beneath our feet on a daily basis. I wanted the ending to reflect that. I felt strongly that this story should mirror our current uncertain reality. That no matter how sure we are of an outcome, or what we think the polls are telling us, we still can't predict what will happen. This is disconcerting, in real life as well as in stories, and I understand that this ending could feel equally so. However, I hope that it creates a dialogue more than any tidy ending could.

I'm optimistic about Charlotte and her future, in or out of politics. I'm also optimistic about all of our futures.

But I want to hear what you think.

In January of 2017, we marched. By January of 2018, a record number of women from both parties were running for state and national office. There are a variety of ways that you can support women running for office. These incredible organizations are a great place to get started.

She Should Run (SheShouldRun.org): She Should Run is a nonpartisan organization committed to getting at least 250,000 women to run by 2030.

EMILY's List (EmilysList.org): EMILY's List recruits and trains pro-choice Democratic women to run for national, state, and local office.

Higher Heights (HigherHeightsForAmerica.org): Higher Heights is building a national infrastructure to harness black women's political power and leadership potential.

Women's Campaign Fund (wcfonline.org): Women's Campaign Fund is a national nonpartisan political organization supporting women at all levels of office.

Emerge America (emerge.ngpvanhost.com): Emerge recruits and trains women leaders from diverse backgrounds.

ACKNOWLEDGMENTS

I wasn't planning to write a novel this year. I was pregnant with my first baby, a little exhausted, and ready for some much-needed time off. But sometimes, as a writer, you feel like you don't have a choice. After watching the election of 2016, marching in Washington in 2017, and hearing stories of the hundreds of women running for office in 2018, I knew that fiction had to tackle the subject of women in politics this year. Thank you to all of the women marching, speaking out, running for office, and writing fearless journalism as the world shifts violently beneath our feet.

Thank you, Christine Pride, for pushing me harder than I've ever been pushed by an editor. I'm fabulously lucky that the wonderful Heather Jackson had a spark of inspiration that the two of us should meet. My agent, Alexandra Machinist, told me over and over again that I could get this book finished before a baby came out of me. Alexandra, I wouldn't want to write books without you. I promise we'll go to Japan soon.

Thank you everyone at Simon & Shuster, including Samantha O'Hara, Elizabeth Breeden, Anduriña Panezo, and many others who helped with this book.

Some of my dearest friends are incredibly astute early readers. Thank you, Tim Kelly, for tirelessly reading every iteration of this manuscript and never being afraid to tell me when I had no idea what I was talking about.

Thank you Glynnis MacNicol, Laura Forman, Emily Foote, Sara Chadwick, Ursula Rouse, Leslie Feingerts, Ivy Givens, Amy Benziger, Jen Doll, Carolyn Murnick, and the one and only Loud Library Lady Kate Olson. Thank you to all the bookstagrammers and tireless booksellers who help readers find my books. You're the reason anyone reads them!

And last but not least, thank you, Nick Aster, for being the most Swedish dad in America and taking our screaming baby away from me at least 50 percent of the time so that I could edit this book and take some naps. You're one of the best copy editors I know and you always know when to feed me cheese. You still make my world make sense.